The Best Crime Stories
of the
Nineteenth Century

Isaac Asimov Presents

THE BEST
CRIME
STORIES
OF THE 19TH CENTURY

EDITED BY ISAAC ASIMOV, CHARLES G. WAUGH,
AND MARTIN H. GREENBERG

DEMBNER BOOKS • New York

DEMBNER BOOKS

Published by Red Dembner Enterprises Corp.,
80 Eighth Avenue, New York, N.Y. 10011
Distributed by W. W. Norton & Company, Inc.,
500 Fifth Avenue, New York, N.Y. 10110

Library of Congress Cataloging-in-Publication Data

The Best crime stories of the nineteenth century.

1. Detective and mystery stories. 2. Fiction—19th
century. I. Asimov, Isaac, 1920–   . II. Greenberg,
Martin Harry. III. Waugh, Charles.
PN6120.95.D45B47 1988   808.83′872   87-30581
ISBN 0-934878-99-4

Design by Antler & Baldwin, Inc.

CONTENTS

INTRODUCTION

From the earliest days of civilization, two chief motifs have run through fiction.

One motif is that of the strong man, the hero, the person who solves problems and achieves victories by means of muscular superiority. That is a surefire way of winning an audience, who never tired of hearing or reading tales of Gilgamesh, of Hercules, of Achilles, of Rustem, of Chuchulain, of Sir Lancelot. Nor do we tire of such things today, for contempory fiction gives us our fill of mindless musclemen from Tarzan and Conan to Superman and Rambo.

Second to this, however, is the motif of the clever man, the shrewd and (perhaps) devious man who solves problems and achieves victories by means of mental superiority. Such are the tales of Odysseus (Ulysses) and Sinbad the Sailor. These stories are more human and offer us a higher ideal.

After all, what right have we to glory in muscular superiority, when Homo sapiens is not by any means supreme in strength? A mature chimpanzee, smaller than ourselves, nevertheless has a much stronger musculature. Tarzan may be able (in fiction) to defeat apes and lions with his bare hands, but even he has no choice but to make friends with elephants.

On the other hand, when it comes to cleverness, human beings bear the prize as compared with all other species, so that the supremely clever person is the true gem of creation.

Of course, one expects a clever person to win out over those who are more muscular than himself, more powerful. He may do this by clever lies, by indirection, even by treachery. Audiences, untroubled by considerations of morality and ethics, applaud. Thus, the great heroes, Achilles, Ajax, and Diomed, could not take Troy with all their martial strength, but Odysseus succeeded by the stratagem of a wooden horse filled with soldiers that the Trojans were talked into bringing into their city.

Ever since, the "Trojan horse" has been a byword for treachery, but Odysseus is admired for his cleverness. And, if it comes to that, few nations at war (or individuals facing difficulties) have refrained from treachery if that would help them to victory.

In the Greek myths, the god, Hermes, when only a day old, stole Apollo's herd of cattle, cleverly sheathing their hooves so that they would yield no tracks to give him away. Apollo found them at last, but clever Hermes had meanwhile invented the lyre and traded it to Apollo for the cattle. Hermes was much admired for all this and made the god of thieves.

On a less exalted scale, Autolycus and Sisyphus were, in Greek legend, clever thieves who constantly tried to outwit each other, and the picaresque tales of their misdeeds were found entertaining by the Greeks. (Autolycus was the grandfather of Odysseus.)

Even in the Bible, the thirtieth Chapter of Genesis, describes how the patriarch, Jacob, outwits his father-in-law, Laban, by what can only be called underhanded ways (and faulty genetics, too). Jacob had also driven a hard bargain with his naive brother, Esau, (see the twenty-fifth chapter) and had tricked his father, Isaac, into giving him, the younger son, the elder's share of the inheritance (see the twenty-seventh chapter).

This sort of thing continues right into modern times. We still admire the resourceful outlaws from Robin Hood to Jesse James, especially if we can convince ourselves, against all the evidence, that they robbed the rich and gave to the poor. We like stories about successful thieves, like Raffles, provided we give it a thin veneer of stealing for righteousness' sake. Again, we enjoy the caper movies in which a bunch of clever rascals plan to steal from a bank or from a museum (or some other faceless victim). Generally, the plan is frustrated at the end, but there is no question that the audience's sympathy is with the malefactors.

It was comparatively late in the game that it dawned upon people that cleverness could be used not to commit crimes, but to thwart it. The first example I can think of is that in the apocryphal Biblical book of "Susannah," which was written about 100 B.C. It tells the tale of two corrupt elders who, thwarted in their attempt to seduce the beautiful and virtuous Susannah, bear false witness against her, accusing her of adultery. A clever young man, Daniel, then questions the elders *separately* and shows that their tales do not match and that, therefore, they are lying. Such tales of clever virtue continued to remain few, however.

Why does virtue limp and lag so badly in its race with vice? We must realize that most societies through history have been terribly unjust, have favored the rich and the well-born, and have treated the poor like animals. One cannot expect that the poor (who have the virtue of numbers, at least) will see it as wicked if one of their own by superior cleverness outwits and discomfits those rich and well-born who oppress him so cruelly and unjustly. Naturally, the "Thief of Bagdad" is the hero of his particular tale, and "Reynard the Fox," that clever, low-born rascal, makes fools of wolves, bears and lions (representing the aristocracy). The aristocracy may applaud the tales of heroes and knights, but the people want to hear of successful thieves and of little tailors who slay giants by trickery.

Occasionally, some societies arise that manage to give most people some feeling that they have a chance, even if poor and low-born, to obtain justice. There has to be a governmental assumption, in theory, at least, that a society is governed by the rule of law, without fear or favor, for rich and poor, for high and low, alike. It is only then that there seems any point to the general population in supporting the law, and only then that it becomes possible to acclaim the clever man who bends his talents to the thwarting of crime.

I would like to suggest that that may be why the "detective story," as opposed to the "crime story," came into prominence first (at least in the western world) in Great Britain and the United States.

It is this that makes the nineteenth century particularly interesting in the history of stories of mystery and crime. In it you can see the slow turn from the clever and daring criminal, to the clever and daring detective.

We get our first clear glimpse of the latter in the works of

Edgar Allen Poe, who wrote three stories of C. Auguste Dupin. Two of these (in my opinion) are long and quite tedious, but the third "The Purloined Letter" is, in every way, a modern story. (You'll find it in this anthology.) The point it makes may not startle you, if only because the story itself has become so famous and has been used as a springboard for so many other stories making use of some variant of Poe's idea but, to my way of thinking, it is the first literary production that unquestionably raises the clever man who supports society above the clever man who fights it.

And a half century after Poe, there came Arthur Conan Doyle, who clinched the victory once and for all. He invented Sherlock Holmes, who, for all time since, has been the quintessential detective, and, many maintain, the most famous fictional character of all time. (Included in this anthology is "The Red-Headed League," viewed by most to be his best short story.)

The Sherlock Holmes stories, all by themselves, persuaded many that there is something admirable in supporting and stabilizing the structure of society. It has not stopped crime (probably nothing ever will) and it doesn't entirely wipe out our sneaking admiration for the one who dares to fight society— which, after all, is never entirely just—but it has probably done more to rally support for the machinery of justice than all the preaching by all the ministers and philosophers in the world.

And that is not a bad accomplishment for a variety of fiction often derided as something suited for an occasional idle hour, and nothing more.

—Isaac Asimov

1834

Mr. Higginbotham's Catastrophe

NATHANIEL HAWTHORNE

A young fellow, a tobacco pedlar by trade, was on his way from Morristown, where he had dealt largely with the Deacon of the Shaker settlement, to the village of Parker's Falls, on Salmon River. He had a neat little cart, painted green, with a box of cigars depicted on each side panel, and an Indian chief, holding a pipe and a golden tobacco stalk, on the rear. The pedlar drove a smart little mare, and was a young man of excellent character, keen at a bargain, but none the worse liked by the Yankees; who, as I have heard them say, would rather be shaved with a sharp razor than a dull one. Especially was he beloved by the pretty girls along the Connecticut, whose favor he used to court by presents of the best smoking tobacco in his stock; knowing well that the country lasses of New England are generally great performers on pipes. Moreover, as will be seen in the course of my story, the pedlar was inquisitive, and something of a tattler, always itching to hear the news and anxious to tell it again.

After an early breakfast at Morristown, the tobacco pedlar, whose name was Dominicus Pike, had travelled seven miles through a solitary piece of woods, without speaking a word to anybody but himself and his little gray mare. It being nearly seven o'clock, he was as eager to hold a morning gossip as a city shopkeeper to read the morning paper. An opportunity seemed at hand when, after lighting a cigar with a sun-glass, he looked up, and perceived a man coming over the brow of the hill, at the foot of which the pedlar had stopped his green cart. Dominicus watched him as he descended, and noticed that he carried a bundle over his shoulder on the end of a stick, and travelled with a weary, yet determined pace. He did not look as if he had started in the freshness of the morning, but had footed it all night, and meant to do the same all day.

"Good morning, mister," said Dominicus, when within speaking distance. "You go a pretty good jog. What's the latest news at Parker's Falls?"

The man pulled the broad brim of a gray hat over his eyes, and answered, rather sullenly, that he did not come from Parker's Falls, which, as being the limit of his own day's journey, the pedlar had naturally mentioned in his inquiry.

"Well, then," rejoined Dominicus Pike, "let's have the latest news where you did come from. I'm not particular about Parker's Falls. Any place will answer."

Being thus importuned, the traveller—who was as ill-looking a fellow as one would desire to meet in a solitary piece of woods—appeared to hesitate a little, as if he was either searching his memory for news, or weighing the expediency of telling it. At last, mounting on the step of the cart, he whispered in the ear of Dominicus, though he might have shouted aloud and no other mortal would have heard him.

"I do remember one little trifle of news," said he. "Old Mr. Higginbotham, of Kimballton, was murdered in his orchard, at eight o'clock last night, by an Irishman and a nigger. They strung him up to the branch of a St. Michael's pear tree, where nobody would find him till the morning."

As soon as this horrible intelligence was communicated, the stranger betook himself to his journey again, with more speed than ever, not even turning his head when Dominicus invited him to smoke a Spanish cigar and relate all the particulars. The pedlar whistled to his mare and went up the hill, pondering on the doleful fate of Mr. Higginbotham, whom he had known in the way of trade, having sold him many a bunch of long nines, and a great deal of pigtail, lady's twist, and fig tobacco. He was rather astonished at the rapidity with which the news had spread. Kimballton was nearly sixty miles distant in a straight line; the murder had been perpetrated only at eight o'clock the preceding night; yet Dominicus had heard of it at seven in the morning, when, in all probability, poor Mr. Higginbotham's own family had but just discovered his corpse, hanging on the St. Michael's pear tree. The stranger on foot must have worn seven-league boots to travel at such a rate.

"Ill news flies fast, they say," thought Dominicus Pike; "but this beats railroads. The fellow ought to be hired to go express with the President's Message."

The difficulty was solved by supposing that the narrator had made a mistake of one day in the date of the occurrence; so that our friend did not hesitate to introduce the story at every tavern and country store along the road, expending a whole bunch of Spanish wrappers among at least twenty horrified audiences. He found himself invariably the first bearer of the intelligence, and was so pestered with questions that he could not avoid filling up the outline, till it became quite a respectable narrative. He met with one piece of corroborative evidence. Mr. Higginbotham was a trader; and a former clerk of his, to whom Dominicus related the facts, testified that the old gentleman was accustomed to return home through the orchard about nightfall, with the money and valuable papers of the store in his pocket. The clerk manifested but little grief at Mr. Higginbotham's catastrophe, hinting, what the pedlar had discovered in his own dealings with him, that he was a crusty old fellow, as close as a vise. His property would descend to a pretty niece, who was now keeping school in Kimballton.

What with telling the news for the public good, and driving bargains for his own, Dominicus was so much delayed on the road that he chose to put up at a tavern about five miles short of Parker's Falls. After supper, lighting one of his prime cigars, he seated himself in the barroom, and went through the story of the murder, which had grown so fast that it took him half an hour to tell. There were as many as twenty people in the room, nineteen of whom received it all for gospel. But the twentieth was an elderly farmer, who had arrived on horseback a short time before, and was now seated in a corner smoking his pipe. When the story was concluded, he rose up very deliberately, brought his chair right in front of Dominicus, and stared him full in the face, puffing out the vilest tobacco smoke the pedlar had ever smelt.

"Will you make affidavit," demanded he, in the tone of a country justice taking an examination, "that old Squire Higginbotham of Kimballton was murdered in his orchard the night before last, and found hanging on his great pear tree yesterday morning?"

"I tell the story as I heard it, mister," answered Dominicus, dropping his half-burnt cigar; "I don't say that I saw the thing done. So I can't take my oath that he was murdered exactly in that way."

"But I can take mine," said the farmer, "that if Squire Higginbotham was murdered night before last, I drank a glass of bitters with his ghost this morning. Being a neighbor of mine, he called me into his store, as I was riding by, and treated me, and then asked me to do a little business for him on the road. He didn't seem to know any more about his own murder than I did."

"Why, then it can't be a fact!" exclaimed Dominicus Pike.

"I guess he'd have mentioned, if it was," said the old farmer; and he removed his chair back to the corner, leaving Dominicus quite down in the mouth.

Here was a sad resurrection of old Mr. Higginbotham! The pedlar had no heart to mingle in the conversation any more, but comforted himself with a glass of gin and water, and went to bed, where, all night long, he dreamed of hanging on the St. Michael's pear tree. To avoid the old farmer (whom he so detested that his suspension would have pleased him better than Mr. Higginbotham's), Dominicus rose in the gray of the morning, put the little mare into the green cart, and trotted swiftly away towards Parker's Falls. The fresh breeze, the dewy road, and the pleasant summer dawn revived his spirits, and might have encouraged him to repeat the old story, had there been anybody awake to hear it. But he met neither ox-team, light wagon chaise, horseman, nor foot traveller, till, just as he crossed Salmon River, a man came trudging down to the bridge with a bundle over his shoulder, on the end of a stick.

"Good morning, mister," said the pedlar, reining in his

mare. "If you come from Kimballton or that neighborhood, may be you can tell me the real fact about this affair of old Mr. Higginbotham. Was the old fellow actually murdered two or three nights ago by an Irishman and a nigger?"

Dominicus had spoken in too great a hurry to observe, at first, that the stranger himself had a deep tinge of negro blood. On hearing this sudden question, the Ethiopian appeared to change his skin, its yellow hue becoming a ghastly white, while, shaking and stammering, he thus replied:

"No! no! There was no colored man! It was an Irishman that hanged him last night, at eight o'clock. I came away at seven! His folks can't have looked for him in the orchard yet."

Scarcely had the yellow man spoken, when he interrupted himself, and though he seemed weary enough before, continued his journey at a pace which would have kept the pedlar's mare on a smart trot. Dominicus stared after him in great perplexity. If the murder had not been committed till Tuesday night, who was the prophet that had foretold it, in all circumstances, on Tuesday morning? If Mr. Higginbotham's corpse were not yet discovered by his own family, how came the mulatto, at above thirty miles' distance, to know that he was hanging in the orchard, especially as he had left Kimballton before the unfortunate man was hanged at all? These ambiguous circumstances, with the stranger's surprise and terror, made Dominicus think of raising a hue and cry after him, as an accomplice in the murder; since a murder, it seemed, had really been perpetrated.

"But let the poor devil go," thought the pedlar. "I don't want his black blood on my head; and hanging the nigger wouldn't unhang Mr. Higginbotham. Unhang the old gentleman! It's a sin, I know; but I should hate to have him come to life a second time, and give me the lie!"

With these meditations, Dominicus Pike drove into the street of Parker's Falls, which, as everybody knows, is as thriving a village as three cotton factories and a slitting mill can make it. The machinery was not in motion, and but a few of the shop doors unbarred, when he alighted in the stable yard of the tavern, and made it his first business to order the mare four quarts of oats. His second duty, of course, was to impart Mr. Higginbotham's catastrophe to the hostler. He deemed it advisable, however, not to be too positive as to the date of the direful fact, and also to be uncertain whether it were perpetrated by an Irishman and a mulatto, or by the son of Erin alone. Neither did he profess to relate it on his own authority, or that of any one person; but mentioned it as a report generally diffused.

The story ran through the town like fire among girdled trees, and became so much the universal talk that nobody could tell whence it originated. Mr. Higginbotham was as well known at Parker's Falls as any citizen of the place, being part owner of the slitting mill, and a considerable stockholder in the cotton factories. The inhabitants felt their own prosperity interested in his fate. Such was the excitement, that the Parker's Falls Gazette anticipated its regular day of publication, and came out with half a form of blank paper and a column of double pica emphasized with capitals, and headed HORRID MURDER OF MR. HIGGINBOTHAM! Among other dreadful details, the printed account described the mark of the cord round the dead man's neck, and stated the number of thousand dollars of which he had been robbed; there was much pathos also about the affliction of his niece, who had gone from one fainting fit to another, ever since her uncle was found hanging on the St. Michael's pear tree with his pockets inside out. The village poet likewise commemorated the young lady's grief in seventeen stanzas of a ballad. The selectmen held a meeting, and, in consideration of Mr. Higginbotham's claims on the town, determined to issue handbills, offering a reward of five hundred dollars for the apprehension of his murderers, and the recovery of the stolen property.

Meanwhile the whole population of Parker's Falls, consisting of shop-keepers, mistresses of boarding houses, factory girls, millmen, and schoolboys, rushed into the street, and kept up such a terrible loquacity as more than compensated for the silence of the cotton machines, which refrained from their usual din out of respect to the deceased. Had Mr. Higginbotham cared about posthumous renown, his untimely ghost would have exulted in this tumult. Our friend Dominicus, in his vanity of heart, forgot his intended precautions, and mounting on the town pump, announced himself as the bearer of the authentic intelligence which had caused so wonderful a sensation. He immediately became the great man of the moment, and had just begun a new edition of the narrative, with a voice like a field preacher, when the mail stage drove into the village street. It had travelled all night, and must have shifted horses at Kimballton, at three in the morning.

"Now we shall hear all the particulars," shouted the crowd.

The coach rumbled up to the piazza of the tavern, followed by a thousand people; for if any man had been minding his own business till then, he now left it at sixes and sevens, to hear the news. The pedlar, foremost in the race, discovered two passengers, both of whom had been startled from a comfortable nap to find themselves in the centre of a mob. Every man assailing them with separate questions, all propounded at once, the couple were struck speechless, though one was a lawyer and the other a young lady.

"Mr. Higginbotham! Mr. Higginbotham! Tell us the particulars about old Mr. Higginbotham!" bawled the mob. "What is the coroner's verdict? Are the murderers apprehended? Is Mr. Higginbotham's niece come out of her fainting fits? Mr. Higginbotham! Mr. Higginbotham!!"

The coachman said not a word, except to swear awfully at the hostler for not bringing him a fresh team of horses. The lawyer inside had generally his wits about him even when asleep; the first thing he did, after learning the cause of the excitement, was to produce a large red pocket-book. Meantime Dominicus Pike, being an extremely polite young man, and also suspecting that a female tongue would tell the story as glibly as a lawyer's, had handed the lady out of the coach. She was a fine, smart girl, now wide awake and bright as a button, and had such a sweet pretty mouth, that Dominicus would almost as lief have heard a love tale from it as a tale of murder.

"Gentlemen and ladies," said the lawyer to the shop-keepers, the millmen, and the factory girls, "I can assure you that some unaccountable mistake, or, more probably, a wilful falsehood, maliciously contrived to injure Mr. Higginbotham's credit, has excited this singular uproar. We passed through Kimballton at three o'clock this morning, and most certainly should have been informed of the murder, had any been perpetrated. But I have proof nearly as strong as Mr. Higginbotham's own oral testimony, in the negative. Here is a note relating to a suit of his in the Connecticut courts, which was delivered me from that gentleman himself. I find it dated at ten o'clock last evening."

So saying, the lawyer exhibited the date and signature of the note, which irrefragably proved, either that this perverse Mr. Higginbotham was alive when he wrote it, or—as some deemed the more probable case, of two doubtful ones—that he was so absorbed in worldly business as to continue to transact it even after his death. But unexpected evidence was forthcoming. The young lady, after listening to the pedlar's explanation, merely seized a moment to smooth her gown and put her curls in order, and then appeared at the tavern door, making a modest signal to be heard.

"Good people," said she, "I am Mr. Higginbotham's niece."

A wondering murmur passed through the crowd on beholding her so rosy and bright; that same unhappy niece, whom they had supposed, on the authority of the Parker's Falls Gazette, to be lying at death's door in a fainting fit. But some shrewd fellows had doubted, all along, whether a young lady would be quite so desperate at the hanging of a rich old uncle.

"You see," continued Miss Higginbotham, with a smile, "that this strange story is quite unfounded as to myself; and I believe I may affirm it to be equally so in regard to my dear uncle Higginbotham. He has the kindness to give me a home in his house, though I contribute to my own support by teaching a school. I left Kimballton this morning to spend the vacation of commencement week with a friend, about five miles from Parker's Falls. My generous uncle, when he heard me on the stairs, called me to his bedside, and gave me two dollars and fifty cents to pay my stage fare, and another dollar for my extra expenses. He then laid his pocket-book under his pillow, shook hands with me, and advised me to take some biscuit in my bag, instead of breakfasting on the road. I feel confident, therefore, that I left my beloved relative alive, and trust that I shall find him so on my return."

The young lady curtsied at the close of her speech, which was so sensible and well worded, and delivered with such grace and propriety, that everybody thought her fit to be preceptress of the best academy in the State. But a stranger would have supposed that Mr. Higginbotham was an object of abhorrence at Parker's Falls, and that a thanksgiving had been proclaimed for his murder; so excessive was the wrath of the inhabitants on learning their mistake. The millmen resolved to bestow public honors on Dominicus Pike, only hesitating whether to tar and feather him, ride him on a rail, or refresh him with an ablution at the town pump, on the top of which he had declared himself the bearer of the news. The selectmen, by advice of the lawyer, spoke of prosecuting him for a misdemeanor, in circulating unfounded reports, to the great disturbance of the peace of the Commonwealth. Nothing saved Dominicus, either from mob law or a court of justice, but an eloquent appeal made by the young lady in his behalf. Addressing a few words of heartfelt gratitude to his benefactress, he mounted the green cart and rode out of town, under a discharge of artillery from the schoolboys, who found plenty of ammunition in the neighboring clay pits and mud holes. As he turned his head to exchange a farewell glance with Mr. Higginbotham's niece, a ball, of the consistence of hasty pudding, hit him slap in the mouth, giving him a most grim aspect. His whole person was so bespattered with the like filthy missiles, that he had almost a mind to ride back, and supplicate for the threatened ablution at the town pump; for, though not meant in kindness, it would now have been a deed of charity.

However, the sun shone bright on poor Dominicus, and the mud, an emblem of all stains of undeserved opprobrium, was easily brushed off when dry. Being a funny rogue, his heart soon cheered up; nor could he refrain from a hearty laugh at the uproar which his story had excited. The handbills of the selectmen would cause the commitment of all the vagabonds in the State; the paragraph in the Parker's Falls Gazette would be reprinted from Maine to Florida, and perhaps form an item in the London newspapers; and many a miser would tremble for his money bags and life, on learning the catastrophe of Mr. Higginbotham. The pedlar meditated with much fervor on the charms of the young schoolmistress, and swore that Daniel Webster never spoke nor looked so like an angel as Miss Higginbotham, while defending him from the wrathful populace at Parker's Falls.

Dominicus was now on the Kimballton turnpike, having all along determined to visit that place, though business had drawn him out of the most direct road from Morristown. As he approached the scene of the supposed murder, he continued to revolve the circumstances in his mind, and was astonished at the aspect which the whole case assumed. Had nothing occurred to corroborate the story of the first traveller, it might now have been considered as a hoax; but the yellow man was evidently acquainted either with the report or the fact; and there was a mystery in his dismayed and guilty look on being abruptly questioned. When, to this singular combination of incidents, it was added that the rumor tallied exactly with Mr. Higginbotham's character and habits of life; and that he had an orchard, and a St. Michael's pear tree, near which he always passed at nightfall: the circumstantial evidence appeared so strong that Dominicus doubted whether the autograph produced by the lawyer, or even the niece's direct testimony, ought to be equivalent. Making cautious inquiries along the road, the pedlar further learned that Mr. Higginbotham had in his service an Irishman of doubtful character, whom he had hired without a recommendation, on the score of economy.

"May I be hanged myself," exclaimed Dominicus Pike aloud, on reaching the top of a lonely hill, "if I'll believe old Higginbotham is unhanged till I see him with my own eyes, and hear it from his own mouth! And as he's a real shaver, I'll have the minister or some other responsible man for an endorser."

It was growing dusk when he reached the tollhouse on Kimballton turnpike, about a quarter of a mile from the village of this name. His little mare was fast bringing him up with a man on horseback, who trotted through the gate a few rods in advance of him, nodded to the toll gatherer, and kept on towards the village. Dominicus was acquainted with the toll man, and, while making change, the usual remarks on the weather passed between them.

"I suppose," said the pedlar, throwing back his whiplash, to bring it down like a feather on the mare's flank, "you have not seen anything of old Mr. Higginbotham within a day or two?"

"Yes," answered the toll gatherer. "He passed the gate just before you drove up, and yonder he rides now, if you can see him through the dusk. He's been to Woodfield his afternoon, attending a sheriff's sale there. The old man generally shakes hands and has a little chat with me; but tonight, he nodded—as if to say, 'Charge my toll,' and jogged on; for wherever he goes, he must always be at home by eight o'clock."

"So they tell me," said Dominicus.

"I never saw a man look so yellow and thin as the squire does," continued the toll gatherer. "Says I to myself, tonight, he's more like a ghost or an old mummy than good flesh and blood."

The pedlar strained his eyes through the twilight, and could just discern the horseman now far ahead on the village road. He seemed to recognize the rear of Mr. Higginbotham; but through the evening shadows, and amid the dust from the horse's feet, the figure appeared dim and unsubstantial; as if the shape of the mysterious old man were faintly moulded of darkness and gray light. Dominicus shivered.

"Mr. Higginbotham has come back from the other world, by way of the Kimballton turnpike," thought he.

He shook the reins and rode forward, keeping about the same distance in the rear of the gray old shadow, till the latter was concealed by a bend of the road. On reaching this point, the pedlar no longer saw the man on horseback, but found himself at the head of the village street, not far from a number of stores and two taverns, clustered round the meeting-house steeple. On his left were a stone wall and a gate, the boundary of a wood lot, beyond which lay an orchard, farther still, a mowing field, and last of all, a house. These were the premises of Mr. Higginbotham, whose dwelling stood beside the old highway, but had been left in the background by the Kimballton turnpike. Dominicus knew the place; and the little mare stopped short by instinct; for he was not conscious of tightening the reins.

"For the soul of me, I cannot get by this gate!" said he, trembling. "I never shall be my own man again, till I see whether Mr. Higginbotham is hanging on the St. Michael's pear tree!"

He leaped from the cart, gave the rein a turn round the gate post, and ran along the green path of the wood lot as if Old Nick were chasing behind. Just then the village clock tolled eight, and as each deep stroke fell, Dominicus gave a fresh bound and flew faster than before, till, dim in the solitary centre of the orchard, he saw the fated pear tree. One great branch stretched from the old contorted trunk across the path, and threw the darkest shadow on that one spot. But something seemed to struggle beneath the branch!

The pedlar had never pretended to more courage than befits a man of peaceable occupation, nor could he account for his valor on this awful emergency. Certain it is, however, that he rushed forward, prostrated a sturdy Irishman with the butt end of his whip, and found—not indeed hanging on the St. Michael's pear tree, but trembling beneath it, with a halter round his neck—the old, identical Mr. Higginbotham!

"Mr. Higginbotham," said Dominicus tremulously, "you're an honest man, and I'll take your word for it. Have you been hanged or not?"

If the riddle be not already guessed, a few words will explain the simple machinery by which this "coming event" was made to "cast its shadow before." Three men had plotted the robbery and murder of Mr. Higginbotham; two of them, successively, lost courage and fled, each delaying the crime one night by their disappearance; the third was in the act of perpetration, when a champion, blindly obeying the call of fate, like the heroes of old romance, appeared in the person of Dominicus Pike.

It only remains to say, that Mr. Higginbotham took the

pedlar into high favor, sanctioned his addresses to the pretty schoolmistress, and settled his whole property on their children, allowing themselves the interest. In due time, the old gentleman capped the climax of his favors by dying a Christian death, in bed, since which melancholy event Dominicus Pike has removed from Kimballton, and established a large tobacco manufactory in my native village.

1844

The Purloined Letter

EDGAR ALLAN POE

Nil sapientiæ odiosius acumine nimio.—*Seneca*

At Paris, just after dark one gusty evening in the autumn of 18–, I was enjoying the twofold luxury of meditation and a meerschaum, in company with my friend, C. Auguste Dupin, in his little back library, or book closet, *au troisième* No. 33 *Rue Dunôt, Faubourg St. Germain*. For one hour at least we had maintained a profound silence; while each, to any casual observer, might have seemed intently and exclusively occupied with the curling eddies of smoke that oppressed the atmosphere of the chamber. For myself, however, I was mentally discussing certain topics which had formed matter for conversation between us at an earlier period of the evening; I mean the affair of the Rue Morgue, and the mystery attending the murder of Marie Rogêt. I looked upon it, therefore, as something of a coincidence, when the door of our apartment was thrown open and admitted our old acquaintance, Monsieur G——, the Prefect of the Parisian police.

We gave him a hearty welcome; for there was nearly half as much of the entertaining as of the contemptible about the man, and we had not seen him for several years. We had been sitting in the dark, and Dupin now arose for the purpose of lighting a lamp, but sat down again, without doing so, upon G.'s saying that he had called to consult us, or rather to ask the opinion of my friend, about some official business which had occasioned a great deal of trouble.

"If it is any point requiring reflection," observed Dupin, as he forebore to enkindle the wick, "we shall examine it to better purpose in the dark."

"That is another of your odd notions," said the Prefect, who had the fashion of calling everything "odd" that was beyond his comprehension, and thus lived amid an absolute legion of "oddities."

"Very true," said Dupin, as he supplied his visitor with a pipe, and rolled toward him a comfortable chair.

"And what is the difficulty now?" I asked. "Nothing more in the assassination way I hope?"

"Oh, no; nothing of that nature. The fact is, the business is *very* simple indeed, and I make no doubt that we can manage it sufficiently well ourselves; but then I thought Dupin would like to hear the details of it, because it is so excessively *odd*."

"Simple and odd," said Dupin.

"Why, yes; and not exactly that either. The fact is, we have all been a good deal puzzled because the affair *is* so simple, and yet baffles us altogether."

"Perhaps it is the very simplicity of the thing which puts you at fault," said my friend.

"What nonsense you *do* talk!" replied the Prefect, laughing heartily.

"Perhaps the mystery is a little *too* plain," said Dupin.

"Oh, good heavens! who ever heard of such an idea?"

"A little *too* self-evident."

"Ha! ha! ha!—ha! ha! ha!—ho! ho! ho!" roared our visitor, profoundly amused, "oh, Dupin, you will be the death of me yet!"

"And what, after all, *is* the matter on hand?" I asked.

"Why, I will tell you," replied the Prefect, as he gave a long, steady, and contemplative puff, and settled himself in his chair. "I will tell you in a few words; but, before I begin, let me caution you that this is an affair demanding the greatest secrecy, and that I should most probably lose the position I now hold, were it known that I confided it to any one."

"Proceed," said I.

"Or not," said Dupin.

"Well, then; I have received personal information, from a very high quarter, that a certain document of the last importance has been purloined from the royal apartments. The individual who purloined it is known; this beyond a doubt; he was seen to take it. It is known, also, that it still remains in his possession."

"How is this known?" asked Dupin.

"It is clearly inferred," replied the Prefect, "from the nature of the document, and from the non-appearance of certain results which would at once arise from its passing *out* of the robber's possession—that is to say, from his employing it as he must design in the end to employ it."

"Be a little more explicit," I said.

"Well, I may venture so far as to say that the paper gives its holder a certain power in a certain quarter where such power is immensely valuable." The Prefect was fond of the cant of diplomacy.

"Still I do not quite understand," said Dupin.

"No? Well; the disclosure of the document to a third person, who shall be nameless, would bring in question the honor of a personage of most exalted station; and this fact gives the holder of the document an ascendancy over the illustrious personage whose honor and peace are so jeopardized."

"But this ascendancy," I interposed, "would depend upon the robber's knowledge of the loser's knowledge of the robber. Who would dare—"

"The thief," said G——, "is the Minister D——, who dares all things, those unbecoming as well as those becoming a man. The method of the theft was not less ingenious than bold. The document in question—a letter, to be frank—had been received by the personage robbed while alone in the royal *boudoir*. During its perusal she was suddenly interrupted by the entrance of the other exalted personage from whom especially it was her wish to conceal it. After a hurried and vain endeavor to thrust it in a drawer, she was forced to place it, open it was, upon a table. The address, however, was uppermost, and, the contents thus unexposed, the letter escaped notice. At this juncture enters the Minister D——. His lynx eye immediately perceives the paper, recognizes the handwriting of the address, observes the confusion of the personage addressed, and fathoms her secret. After some business transactions, hurried through in his ordinary manner, he produces a letter somewhat similar to the one in question, opens it, pretends to read it, and then places it in close juxtaposition to the other. Again he converses, for some fifteen minutes, upon the public affairs. At length, in taking leave, he takes also from the table the letter to which he had no claim. Its rightful owner saw, but, of course, dared not call attention to the act, in the presence of the third personage who stood at her elbow. The minister decamped; leaving his own letter—one of no importance—upon the table."

"Here, then," said Dupin to me, "you have precisely what you demand to make the ascendancy complete—the robber's knowledge of the loser's knowledge of the robber."

"Yes," replied the Prefect; "and the power thus attained has, for some months past, been wielded, for political purposes, to a very dangerous extent. The personage robbed is more thoroughly convinced, every day, of the necessity of reclaiming her letter. But this, of course, cannot be done openly. In fine, driven to despair, she has committed the matter to me."

"Than whom," said Dupin, amid a perfect whirlwind of smoke, "no more sagacious agent could, I suppose, be desired, or even imagined."

"You flatter me," replied the Prefect; "but it is possible that some such opinion may have been entertained."

"It is clear," said I, "as you observe, that the letter is still in the possession of the minister; since it is this possession, and not any employment of the letter, which bestows the power. With the employment the power departs."

"True," said G.; "and upon this conviction I proceeded. My first care was to make thorough search of the minister's hotel; and here my chief embarrassment lay in the necessity of searching without his knowledge. Beyond all things, I have been warned of the danger which would result from giving him reason to suspect our design."

"But," said I, "you are quite *au fait* in these investigations. The Parisian police have done this thing often before."

"Oh, yes; and for this reason I did not despair. The habits of the minister gave me, too, a great advantage. He is frequently absent from home all night. His servants are by no means numerous. They sleep at a distance from their master's apartment, and, being chiefly Neapolitans, are readily made drunk. I have keys, as you know, with which I can open any chamber or cabinet in Paris. For three months a night has not passed, during the greater part of which I have not been engaged, personally, in ransacking the D——Hotel. My honor is interested, and, to mention a great secret, the reward is enormous. So I did not abandon the search until I had become fully satisfied that the thief is a more astute man than myself. I fancy that I have investigated every nook and corner of the premises in which it is possible that the paper can be concealed."

"But it is not possible," I suggested, "that although the letter may be in possession of the minister, as it unquestionably is, he may have concealed it elsewhere than upon his own premises?"

"This is barely possible," said Dupin. "The present peculiar condition of affairs at court, and especially of those intrigues in which D——is known to be involved, would render the instant availability of the document—its susceptibility of being produced at a moment's notice—a point of nearly equal importance with its possession."

"Its susceptibility of being produced?" said I.

"That is to say, of being *destroyed*," said Dupin.

"True," I observed; "the paper is clearly then upon the premises. As for its being upon the person of the minister, we may consider that as out of the question."

"Entirely," said the Prefect. "He has been twice waylaid, as if by footpads, and his person rigidly searched under my own inspection."

"You might have spared yourself this trouble," said Dupin. "D——, I presume, is not altogether a fool, and, if not, must have anticipated these waylayings, as a matter of course."

"Not *altogether* a fool," said G., "but then he is a poet, which I take to be only one remove from a fool."

"True," said Dupin, after a long and thoughtful whiff from

his meerschaum, "although I have been guilty of certain doggerel myself."

"Suppose you detail," said I, "the particulars of your search."

"Why, the fact is, we took our time, and we searched *everywhere*. I have had long experience in these affairs. I took the entire building, room by room; devoting the nights of a whole week to each. We examined, first, the furniture of each apartment. We opened every possible drawer; and I presume you know that, to a properly trained police agent, such a thing as a *'secret'* drawer is impossible. Any man is a dolt who permits a 'secret' drawer to escape him in a search of this kind. The thing is *so* plain. There is a certain amount of bulk—of space—to be accounted for in every cabinet. Then we have accurate rules. The fiftieth part of a line could not escape us. After the cabinets we took the chairs. The cushions we probed with the fine long needles you have seen me employ. From the tables we removed the tops."

"Why so?"

"Sometimes the top of a table, or other similarly arranged piece of furniture, is removed by the person wishing to conceal an article; then the leg is excavated, the article deposited within the cavity, and the top replaced. The bottoms and tops of bedposts are employed in the same way."

"But could not the cavity be detected by sounding?" I asked.

"By no means, if, when the article is deposited, a sufficient wadding of cotton be placed around it. Besides, in our case, we were obliged to proceed without noise."

"But you could not have removed—you could not have taken to pieces *all* articles of furniture in which it would have been possible to make a deposit in the manner you mention. A letter may be compressed into a thin spiral roll, not differing much in shape or bulk from a large knitting needle, and in this form it might be inserted into the rung of a chair, for example. You did not take to pieces all the chairs?"

"Certainly not; but we did better—we examined the rungs of every chair in the hotel, and, indeed, the jointings of every description of furniture, by the aid of a most powerful micro-scope. Had there been any traces of recent disturbance we should not have failed to detect it instantly. A single grain of gimlet dust, for example, would have been as obvious as an apple. Any disorder in the gluing—any unusual gaping in the joints—would have sufficed to insure detection."

"I presume you looked to the mirrors, between the boards and the plates, and you probed the beds and the bedclothes, as well as the curtains and carpets."

"That of course; and when we had absolutely completed every particle of the furniture in this way, then we examined the house itself. We divided its entire surface into compartments, which we numbered, so that none might be missed; then we scrutinized each individual square inch throughout the premis-es, including the two houses immediately adjoining, with the microscope, as before."

"The two houses adjoining!" I exclaimed; "you must have had a great deal of trouble."

"We had; but the reward offered is prodigious."

"You include the *grounds* about the houses?"

"All the grounds are paved with brick. They gave us comparatively little trouble. We examined the moss between the bricks, and found it undisturbed."

"You looked among D——'s papers, of course, and into the books of the library?"

"Certainly; we opened every package and parcel; we not only opened every book, but we turned over every leaf in each volume, not contenting ourselves with a mere shake, according to the fashion of some of our police officers. We also measured the thickness of every book-*cover*, with the most accurate admeasurement, and applied to each the most jealous scrutiny of the microscope. Had any of the bindings been recently meddled with, it would have been utterly impossible that the fact should have escaped observation. Some five to six volumes, just from the hands of the binder, we carefully probed, longitudinally, with the needles."

"You explored the floors beneath the carpets?"

"Beyond doubt. We removed every carpet, and examined the boards with the microscope."

"And the paper on the walls?"

"Yes."

"You looked into the cellars?"

"We did."

"Then," I said, "you have been making a miscalculation, and the letter is *not* upon the premises, as you suppose."

"I fear you are right there," said the Prefect. "And now, Dupin, what would you advise me to do?"

"To make a thorough research of the premises."

"That is absolutely needless," replied G——. "I am not more sure that I breathe than I am that the letter is not at the hotel."

"I have no better advice to give you," said Dupin. "You have, of course, an accurate description of the letter?"

"Oh, yes!"—And here the Prefect, producing a memorandum book, proceeded to read aloud a minute account of the internal, and especially of the external, appearance of the missing document. Soon after finishing the perusal of this description, he took his departure, more entirely depressed in spirits than I had ever known the good gentlemen before.

In about a month afterward he paid us another visit, and found us occupied very nearly as before. He took a pipe and a chair and entered into some ordinary conversation. At length I said:

"Well, but G., what of the purloined letter? I presume you have at last made up your mind that there is no such thing as overreaching the Minister?"

"Confound him, say I—yes; I made the re-examination, however, as Dupin suggested—but it was all labor lost, as I knew it would be."

"How much was the reward offered, did you say?" asked Dupin.

"Why, a very great deal—a *very* liberal reward—I don't like to say how much, precisely; but one thing I *will* say, that I wouldn't mind giving my individual check for fifty thousand francs to any one who could obtain me that letter. The fact is, it is becoming of more and more importance every day; and the reward has been lately doubled. If it were trebled, however, I could do no more than I have done."

"Why, yes," said Dupin, drawlingly, between the whiffs of his meerschaum, "I really—think, G., you have not exerted yourself—to the utmost in this matter. You might—do a little more, I think, eh?"

"How?—in what way?"

"Why—*puff, puff*—you might—*puff, puff*—employ counsel in the matter, eh?—*puff, puff, puff.* Do you remember the story they tell of Abernethy?"

"No; hang Abernethy!"

"To be sure! hang him and welcome. But, once upon a time, a certain rich miser conceived the design of spunging upon this Abernethy for a medical opinion. Getting up, for this purpose, an ordinary conversation in a private company, he insinuated his case to the physician, as that of an imaginary individual.

"'We will suppose,' said the miser, 'that his symptoms are such and such; now, doctor, what would *you* have directed him to take?'

"'Take!' said Abernethy, 'why, take *advice* to be sure.'"

"But," said the Prefect, a little discomposed, "I am *perfectly* willing to take advice, and to pay for it. I would *really* give fifty thousand francs to any one who would aid me in the matter."

"In that case," replied Dupin, opening a drawer, and producing a checkbook, "you may as well fill me up a check for the amount mentioned. When you have signed it, I will hand you the letter."

I was astounded. The Prefect appeared absolutely thunder-stricken. For some minutes he remained speechless and motion-less, looking incredously at my friend with open mouth, and eyes that seemed starting from their sockets; then apparently recovering himself in some measure, he seized a pen, and after several pauses and vacant stares, finally filled up and signed a check for fifty thousand francs, and handed it across the table to Dupin. The latter examined it carefully and deposited it in his pocket-book; then, unlocking an *escritoire*, took thence a letter and gave it to the Prefect. This functionary grasped it in a perfect agony of joy, opened it with a trembling hand, cast a rapid glance at its contents, and then, scrambling and struggling to the door, rushed at length unceremoniously from the room and from the house, without having uttered a syllable since Dupin had requested him to fill up the check.

When he had gone, my friend entered into some explanations.

"The Parisian police," he said, "are exceedingly able in their way. They are persevering, ingenious, cunning, and thoroughly versed in the knowledge which their duties seem chiefly to demand. Thus, when G—— detailed to us his mode of searching the premises at the Hotel D——, I felt entire confidence in his having made a satisfactory investigation—so far as his labors extended."

"So far as his labors extended?" said I.

"Yes," said Dupin. "The measures adopted were not only the best of their kind, but carried out to absolute perfection. Had the letter been deposited within the range of their search, these fellows would, beyond a question, have found it."

I merely laughed—but he seemed quite serious in all that he said.

"The measures, then," he continued, "were good in their kind, and well executed; their defect lay in their being inapplicable to the case and to the man. A certain set of highly ingenious resources are, with the Prefect, a sort of Procrustean bed, to which he forcibly adapts his designs. But he perpetually errs by being too deep or too shallow for the matter in hand; and many a schoolboy is a better reasoner than he. I knew one about eight years of age, whose success at guessing in the game of 'even and odd' attracted universal admiration. This game is simple, and is played with marbles. One player holds in his hand a number of these toys, and demands of another whether that number is even or odd. If the guess is right, the guesser wins one; if wrong, he loses one. The boy to whom I allude won all the marbles of the school. Of course he had some principle of guessing; and this lay in mere observation and admeasurement of the astuteness of his opponents. For example, an arrant simpleton is his opponent, and, holding up his closed hand, asks, 'Are they even or odd?' Our school-boy replies, 'Odd,' and loses; but upon the second trial he wins, for he then says to himself: 'The simpleton had them even upon the first trial, and his amount of cunning is just sufficient to make him have them odd upon the second; I will therefore guess odd';—he guesses odd, and wins. Now, with a simpleton a degree above the first, he would have reasoned thus: 'This fellow finds that in the first instance I guessed odd, and, in the second, he will propose to himself, upon the first impulse, a simple variation from even to odd, as did the first simpleton; but then a second thought will suggest that this is too simple a variation, and finally he will decide upon putting it even as before. I will therefore guess even';—he guesses even, and wins. Now this mode of reasoning in the schoolboy, whom his fellows termed 'lucky,'—what, in its last analysis, is it?"

"It is merely," I said, "an identification of the reasoner's intellect with that of his opponent."

"It is," said Dupin; "and, upon inquiring of the boy by what means he effected the *thorough* identification in which his success consisted, I received answer as follows: 'When I wish to find out how wise, or how stupid, or how good, or how wicked is any one, or what are his thoughts at the moment, I fashion the expression of my face, as accurately as possible, in accordance with the expression of his, and then wait to see what thoughts or sentiments arise in my mind or heart, as if to match or correspond with the expression.' This response of the schoolboy lies at the bottom of all the spurious profundity which has been attributed to Rochefoucault, to La Bougive, to Machiavelli, and to Campanella."

"And the indentification," I said, "of the reasoner's intellect with that of his opponent, depends, if I understand you aright, upon the accuracy with which the opponent's intellect is admeasured."

"For its practical value it depends upon this," replied Dupin; "and the Prefect and his cohort fail so frequently, first, by default of this identification, and, secondly, by ill-admeasurement, or rather through nonadmeasurement, of the intellect with which they are engaged. They consider only their *own* ideas of ingenuity; and, in searching for any thing hidden, advert only to the modes in which *they* would have hidden it. They are right in this much—that their own ingenuity is a faithful representative of that of *the mass;* but when the cunning of the individual felon is diverse in character from their own, the felon foils them, of course. This always happens when it is above their own, and very usually when it is below. They have no variation of principle in their investigations; at best, when urged by some unusual emergency—by some extraordinary reward—they extend or exaggerate their old modes of *practice,* without touching their principles. What, for example, in this case of D——, has been done to vary the principle of action? What is all this boring, and probing, and sounding, and scrutinizing with the microscope, and dividing the surface of the building into registered square inches—what is it all but an exaggeration *of the application* of the one principle or set of principles of search, which are based upon the one set of notions regarding human ingenuity, to which the Prefect, in the long routine of his duty, has been accustomed? Do you not see he has taken it for granted that *all* men proceed to conceal a letter, not exactly in a gimlet hole bored in a chair leg, but, at least, in *some* out-of-the-way hole or corner suggested by the same tenor of thought which would urge a man to secrete a letter in a gimlet hole bored in a chair-leg? And do you not see also, that such *recherchés* nooks for concealment are adapted only for ordinary occasions, and would be adopted only by ordinary intellects; for, in all cases of concealment, a disposal of the article concealed—a disposal of it in this *recherché* manner,— is, in the very first instance, presumable and presumed; and thus its discovery depends, not at all upon the acumen, but altogether upon the mere care, patience, and determination of the seekers; and where the case is of importance—or, what amounts to the same thing in the political eyes, when the reward is of magnitude,—the qualities in question have *never* been known to fail. You will now understand what I meant in suggesting that, had the purloined letter been hidden anywhere within the limits of the Prefect's examination—in other words, had the principle of its concealment been comprehended within the principles of the Prefect—its discovery would have been a matter altogether beyond question. This functionary, however, has been thoroughly mystified; and the remote source of his defeat lies in the supposition that the Minister is a fool, because he has acquired renown as a poet. All fools are poets; this the Prefect *feels;* and he is merely guilty of a *non distributio medii* in thence inferring that all poets are fools."

"But is this really the poet?" I asked. "There are two brothers, I know; and both have attained reputation in letters. The Minister I believe has written learnedly on the Differential Calculus. He is a mathematician, and no poet."

"You are mistaken; I know him well; he is both. As poet *and* mathematician, he would reason well; as mere mathematician, he could not have reasoned at all, and thus would have been at the mercy of the Prefect."

"You surprise me," I said, "by these opinions, which have been contradicted by the voice of the world. You do not mean to set at naught the well-digested idea of centuries. The mathematical reason has long been regarded as *the* reason *par excellence.*"

" '*Il y a à parier,*'" replied Dupin, quoting from Chamfort, " '*que toute idée publique, toute convention reçue, est une sottise, car elle a convenue au plus grand nombre.*' The mathematicians, I grant you, have done their best to promulgate the popular error to which you allude, and which is none the less an error for its promulgation as truth. With an art worthy a better cause, for example, they have insinuated the term 'analysis' into application to algebra. The French are the originators of this particular deception; but if a term is of any importance—if words derive any value from applicability—then 'analysis' conveys 'algebra' about as much as, in Latin, '*ambitus*' implies 'ambition,' '*religio*' 'religion,' or '*homines honesti*' a set of *honorable* men."

"You have a quarrel on hand, I see," said I, "with some of the algebraists of Paris; but proceed."

"I dispute the availability, and thus the value, of that reason which is cultivated in any especial form other than the abstractly logical. I dispute, in particular, the reason educed by mathematical study. The mathematics are the science of form and quantity; mathematical reasoning is merely logic applied to observation upon form and quantity. The great error lies in supposing that even the truths of what is called *pure* algebra are abstract or general truths. And this error is so egregious that I am confounded at the universality with which it has been received. Mathematical axioms are *not* axioms of general truth. What is true of *relation*—or form and quantity—is often grossly false in regard to morals, for example. In this latter science it is very usually *un*true that the aggregated parts are equal to the whole. In chemistry also the axiom fails. In consideration of motive it fails; for two motives, each of a given value, have not, necessarily, a value when united, equal to the sum of their values apart. There are numerous other mathematical truths which are only truths within the limits of *relation*. But the mathematician argues from his *finite truths*, through habit, as if they were of an absolutely general applicability—as the world indeed imagines them to be. Bryant, in his very learned 'Mythology,' mentions an analogous source of error, when he says that 'although the pagan fables are not believed, yet we forget ourselves continually, and make inferences from them as existing realities.' With the algebraists, however, who are pagans themselves, the 'pagan fables' *are* believed, and the inferences are made, not so much through lapse of memory as through an unaccountable addling of the brains. In short, I never yet encountered the mere mathematician who would be trusted out of equal roots, or one who did not clandestinely hold it as a point of his faith that $x^2 + px$ was absolutely and unconditionally equal to q. Say to one these gentlemen, by way of experiment, if you please, that you believe occasions may occur where $x^2 + px$ is *not* altogether equal to q, and, having made him understand what you mean, get out of his reach as speedily as convenient, for, beyond doubt, he will endeavor to knock you down.

"I mean to say," continued Dupin, while I merely laughed at his last observations, "that if the Minister had been no more than a mathematician, the Prefect would have been under no necessity of giving me this check. I knew him, however, as both mathematician and poet, and my measures were adapted to his capacity, with reference to the circumstances by which he was surrounded. I knew him as a courtier, too, and as a bold *intriguant*. Such a man, I considered, could not fail to be aware of the ordinary policial modes of action. He could not have failed to anticipate—and events have proved that he did not fail to anticipate—the waylayings to which he was subjected. He must have foreseen, I reflected, the secret investigations of his premises. His frequent absences from home at night, which were hailed by the Prefect as certain aids to his success, I regarded only as *ruses*, to afford opportunity for thorough search to the police, and thus the sooner to impress them with the conviction to which G——, in fact, did finally arrive—the conviction that the letter was not upon the premises. I felt, also, that the whole train of thought, which I was at some pains in detailing to you just now, concerning the invariable principle of policial action in searches for articles concealed—I felt that this whole train of thought would necessarily pass through the mind of the minister. It would imperatively lead him to despise all the ordinary *nooks* of concealment. *He* could not, I reflected, be so weak as not to see that the most intricate and remote recess of his hotel would be as open as his commonest closets to the eyes, to the probes, to the gimlets, and to the microscopes of the Prefect. I saw, in fine, that he would be driven, as a matter of course, to *simplicity*, if not deliberately induced to it as a matter of choice. You will remember, perhaps, how desperately the Prefect laughed when I suggested, upon our first interview, that it was just possible this mystery troubled him so much on account of its being so *very* self-evident."

"Yes," said I, "I remember his merriment well. I really thought he would have fallen into convulsions."

"The material world," continued Dupin, "abounds with very strict analogies to the immaterial; and thus some color of truth has been given to the rhetorical dogma, that metaphor, or simile, may be made to strengthen an argument as well as to embellish a description. The principle of the *vis inertiæ*, for example, seems to be identical in physics and metaphysics. It is not more true in the former, that a large body is with more difficulty set in motion than a smaller one, and that its subsequent *momentum* is commensurate with this difficulty, that it is, in the latter, that intellects of the vaster capacity, while more forcible, more constant, and more eventful in their movements than those of inferior grade, are yet the less readily moved, and more embarrassed, and full of hesitation in the first few steps of their progress. Again: have you ever noticed which of the street signs, over the shop doors, are the most attractive of attention?"

"I have never given the matter a thought," I said.

"There is a game of puzzles," he resumed, "which is played upon a map. One party playing requires another to find a given word—the name of town, river, state, or empire—any word, in short, upon the motley and perplexed surface of the chart. A novice in the game generally seeks to embarrass his opponents by giving them the most minutely lettered names; but the adept selects such words as stretch, in large characters, from one end of the chart to the other. These, like the over-largely lettered signs and placards of the street, escape observation by dint of being excessively obvious; and here the physical oversight is precisely analogous with the moral inapprehension by which the intellect suffers to pass unnoticed those considerations which are too obtrusively and too palpably self-evident. But this is a point, it appears, somewhat above or beneath the understanding of the Prefect. He never once thought it probable, or possible, that the minister had deposited the letter immediately beneath the nose of the whole world, by way of best preventing any portion of that world from perceiving it.

But the more I reflected upon the daring, dashing, and discriminating ingenuity of D——; upon the fact that the document must always have been *at hand*, if he intended to use it to good purpose; and upon the decisive evidence, obtained by the Prefect, that it was not hidden within the limits of that dignitary's ordinary search—the more satisfied I became that, to conceal this letter, the minister had resorted to the comprehensive and sagacious expedient of not attempting to conceal it at all.

"Full of these ideas, I prepared myself with a pair of green spectacles, and called one fine morning, quite by accident, at the Ministerial hotel. I found D——at home, yawning, lounging, and dawdling, as usual, and pretending to be in the last extremity of *ennui*. He is, perhaps, the most really energetic human being now alive—but that is only when nobody sees him.

"To be even with him, I complained of my weak eyes, and lamented the necessity of the spectacles, under cover of which I cautiously and thoroughly surveyed the whole apartment, while seemingly intent only upon the conversation of my host.

"I paid especial attention to a large writing table near which he sat, and upon which lay confusedly, some miscellaneous letters and other papers, with one or two musical instruments and a few books. Here, however, after a long and very deliberate scrutiny, I saw nothing to excite particular suspicion.

"At length my eyes, in going the circuit of the room, fell upon a triumphery filigree card-rack of pasteboard, that hung dangling by a dirty blue ribbon, from a little brass knob just beneath the middle of the mantelpiece. In this rack, which had three or four compartments, were five or six visiting cards and a solitary letter. This last was much soiled and crumpled. It was torn nearly in two, across the middle—as if a design, in the first instance, to tear it entirely up as worthless, had been altered, or stayed, in the second. It had a large black seal, bearing the D——cipher *very* conspicuously, and was addressed, in a diminutive female hand, to D——, the minister, himself. It was thrust carelessly, and even, as it seemed, contemptuously, into one of the uppermost divisions of the rack.

"No sooner had I glanced at this letter than I concluded it to be that of which I was in search. To be sure, it was, to all appearance, radically different from the one of which the Prefect had read us so minute a description. Here the seal was large and black, with the D——cipher; there it was small and red, with the ducal arms of the S——family. Here, the address, to the minister, was diminutive and feminine; there the superscription, to a certain royal personage, was markedly bold and decided; the size alone formed a point of correspondence. But, then, the *radicalness* of these differences, which was excessive; the dirt; the soiled and torn condition of the paper, so inconsistent with the *true* methodical habits of D——, and so suggestive of a design to delude the beholder into an idea of the worthlessness of the document;—these things, together with the hyperobtrusive situation of this document, full in the view of every visitor, and thus exactly in accordance with the conclusions to which I had previously arrived; these things, I say, were strongly corroborative of suspicion, in one who came with the intention to suspect.

"I protracted my visit as long as possible, and, while I maintained a most animated discussion with the minister, upon a topic which I knew well had never failed to interest and excite him, I kept my attention really riveted upon the letter. In this examination, I committed to memory its external appearance and arrangement in the rack; and also fell, at length, upon a discovery which set at rest whatever trivial doubt I might have entertained. In scrutinizing the edges of the paper, I observed them to be more *chafed* than seemed necessary. They presented the *broken* appearance which is manifested when a stiff paper, having been once folded and pressed with a folder, is refolded in a reversed direction, in the same creases or edges which had formed the original fold. This discovery was sufficient. It was clear to me that the letter had been turned, as a glove, inside out, redirected and resealed. I bade the minister good morning, and took my departure at once, leaving a gold snuff box upon the table.

"The next morning I called for the snuff box, when we resumed, quite eagerly, the conversation of the preceding day. While thus engaged, however, a loud report, as if of a pistol, was heard immediately beneath the windows of the hotel, and was succeeded by a series of fearful screams, and the shoutings of a terrified mob. D——rushed to a casement, threw it open, and looked out. In the meantime I stepped to the card-rack, took the letter, put it in my pocket, and replaced it by a *facsimile*, (so far as regards externals) which I had carefully prepared at my lodgings—imitating the D——cipher, very readily, by means of a seal formed of bread.

"The disturbance in the street had been occasioned by the frantic behavior of a man with a musket. He had fired it among a crowd of women and children. It proved, however, to have been without ball, and the fellow was suffered to go his way as a lunatic or a drunkard. When he had gone, D——came from the window, whither I had followed him immediately upon securing the object in view. Soon afterward I bade him farewell. The pretended lunatic was a man in my own pay."

"But what purpose had you," I asked, "in replacing the letter by a *facsimile?* Would it not have been better, at the first visit, to have seized it openly, and departed?"

"D——," replied Dupin, "is a desperate man, and a man of nerve. His hotel, too, is not without attendants devoted to his interests. Had I made the wild attempt you suggest, I might never have left the Ministerial presence alive. The good people of Paris might have heard of me no more. But I had an object apart from these considerations. You know my political prepossessions. In this matter, I act as a partisan of the lady concerned. For eighteen months the Minister has had her in his power. She has now him in hers—since, being unaware that the letter is not in his possession, he will proceed with his exactions as if it was. Thus will he inevitably commit himself, at once, to his political destruction. His downfall, too, will not be more precipitate than awkward. It is all very well to talk about the *facilis descensus Averni;* but in all kinds of climbing, as Catalani said of singing, it is far more easy to get up than to come down. In the present instance I have no sympathy—at least no pity—for him who descends. He is that *monstrum horrendum*, an unprincipled man of genius. I confess, however, that I should like very well to know the precise character of his thoughts, when, being defied by her whom the Prefect terms 'a certain personage,' he is reduced to opening the letter which I left for him in the card-rack."

"How? did you put any thing particular in it?"

"Why—it did not seem altogether right to leave the interior blank—that would have been insulting. D——, at Vienna once, did me an evil turn, which I told him, quite good-humoredly, that I should remember. So, as I knew he would feel some curiosity in regard to the identity of the person who had outwitted him, I thought it a pity not to give him a clue. He is well acquainted with my MS., and I just copied into the middle of the blank sheet the words—

"'_____   ——Un dessein si funeste,
S'il n'est digne d'Atrée, est digne de Thyeste.'

They are to be found in Crébillon's 'Atrée.'"

1852

A Terribly Strange Bed

WILKIE COLLINS

Shortly after my education at college was finished, I happened to be staying at Paris with an English friend. We were both young men then, and lived, I am afraid, rather a wild life, in the delightful city of our sojourn. One night we were idling about the neighborhood of the Palais Royal, doubtful to what amusement we should next betake ourselves. My friend proposed a visit to Frascati's, but his suggestion was not to my taste. I knew Frascati's, as the French saying is, by heart; had lost and won plenty of five-franc pieces there, merely for amusement's sake, until it was amusement no longer, and was thoroughly tired, in fact, of all the ghastly respectabilities of such a social anomaly as a respectable gambling-house. "For heaven's sake," said I to my friend, "let us go somewhere where we can see a little genuine, blackguard, poverty-stricken gaming with no false gingerbread glitter thrown over it at all. Let us get away from fashionable Frascati's, to a house where they don't mind letting in a man with a ragged coat, or a man with no coat, ragged or otherwise."—"Very well," said my friend, "we needn't go out of the Palais Royal to find the sort of company you want. Here's the place just before us; as blackguard a place, by all report, as you could possibly wish to see." In another minute we arrived at the door, and entered the house.

When we got up stairs, and had left our hats and sticks with the doorkeeper, we were admitted into the chief gambling room. We did not find many people assembled there. But, few as the men were who looked up at us on our entrance, they were all types, lamentably true types, of their respective classes.

34

We had come to see blackguards; but these men were something worse. There is a comic side, more or less appreciable, in all blackguardism. Here there was nothing but tragedy—mute, weird tragedy. The quiet in the room was horrible. The thin, haggard, long-haired young man, whose sunken eyes fiercely watched the turning-up of the cards, never spoke; the flabby, fat-faced, pimply player, who picked his piece of pasteboard perseveringly, to register how often black won, and how often red, never spoke; the dirty, wrinkled old man, with the vulture eyes, and the darned greatcoat, who had lost his last *sou*, and still looked on desperately, after he could play no longer, never spoke. Even the voice of the croupier sounded as if it were strangely dulled and thickened in the atmosphere of the room. I had entered the place to laugh; but the spectacle before me was something to weep over. I soon found it necessary to take refuge, in excitement, from the depression of spirits which was fast stealing on me. Unfortunately I sought the nearest excitement by going to the table, and beginning to play. Still more unfortunately, as the event will show, I won—won prodigiously; won incredibly; won at such a rate, that the regular players at the table crowded round me, and staring at my stakes with hungry, superstitious eyes, whispered to one another, that the English stranger was going to break the bank.

The game was *Rouge et Noir*. I had played at it in every city in Europe, without, however, the care or the wish to study the theory of chances, that philosopher's stone of all gamblers. And a gambler, in the strict sense of the word, I had never been. I was heart-whole from the corroding passion for play. My gaming was a mere idle amusement. I never resorted to it by necessity, because I never knew what it was to want money. I never practised it so incessantly as to lose more than I could afford, or to gain more than I could coolly pocket without being thrown off my balance by my good luck. In short, I had hitherto frequented gambling tables, just as I frequented ball rooms and opera houses, because they amused me, and because I had nothing better to do with my leisure hours.

But on this occasion it was very different. Now, for the first time in my life, I felt what the passion for play really was. My success first bewildered, and then, in the most literal meaning of the word, intoxicated me. Incredible as it may appear, it is nevertheless true, that I only lost when I attempted to estimate chances, and played according to previous calculation. If I left everything to luck, and staked without any care or consideration, I was sure to win—to win in the face of every recognized probability in favor of the bank. At first some of the men present ventured their money safely enough on my color; but I speedily increased my stakes to sums which they dared not risk. One after another, they left off playing, and breathlessly looked on at my game.

Still, time after time, I staked higher and higher, and still won. The excitement in the room rose to fever pitch. The silence was interrupted by a deep, muttered chorus of oaths and exclamations in different languages, every time the gold was shovelled across to my side of the table. Even the imperturbable croupier dashed his rake on the floor in a (French) fury of astonishment at my success. But one man present preserved his self-possession; and that man was my friend. He came to my side, and, whispering in English, begged me to leave the place satisfied with what I had already gained. I must do him the justice to say that he repeated his warnings and entreaties several times; and only left me, and went away, after I had rejected his advice (I was, to all intents and purposes, gambling-drunk) in terms which rendered it impossible for him to address me again that night.

Shortly after he had gone, a hoarse voice behind me cried, "Permit me, my dear sir, permit me to restore to their proper place two Napoleons which you have dropped. Wonderful luck, sir! I pledge you my word of honor as an old soldier, in the course of my long experience in this sort of thing, I never saw such luck as yours, never! Go on, sir; *sacré mille bombes!* Go on boldly, and break the bank!"

I turned round, and saw, nodding and smiling at me with inveterate civility, a tall man, dressed in a frogged and braided surtout.

If I had been in my senses, I should have considered him, personally, as being rather a suspicious specimen of an old soldier. He had goggling, bloodshot eyes, mangy mustachios, and a broken nose. His voice betrayed a barrack-room intonation of the worst order; and he had the dirtiest pair of hands I ever saw, even in France. These little personal peculiarities exercised, however, no repelling influence on me. In the mad excitement, the reckless triumph, of that moment, I was ready to "fraternize" with anybody who encouraged me in my game. I accepted the old soldier's proffered pinch of snuff, clapped him on the back, and swore he was the honestest fellow in the world—the most glorious relic of the Grand Army that I had ever met with. "Go on!" cried my military friend, snapping his fingers in ecstasy—"go on, and win! Break the bank; *mille tonnerres!* My gallant English comrade, break the bank!"

And I *did* go on—went on at such a rate, that in another quarter of an hour the croupier called out, "Gentlemen, the bank has discontinued for tonight!" All the notes, and all the gold in that "bank," now lay in a heap under my hands; the whole floating capital of the gambling house was waiting to pour into my pockets.

"Tie up the money in your pocket-handkerchief, my worthy sir," said the old soldier, as I wildly plunged my hands into my heap of gold. "Tie it up as we used to tie up a bit of dinner in the Grand Army: your winnings are too heavy for any breeches-pockets that ever were sewed. There, that's it. Shovel them in, notes and all. *Credié!* what luck! Stop! another Napoleon on the floor! *Ah! sacré petit polisson de Napoleon!* have I found thee at last? Now then, sir, two tight double-knots each way, with your honorable permission, and the money's safe. Feel it! feel it, fortunate sir! hard and round as a cannon-ball. *Ah, bah!* if they had only fired such cannon-balls at us at Austerlitz! *nom d'une pipe!* if they only had! And now, as an ancient grenadier, as an ex-brave of the French army, what remains for me to do? I ask what? Simply this: to entreat my valued English friend to drink a bottle of champagne with me, and toast the goddess Fortune in foaming goblets before we part!"

"Excellent ex-brave! Convivial ancient grenadier! Champagne by all means! An English cheer for an old soldier! Hurrah! hurrah! Another English cheer for the goddess Fortune! Hurrah! hurrah! hurrah!"

"Bravo! the Englishman; the amiable, gracious Englishman, in whose veins circulates the vivacious blood of France! Another glass? *Ah, bah!* the bottle is empty. Never mind! *Vive le vin!* I, the old soldier, order another bottle, and half a pound of *bonbons* with it!"

"No, no, ex-brave; never, ancient grenadier! *Your* bottle last time; *my* bottle this. Behold it! Toast away! The French army! the great Napoleon! the present company! the croupier! the honest croupier's wife and daughters—if he has any! the ladies generally! Everybody in the world!"

By the time the time the second bottle of champagne was emptied, I felt as if I had been drinking liquid fire: my brain seemed all aflame. No excess in wine had ever had this effect on me before in my life. Was it the result of a stimulant acting upon my system when I was in a highly excited state? Was my stomach in a particularly disordered condition? Or was the champagne amazingly strong?

"Ex-brave of the French army!" cried I, in a mad state of exhilaration, "*I am* on fire! how are *you?* You have set me on fire! Do you hear, my hero of Austerlitz? Let us have a third bottle of champagne to put the flame out!"

The old soldier wagged his head, rolled his goggle eyes, until I expected to see them slip out of their sockets; placed his dirty forefinger by the side of his broken nose; solemnly ejaculated "Coffee!" and immediately ran off into an inner room.

The word pronounced by the eccentric veteran seemed to have a magical effect on the rest of the company present. With one accord they all rose to depart. Probably they had expected to profit by my intoxication; but, finding that my new friend was benevolently bent on preventing me from getting dead drunk, had now abandoned all hope of thriving pleasantly on my winnings. Whatever their motive might be, at any rate they went away in a body. When the old soldier returned, and sat down again opposite me at the table, we had the room to ourselves. I could see the croupier, in a sort of vestibule which opened out of it, eating his supper in solitude. The silence was now deeper than ever.

A sudden change, too, had come over the "ex-brave." He

assumed a portentously solemn look; and, when he spoke to me again, his speech was ornamented by no oaths, enforced by no finger-snapping, enlivened by no apostrophes or exclamations.

"Listen, my dear sir," he said, in mysteriously confidential tones—"listen to an old soldier's advice. I have been to the mistress of this house (a very charming woman, with a genius for cookery), to impress on her the necessity of making us some particularly strong and good coffee. You must drink this coffee in order to get rid of your little amiable exaltation of spirits before you think of going home—you *must*, my good and gracious friend! With all that money to take home tonight, it is a sacred duty to yourself to have your wits about you. You are known to be a winner, to an enormous extent, by several gentlemen present tonight, who, in a certain point of view, are very worthy and excellent fellows; but they are mortal men, my dear sir, and they have their amiable weaknessess! Need I say more? Ah, no, no! you understand me. Now, this is what you must do,—send for a cabriolet when you feel quite well again, draw up all the windows when you get into it, and tell the driver to take you home only through the large and well-lighted thoroughfares. Do this, and you and yor money will be safe. Do this, and tomorrow you will thank an old soldier for giving you a word of honest advice."

Just as the ex-brave ended his oration in very lachrymose tones, the coffee came in, ready poured out in two cups. My attentive friend handed me one of the cups with a bow. I was parched with thirst, and drank it off at a draught. Almost instantly afterwards, I was seized with a fit of giddiness, and felt more completely intoxicated than ever. The room whirled round and round furiously; the old soldier seemed to be regularly bobbing up and down before me like the piston of the steam-engine. I was half deafened by a violent singing in my ears; a feeling of utter bewilderment, helplessness, idiocy, overcame me. I rose from my chair, holding on by the table to keep my balance; and stammered out, that I felt dreadfully unwell—so unwell that I did not know how I was to get home.

"My dear friend," answered the old soldier, and even his voice seemed to be bobbing up and down as he spoke, "my dear friend, it would be madness to go home in *your* state; you would be sure to lose your money; you might be robbed and murdered with the greatest ease. *I* am going to sleep here: do *you* sleep here too. They make up capital beds in this house: take one, sleep off the effects of the wine, and go home safely with your winnings tomorrow—tomorrow, in broad daylight."

I had but two ideas left—one, that I must never let go hold of my handkerchief full of money; the other, that I must lie down somewhere immediately, and fall off into a comfortable sleep. So I agreed to the proposal about the bed, and took the offered arm of the old soldier, carrying my money with my disengaged hand. Preceded by the croupier, we passed along some passages, and up a flight of stairs, into the bedroom which I was to occupy. The ex-brave shook me warmly by the hand, proposed that we should breakfast together, and then, followed by the croupier, left me for the night.

I ran to the wash-stand; drank some of the water in my jug; poured the rest out, and plunged my face into it; then sat down in a chair, and tried to compose myself. I soon felt better. The change for my lungs, from the fetid atmosphere of the gambling-room to the cool air of the apartment I now occupied; the almost equally refreshing change for my eyes, from the glaring gas lights of the "salon" to the dim, quiet flicker of one bedroom candle—aided wonderfully the restorative effects of cold water. The giddiness left me, and I began to feel a little like a reasonable being again. My first thought was of the risk of sleeping all night in a gambling house; my second, of the still greater risk of trying to get out after the house was closed, and of going home alone at night, through the streets of Paris, with a large sum of money about me. I had slept in worse places than this on my travels: so I determined to lock, bolt, and barricade my door, and take my chance till the next morning.

Accordingly, I secured myself against all intrusion; looked under the bed, and into the cupboard; tried the fastening of the window; and then, satisfied that I had taken every proper precaution, pulled off my upper clothing, put my light, which was a dim one, on the hearth among a feathery litter of wood-ashes, and got into bed, with the handkerchief full of money under my pillow.

I soon felt not only that I could not go to sleep, but that I could not even close my eyes. I was wide awake, and in a high fever. Every nerve in my body trembled; every one of my senses seemed to be preternaturally sharpened. I tossed and rolled, and tried every kind of position, and perseveringly sought out the cold corners of the bed, and all to no purpose. Now I thrust my arms over the clothes; now I poked them under the clothes. Now I violently shot my legs straight out down to the bottom of the bed; now I convulsively coiled them up as near my chin as they would go. Now I shook out my crumpled pillow, changed it to the cool side, patted it flat, and lay down quietly on my back; now I fiercely doubled it in two, set it up on end, thrust it against the board of the bed, and tried a sitting-posture. Every effort was in vain. I groaned with vexation, as I felt that I was in for a sleepless night.

What could I do? I had no book to read. And yet, unless I found out some method of diverting my mind, I felt certain that I was in the condition to imagine all sorts of horror, to rack my brain with forebodings of every possible and impossible danger, in short, to pass the night in suffering all conceivable varieties of nervous terror.

I raised myself on my elbow, and looked about the room, which was brightened by a lovely moonlight pouring straight through the window, to see if it contained any pictures or ornaments that I could at all clearly distinguish. While my eyes wandered from wall to wall, a remembrance of Le Maistre's delightful little book, "Voyage autour de ma Chambre," occurred to me. I resolved to imitate the French author, and find occupation and amusement enough to relieve the tedium of my wakefulness, by making a mental inventory of every article of furniture I could see, and by following up to their sources the multitude of associations which even a chair, a table, or a wash-hand stand may be made to call forth.

In the nervous, unsettled state of my mind at that moment, I found it much easier to make my inventory than to make my reflections, and thereupon soon gave up all hope of thinking in Le Maistre's fanciful track, or, indeed, of thinking at all. I looked about the room at the different articles of furniture, and did nothing more.

There was, first, the bed I was lying in—a four-post bed, of all things in the world, to meet with in Paris! yes, a thorough, clumsy British four-poster, with the regular top lined with chintz, the regular fringed valance all around, the regular stifling, unwholesome curtains, which I remembered having mechanically drawn back against the post, without particularly noticing the bed, when I first got into the room. Then there was the marble-topped wash-hand stand, from which the water I had spilt, in my hurry to pour it out, was still dripping, slowly and more slowly, on to the brick floor. Then two small chairs with my coat, waistcoat, and trousers flung on them. Then a large elbow-chair, covered with dirty white dimity, with my cravat and shirt-collar thrown over the back. Then a chest of drawers with two of the brass handles off, and a tawdry, broken china inkstand placed on it by way of ornament for the top. Then the dressing table, adorned by a very small looking glass, and a very large pincushion. Then the window, an unusually large window. Then a dark old picture, which the feeble candle dimly showed me. It was the picture of a fellow in a high Spanish hat, crowned with a plume of towering feathers. A swarthy, sinister ruffian, looking upward, shading his eyes with his hand, and looking intently upward, it might be at some tall gallows at which he was going to be hanged. At any rate, he had the appearance of thoroughly deserving it.

The picture put a kind of constraint upon me to look upward, too, at the top of the bed. It was a gloomy, and not an interesting object; and I looked back at the picture. I counted the feathers in the man's hat: they stood out in relief—three white, two green. I observed the crown of his hat, which was of a conical shape, according to the fashion supposed to have been favored by Guido Fawkes. I wondered what he was looking at. It couldn't be at the star: such a desperado was neither astrologer nor astronomer. It must be at the high gallows, and he was going to be hanged presently. Would the executioner come into possession of his conical crowned hat, and plume of feathers? I counted the feathers again—three white, two green.

While I still lingered over this very improving and intellectual employment, my thoughts insensibly began to wander. The moonlight shining into the room reminded me of a certain moonlight night in England, the night after a picnic party in a Welsh valley. Every incident of the drive homeward through lovely scenery, which the moonlight made lovelier than ever, came back to my remembrance, though I had never given the picnic a thought for years; though, if I had *tried* to recollect it, I could certainly have recalled little or nothing of that scene long past. Of all the wonderful faculties that help to tell us we are immortal, which speaks the sublime truth more eloquently than memory? Here was I, in a strange house of the most suspicious character, in a situation of uncertainty, and even of peril, which might seem to make the cool exercise of my recollection almost out of the question; nevertheless remembering, quite involuntarily, places, people, conversations, minute circumstances of every kind, which I had thought forgotten forever, which I could not possibly have recalled at will, even under the most favorable auspices. And what cause had produced, in a moment, the whole of this strange, complicated, mysterious effect? Nothing but some rays of moonlight shining in at my bedroom window.

I was still thinking of the picnic, of our merriment on the drive home, of the sentimental young lady who *would* quote Childe Harold because it was moonlight; I was absorbed by these past scenes and past amusements,—when, in an instant, the thread on which my memories hung snapped asunder; my attention immediately came back to present things more vividly than ever; and I found myself, I neither knew why nor wherefore, looking hard at the picture again.

Looking for what?

Good God! the man had pulled his hat down on his brows! No, the hat itself was gone! Where was the conical crown? Where the feathers—three white, two green? Not there. In place of the hat and feathers, what dusky object was it that now hid his forehead, his eyes, his shading hand?

Was the bed moving?

I turned on my back, and looked up. Was I mad? drunk? dreaming? giddy again? Or was the top of the bed really moving down, sinking slowly, regularly, silently, horribly, right down throughout the whole of its length and breadth, right down upon me, as I lay underneath?

My blood seemed to stand still. A deadly, paralyzing coldness stole all over me, as I turned my head round on the pillow, and determined to test whether the bed-top was really moving or not, by keeping my eye on the man in the picture. The next look in that direction was enough. The dull, black, frowzy outline of the valance above me was within an inch of being parallel with his waist. I still looked breathlessly; and steadily, and slowly, very slowly, I saw the figure, and the line of frame below the figure, vanish, as the valance moved down before it.

I am, constitutionally, anything but timid. I have been, on more than one occasion, in peril of my life, and have not lost my self-possession for an instant; but when the conviction first settled on my mind that the bed-top was really moving, was steadily and continuously sinking down upon me, I looked up shuddering, helpless, panic-stricken, beneath the hideous machinery for murder, which was advancing closer and closer to suffocate me where I lay.

I looked up motionless, speechless, breathless. The candle, fully spent, went out; but the moonlight still brightened the room. Down and down, without pausing and without sounding, came the bed-top; and still my panic-terror seemed to bind me faster and faster to the mattress on which I lay. Down and down it sank, till the dusty odor from the lining of the canopy came stealing into my nostrils.

At that final moment, the instinct of self-preservation startled me out of my trance, and I moved at last. There was just room for me to roll myself sideways off the bed. As I dropped noiselessly to the floor, the edge of the murderous canopy touched me on the shoulder.

Without stopping to draw my breath, without wiping the cold sweat from my face, I rose instantly on my knees to watch the bed-top. I was literally spellbound by it. If I had heard footsteps behind me, I could not have turned round; if a means of escape had been miraculously provided for me, I could not have moved to take advantage of it. The whole life in me was, at that moment, concentrated in my eyes.

It descended; the whole canopy, with the fringe around it,

came down, down, close down, so close that there was not room now to squeeze my finger between the bed-top and the bed. I felt at the sides, and discovered that what had appeared to me, from beneath, to be the ordinary light canopy of a four-post bed, was in reality a thick, broad mattress, the substance of which was concealed by the valance and its fringe. I looked up, and saw the four posts rising hideously bare. In the middle of the bed-top was a huge wooden screw that had evidently worked it down through a hole in the ceiling, just as ordinary presses are worked down on the substance selected for compression. The frightful apparatus moved without making the faintest noise. There had been no creaking as it came down: there was now not the faintest sound from the room above. Amid a dead and awful silence, I beheld before me, in the nineteenth century, and in the civilized capital of France, such a machine for secret murder by suffocation as might have existed in the worst days of the Inquisition, in the lonely inns among the Harz Mountains, in the mysterious tribunals of Westphalia! Still, as I looked on it, I could not move; I could hardly breathe; but I began to recover the power of thinking, and in a moment I discovered the murderous conspiracy framed against me, in all its horror.

My cup of coffee had been drugged, and drugged too strongly. I had been saved from being smothered by having taken an overdose of some narcotic. How I had chafed and fretted at the fever-fit which had preserved my life by keeping me awake! How recklessly I had confided myself to the two wretches who had led me into this room, determined, for the sake of my winnings, to kill me in my sleep by the surest and most horrible contrivance for secretly accomplishing my destruction! How many men, winners like me, had slept, as I had proposed to sleep, in that bed, and had never been seen or heard of more! I shuddered at the bare idea of it.

But, ere long, all thought was again suspended by the sight of the murderous canopy moving once more. After it had remained on the bed, as nearly as I could guess, about ten minutes, it began to move up again. The villains who worked it from above evidently believed that their purpose was now accomplished. Slowly and silently, as it had descended, that horrible bed-top rose towards its former place. When it reached the upper extremities of the four posts, it reached the ceiling too. Neither hole nor screw could be seen; the bed became, in appearance, an ordinary bed again, the canopy an ordinary canopy, even to the most suspicious eyes.

Now, for the first time, I was able to move, to rise from my knees, to dress myself in my upper clothing, and to consider of how I should escape. If I betrayed, by the slightest noise, that the attempt to suffocate me had failed, I was certain to be murdered. Had I made any noise already? I listened intently, looking towards the door.

No! no footsteps in the passage outside; no sound of a tread, light or heavy, in the room above: absolute silence everywhere. Besides locking and bolting my door, I had moved an old wooden chest against it, which I had found under the bed. To remove this chest (my blood ran cold as I thought what its contents *might* be), without making some disturbance, was impossible; and, moreover, to think of escaping through the house, now barred up for the night, was sheer insanity. Only one chance was left for me—the window. I stole to it on tiptoe.

My room was on the second floor, above an *entresol*, and looked into the back street. I raised my hand to open the window, knowing that on that action hung, by the merest hair's breadth, my chance of safety. They keep vigilant watch in a house of murder. If any part of the frame cracked, if the hinge creaked, I was a lost man! It must have occupied me at least five minutes, reckoning by time—five *hours*, reckoning by suspense—to open that window. I succeeded in doing it silently, in doing it with all the dexterity of a housebreaker, and then looked down into the street. To leap the distance beneath me would be almost certain destruction. Next I looked round at the sides of the house. Down the left side ran a thick water-pipe: it passed close by the outer edge of the window. The moment I saw the pipe, I knew I was saved. My breath came and went freely for the first time since I had seen the canopy of the bed moving down upon me.

To some men, the means of escape which I had discovered

might have seemed difficult and dangerous enough: to *me*, the prospect of slipping down the pipe into the street did not suggest even a thought of peril. I had always been accustomed, by the practice of gymnastics, to keep up my schoolboy powers as a daring and expert climber; and knew that my head, hands, and feet would serve me faithfully in any hazards of ascent or descent. I had already got one leg over the window sill, when I remembered the handkerchief filled with money under my pillow. I could well have afforded to leave it behind me; but I was revengefully determined that the miscreants of the gambling house should miss their plunder, as well as their victim. So I went back to the bed, and tied the heavy handkerchief at my back by my cravat.

Just as I had made it tight, and fixed it in a comfortable place, I thought I heard a sound of breathing outside the door. The chill feeling of horror ran through me again as I listened. No! dead silence still in the passage: I had only heard the night air blowing softly into the room. The next moment I was on the window sill; and the next I had a firm grip on the water-pipe with my hands and knees.

I slid down into the street easily and quietly, as I thought I should, and immediately set off, at the top of my speed, to a branch "prefecture" of police, which I knew was situated in the immediate neighborhood. A "sub-prefect," and several picked men among his subordinates, happened to be up, maturing, I believe, some scheme for discovering the perpetrator of a mysterious murder which all Paris was talking of just then. When I began my story in a breathless hurry, and in very bad French, I could see that the sub-prefect suspected me of being a drunken Englishman who had robbed somebody; but he soon altered his opinion as I went on; and, before I had anything like concluded, he shoved all the papers before him into a drawer, put on his hat, supplied me with another (for I was bareheaded), ordered a file of soldiers, desired his expert followers to get ready all sorts of tools for breaking open doors, and ripping up brick flooring, and took my arm, in the most friendly and familiar manner possible, to lead me with him out of the house. I will venture to say, that when the sub-prefect was a little boy, and was taken for the first time to the play, he was not half as much pleased as he was now at the job in prospect for him at the gambling-house.

Away we went through the streets, the sub-prefect cross-examining and congratulating me in the same breath, as we marched at the head of our formidable *posse comitatus*. Sentinels were placed at the back and front of the house the moment we got to it. A tremendous battery of knocks was directed against the door; a light appeared at the window; I was told to conceal myself behind the police. Then came more knocks, and a cry of "Open, in the name of the law!" At that terrible summons, bolts and locks gave way before an invisible hand; and, the moment after, the sub-prefect was in the passage, confronting a waiter, half-dressed, and ghastly pale. This was the short dialogue which immediately took place:—

"We want to see the Englishman who is sleeping in this house."

"He went away hours ago."

"He did no such thing. His friend went away: *he* remained. Show us to his bedroom."

"I swear to you, M. le Sous-prefet, he is not here. He—"

"I swear to you, M. le Garçon, he is. He slept here; he didn't find your bed comfortable; he came to us to complain of it; here he is, among my men; and here am I, ready to look for a flea or two in his bedstead. Renaudin!" (calling to one of the subordinates and pointing to the waiter), "collar that man, and tie his hands behind him. Now, then, gentlemen, let us walk upstairs."

Every man and woman in the house was secured—the "old soldier" the first. Then I identified the bed in which I had slept; and then we went into the room above.

No object that was at all extraordinary appeared in any part of it. The sub-prefect looked round the place, commanded everybody to be silent, stamped twice on the floor, called for a candle, looked attentively at the spot he had stamped on, and ordered the flooring there to be carefully taken up. This was done in no time. Lights were produced; and we saw a deep, raftered cavity between the floor of this room, and the ceiling of the room beneath. Through this cavity, there ran perpendicularly a sort of case of iron, thickly greased; and inside the case appeared the screw, which communicated with the bed-top below. Extra lengths of screw, freshly oiled; levers, covered with felt; all the complete upper works of a heavy press, constructed with infernal ingenuity so as to join the fixtures below, and when taken to pieces again, to go into the smallest possible compass—were next discovered, and pulled out upon the floor. After some little difficulty, the sub-prefect succeeded in putting the machinery together, and, leaving his men to work it, descended with me to the bedroom. The smothering canopy was then lowered, but not so noiselessly as I had seen it lowered. When I mentioned this to the sub-prefect, his answer, simple as it was, had a terrible significance. "My men," said he, "are working down the bed-top for the first time: the men whose money you won were in better practice."

We left the house in the sole possession of two police-agents, every one of the inmates being removed to prison on the spot. The sub-prefect, after taking down my *procès verbal* in his office, returned with me to my hotel to get my passport. "Do you think," I asked, as I gave it to him, "that any men have really been smothered in that bed, as they tried to smother *me?*"

"I have seen dozens of drowned men laid out at the Morgue," answered the sub-prefect, "in whose pocket-books were found letters, stating that they had committed suicide in the Seine, because they had lost everything at the gaming table. Do I know how many of those men entered the same gambling house that *you* entered, won as *you* won, took that bed as *you* took it, slept in it, were smothered in it, and were privately thrown into the river, with a letter of explanation written by the murderers, and placed in their pocket-books? No man can say how many, or how few, have suffered the fate from which you have escaped. The people of the gambling house kept their bedstead-machinery a secret from *us*, even from the police. The dead kept the rest of the secret from them. Good night, or, rather, good morning, Mr. Faulkner! Be at my office again at nine o'clock. In the meantime, *au revoir!*"

The rest of my story is soon told. I was examined and re-examined; the gambling house was strictly searched all through, from top to bottom; the prisoners were separately interrogated; and two of the less guilty among them made a confession. *I* discovered that the old soldier was the master of the gambling house: *justice* discovered that he had been drummed out of the army, as a vagabond, years ago; that he had been guilty of all sorts of villainies since, that he was in possession of stolen property, which the owners identified; and that he, the croupier, another accomplice, and the woman who had made my cup of coffee, were all in the secret of the bedstead. There appeared some reason to doubt whether the inferior persons attached to the house knew anything of the suffocating machinery; and they received the benefit of that doubt, by being treated simply as thieves and vagabonds. As for the old soldier and his two head-myrmidons, they went to the galleys; the woman who had drugged my coffee was imprisoned for I forget how many years; the regular attendants at the gambling house were considered "suspicious," and placed under "surveillance"; and I became, for one whole week (which is a long time), the head "lion" in Parisian society. My adventure was dramatized by three illustrious playmakers, but never saw theatrical daylight; for the censorship forbade the introduction, on the stage, of a correct copy of the gambling house bedstead.

One good result was produced by my adventure, which any censorship must have approved: it cured me of ever again trying *Rouge et Noir* as an amusement. The sight of a green cloth, with packs of cards and heaps of money on it, will henceforth be forever associated, in my mind, with the sight of a bed canopy descending to suffocate me in the silence and darkness of the night.

1862

Murder Under the Microscope

WILLIAM RUSSELL

In a straggling, sandy district known as Stape Hill, not far from Poole, Dorsetshire, there dwelt in 1844, a man not more than forty years of age, if so much, but so bowed, withered by care and disappointment that he looked to be sixty at the very least. His name was Joseph Gibson, and he had once carried on business as an oil and colorman, in High-street, Islington. He failed in 1843, but managed, by effecting a compromise with his chief creditors, to save about four hundred pounds from the wreck. He had been some years separated from his wife, an attractive woman, by whom he had one pretty, delicate girl at the time of the failure. His own life was wrapped up in that of Catherine; and medical authority warned him only country air, and that for some years to come, could permanently establish her health. Whilst earnestly pondering how their future lives could be shaped so as to secure that primary object, his eye hit upon an advertisement in the *Times,* announcing to agriculturists and others that a farm of one hundred acres, partly arable, partly pasture, with convenient dwelling-house, out-buildings, &c, situate at Stape Hill, market town of Poole, was to be let on lease, at the low rental of fifty pounds per annum. The stock, implements, &c, were to be taken at a valuation, which would certainly not exceed three hundred pounds, including the growing crops, the season being late in the year; possession to be given on Michaelmas-day, then ten days distant only. Satisfactory reasons for the throwing up of so desirable a homestead by the last tenant would be given, and so on after the manner of such schemes for gulling the unwary. A transparent trap like that could not have imposed upon the least intelligent of practical farmers. He would have known that you might as well have attempted to cultivate seashore sand as arable and pasture land near a populous English market town, inclusive of a convenient dwelling-house and requisite out-buildings, which the proprietor was willing to let at ten shillings annual rent per acre. But to town folk there is a fascination in the prospect of occupying land which blinds them to the most self-evident facts. Application in person only was to be made to Mr. Arthur Blagden, of Finsbury-square. This gentleman was a solicitor retired from business, and a native of Dorsetshire, in which county he possessed large property, especially in Poole and its vicinity. He was a man of somewhat eccentric habits, and very close, almost penurious, in his expenditure. The Dorsetshire rents he always collected twice a year in person.

The Stape Hill Farm appeared to be precisely suited to Gibson; it being, the advertisement stated, one of the healthiest places in the United Kingdom, and apparently requiring no more capital than he possessed for adequate cultivation. As to not being himself a practical agriculturist, that deficiency the diligent study of books as "Farming for the million," &c., would quickly supply. Joseph Gibson having so resolved, betook himself to Finsbury-square without delay, saw Mr. Blagden, who, when informed that the applicant really possessed four hundred pounds in cash, readily accepted him as a tenant for Stape Hill Farm, a coloured drawing of which he placed before Gibson, who was so delighted with the picture of rural felicity which it presented that he carried it away to show his child. A lease for fourteen years was to be immediately prepared at the tenant's cost, and on the twenty-eighth of September Mr. Blagden would go down with him to Dorsetshire to give possession of the estate and stock.

The preceding tenant, Mr. Blagden candidly informed Gibson, had not prospered at the farm—was, in fact, at that moment a prisoner for debt; but he was an idle, dissolute fellow; encumbered, too, with a large, idle family, and a slatternly wife, who would never do well anywhere. Mr. Blagden had gladly taken the farm and stock off his hands—pleased to be shut of Edward Ridges, even at a considerable sacrifice.

Possession was given—Joseph Gibson installed in his rural domain—monarch of all he surveyed; spavined horses; lean and for the most part, barren cows, a score of decent pigs; and growing crops, such as they were; inclusive. Three labourers (one of them of the name of Somers) on the farm; and Jane Somers (an elderly maid-of-all-work and dairy-woman) were retained. Somers and his wife slept on the premises.

A very short time sufficed to dissipate the fond illusions which the swindled oil and colorman had indulged in. Staple Hill Farm would have consigned any man to a debtor's prison who could not afford to lose at least one hundred pounds per annum upon it. It was a sad awakening from a pleasant dream. His eyes were suddenly opened to the bare-faced fraud practised upon him by Mr. Blagden on the very next market day, in Poole, after that gentleman, having collected his rents, left for London. The poor victim, who zealously falling in at once with market habits, dropped in at the Roebuck—an inn patronised by the bulk of the farmers, to not one of whom he was personally known—had the pleasure of listening to a very enlightening conversation, carried on in undertone by two or three of the guests. One asked who it was that that cunning devil, Blagden, had let Stape Hill Farm to? To which the reply was: "A Cockney tailor, or something of the sort, who had got a few hundreds, which the avaricious old leech would soon suck him dry of. He had taken handsome hansel already, by making out that the stock on the place was worth three hundred pounds, and had got the rhino, so at least Jem Somers said—the covetous old hawk's factotum, sly as his master, and a sweet nut for the devil to crack some day or other." "Three hundred pounds!" says another; "the unconscionable, thieving skinflint. Why it was all valleyed to Blagden by poor Ridge's creditors for as hundred and forty pounds! and money enough too. Ah, well! the London tailor must soon take to his goose again; though he be goose enough himself, for that matter. Well, if folks will meddle with things they don't understand, they must pay their account with being done uncommon brown, especially if they come in old Blagden's way."

This was something like the substance of the conversation, as related to me about a twelvemonth after it occurred, by Nicholas Price, one of the interlocutors; my business in Poole being to ascertain if any ill-blood had existed by Gibson and Blagden, how engendered, and how hot—inflamed. "Something turned the talk," Price said, "to other matters, and about two hours passed—the silent stranger, as he and others noticed, drinking hot brandy-and-water as if it were so much water— when, all in a minute, up the said stranger speaks, says he's the Cockney tailor they had been talking about, and wants to know if it was positive true that Blagden was such a swindling blackguard as they made out. 'If so,' said the excited stranger, 'I am a ruined man! My name is Joseph Gibson. It is I who have taken the Stape Hill Farm; and if what you have said is true, may God do so to me and more also but I will have the villain's heart's blood before many months have passed!'" Genuine fury, earnest passion always impresses, rebukes men for a time to silence, and no one spoke in answer. Price and his companions were not desirous that their confidential chat with each other should be made a town-talk of. Everybody disliked Blagden, but few would have chosen to make him their personal enemy. "What I want to know is," continued Gibson, who did not appear to be exactly drunk, though he had really tossed down his throat during those two hours nine shilling glasses of brandy-and-water—his speech, his legs being steady, firm (the devil of drink, as frequently happens, was mastered by the far mightier demon of revengeful rage)—"what I want to know, and will know, is, whether or not the stock and growing crops at Stape Hill Farm were valued to Blagden at one hundred and forty pounds?" This fierce query was replied to by Mr. Philips, a master-harness-maker at Poole, who had before spoken upon the subject. "That is Gospel-truth," said he. "I am one of Ridge's creditors, under the assignment which he made for the benefit of all (though some haven't accepted it), and my name is to the receipt for the one hundred and forty pounds paid by Blagden, just three weeks agone, for the stock and crops upon them acres of hungry sand which he calls Stape Hill Farms. A precious farm! It was plenty of money too. Let me advise the gentleman from London," continued Mr. Phillips, in the very words he used, as well as his memory served him, "that if he have given three hundred pounds, as some say he have, for what will not bring in more than a hundred odd, to throw up the place at once, and let first loss be last loss. As for taking Blagden's heart's blood, that is very wild, foolish talk."

At hearing that, Gibson dropped back into his chair without speaking a word, motioned a person near a bell to ring it, signed to the answering waiter for another glass of brandy-and-water, and sat drinking till he fell, helplessly drunk, upon the floor, and was carried to bed. It was late the next day when he left the Roebuck, and he was never again seen in the house.

Gibson had never been addicted to drink; and in ordinary circumstances, till of late years, when misfortunes gathering thickly about him cankered his temper as it bowed his form, as it blanched his hair—had been a man of generally placid demeanour, though capable, when roused, of rushing into the most violent extremes. This I ascertained from his former neighbors in Islington. It must not be forgotten either, that he had set his life—more than his own, his child's life—upon the desperate cast of success in the farming experiment. To play falsely with such a man, in such a mood of mind, was playing with fire.

Somers and his wife managed to pacify him for a time by confident assertions that the land was very fair land, and the stock, properly tended, would realize a profit upon the three hundred pounds. What he had heard at the Roebuck was mere malicious gossip; nothing more. Thus heartened, Gibson persevered; working, at such labor as he was fit for, like a slave. He had one prime source of consolation, which could be no deception—Catherine's health improved wonderfully at Stape Hill; and could he but manage to make both ends meet, he should be well content with his bargain.

That he soon found to be impossible. Wages, manure, horse-keep, his own domestic expenses—trifling as was the last item—quickly ate up his ridiculously insufficient capital. Stock, half-fattened, was sold at ruinous prices; and two months before Michaelmas 1845, he, after looking carefully and boldly into the state of his affairs, was fain to recognize the terrible fact, that he must give up the farm; and, with scarcely a sovereign in his pocket, return to dingy, stifling London, with his now blooming daughter; to seek there means of eking out miserable life, and die there. Catherine soon as he, perhaps sooner; The slightest hint of leaving Stape Hill pales the newly blown roses on her cheeks, one of the reasons why being that she, on most fine evenings met "William down at the stile," the said William being the blithe-looking, well-respected son of a building carpenter and timber-merchant, whose place of business was less than a mile distant from Stape Hill Farm.

This success induced Gibson to again go minutely over his accounts, and the result this time was, that if Mr. Blagden could be persuaded to let the rent—the whole twelve months' rent—stand over to the following year, he might rub on, and eventually by growing only root crops, pull through. But if the retired attorney would insist upon being paid the fifty pounds, the amateur agriculturist did not see how it would be possible to get through the year whilst the crops were growing; hardly then. Still, it might be barely possible to do so.

On the thirtieth of September 1845, Blagden, (arrived from London on the previous day) called at Stape Hill for the year's rent. He came in a one-horse gig, which, as he was in the habit of doing, he had hired at the Roebuck, Poole. It was growing dusk when he reached the place; he stayed about two hours, and it was quite dark, except for a faint starlight, when he left in high dudgeon.

There had been a stormy scene between him and Joseph Gibson, at which were present Catherine Gibson and James Somers, who had cleverly or cunningly, managed to keep well both with the tenant and the proprietor.

Blagden flatly refused to wait one day longer for his rent. The terrified tenant's beseeching remonstrances; the daughter's tears; even the pretty positive opinion of Somers that were the time asked for granted, Mr. Gibson might come round—had no effect upon the retired lawyer. To end the matter, he took his pocket-book, which being stuffed with Bank of England notes, he ostentatiously spread open, selected a ready-drawn, stamped receipt for fifty pounds from a number of others, placed it upon the table, drew forth his watch, and said he would just wait half an hour for the money; if it were not then forthcoming, he should leave, and on the morrow an execution for the amount and costs would be put in. Furious, maddened with rage and disappointment, Gibson leapt at his landlord, and inflicted a severe blow upon his face, at the same time howling forth threats of direst vengeance.

The midguided man was forcibly separated from Blagden by his daughter and James Somers. The landlord (Catherine afterward told me) remained quite cool; and but for the quiver of his ashen lips, the calm, deadly ferocity which gleamed in his gray eyes, any one might have believed that the assault was a trifling matter, of no importance whatever.

There was a slight lull after the storm and Catherine, taking advantage of it, said:—"I will go and ask Mr. Finch to advance my father forty pounds upon the piece of carrots he has bought. They will be digged next week. We have quite ten pounds in the house, and shall then be able to pay the rent in full."

"You have just twenty minutes, Miss Gibson," said the inperturbable lawyer. "Just twenty minutes—not one more or less. The cowardly assault committed upon me," he added, with a flash of hell-fire at his tenants, "a court of law shall pronounce upon! Somers, see the horse is put into the trap."

Somers said that should be done, and left the room to do it. Miss Gibson left at the same time. She was gone but a quarter of an hour. Mr. Finch was out, and Mrs. Finch said he never paid money till he was in possession of the goods purchased. Mr. Blagden took no apparent notice of what Catherine Gibson said, waited till the half-hour was exactly expired, took up his watch, wrapped his long fur-collar about him, and left.

Soon after it was light the next morning, two sailors on their way to join a vessel in the harbor of Poole came upon the dead body of Mr. Blagden, lying across the narrow but high road. A little distance off was the horse and gig; the animal, one of its forelegs broken, was suffering great torture; and both shafts of the gig were broken. Immediate alarm was given, and before long a number of people came up, by whom it was at first supposed that Mr. Blagden had met his death by accident. The horse, a high-spirited animal, had perhaps bolted, and the gig coming in contact with one of the trees, which dotted each side of the road, had been turned over with great violence, and Mr. Blagden, hurled upon the hard road, had probably been killed instantaneously. A very cursory examination sufficed to show the fallacy of that surmise. There was a deep wound in the back of the dead man's neck—apparently delivered by a sharp axe, which had cut through the stand-up collar of the cloak he wore. No question that he had been struck from behind. Robbery had been added to murder; the deceased gentleman's pocket-book, purse, and gold watch were gone. There was another wound in the crown scalp, sufficient in itself to cause death, and which must have been inflicted when the head was bare, as there was not the slightest cut visible in the texture of the hat, which was found some yards off. The murdered man's clenched hands were filled with the gravel of the road, grasped no doubt in his agony, and suggestive that he must have been either forced upon the ground or kneeling when the mortal blow was dealt. But how had the gig been stopped—the horse flung down, and reduced to so pitiable state? A question that not very readily answered. Two or three days subsequently a clothesline, almost new, one end of which had been recently cut, was found by a woman, buried under the hedge of a cottage, situated between the spot where the murder was committed and Stape Hill Farm. One of the woman's hens, in scratching under the hedge, had brought it to the surface. The circumstance was spoken of, but no importance was attached to it. The murdered man had not been strangled. The buried cord could not therefore have been the instrument or one of the instruments, of death! Still, it was odd that the full half of a long, new clothesline should have been carefully buried near the scene of the awful crime!

No sooner was the murder, and the circumstances connected with it, known at Poole, than every finger pointed to Joseph Gibson, the tenant of the Stape Hill Farm, as the murderer. His savage threat at the Roebuck was remembered;

and it was known to several persons that his sole chance, admitted to be so by himself, was that Blagden should let the year's rent then due stand over till the following Michaelmas! One person, of the name of Frost, who had done some smith's work for Gibson, having told him he was trusting to a broken-reed in relying upon lawyer Blagden's generosity, received for reply, that "Blagden would be very unwise to provoke him too far!" This expression was held to indicate a settled determination in Gibson's mind to kill his landlord, should the required favor be refused. A skilled detective would have drawn an inference just the reverse of that. No man, unless he be delirious with drink or rage, hints of his intention, under certain contingencies, to commit murder!

Joseph Gibson, unprovided with professional aid, was taken before the coroner's inquest, and the cumulative evidence brought against him was certainly staggering. The scene at Stape Hill, already given—the assault by Gibson upon the attorney, and his ferocious menaces—Blagden's threat to distrain early in the next day—the vain attempt by Catherine Gibson to borrow money of Mr. Finch to make up the rent—were capped by the discovery, in Gibson's bureau in his bedroom, Stape Hill, by the Poole police, of the genuine stamped receipt for the money, which Blagden had placed tauntingly upon the table, and taken away with him. Unceremonious verdict of wilful murder against Joseph Gibson, who was forthwith committed on the coroner's warrant to Dorchester jail!

This narrative I heard from the daughter, with exception of the conversation at the Roebuck, of which she herself had heard but a vague, indistinct report from her father.

It has been stated that Mr. Joseph Gibson was and had been long separated from his wife, a person of remarkable personal attractions. Neither her maiden name nor that which she has since the separation passed under need be printed in these pages. It is sufficient to say she was an orphan girl and a milliner's assistant when Gibson foolishly fell in love with and married her. As often happens in such cases, the disappointment was mutual. Gibson at the time had quite a splendid shop, was in the first flush of a year's promising business, kept two servants; which items summed up meant, of course, nothing to do, a well-furnished table, silk and satin dresses, cabs to theatres, &c. In short, the life of a ladyship, *minus* only the title. And the bridegroom, no doubt, expected to be imparadised in the smiles and endearments of the entrancing milliner's assistant to the full end and term of his natural life. Well, the business did not answer so well as might have been reasonably expected—one servant was first lopped off, omnibus must serve for a cab, with the rest of such disagreeable declines in life. The husband (time and familiarity are such disenchanters) discovered that his wife was not quite the angel he had supposed, and—and the young lady was frail. A separation took place, and the guilty wife had since continued to live in splendid sin. Twenty years ago only a rich man could obtain a divorce—the matrimonial chain yielded only to a golden file—and Mr. and Mrs. Gibson were still of course, in legal parlance, man and wife. The woman, however, was not all bad; few are—neither man nor woman, none that I have known; and having read the report, copied into the London papers from the *Poole Herald*, of the proceedings at the inquest of Blagden's death, she forwarded to her daughter Catherine, a draft, in a feigned name, for one hundred pounds; and at the same time, so influenced—not directly, of course—influential persons, that I was commanded to proceed to Poole and Stape Hill, and minutely investigate the case. A letter from "the friend" who had forwarded the one hundred pound draft, addressed to Miss Gibson, preceded me; and I was welcomed with tears of trembling hope. I think that Catherine guessed that "the friend" was her fallen mother; but she hinted nothing of the kind, and indeed it was not till all was over that I myself had any notion—a matter after all of supreme indifference—as to who pulled the strings by which I was set in motion.

It was a very, very ugly affair. Before going into the business with Miss Gibson, I, in accordance with invariable tactics, made myself thoroughly acquainted with the case against us—in this instance the case for the Crown. A sight of your adversary's cards is a good step towards winning the game. The sight,

however, of the formidable cards held by the Crown in "Regina
v. Gibson" did not at all reassure me.

The Poole police had not only deposed that the prisoner,
when surprised in his bed on the morning of the murder, so late
as eleven o'clock—he that usually rose by six at latest—
exclaimed when he saw the officers, who had not spoken a
syllable respecting the murder of Blagden, not even mentioned
that gentleman's name, opening his bureau, he cried out, "Ah!
it's all over with me. I shall be hanged, I suppose, for that devil
Blagden. Take me away at once." After that betraying avowal,
he assumed the mask of sudden silence—not speaking another
word except when, as they were going along the road with him,
in a chaise cart, towards Poole, one of them, when passing or
nearing the spot where the crime had been committed, said, "I
can't but think Blagden fought hard for his life, whoever
murdered him."

"Whoever murdered Blagden!" exclaimed Gibson with a
fearful start, "what are you talking of? Robbed him perhaps?"
"Murdered and robbed him," said the officer; "but, mind, no
one asks you to let out about it." At hearing which, the prisoner
gave a loud cry, and fainted or pretened to faint away.

Since then he had not said a word upon the subject; the
attorney who appeared for him when he was examined before
the magistrates having "reserved his client's defence." Since
then there had been found at Stape Hill, in an outhouse, a sharp
billhook, the blade and handle of which were stained with
blood. It was such an instrument as might, the surgeon who had
examined the body deposed, have inflicted the wound which
deprived the deceased Blagden of life; and thrust away amongst
old rags and other lumber, in a place which Miss Gibson
admitted her father could only have access to, was an old apron,
just such a one as the prisoner sometimes wore, covered with
bloodstains. These evidences—dumb, yet endowed with miraculous voice—had been carefully sealed up, and remained in
possession of the local police. Catherine Gibson endeavoured to
account for the blood upon the finely sharpened billhook, by
saying that her father had a few days before the death of Mr.
Blagden chopped off the head of a gander, which bled very

much. Gibson did not however, she admitted, wear the bloody apron upon that occasion. None of the money belonging to Mr. Blagden, neither notes nor coin—he had a small canvass bag full, or nearly so, of sovereigns—had been found, nor had the gold watch. It had, no doubt, been cunningly concealed; but he (the officer with whom I was conversing) had little doubt that with patience and perseverence they should discover the hiding hole.

"Does it not strike you as somewhat remarkable," said I, "that Gibson did not also cunningly conceal the stamped receipt, the most damning piece of evidence against him? It *might* be legally impossible to prove that the notes and gold, even the watch, belonged to Mr. Blagden; *might* be I say— though that, as regards the watch, is a violent supposition. But the receipt, about which there can be no mistake—the man must have lost his head not to have concealed or destroyed that."

"He, no doubt, intended to produce it in bar of the claim for rent which would be made by the deceased's representatives!"

"Although Somers could prove that he had not paid the rent, and Mrs. Finch that she had refused to Catherine Gibson the means of doing so? Queer to my mind that. Still the easily discoverable possession of the receipt is, however looked at, unaccountable. It can only be explained by the axiom that whom God determines to destroy he first deprives of reason. Did I understand you to say that the prisoner had been fully committed for trial by the magistrates as well as by the coroner?"

"Yes; fully committed in reality, not formally. The magistrates, having no doubt whatever of the prisoner's guilt, declared their intention of fully committing him for wilful murder; but he will be again brought before them the day after to-morrow, for the completion of the depositions. At present he remains in Poole Jail."

"The day after tomorrow! Oh, by-the-bye, is the clothesline, or half of a clothesline, scratched out by a hen from under a hedge, handy?"

"Yes, it is here. I will show it you. But I really do not see what possible connection that can have with the murder."

"I do not say it has; still I should like to see it."

It was shown me.

"Humph! A new line—one of the best make. A new line spoiled to no purpose. This piece is not above six yards long; sharply severed, too; and there is a slip-noose at one end!"

"True enough; but what use could have been made of it in effecting the murder?"

"Well, a very efficient use; but we will speak of that hereafter. Keep it safe if you please. The hedge where it was scratched up was not road gravel, I suppose; and there are many particles of road gravel, sticking to this line, or I am mistaken. Have you leisure to go with me to the scene of the murder?"

"Yes," replied the officer, "I will go with much pleasure."

The notion which had struck me about the clothesline was derived from a former police experience near Hereford. How the horse had been thrown down with such violence as to break one of its legs—a singularly sure-footed animal too—had puzzled the natives. Now, it had come out in the Hereford business— which ended in nothing, the person robbed having refused to prosecute—that the robbers had, in that case, thrown the gentleman's horse (he also drove a gig) down by a very simple expedient. A line was dropped in the dark across the road, attached by a running noose at one end to the stump of a tree, at about two feet from the ground, which suddenly tightened as the horse came swiftly up, would bring down the surest-footed beast in the world, with terrible violence. The same trick might have been played upon this occasion. I was pretty sure it had been; and the other portion of the clothes-line might suffice to hang whoever could be proved to have had it in his possession on the night of the murder.

The place where the horse must have fallen was just the spot where such a device might be resorted to with success. The road was narrow, level; the horse would be going at its swiftest pace; and there was an oak-sapling on one side, round which the running noose could be slipped, and fixed at any height. One man, having the other end in his hand, and *seizing the exact moment* for raising it, could throw any swift horse down. Yes; but to do so was scarcely to be expected of a Cockney oil and colorman—one too prematurely feeble, aged. No, no; if that trick had been played, it was by some one whose eyes could see in the dark as well as by daylight; one possessed of nerve, quickness, decision, which would bring down a partridge before it had fluttered its wings thrice.

"Clever poachers about here?" I carelessly remarked, speaking to my brother officer.

"I should think so. Rum fellows to meet with of a dark night too!"

"Mr. Gibson, the prisoner, can hardly be one of that sort, I should think?"

"God bless you! No. I should hardly think he knows a snipe from a partridge, except when they are cooked; nor how to so much as load a gun."

"Have you any first-rate moonlight fellows about here?"

"Yes; but the cleverest, by a long chalk, is gone out of that line—Jem Somers, as live at Stape Hill. He used to be an out-and-outer. He's not exactly such a bad sort," continued the officer, "as everybody, or almost everybody (Mr. Blagden liked him very much) says he is. He's very sorry, seems almost heart-broken about this horrible affair—Mr. Gibson and his daughter having been, he says, so very kind to him. He thinks, if he can't get a tolerable situation, which he can hardly expect now Mr. Blagden is dead, of going to America."

"America! Well, he'll have plenty of sport there. I suppose such a tender-hearted gentleman would be most grieved for the fate of his oldest friend Mr. Blagden."

"No, really, no. He is most distressed about Gibson and his daughter. Tears come into his eyes every time he speaks about them. Why," continued the greenly guileless officer, "Why to get out of him, before the coroner and magistrates, about what passed at Stape Hill between Gibson and Blagden, when there was such a row because Gibson could not pay his rent was like pulling the very teeth out of his head."

"But it came out, as the teeth would, at last. He's a 'cute chap, too, I am pretty sure, as well as soft-hearted?"

" 'Cute, I should think so! Catch a weasel asleep, and you may chance to drop upon Jim Somers when he's got one eye shut."

"He lives, you say, in the same house with the Gibsons?"

"Yes; but not exactly. They have a place to themselves that joins on like to the farmhouse, but yet separated from it."

"I understand. They have their castle. Every Englishman— the humblest—likes that, if the castle is a wooden one, the roof thatched with furze. Their own poultry, pig, and washing yard also, I suppose?"

"Yes; quite distinct from the farmhouse. Jim's wife showed me over it the other day."

I was pleased at that; for it had occurred to me that I should like to *see Jim Somers' last new clothesline or what remained of it.*

I had a long conference with Catherine Gibson; but it was far from a heartening one. When she had done, I said:

"There is one circumstance I should be glad to hear from your own lips, if you choose to honor me with your confidence. I mean, of course, if you can throw any light upon the seeming mystery. It is this: how came the receipt for the rent due (fifty pounds) in your father's possession!"

The young woman's face flushed—the flush, I was sure, of shame. She cast down her eyes, and remained silent.

"If I am to be of any service, I must know *all*," said I, gently, but firmly.

"I understand that," said Catherine Gibson, not uplifting her eyes. "I will tell you. Mr. Blagden, in his hurry and passion, did not observe that it had dropped on the floor; and left, supposing, no doubt, that he had replaced it in his pocket-book. After he was some time gone, my father saw the piece of paper, picked it up, and—and—"

"Appropriated it, you mean to say; or had some indistinct notion—a very foolish notion—that it might be a bar to the execution to be put in on the morrow. And when the police called on the morrow, the still wilder notion arose in his mind, that an intention, if he had really intended such a crime, of *stealing* the receipt, was equivalent, under the circumstances, of having really done so. Absurd! but I can readily understand such a feeling. Your father, perhaps, drank more than usual that night, after Mr. Blagden's departure?"

"Oh! more, much more. My father is a very abstemious man."

"So I have been told. The receipt stumbling block, as far as I am concerned, is removed. The man Somers and his wife are, I am told, very kind and serviceable to you in this sad crisis?"

"Very kind and attentive; more so than ever they were."

"I should much like to see Somers. Perhaps I could glean something from him or his wife which, though deemed unimportant by you and them, might in my eyes be of significance. Is he within?"

"His wife is not, but he is—in the next building which adjoins this. Shall I say who you are?"

"Not that I am a detective-officer, if you please. It would not, perhaps, so much matter that Somers should know my vocation; but if I am to serve your father, I must work, like a mole, in the dark. Say simply, and which is the truth, that I am a friend from London, anxious to assist your father in his, I trust, passing trouble."

"I will do so. He will be here in three minutes."

"Not of the least use, James Somers, to fence with me with that smoothly loose tongue of yours; to look modestly, sorrowfully upon the floor with those catlike eyes. *I know you, and that you are the murderer of Mr. Blagden!*

"A moment after Miss Gibson passed out at the front, I left by the back door, making a trivial excuse to the servant, and saying I would return in a moment. You came out of your house with Miss Gibson, and I took the liberty of walking in. Had I been seen by either of you, it would have been easy to say that I went to tell you I would prefer seeing you and Mrs. Somers (she not being then in the way) on the morrow. Neither of you did see me. But I saw in a large table drawer, which I took the liberty of inspecting, the longest half of a clothesline, sharply cut, of the newness, color, and, I think, rather peculiar twist of that found under the hedge. It's not likely you'll miss it before it has answered the present purpose I shall put it to; and if you do, the last thought that will enter the cunning—but, as I can see plainly enough through the flat-crowned, animally shaped skull— uneasy, palpitating brain of yours, that it is now in the coat-pocket of a London detective officer. Though of itself hardly strong enough to make a halter for that bull-neck of yours, it will perhaps enable me to find something that will. Oh! you have nothing more to say, except to repeat how "mortal sorry" you be for the young missus, and for Mr. Gibson too! I have no doubt, Somers, you are a feeling man, and especially just now you must feel very strongly. I am sure you do. I have nothing more to ask. Miss Gibson is positive that her father is innocent, and we must trust to Providence to make the truth manifest. Tomorrow I may, or may not, call to see your wife. Good day, Miss Gibson. I have promised to dine with an acquaintance in Poole, and must be gone."

The end of the clothesline which I had brought away from Somers' place precisely matched with that in possession of the Poole police; colour, size, twist were identical, and both pieces made up in length that of an ordinary clothesline. If the county magistrate—to whom the officer I had previously spoken with, whose name I forget, volunteered to introduce me—had any brains in his head, he would, in a case involving such issues, grant a warrant to search Somers' premises. The magistrate fortunately had brains in his head. I mentioned the Hereford affair, showed him the sundered clothes cord, and declared my willingness to make oath that I had sufficient grounds for suspecting James Somers of having murdered and robbed Mr. Arthur Blagden, to justify the issuing of a search warrant. I had brought written testimony as to my detective acumen, signed "Richard Mayne;" and it is probable that that as much, if not more than the evidence of the clothesline, decided him to grant the warrant, which was placed at once in the hands of the police officer, whose name I have forgotten, and off we both set without delay for Stape Hill.

Somers and his wife were greatly scared by our visit, the man especially so, upon finding that Miss Gibson's friend was a London detective.

Our search was ineffectual, so far as that no property of the murdered man could be found; neither notes, gold, or watch; but a very sharply ground hand-axe, put away in a corner-cupboard, attracted my attention. "This is your husband's axe?"

"O yes; our axe!" I examined it minutely. First with the naked eye, then with a strong magnifier, which I was seldom or never without. The axe had been washed, not so very long ago; and, though nothing was visible to the naked eye, my magnifier discovered upon the blade, not only spots of red rust, which might not be stains of blood, but a number of what looked to be minute fibres of fur sticking to the stains. On removing the wooden handle, we saw distinct marks of blood, which I concluded had been washed, as it were, into the socket. The man saw those marks, and turning cadaverously white, exclaimed that he had killed a snared rabbit with it not long before.

"A rabbit?"

"Yes, a snared rabbit."

"You have killed nothing else with it?"

"Oh no!"

"You had better take this axe with you, at all events," said I to the local officer. "It may be of no consequence; still you had better take possession of the instrument."

Once when I attended a lecture by a celebrated man, he had stated that every animal had in its blood globules differing in size from those of any other kind. This knowledge had been arrived at by very slow steps. There was no doubt, however, of its scientific accuracy, or that with the aid of a powerful microscope a professional man of skill and experience could decide, without chance of committing a mistake, from the slightest stain whether the blood, if blood, had flowed in the veins of a human being or other animal. It was the same with minute fibres of fur, hair, &c. This he had said was a most valuable discovery, and he instanced the fact that in France an innocent man might have been convicted of murder owing to a knife having been found in his possession stained with what had every appearance of blood, which stain examined by a skilled gentleman through the miscroscope was proved to be lime juice.

The lecture had made a great impression on me at that time, and it occurred to me that here was a case in which such a discovery, such a power, would prove invaluable. The fur cloak collar of the murdered man, it will be remembered, had been cut through; the skull had also been split by the assassin. Were those minute fibres of fur sticking on the blade of the axe, fibres of rabbit fur, or of that, whatever it might be, of which the cloak collar was made? and were there any, the slightest shreds of human hair mingled with those particles of fur? Then as to the blood upon Gibson's billhook, and upon the old rag of an apron; was that human blood?

In the scientific replies to these questions lay the issues of life and death as regarded the prisoner Gibson; and as, although not knowing *who* "the friend" was that sent Miss Gibson the one hundred pound draft, I knew how to communicate with him or her, I determined to do so without delay, and I started in a gig for Dorchester ten minutes after I had so determined, there not being a moment to spare—reached London by train, and with the potent agency of "A Friend's" purse, engaged the services of the most eminent professor of that especial branch of anatomical science in the metropolis, with whom I returned to Poole.

The court was crowded on the day when it had been expected that Joseph Gibson would be finally committed for trial—a rumor having got afloat, that owing to the Dectective that had been sent down from London, strange discoveries had been made. Poor Gibson looked more like a ghost than a man. He believed himself to be the doomed victim of a relentless fate—that nothing, no accident could—that God would not reveal the truth.

The billhook, the apron, the axe were placed upon the table, and Professor Ansted (by whom they had been carefully examined) gave his evidence: it was clear, decisive. The blood upon the billhook was *not* human blood; of that he said there could be no possible doubt. The stains upon the apron were red paint, containing peroxide or iron. (Gibson, when oil and colorman, no doubt had to grind his own paints, and when so occupied used the apron.) The stains upon the axe, found in the house of Somers, were human blood (there were human hairs sticking on them); and the particles of fur were not rabbit but squirrel fur the fur of which the murdered man's cloak collar was made!

Seldom has evidence—almost supernatural it seemed to the

astounded audience—produced a deeper impression than did Professor Ansted's. The finger of God appeared to be visible in it! "William," who had proved himself a true lover through out, burst into tears, as he pressed forward and shook the prisoner, and his daughter, standing close to her father, warmly by the hands.

The magistrates, who appeared to be somewhat mystified, bewildered, retired to consult with each other. Returning into court, the chairman announced, that relying upon the evidence of so distinguished a gentleman as Professor Ansted, a warrant for the apprehension of James Somers would be immediately issued; but that for the present it was not thought prudent to discharge the prisoner Joseph Gibson. The case would be adjourned for three days.

The magistrates were saved any further trouble in the matter by the murderer himself. An acquaintance in court, specially employed for that purpose, had ridden off to Stape Hill directly the decision of the magistrates were declared; who, of course, apprised Somers that a warrant was out against him for wilful murder, and that the officers would be there almost immediately to arrest him. The despairing felon heard the news with a savage growl, and a moment or so afterwards desired to be left alone.

The door of the room, in which his wife (weeping, sobbing, wringing her hands the while) said we should find him, was fastened on the inside. We burst it open; and a shocking spectacle presented itself. Somers was lying dead on the floor, in a pool of blood, selfmurdered; he had cut his throat with a razor. On a small table we found a scrap of writing in his hand: "It was I, not Gibson, that killed Blagden. I had owed him a bitter grudge a long time, though he didn't think it. D–n him, he ruined me body and soul when he sold me up eight years ago. What I wish particularly to say is, that my wife is as innocent as a babe in the business. She don't even know where the money and watch is, or that I have such things. They are hidden away in a box under the flagstones of one of my pig-styes—the right hand one going out. That is all I have to say. I thought of going to America; and now I'm going to——, if there is such a place, which I don't believe. The Peeler was right about the clothes line; that was just how it was done.———J. S."

The money, watch, &c., we found as indicated. All doubt respecting the terrible business being at the end, Joseph Gibson was forthwith discharged from prison. His case excited much sympathy. The executors of Arthur Blagden allowed him to throw up his farm, forgiving him the arrears of rent; and he, with the help, I believe anonymously conveyed through the daughter of "A Friend," took a smaller and culturable one not very far off from Stape Hill; and has since, I have been told, prospered tolerably. His daughter, I saw by the local paper which some of them sent me now and then, married "William."

1883

The Three Strangers

THOMAS HARDY

Among the few features of agricultural England which
retain an appearance but little modified by the lapse of centuries, may be reckoned the high, grassy and furzy downs,
coombs, or ewe-leases, as they are indifferently called, that fill a
large area of certain counties in the south and southwest. If any
mark of human occupation is met with hereon, it usually takes
the form of the solitary cottage of some shepherd.

Fifty years ago such a lonely cottage stood on such a down,
and may possibly be standing there now. In spite of its
loneliness, however, the spot, by actual measurement, was not
more than five miles from a county town. Yet that affected it
little. Five miles of irregular upland, during the long inimical
seasons, with their sleets, snows, rains, and mists, afford
withdrawing space enough to isolate a Timon or a Nebuchad-
nezzar; much less, in fair weather, to please that less repellent
tribe, the poets, philosophers, artists, and others who "conceive
and meditate of pleasant things."

Some old earthen camp or barrow, some clump of trees, at
least some starved fragment of ancient hedge is usually taken
advantage of in the erection of these forlorn dwellings. But, in
the present case, such a kind of shelter had been disregarded.
Higher Crowstairs, as the house was called, stood quite detached and undefended. The only reason for its precise situation
seemed to be the crossing of two footpaths at right angles hard
by, which may have crossed there and thus for a good five
hundred years. Hence the house was exposed to the elements
on all sides. But, though the wind up here blew unmistakably

when it did blow, and the rain hit hard whenever it fell, the various weathers of the winter season were not quite so formidable on the coomb as they were imagined to be by dwellers on low ground. The raw rimes were not so pernicious as in the hollows, who tenanted the house were pitied for their sufferings from the exposure, they said that upon the whole they were less inconvenienced by "wuzzes and flames" (hoarses and phlegms) than when they had lived by the stream of a snug neighboring valley.

The night of March 28, 182–, was precisely one of the nights that were wont to call forth these expressions of commiseration. The level rainstorm smote walls, slopes, and hedges like the clothyard shafts of Senlac and Crecy. Such sheep and outdoor animals as had no shelter stood with their buttocks to the winds; while the tails of little birds trying to roost on some scraggy thorn were blown inside-out like umbrellas. The gable-end of the cottage was stained with wet, and the eavesdroppings flapped against the wall. Yet never was commiseration for the shepherd more misplaced. For that cheerful rustic was entertaining a large party in glorification of the christening of his second girl.

The guests had arrived before the rain began to fall, and they were all now assembled in the chief or living room of the dwelling. A glance into the apartment at eight o'clock on this evening would have resulted in the opinion that it was as cozy and comfortable a nook as could be wished for in boisterous weather. The calling of its inhabitant was proclaimed by a number of highly-polished sheep-crooks without stems that were hung ornamentally over the fireplace, the curl of each shining crook varying from the antiquated type engraved in the patriarchal pictures of old family Bibles to the most approved fashion of the last local sheep-fair. The room was lighted by half-a-dozen candles, having wicks only a trifle smaller than the grease which enveloped them, in candlesticks that were never used but at high-days, holy-days, and family feasts. The lights were scattered about the room, two of them standing on the chimney-piece. This position of candles was in itself magnificent. Candles on the chimney-piece always meant a party.

On the hearth, in front of a back-brand to give substance, blazed a fire of thorns, that crackled "like the laughter of the fool."

Nineteen persons were gathered there. Of these, five women, wearing gowns of various bright hues, sat in chairs along the wall; girls shy and not shy filled the window-bench; four men, including Charley Jake the hedge-carpenter, Elijah New the parish-clerk, and John Pitcher, a neighboring dairyman, the shepherd's father-in-law, lolled in the settle; a young man and maid, who were blushing over tentative *pourparlers* on a life-companionship, sat beneath the corner-cupboard; and an elderly engaged man of fifty or upward moved restlessly about from spots where his betrothed was not to the spot where she was. Enjoyment was pretty general, and so much the more prevailed in being unhampered by conventional restrictions. Absolute confidence in each other's good opinion begat perfect ease, while the finishing stroke of manner, amounting to a truly princely serenity, was lent to the majority by the absence of any expression or trait denoting that they wished to get on in the world, enlarge their minds, or do any eclipsing thing whatever—which nowadays so generally nips the bloom and *bonhomie* of all except the two extremes of the social scale.

Shepherd Fennel had married well, his wife being a dairyman's daughter from a vale at a distance, who brought fifty guineas in her pocket—and kept them there, till they should be required for ministering to the needs of a coming family. This frugal woman had been somewhat exercised as to the character that should be given to the gathering. A sit-still party had its advantages; but an undisturbed position of ease in chairs and settles was apt to lead on the men to such an unconscionable deal of toping that they would sometimes fairly drink the house dry. A dancing-party was the alternative; but this, while avoiding the foregoing objection on the score of good drink, had a counterbalancing disadvantage in the matter of good victuals, the ravenous appetites engendered by the exercise causing immense havoc in the buttery. Shepherdess Fennel fell back upon the intermediate plan of mingling short dances with short periods of talk and singing, so as to hinder any ungovernable rage in either. But this scheme was entirely confined to her own gentle mind: the shepherd himself was in the mood to exhibit the most reckless phases of hospitality.

The fiddler was a boy of those parts, about twelve years of age, who had a wonderful dexterity in jigs and reels, though his fingers were so small and short as to necessitate a constant shifting for the high notes, from which he scrambled back to the first position with sounds not of unmixed purity of tone. At seven the shrill tweedle-dee of this youngster had begun, accompanied by a booming ground-bass from Elijah New, the parish-clerk, who had thoughtfully brought with him his favorite musical instrument, the serpent. Dancing was instantaneous, Mrs. Fennel privately enjoining the players on no account to let the dance exceed the length of a quarter of an hour.

But Elijah and the boy, in the excitement of their position, quite forgot the injunction. Moreover, Oliver Giles, a man of seventeen, one of the dancers, who was enamored of his partner, a fair girl of thirty-three rolling years, had recklessly handed a new crown-piece to the musicians, as a bribe to keep going as long as they had muscle and wind. Mrs. Fennel, seeing the steam begin to generate on the countenances of her guests, crossed over and touched the fiddler's elbow and put her hand on the serpent's mouth. But they took no notice, and fearing she might lose her character of genial hostess if she were to interfere too markedly, she retired and sat down helpless. And so the dance whizzed on with cumulative fury, the performers moving in their planet-like courses, direct and retrograde, from apogee to perigee, till the hand of the well-kicked clock at the bottom of the room had travelled over the circumference of an hour.

While these cheerful events were in course of enactment within Fennel's pastoral dwelling, an incident having considerable bearing on the party had occurred in the gloomy night without. Mrs. Fennel's concern about the growing fierceness of the dance corresponded in point of time with the ascent of a human figure to the solitary hill of Higher Crowstairs from the direction of the distant town. This personage strode on through the rain without a pause, following the little-worn path which, further on in its course, skirted the shepherd's cottage.

It was nearly the time of full moon, and on this account, though the sky was lined with a uniform sheet of dripping cloud, ordinary objects out of doors were readily visible. The sad wan light revealed the lonely pedestrian to be a man of supple frame; his gait suggested that he had somewhat passed the period of perfect and instinctive agility, though not so far as to be otherwise than rapid of motion when occasion required. At a rough guess, he might have been about forty years of age. He appeared tall, but a recruiting sergeant, or other person accustomed to the judging of men's heights by the eye, would have discerned that this was chiefly owing to his gauntness, and that he was not more than five-feet-eight or nine.

Notwithstanding the regularity of his tread, there was caution in it, as in that of one who mentally feels his way; and despite the fact that it was not a black coat nor a dark garment of any sort that he wore, there was something about him which suggested that he naturally belonged to the black-coated tribes of men. His clothes were of fustian, and his boots hobnailed, yet in his progress he showed not the mud-accustomed bearing of hobnailed and fustianed peasantry.

By the time that he had arrived abreast of the shepherd's premises the rain came down, or rather came along, with yet more determined violence. The outskirts of the little settlement partially broke the force of wind and rain, and this induced him to stand still. The most salient of the shepherd's domestic erections was an empty sty at the forward corner of his hedgeless garden, for in these latitudes the principle of masking the homelier features of your establishment by a conventional frontage was unknown. The traveler's eye was attracted to this small building by the pallid shine of the wet slates that covered it. He turned aside, and, finding it empty, stood under the pent-roof for shelter.

While he stood, the boom of the serpent within the adjacent house, and the lesser strains of the fiddler, reached the spot as an accompaniment to the surging hiss of the flying rain on the sod, its louder beating on the cabbage-leaves of the garden, on the eight or ten beehives just discernible by the path, and its dripping from the eaves into a row of buckets and pans that had been placed under the walls of the cottage. For at Higher Crowstairs, as at all such elevated domiciles, the grand difficulty of housekeeping was an insufficiency of water; and a casual rainfall was utilized by turning out, as catchers, every utensil that the house contained. Some queer stories might be told of the contrivances for economy in suds and dish-waters that are absolutely necessitated in upland habitations during the droughts of summer. But at this season there were no such exigencies; a mere acceptance of what the skies bestowed was sufficient for an abundant store.

At last the notes of the serpent ceased and the house was silent. This cessation of activity aroused the solitary pedestrian from the reverie into which he had lapsed, and, emerging from the shed, with an apparently new intention, he walked up the path to the house-door. Arrived here, his first act was to kneel down on a large stone beside the row of vessels, and to drink a copious draught from one of them. Having quenched his thirst he rose and lifted his hand to knock, but paused with his eye upon the panel. Since the dark surface of the wood revealed absolutely nothing, it was evident that he must be mentally looking through the door, as if he wished to measure thereby all the possibilities that a house of this sort might include, and how they might bear upon the question of his entry.

In his indecision he turned and surveyed the scene around. Not a soul was anywhere visible. The garden-path stretched downward from his feet, gleaming like the track of a snail; the roof of the little well (mostly dry), the well-cover, the top rail of the garden-gate, were varnished with the same dull liquid glaze; while, far away in the vale, a faint whiteness of more than usual extent showed that the rivers were high in the meads. Beyond all this winked a few bleared lamplights through the beating drops—lights that denoted the situation of the county-town from which he had appeared to come. The absence of all notes of life in that direction seemed to clinch his intentions, and he knocked at the door.

Within, a desultory chat had taken the place of movement

and musical sound. The hedge-carpenter was suggesting a song to the company, which nobody just then was inclined to undertake, so that the knock afforded a not unwelcome diversion.

"Walk in!" said the shepherd promptly.

The latch clicked upward, and out of the night our pedestrian appeared upon the door-mat. The shepherd arose, snuffed two of the nearest candles, and turned to look at him.

Their light disclosed that the stranger was dark in complexion and not unprepossesing as to feature. His hat, which for a moment he did not remove, hung low over his eyes, without concealing that they were large, open, and determined, moving with a flash rather than a glance round the room. He seemed pleased with his survey, and, baring his shaggy head, said, in a rich deep voice, "The rain is so heavy, friends, that I ask leave to come in and rest awhile."

"To be sure, stranger," said the shepherd. "And faith, you've been lucky in choosing your time, for we are having a bit of a fling for a glad cause—though, to be sure, a man could hardly wish that glad cause to happen more than once a year."

"Nor less," spoke up a woman. "For 'tis best to get your family over and done with, as soon as you can, so as to be all the earlier out of the fag o't."

"And what may be this glad cause?" asked the stranger.

"A birth and christening," said the shepherd.

The stranger hoped his host might not be made unhappy either by too many or too few of such episodes, and being invited by a gesture to a pull at the mug, he readily acquiesced. His manner, which, before entering, had been so dubious, was now altogether that of a careless and candid man.

"Late to be traipsing athwart this coomb—hey?" said the engaged man of fifty.

"Late it is, master, as you say.—I'll take a seat in the chimney-corner, if you have nothing to urge against it, ma'am; for I am a little moist on the side that was next the rain."

Mrs. Shepherd Fennel assented, and made room for the self-invited comer, who, having got completely inside the chimney-corner, stretched out his legs and his arms with the expansiveness of a person quite at home.

"Yes, I am rather cracked in the vamp," he said freely, seeing that the eyes of the shepherd's wife fell upon his boots, "and I am not well fitted either. I have had some rough times lately, and have been forced to pick up what I can get in the way of wearing, but I must find a suit better fit for working-days when I reach home."

"One of hereabouts?" she inquired.

"Not quite that—further up the county."

"I thought so. And so be I; and by your tongue you come from my neighborhood."

"But you would hardly have heard of me," he said quickly. "My time would be long before yours, ma'am, you see."

This testimony to the youthfulness of his hostess had the effect of stopping her cross-examination.

"There is only one thing more wanted to make me happy," continued the new-comer. "And that is a little baccy, which I am sorry to say I am out of."

"I'll fill your pipe," said the shepherd.

"I must ask you to lend me a pipe likewise."

"A smoker, and no pipe about 'ee?"

"I have dropped it somewhere on the road."

The shepherd filled and handed him a new clay pipe, saying, as he did so, "Hand me your baccy-box—I'll fill that too, now I am about it."

The man went through the movement of searching his pockets.

"Lost that too?" said his entertainer, with some surprise.

"I am afraid so," said the man with some confusion. "Give it to me in a screw of paper." Lighting his pipe at the candle with a suction that drew the whole flame into the bowl, he resettled himself in the corner and bent his looks upon the faint steam from his damp legs, as if he wished to say no more.

Meanwhile the general body of guests had been taking little notice of this visitor by reason of an absorbing discussion in which they were engaged with the band about a tune for the next dance. The matter being settled, they were about to stand up when an interruption came in the shape of another knock at the door.

At sound of the same the man in the chimney-corner took up the poker and began stirring the brands as if doing it thoroughly were the one aim of his existence; and a second time the shepherd said, "Walk in!" In a moment another man stood upon the straw-woven door-mat. He too was a stranger.

This individual was one of a type radically different from the first. There was more of the commonplace in his manner, and a certain jovial cosmopolitanism sat upon his features. He was several years older than the first arrival, his hair being slightly frosted, his eyebrows bristly, and his whiskers cut back from his cheeks. His face was rather full and flabby, and yet it was not altogether a face without power. A few grog-blossoms marked the neighborhood of his nose. He flung back his long drab greatcoat, revealing that beneath it he wore a suit of cinder-gray shade throughout, large heavy seals, of some metal or other that would take a polish, dangling from his fob as his only personal ornament. Shaking the water-drops from his low-crowned glazed hat, he said, "I must ask for a few minutes' shelter, comrades, or I shall be wetted to my skin before I get to Casterbridge."

"Make yourself at home, master," said the shepherd, perhaps a trifle less heartily than on the first occasion. Not that Fennel had the least tinge of niggardliness in his composition; but the room was far from large, spare chairs were not numerous, and damp companions were not altogether desirable at close quarters for the women and girls in their bright-colored gowns.

However, the second comer, after taking off his greatcoat, and hanging his hat on a nail in one of the ceiling-beams as if he had been specially invited to put it there, advanced and sat down at the table. This had been pushed so closely into the chimney-corner, to give all available room to the daners, that its inner edge grazed the elbow of the man who had ensconced himself by the fire; and thus the two strangers were brought into close companionship. They nodded to each other by way of breaking the ice of unacquaintance, and the first stranger handed his neighbor the family mug—a huge vessel of brown ware, having its upper edge worn away like a threshold by the rub of whole generations of thirsty lips that had gone the way of all flesh, and bearing the following inscription burnt upon its rotund side in yellow letters:

THERE IS NO FUN
UNTIL i CUM.

The other man, nothing loath, raised the mug to his lips, and drank on, and on, and on—till a curious blueness overspread the countenance of the shepherd's wife, who had regarded with no little surprise the first stranger's free offer to the second of what did not belong to him to dispense.

"I knew it!" said the toper to the shepherd with much satisfaction. "When I walked up your garden before coming in, and saw the hives all of a row, I said to myself, 'Where there's bees there's honey, and where there's honey there's mead.' But mead of such a truly comfortable sort as this I really didn't expect to meet in my older days." He took yet another pull at the mug, till it assumed an ominous elevation.

"Glad you enjoy it!" said the shepherd warmly.

"It is goodish mead," assented Mrs. Fennel, with an absence of enthusiasm which seemed to say that it was possible to buy praise for one's cellar at too heavy a price. "It is trouble enough to make—and really I hardly think we shall make any more. For honey sells well, and we ourselves can make shift with a drop o' small mead and metheglin for common use from the comb-washings."

"Oh, but you'll never have the heart!" reproachfully cried the stranger in cinder-gray, after taking up the mug a third time and setting it down empty. "I love mead, when 'tis old like this, as I love to go to church o' Sundays, or to relieve the needy any day of the week."

"Ha, ha, ha!" said the man in the chimney-corner, who in spite of the taciturnity induced by the pipe of tobacco, could not or would not refrain from this slight testimony to his comrade's humor.

Now the old mead of those days, brewed of the purest first-year or maiden honey, four pounds to the gallon—with its due complement of white of eggs, cinnamon, ginger, cloves, mace, rosemary, yeast, and processes of working, bottling, and cellaring—tasted remarkably strong; but it did not taste so strong as it actually was. Hence, presently, the stranger in cinder-gray at the table, moved by its creeping influence, unbuttoned his waistcoat, threw himself back in his chair, spread his legs, and made his presence felt in various ways.

"Well, well, as I say," he resumed, "I am going to Casterbridge, and to Casterbridge I must go. I should have been almost there by this time; but the rain drove me into your dwelling, and I'm not sorry for it."

"You don't live in Casterbridge?" said the shepherd.

"Not as yet; though I shortly mean to move there."

"Going to set up in trade, perhaps?"

"No, no," said the shepherd's wife. "It is easy to see that the gentleman is rich, and don't want to work at anything."

The cinder-gray stranger paused, as if to consider whether he would accept that definition of himself. He presently rejected it by answering, "Rich is not quite the word for me, dame. I do work, and I must work. And even if I only get to Casterbridge by midnight I must begin work there at eight tomorrow morning. Yes, het or wet, blow or snow, famine or sword, my day's work tomorrow must be done."

"Poor man! Then, in spite o' seeming, you be worse off than we?" replied the shepherd's wife.

"'Tis the nature of my trade, men and maidens. 'Tis the nature of my trade more than my poverty. . . . But really and truly I must up and off, or I shan't get a lodging in the town." However, the speaker did not move, and directly added, "There's time for one more draught of friendship before I go; and I'd perform it at once if the mug were not dry."

"Here's a mug o' small," said Mrs. Fennel. "Small, we call it, though to be sure 'tis only the first wash o' the combs."

"No," said the stranger disdainfully. "I won't spoil your first kindness by partaking o' your second."

"Certainly not," broke in Fennel. "We don't increase and multiply every day, and I'll fill the mug again." He went away to the dark place under the stairs where the barrel stood. The shepherdess followed him.

"Why should you do this?" she said reproachfully, as soon as they were alone. "He's emptied it once, though it held enough for ten people; and now he's not contented wi' the small, but must needs call for more o' the strong! And a stranger unbeknown to any of us. For my part, I don't like the look o' the man at all."

"But he's in the house, my honey; and 'tis a wet night, and a christening. Daze it, what's a cup of mead more or less? There'll be plenty more next bee-burning."

"Very well—this time, then," she answered, lookingly wistfully at the barrel. "But what is the man's calling, and where is he one of, that he should come in and join us like this?"

"I don't know. I'll ask him again."

The catastrophe of having the mug drained dry at one pull by the stranger in cinder-gray was effectually guarded against this time by Mrs. Fennel. She poured out his allowance in a small cup, keeping the large one at a discreet distance from him. When he had tossed off his portion the shepherd renewed his inquiry about the stranger's occupation.

The latter did not immediately reply, and the man in the chimney-corner, with sudden demonstrativeness, said, "Anybody may know my trade—I'm a wheelwright."

"A very good trade for these parts," said the shepherd.

"And anybody may know mine—if they've the sense to find it out," said the stranger in cinder-gray.

"You may generally tell what a man is by his claws," observed the hedge-carpenter, looking at his own hands. "My fingers be as full of thorns as an old pin-cushion is of pins."

The hands of the man in the chimney-corner instinctively sought the shade, and he gazed into the fire as he resumed his pipe. The man at the table took up the hedge-carpenter's remark, and added smartly, "True; but the oddity of my trade is that, instead of setting a mark upon me, it sets a mark upon my customers."

No observation being offered by anybody in elucidation of this enigma, the shepherd's wife once more called for a song.

The same obstacles presented themselves as at the former time—one had no voice, another had forgotten the first verse. The stranger at the table, whose soul had now risen to a good working temperature, relieved the difficulty by exclaiming that, to start the company, he would sing himself. Thrusting one thumb into the arm-hole of his waistcoat, he waved the other hand in the air, and, with an extemporizing gaze at the shining sheep-crooks above the mantelpiece, began:

> O my trade it is the rarest one,
>   Simple shepherds all—
> My trade is a sight to see;
> For my customers I tie, and take them up on high,
>   And waft'em to a far countree!"

The room was silent when he had finished the verse—with one exception, that of the man in the chimney-corner, who, at the singer's word, "Chorus!" joined him in a deep bass voice of musical relish—

> And waft 'em to a far countree!"

Oliver Giles, John Pitcher the dairyman, the parish-clerk, the engaged man of fifty, the row of young women against the wall, seemed lost in thought not of the gayest kind. The shepherd looked meditatively on the ground, the shepherdess gazed keenly at the singer, and with some suspicion; she was doubting whether this stranger were merely singing an old song from recollection, or was composing one there and then for the occasion. All were as perplexed at the obscure revelation as the guests at Belshazzar's Feast, except the man in the chimney-corner, who quietly said, "Second verse, stranger," and smoked on.

The singer thorougly moistened himself from his lips inwards, and went on with the next stanza as requested:

> My tools are but common ones,
>   Simple shepherds all—

> My tools are no sight to see:
> A little hempen string, and a post whereon to swing,
> Are implements enough for me!

Shepherd Fennel glanced round. There was no longer any doubt that the stranger was answering his question rhythmically. The guests one and all started back with suppressed exclamations. The young woman engaged to the man of fifty fainted half-way, and would have proceeded, but finding him wanting in alacrity for catching her she sat down trembling.

"Oh, he's the—!" whispered the people in the background, mentioning the name of an ominous public officer. "He's come to do it! 'Tis to be at Casterbridge jail tomorrow—the man for sheep-stealing—the poor clockmaker we heard of, who used to live away at Shottsford and had no work to do—Timothy Summers, whose family were a-starving, and so he went out of Shottsford by the high road, and took a sheep in open daylight defying the farmer and the farmer's wife and the farmer's lad, and every man jack among 'em. He" (and they nodded towards the stranger of the deadly trade) "is come from up the country to do it because there's not enough to do in his own county-town, and he's got the place here now our own county man's dead; he's going to live in the same cottage under the prison wall."

The stranger in cinder-gray took no notice of this whispered string of observations, but again wetted his lips. Seeing that his friend in the chimney-corner was the only one who reciprocated his joviality in any way, he held out his cup towards that appreciative comrade, who also held out his own. They clinked together, the eyes of the rest of the room hanging upon the singer's actions. He parted his lips for the third verse; but at that moment another knock was audible upon the door. This time the knock was faint and hesitating.

The company seemed scared; the shepherd looked with consternation towards the entrance, and it was with some effort that he resisted his alarmed wife's deprecatory glance, and uttered for the third time the welcoming words "Walk in!"

The door was gently opened, and another man stood upon the mat. He, like those who had preceded him, was a stranger.

This time it was a short, small personage, of fair complexion, and dressed in a decent suit of dark clothes.

"Can you tell me the way to—" he began: when, gazing round the room to observe the nature of the company amongst whom he had fallen, his eyes lighted on the stranger in cinder-gray. It was just at the instant when the latter, who had thrown his mind into his song with such a will that he scarcely heeded the interruption, silenced all whispers and inquireies by bursting into his third verse:

> Tomorrow is my working day,
> Simple shepherds all—
> Tomorrow is a working day for me:
> For the farmer's sheep is slain, and the lad who did it ta'en,
> And on his soul may God ha' merc-y!

The stranger in the chimney-corner, waving cups with the singer so heartily that his mead splashed over on the hearth, repeated in his bass voice as before:

> And on his soul may God ha' merc-y!

All this time the third stranger had been standing in the doorway. Finding now that he did not come forward or go on speaking, the guests particularly regarded him. They noticed to their surprise that he stood before them the picture of abject terror—his knees trembling, his hand shaking so violently that the door-latch by which he supported himself rattled audibly: his white lips were parted, and his eyes fixed on the merry officer of justice in the middle of the room. A moment more and he had turned, closed the door, and fled.

"What a man can it be?" said the shepherd.

The rest, between the awfulness of their late discovery and the odd conduct of this third visitor, looked as if they knew not what to think, and said nothing. Instinctively they withdrew further and further from the grim gentleman in their midst, whom some of them seemed to take for the Prince of Darkness himself, till they formed a remote circle, an empty space of floor being left between them and him—

　　. . . circulus, cujus centrum diabolus.

The room was so silent—though there were more than twenty people in it—that nothing could be heard but the patter of the rain against the window-shutters, accompanied by the occasional hiss of a stray drop that fell down the chimney into the fire, and the steady puffing of the man in the corner, who had now resumed his long pipe of clay.

The stillness was unexpectedly broken. The distant sound of a gun reverberated through the air—apparently from the direction of the county town.

"Be jiggered!" cried the stranger who had sung the song, jumping up.

"What does that mean?" asked several.

"A prisoner escaped from the jail—that's what it means."

All listened. The sound was repeated, and none of them spoke but the man in the chimney-corner, who said quietly, "I've often been told that in this county they fire a gun at such times; but I never heard it till now."

"I wonder if it is *my* man?" murmured the personage in cinder-gray.

"Surely it is!" said the shepherd involuntarily. "And surely we've zeed him! That little man who looked in at the door by now, and quivered like a leaf when he zeed ye and heard your song!"

"His teeth chattered, and the breath went out of his body," said the dairyman.

"And his heart seemed to sink within him like a stone," said Oliver Giles.

"And he bolted as if he'd been shot at," said the hedge-carpenter.

"True—his teeth chattered, and his heart seemed to sink; and he bolted as if he'd been shot at," slowly summed up the man in the chimney-corner.

"I didn't notice it," remarked the hangman.

"We were all a-wondering what made him run off in such a fright," faltered one of the women against the wall, "and now 'tis explained!"

The firing of the alarm-gun went on at intervals, low and sullenly, and their suspicions became a certainty. The sinister gentleman in cinder-gray roused himself. "Is there a constable here?" he asked, in thick tones. "If so, let him step forward."

The engaged man of fifty stepped quavering out from the wall, his betrothed beginning to sob on the back of the chair.

"You are a sworn constable?"

"I be, sir."

"Then pursue the criminal at once, with assistance, and bring him back here. He can't have gone far."

"I will, sir, I will—when I've got my staff. I'll go home and get it, and come sharp here, and start in a body."

"Staff!—never mind your staff; the man'll be gone!"

"But I can't do nothing without my staff—can I, William, and John, and Charles Jake? No; for there's the king's royal crown a painted on en in yaller and gold, and the lion and the unicorn, so as when I raise en up and hit my prisoner, 'tis made a lawful blow thereby. I wouldn't 'tempt to take up a man without my staff—no, not I. If I hadn't the law to gie me courage, why, instead o' my taking up him he might take up me!"

"Now, I'm a king's man myself, and can give you authority enough for this," said the formidable officer in gray. "Now then, all of ye, be ready. Have ye any lanterns?"

"Yes—have ye any lanterns?—I demand it!" said the constable.

"And the rest of you able-bodied—"

"Able-bodied men—yes—the rest of ye!" said the constable.

"Have you some good stout staves and pitchforks—"

"Staves and pitchforks—in the name o' the law! And take 'em in yer hands and go in quest, and do as we in authority tell ye!"

Thus aroused, the men prepared to give chase. The evidence was, indeed, though circumstantial, so convincing, that but little argument was needed to show the shepherd's guests that after what they had seen it would look very much like connivance if they did not instantly pursue the unhappy third stranger, who could not as yet have gone more than a few hundred yards over such uneven country.

A shepherd is always well provided with lanterns; and, lighting these hastily, and with hurdle-staves in their hands, they poured out of the door, taking a direction along the crest of the hill, away from the town, the rain having fortunately a little abated.

Disturbed by the noise, or possibly by unpleasant dreams of her baptism, the child who had been christened began to cry heart-brokenly in the room overhead. These notes of grief came down through the chinks of the floor to the ears of the women below, who jumped up one by one, and seemed glad of the excuse to ascend and comfort the baby, for the incidents of the last half-hour greatly oppressed them. Thus in the space of two or three minutes the room on the ground-floor was deserted quite.

But it was not for long. Hardly had the sound of footsteps died away when a man returned round the corner of the house from the direction the pursuers had taken. Peeping in at the door, and seeing nobody there, he entered leisurely. It was the stranger of the chimney-corner, who had gone out with the rest. The motive of his return was shown by his helping himself to a cut piece of skimmer-cake that lay on a ledge beside where he had sat, and which he had apparently forgotten to take with him. He also poured out half a cup more mead from the quantity that remained, ravenously eating and drinking these as he stood. He had not finished when another figure came in just as quietly—his friend in cinder-gray.

"Oh—you here?" said the latter, smiling. "I thought you had gone to help in the capture." And this speaker also revealed the object of his return by looking solicitously round for the fascinating mug of old mead.

"And I thought you had gone," said the other, continuing his skimmer-cake with some effort.

"Well, on second thoughts, I felt there were enough

without me," said the first confidentially, "and such a night as it is, too. Besides, 'tis the business o' the Government to take care of its criminals—not mine."

"True; so it is. And I felt as you did, that there were enough without me."

"I don't want to break my limbs running over the humps and hollows of this wild country."

"Nor I neither, between you and me."

"These shepherd-people are used to it—simple-minded souls, you know, stirred up to anything in a moment. They'll have him ready for me before the morning, and no trouble to me at all."

"They'll have him, and we shall have saved ourselves all labor in the matter."

"True, true. Well, my way is to Casterbridge; and 'tis as much as my legs will do to take me that far. Going the same way?"

"No, I am sorry to say! I have to get home over there" (he nodded indefinitely to the right), "and I feel as you do, that it is quite enough for my legs to do before bedtime."

The other had by this time finished the mead in the mug, after which, shaking hands heartily at the door, and wishing each other well, they went their several ways.

In the meantime the company of pursuers had reached the end of the hog's-back elevation which dominated this part of the down. They had decided on no particular plan of action; and, finding that the man of the baleful trade was no longer in their company, they seemed quite unable to form any such plan now. They descended in all directions down the hill, and straightway several of the party fell into the snare set by Nature for all misguided midnight ramblers over this part of the cretaceous formation. The "lanchets," or flint slopes, which belted the escarpment at intervals of a dozen yards, took the less cautious ones unawares, and losing their footing on the rubbly steep they slid sharply downwards, the lanterns rolling from their hands to the bottom, and there lying on their sides till the horn was scorched through.

When they had again gathered themselves together, the

shepherd, as the man who knew the country best, took the lead, and guided them round these treacherous inclines. The lanterns, which seemed rather to dazzle their eyes and warn the fugitive than to assist them in the exploration, were extinguished, due silence was observed; and in this more rational order they plunged into the vale. It was grassy, briery, moist defile, affording some shelter to any person who had sought it; but the party perambulated it in vain, and ascended on the other side. Here they wandered apart, and after an interval closed together again to report progress. At the second time of closing in they found themselves near a lonely ash, the single tree on this part of the coomb, probably sown there by a passing bird some fifty years before. And here, standing a little to one side of the trunk, as motionless as the trunk itself, appeared the man they were in quest of, his outline being well defined against the sky beyond. The band noiselessly drew up and faced him.

"Your money or your life!" said the constable sternly to the still figure.

"No, no," whispered John Pitcher. " 'Tisn't our side ought to say that. That's the doctrine of vagabonds like him, and we be on the side of the law."

"Well, well," replied the constable impatiently; "I must say something, mustn't I? and if you had all the weight o' this undertaking upon your mind, perhaps you'd say the wrong thing too!—Prisoner at the bar, surrender, in the name of the Father—the Crown, I mane!"

The man under the tree seemed now to notice them for the first time, and, giving them no opportunity whatever for exhibiting their courage, he strolled slowly towards them. He was, indeed, the little man, the third stranger; but his trepidation had in a great measure gone.

"Well, travelers," he said, "did I hear ye speak to me?"

"You did: you've got to come and be our prisoner at once!" said the constable. "We arrest 'ee on the charge of not biding in Casterbridge jail in a decent proper manner to be hung tomorrow morning. Neighbors, do your duty, and seize the culpet!"

On hearing the charge, the man seemed enlightened, and,

saying not another word, resigned himself with preternatural civility to the search-party, who, with their staves in their hands, surrounded him on all sides, and marched him back towards the shepherd's cottage.

It was eleven o'clock by the time they arrived. The light shining from the open door, a sound of men's voices within, proclaimed to them as they approached the house that some new events had arisen in their absence. On entering they discovered the shepherd's living room to be invaded by two officers from Casterbridge jail, and a well-known magistrate who lived at the nearest country-seat, intelligence of the escape having become generally circulated.

"Gentlemen," said the constable, "I have brought back your man—not without risk and danger; but every one must do his duty! He is inside this circle of able-bodied persons, who have lent me useful aid, considering their ignorance of Crown work. Men, bring forward your prisoner!" And the third stranger was led to the light.

"Who is this?" said one of the officials.

"The man," said the constable.

"Certainly not," said the turnkey; and the first corroborated his statement.

"But how can it be otherwise?" asked the constable. "Or why was he so terrified at sight o' the singing instrument of the law who sat there?" Here he related the strange behavior of the third stranger on entering the house during the hangman's song.

"Can't understand it," said the officer coolly. "All I know is that it is not the condemned man. He's quite a different character from this one; a gauntish fellow, with dark hair and eyes, rather good-looking, and with a musical bass voice that if you heard it once you'd never mistake as long as you lived."

"Why, souls—'twas the man in the chimney-corner!"

"Hey—what?" said the magistrate, coming forward after inquiring particulars from the shepherd in the background. "Haven't you got the man after all?"

"Well, sir," said the constable, "he's the man we were in

search of, that's true; and yet he's not the man we were in search of. For the man we were in search of was not the man we wanted, sir, if you understand my everyday way; for 'twas the man in the chimney-corner!"

"A pretty kettle of fish altogether!" said the magistrate. "You had better start for the other man at once."

The prisoner now spoke for the first time. The mention of the man in the chimney-corner seemed to have moved him as nothing else could do. "Sir," he said, stepping forward to the magistrate, "take no more trouble about me. The time is come when I may as well speak. I have done nothing; my crime is that the condemned man is my brother. Early this afternoon I left home at Shottsford to tramp it all the way to Casterbridge jail to bid him farewell. I was benighted, and called here to rest and ask the way. When I opened the door I saw before me the very man, my brother, that I thought to see in the condemned cell at Casterbridge. He was in this chimney-corner; and jammed close to him, so that he could not have got out if he had tried, was the executioner who'd come to take his life, singing a song about it and not knowing that it was his victim who was close by, joining in to save appearances. My brother looked a glance of agony at me, and I knew he meant, 'Don't reveal what you see; my life depends on it.' I was so terror-struck that I could hardly stand, and, not knowing what I did, I turned and hurried away."

The narrator's manner and tone had the stamp of truth, and his story made a great impression on all around. "And do you know where your brother is at the present time?" asked the magistrate.

"I do not. I have never seen him since I closed this door."

"I can testify to that, for we've been between ye ever since," said the constable.

"Where does he think to fly to?—what is his occupation?"

"He's a watch-and-clock-maker, sir."

"'A said 'a was a wheelwright—a wicked rogue," said the constable.

"The wheels of clocks and watches he meant, no doubt," said Shepherd Fennel. "I thought his hands were palish for's trade."

"Well, it appears to me that nothing can be gained by retaining this poor man in custody," said the magistrate; "your business lies with the other, unquestionably."

And so the little man was released off-hand; but he looked nothing the less sad on that account, it being beyond the power of magistrate or constable to raze out the written troubles in his brain, for they concerned another whom he regarded with more solicitude than himself. When this was done, and the man had gone his way, the night was found to be so far advanced that it was deemed useless to renew the search before the next morning.

Next day, accordingly, the quest for the clever sheep-stealer became general and keen, to all appearance at least. But the intended punishment was cruelly disproportioned to the transgression, and the sympathy of a great many country-folk in that district was strongly on the side of the fugitive. Moreover, his marvelous coolness and daring in hob-and-nobbing with the hangman, under the unprecedented circumstances of the shepherd's party, won their admiration. So that it may be questioned if all those who ostensibly made themselves so busy in exploring woods and fields and lanes were quite so thorough when it came to the private examination of their own lofts and outhouses. Stories were afloat of a mysterious figure being occasionally seen in some old overgrown trackway or other, remote from turnpike roads; but when a search was instituted in any of these suspected quarters nobody was found. Thus the days and weeks passed without tidings.

In brief, the bass-voiced man of the chimney-corner was never recaptured. Some said that he went across the sea, others that he did not, but buried himself in the depths of a populous city. At any rate, the gentleman in cinder-gray never did his morning's work at Casterbridge, nor met anywhere at all, for business purposes, the genial comrade with whom he had passed an hour of relaxation in the lonely house on the coomb.

The grass has long been green on the graves of Shepherd Fennel and his frugal wife; the guests who made up the christening party have mainly followed their entertainers to the tomb; the baby in whose honor they all had met is a matron in the sere and yellow leaf. But the arrival of the three strangers at the shepherd's that night, and the details connected therewith, is a story as well known as ever in the country about Higher Crowstairs.

1890

Gallegher

RICHARD HARDING DAVIS

We had had so many office-boys before Gallegher came among us that they had begun to lose the characteristics of individuals, and became merged in a composite photograph of small boys, to whom we applied the generic title of "Here, you"; or "You, boy."

We had had sleepy boys, and lazy boys, and bright, "smart" boys, who became so familiar on so short an acquaintance that we were forced to part with them to save our own self-respect.

They generally graduated into district-messenger boys, and occasionally returned to us in blue coats with nickel-plated buttons, and patronized us.

But Gallegher was something different from anything we had experienced before. Gallegher was short and broad in build, with a solid, muscular broadness, and not a fat and dumpy shortness. He wore perpetually on his face a happy and knowing smile, as if you and the world in general were not impressing him as seriously as you thought you were, and his eyes, which were very black and very bright, snapped intelligently at you like those of a little black-and-tan terrier.

All Gallegher knew had been learnt on the streets; not a very good school in itself, but one that turns out very knowing scholars. And Gallegher had attended both morning and evening sessions. He could not tell you who the Pilgrim Fathers were, nor could he name the thirteen original States, but he knew all the officers of the twenty-second police district by name, and he could distinguish the clang of a fire-engine's gong from that of a patrol-wagon or an ambulance fully two blocks distant. It was Gallegher who rang the alarm when the Woolwich Mills caught fire, while the officer on the beat was asleep, and it was Gallegher who led the "Black Diamonds" against the "Wharf Rats," when they used to stone each other to their hearts' content on the coal wharves of Richmond.

I am afraid, now that I see these facts written down, that Gallegher was not a reputable character; but he was so very young and so very old for his years that we all liked him very much nevertheless. He lived in the extreme northern part of Philadelphia, where the cotton and woollen mills run down to the river, and how he ever got home after leaving the *Press* building at two in the morning, was one of the mysteries of the office. Sometimes he caught a night car, and sometimes he walked all the way, arriving at the little house, where his mother and himself lived alone, at four in the morning. Occasionally he was given a ride on an early milk cart, or on one of the newspaper delivery wagons, with its high piles of papers still damp and sticky from the press. He knew several drivers of "night hawks"—those cabs that prowl the streets at night looking for belated passengers—and when it was a very cold morning he would not go home at all, but would crawl into one of these cabs and sleep, curled up on the cushions, until daylight.

Besides being quick and cheerful, Gallegher possessed a power of amusing the *Press*'s young men to a degree seldom attained by the ordinary mortal. His clog-dancing on the city editor's desk, when that gentleman was upstairs fighting for two more columns of space, was always a source of innocent joy to us, and his imitations of the comedians of the variety halls delighted even the dramatic critic, from whom the comedians themselves failed to force a smile.

But Gallegher's chief characteristic was his love for that element of news generically classed as "crime."

Not that he ever did anything criminal himself. On the contrary, his was rather the work of the criminal specialist, and his morbid interest in the doings of all queer characters, his knowledge of their methods, their present whereabouts, and their past deeds of transgression often rendered him a valuable ally to our police reporter, whose daily feuilletons were the only portion of the paper Gallegher deigned to read.

In Gallegher the detective element was abnormally developed. He had shown this on several occasions, and to excellent purpose.

Once the paper had sent him into a Home for Destitute Orphans which was believed to be grievously mismanaged, and Gallegher, while playing the part of a destitute orphan, kept his eyes open to what was going on around him so faithfully that the story he told of the treatment meted out to the real orphans was sufficient to rescue the unhappy little wretches from the individual who had them in charge, and to have the individual himself sent to jail.

Gallegher's knowledge of the aliases, terms of imprisonment, and various misdoings of the leading criminals in Philadelphia was almost as thorough as that of the chief of police himself, and he could tell to an hour when "Dutchy Mack" was to be let out of prison, and could identify at a glance "Dick Oxford, confidence man," as "Gentleman Dan, petty thief."

There were, at this time, only two pieces of news in any of the papers. The least important of the two was the big fight between the Champion of the United States and the Would-be Champion, arranged to take place near Philadelphia; the second was the Burrbank murder, which was filling space in newspapers all over the world, from New York to Bombay.

Richard F. Burrbank was one of the most prominent of New York's railroad lawyers; he was also, a matter of course, an owner of much railroad stock, and and a very wealthy man. He had been spoken of as a political possibility for many high offices, and, as the counsel for a great railroad, was known even further than the great railroad itself had stretched its system.

At six o'clock one morning he was found by his butler lying at the foot of the hall stairs with two pistol wounds above his heart. He was quite dead. His safe, to which only he and his secretary had the keys, was found open, and $200,000 in bonds, stocks, and money, which had been placed there only the night before, was found missing. The secretary was missing also. His name was Stephen S. Hade, and his name and his description had been telegraphed and cabled to all parts of the world. There was enough circumstantial evidence to show, beyond any question or possibility of mistake, that he was the murderer.

It made an enormous amount of talk, and unhappy individuals were being arrested all over the country, and sent on to New York for identification. Three had been arrested at Liverpool, and one man just as he landed at Sydney, Australia. But so far the murderer had escaped.

We were talking about it one night, as everybody else was all over the country, in the local room, and the city editor said it was worth a fortune to any one who chanced to run across Hade and succeeded in handing him over to the police. Some of us thought Hade had taken passage from some one of the smaller seaports, and others were of the opinion that he had buried himself in some cheap lodging-house in New York, or in one of the smaller towns in New Jersey.

"I shouldn't be surprised to meet him out walking, right here in Philadelphia," said one of the staff. "He'll be disguised, of course, but you could always tell him by the absence of the trigger finger on his right hand. It's missing, you know; shot off when he was a boy."

"You want to look for a man dressed like a tough," said the city editor; "for as this fellow is to all appearances a gentleman, he will try to look as little like a gentleman as possible."

"No, he won't," said Gallegher, with that calm impertinence that made him dear to us. "He'll dress just like a gentleman. Toughs don't wear gloves, and you see he's got to wear 'em. The first thing he thought of after doing for Burrbank was of that gone finger, and how he was to hide it. He stuffed the finger of that glove with cotton so's to make it look like a whole finger, and the first time he takes off that glove they've got him—see, and he knows it. So what youse want to do is to look for a man with gloves on. I've been a-doing it for two weeks now, and I can tell you it's hard work, for everybody wears gloves this kind of weather. But if you look long enough you'll find him. And when you think it's him, go up to him and hold out your hand in a friendly way, like a bunco-steerer, and shake his hand; and if you feel that his forefinger ain't real flesh, but just wadded cotton, then grip to it with your right and grab his throat with your left, and holler for help."

There was an appreciative pause.

"I see, gentlemen," said the city editor, dryly, "that Gallegher's reasoning has impressed you; and I also see that before the week is out all of my young men will be under bonds for assaulting innocent pedestrians whose only offence is that they wear gloves in midwinter."

It was about a week after this that Detective Hefflefinger, of Inspector Byrnes's staff, came over to Philadelphia after a burglar, of whose whereabouts he had been misinformed by telegraph. He brought the warrant, requisition, and other necessary papers about him, but the burglar had flown. One of our reporters had worked on a New York paper, and knew Hefflefinger, and the detective came to the office to see if he could help him in his so far unsuccessful search.

He gave Gallegher his card, and after Gallegher had read it, and had discovered who the visitor was, he became so demoralized that he was absolutely useless.

"One of Byrnes's men" was a much more awe-inspiring individual to Gallegher than a member of the Cabinet. He accordingly seized his hat and overcoat, and leaving his duties to be looked after by others, hastened out after the object of his admiration, who found his suggestions and knowledge of the city so valuable, and his company so entertaining, that they became very intimate, and spent the rest of the day together.

In the meanwhile the managing editor had instructed his subordinates to inform Gallegher, when he condescended to return, that his services were no longer needed. Gallegher had played truant once too often. Unconscious of this, he remained with his new friend until late the same evening, and started the next afternoon toward the *Press* office.

As I have said, Gallegher lived in the most distant part of the city, not many minutes' walk from the Kensington railroad station, where trains ran into the suburbs and on to New York.

It was in front of this station that a smoothly shaven, well-dressed man brushed past Gallegher and hurried up the steps to the ticket office.

He held a walking stick in his right hand, and Gallegher, who now patiently scrutinized the hands of every one who wore gloves, saw that while three fingers of the man's hand were closed around the cane, the fourth stood out in almost a straight line with his palm.

Gallegher stopped with a gasp and with a trembling all over his little body, and his brain asked with a throb if it could be possible. But possibilities and probabilities were to be discovered later. Now was the time for action.

He was after the man in a moment, hanging at his heels and his eyes moist with excitement.

He heard the man ask for a ticket to Torresdale, a little station just outside of Philadelphia, and when he was out of hearing, but not out of sight, purchased one for the same place.

The stranger went into the smoking-car, and seated himself at one end toward the door. Gallegher took his place at the opposite end.

He was trembling all over, and suffered from a slight feeling of nausea. He guessed it came from fright, not of any bodily harm that might come to him, but at the probability of failure in his adventure and of its most momentous possibilities.

The stranger pulled his coat collar up around his ears, hiding the lower portion of his face, but not concealing the resemblance in his troubled eyes and close-shut lips to the likenesses of the murderer Hade.

They reached Torresdale in half an hour, and the stranger, alighting quickly, struck off at a rapid pace down the country road leading to the station.

Gallegher gave him a hundred yards' start, and then followed slowly after. The road ran between fields and past a few frame-houses set far from the road in kitchen gardens.

Once or twice the man looked back over his shoulder, but he saw only a dreary length of road with a small boy splashing through the slush in the midst of it and stopping every now and again to throw snowballs at belated sparrows.

After a ten minutes' walk the stranger turned into a side

road which led to only one place, the Eagle Inn, an old roadside
hostelry known now as the headquarters for pothunters from
the Philadelphia game market and the battle ground of many a
cockfight.

Gallegher knew the place well. He and his young companions had often stopped there when out chestnutting on holidays
in the autumn.

The son of the man who kept it had often accompanied
them on their excursions, and though the boys of the city streets
considered him a dumb lout, they respected him somewhat
owing to his inside knowledge of dog and cockfights.

The stranger entered the inn at a side door, and Gallegher,
reaching it a few minutes later, let him go for the time being, and
set about finding his occasional playmate, young Keppler.

Keppler's offspring was found in the woodshed.

" 'Tain't hard to guess what brings you out here," said the
tavern keeper's son, with a grin; "it's the fight."

"What fight?" asked Gallegher, unguardedly.

"What fight? Why, *the* fight," returned his companion, with
the slow contempt of superior knowledge. "It's to come off here
to-night. You knew that as well as me; anyway your sportin'
editor knows it. He got the tip last night, but that won't help you
any. You needn't think there's any chance of your getting a peep
at it. Why, tickets is two hundred and fifty apiece!"

"Whew!" whistled Gallegher, "where's it to be?"

"In the barn," whispered Keppler. "I helped 'em fix the
ropes this morning, I did."

"Gosh, but you're in luck," exclaimed Gallegher, with
flattering envy. "Couldn't I jest get a peep at it?"

"Maybe," said the gratified Keppler. "There's a winder with
a wooden shutter at the back of the barn. You can get in by it, if
you have some one to boost you up to the sill."

"Sa-a-y," drawled Gallegher, as if something had but just
that moment reminded him. "Who's that gent who come down
the road just a bit ahead of me—him with the cape-coat! Has he
got anything to do with the fight?"

"Him?" repeated Keppler in tones of sincere disgust. "No-
oh, he ain't no sport. He's queer, Dad thinks. He come here one

day last week about ten in the morning, said his doctor told him to go out 'en the country for his health. He's stuck up and citified, and wears gloves, and takes his meals private in his room, and all that sort of ruck. They was saying in the saloon last night that they thought he was hiding from something, and Dad, just to try him, asks him last night if he was coming to see the fight. He looked sort of scared, and said he didn't want to see no fight. And then Dad says, 'I guess you mean you don't want no fighters to see you.' Dad didn't mean no harm by it, just passed it as a joke; but Mr. Carleton, as he calls himself, got white as a ghost an' says, 'I'll go to the fight willing enough,' and begins to laugh and joke. And this morning he went right into the bar-room, where all the sports were setting, and said he was going into town to see some friends; and as he starts off he laughs an' says, 'This don't look as if I was afraid of seeing people, does it?' but Dad says it was just bluff that made him do it, and Dad thinks that if he hadn't said what he did, this Mr. Carleton wouldn't have left his room at all."

Gallegher had got all he wanted, and much more than he had hoped for—so much more that his walk back to the station was in the nature of a triumphal march.

He had twenty minutes to wait for the next train, and it seemed an hour. While waiting he sent a telegram to Hefflefinger at his hotel. It read: "Your man is near the Torresdale station, on Pennsylvania Railroad; take cab, and meet me at station. Wait until I come. GALLEGHER."

With the exception of one at midnight, no other train stopped at Torresdale that evening, hence the direction to take a cab.

The train to the city seemed to Gallegher to drag itself by inches. It stopped and backed at purposeless intervals, waited for an express to precede it, and dallied at stations, and when, at last, it reached the terminus, Gallegher was out before it had stopped and was in the cab and off on his way to the home of the sporting editor.

The sporting editor was at dinner and came out in the hall to see him, with his napkin in his hand. Gallegher explained breathlessly that he had located the murderer for whom the police of two continents were looking, and that he believed, in order to quiet the suspicions of the people with whom he was hiding, that he would be present at the fight that night.

The sporting editor led Gallegher into his library and shut the door. "Now," he said, "go over all that again."

Gallegher went over it again in detail, and added how he had sent for Hefflefinger to make the arrest in order that it might be kept from the knowledge of the local police and from the Philadelphia reporters.

"What I want Hefflefinger to do is to arrest Hade with the warrant he has for the burglar," explained Gallegher; "and to take him on to New York on the owl train that passes Torresdale at one. It don't get to Jersey City until four o'clock, one hour after the morning papers go to press. Of course, we must fix Hefflefinger so's he'll keep quiet and not tell who his prisoner really is."

The sporting editor reached his hand out to pat Gallegher on the head, but changed his mind and shook hands with him instead.

"My boy," he said, "you are an infant phenomenon. If I can pull the rest of this thing off tonight it will mean the $5,000 reward and fame galore for you and the paper. Now, I'm going to write a note to the managing editor, and you can take it around to him and tell him what you've done and what I am going to do, and he'll take you back on the paper and raise your salary. Perhaps you didn't know you've been discharged?"

"Do you think you ain't a-going to take me with you?" demanded Gallegher.

"Why, certainly not. Why should I? It all lies with the detective and myself now. You've done your share, and done it well. If the man's caught, the reward's yours. But you'd only be in the way now. You'd better go to the office and make your peace with the chief."

"If the paper can get along without me, I can get along without the old paper," said Gallegher, hotly. "And if I ain't a-going with you, you ain't neither, for I know where Hefflefinger is to be, and you don't, and I won't tell you."

"Oh, very well, very well," replied the sporting editor,

weakly capitulating. "I'll send the note by a messenger; only mind, if you lose your place, don't blame me."

Gallegher wondered how this man could value a week's salary against the excitement of seeing a noted criminal run down, and of getting the news to the paper, and to that one paper alone.

From that moment the sporting editor sank in Gallegher's estimation.

Mr. Dwyer sat down at his desk and scribbled off the following note:

"I have received reliable information that Hade, the Burr-bank murderer, will be present at the fight tonight. We have arranged it so that he will be arrested quietly and in such a manner that the fact may be kept from all other papers. I need not point out to you that this will be the most important piece of news in the country tomorrow.

"Yours, etc.,   Michael E. Dwyer."

The sporting editor stepped into the waiting cab, while Gallegher whispered the directions to the driver. He was told to go first to a district messenger office, and from there up to the Ridge Avenue Road, out Broad Street, and on to the old Eagle Inn, near Torresdale.

It was a miserable night. The rain and snow were falling together, and freezing as they fell. The sporting editor got out to send his message to the *Press* office, and then lighting a cigar, and turning up the collar of his great-coat, curled up in the corner of the cab.

"Wake me when we get there, Gallegher," he said. He knew he had a long ride, and much rapid work before him, and he was preparing for the strain.

To Gallegher the idea of going to sleep seemed almost criminal. From the dark corner of the cab his eyes shone with excitement, and with the awful joy of anticipation. He glanced every now and then to where the sporting editor's cigar shone in the darkness, and watched it as it gradually burnt more dimly and went out. The lights in the shop windows threw a broad glare across the ice on the pavements, and the lights from the lamp posts tossed the distorted shadow of the cab, and the horse, and the motionless driver, sometimes before and sometimes behind them.

After half an hour Gallegher slipped down to the bottom of the cab and dragged out a lap-robe, in which he wrapped himself. It was growing colder, and the damp, keen wind swept in through the cracks until the window-frames and woodwork were cold to the touch.

An hour passed, and the cab was still moving more slowly over the rough surface of partly paved streets, and by single rows of new houses standing at different angles to each other in fields covered with ash-heaps and brick-kilns. Here and there the gaudy lights of a drug-store, and the forerunner of suburban civilization, shone from the end of a new block of houses, and the rubber cape of an occasional policeman showed in the light of the lamp-post that he hugged for comfort.

Then even the houses disappeared, and the cab dragged its way between truck farms, with desolate-looking glass-covered beds, and pools of water, half-caked with ice, and bare trees, and interminable fences.

Once or twice the cab stopped altogether, and Gallegher could hear the driver swearing to himself, or at the horse, or the roads. At last they drew up before the station at Torresdale. It was quite deserted, and only a single light cut a swath in the darkness and showed a portion of the platform, the ties, and the rails glistening in the rain. They walked twice past the light before a figure stepped out of the shadow and greeted them cautiously.

"I am Mr. Dwyer, of the *Press*," said the sporting editor, briskly. "You've heard of me, perhaps. Well, there shouldn't be any difficulty in our making a deal, should there? This boy here has found Hade, and we have reason to believe he will be among the spectators at the fight tonight. We want you to arrest him quietly, and as secretly as possible. You can do it with your papers and your badge easily enough. We want you to pretend that you believe he is this burglar you came over after. If you will do this, and take him away without any one so much as suspecting who he really is, and on the train that passes here at 1.20 for New York, we will give you $500 out of the $5,000 reward. If, however, one other paper, either in New York or Philadelphia, or anywhere else, knows of the arrest, you won't get a cent. Now, what do you say?"

The detective had a great deal to say. He wasn't at all sure the man Gallegher suspected was Hade; he feared he might get himself into trouble by making a false arrest, and if it should be the man, he was afraid the local police would interfere.

"We've no time to argue or debate this matter," said Dwyer, warmly. "We agree to point Hade out to you in the crowd. After the fight is over you arrest him as we have directed, and you get the money and the credit of the arrest. If you don't like this, I will arrest the man myself, and have him driven to town, with a pistol for a warrant."

Hefflefinger considered in silence and then agreed unconditionally. "As you say, Mr. Dwyer," he returned. "I've heard of you for a thoroughbred sport. I know you'll do what you say you'll do; and as for me I'll do what you say and just as you say, and it's a very pretty piece of work as it stands."

They all stepped back into the cab, and then it was that they were met by a fresh difficulty, how to get the detective into the barn where the fight was to take place, for neither of the two men had $250 to pay for his admittance.

But this was overcome when Gallegher remembered the window of which young Keppler had told him.

In the event of Hade's losing courage and not daring to show himself in the crowd around the ring, it was agreed that Dwyer should come to the barn and warn Hefflefinger; but if he should come, Dwyer was merely to keep near him and to signify by a prearranged gesture which one of the crowd he was.

They drew up before a great black shadow of a house, dark, forbidding, and apparently deserted. But at the sound of the wheels on the gravel the door opened, letting out a stream of warm, cheerful light, and a man's voice said, "Put out those lights. Don't youse know no better than that?" This was Keppler, and he welcomed Mr. Dwyer with effusive courtesy.

The two men showed in the stream of light, and the door closed on them, leaving the house as it was at first, black and silent, save for the dripping of the rain and snow from the eaves.

The detective and Gallegher put out the cab's lamps and led the horse toward a long, low shed in the rear of the yard, which they now noticed was almost filled with teams of many different makes, from the Hobson's choice of a livery stable to the brougham of the man about town.

"No," said Gallegher, as the cabman stopped to hitch the horse beside the others, "we want it nearest that lower gate. When we newspaper men leave this place we'll leave it in a hurry, and the man who is nearest town is likely to get there first. You won't be a-following of no hearse when you make your return trip."

Gallegher tied the horse to the very gate-post itself, leaving the gate open and allowing a clear road and a flying start for the prospective race to Newspaper Row.

The driver disappeared under the shelter of the porch, and Gallegher and the detective moved off cautiously to the rear of the barn. "This must be the window," said Hefflefinger, pointing to a broad wooden shutter some feet from the window.

"Just you give me a boost once, and I'll get that open in a jiffy," said Gallegher.

The detective placed his hands on his knees, and Gallegher stood upon his shoulders, and with the blade of his knife lifted the wooden button that fastened the window on the inside, and pulled the shutter open.

Then he put one leg inside over the sill, and leaning down helped to draw his fellow-conspirator up to a level with the window. "I feel just like I was burglarizing a house," chuckled Gallegher, as he dropped noiselessly to the floor below and refastened the shutter. The barn was a large one, with a row of stalls on either side in which horses and cows were dozing. There was a haymow over each row of stalls, and at one end of the barn a number of fence-rails had been thrown across from one mow to the other. These rails were covered with hay.

In the middle of the floor was the ring. It was not really a ring, but a square, with wooden posts at its four corners through which ran a heavy rope. The space inclosed by the rope was covered with sawdust.

Gallegher could not resist stepping into the ring, and after stamping the sawdust once or twice, as if to assure himself that he was really there, began dancing around it, and indulging in such a remarkable series of fistic manœuvres with an imaginary adversary that the unimaginative detective precipitately backed into a corner of the barn.

"Now, then," said Gallegher, having apparently vanquished his foe, "you come with me." His companion followed quickly as Gallegher climbed to one of the haymows, and crawling carefully out on the fence-rail, stretched himself at full length, face downward. In this position, by moving the straw a little, he could look down, without being himself seen, upon the heads of whomsoever stood below. "This is better'n a private box, ain't it?" said Gallegher.

The boy from the newspaper office and the detective lay there in silence, biting at straws and tossing anxiously on their comfortable bed.

It seemed fully two hours before they came. Gallegher had listened without breathing, and with every muscle on a strain, at least a dozen times, when some movement in the yard had led him to believe that they were at the door.

And he had numerous doubts and fears. Sometimes it was that the police had learnt of the fight, and had raided Keppler's in his absence, and again it was that the fight had been postponed, or, worst of all, that it would be put off until so late that Mr. Dwyer could not get back in time for the last edition of the paper. Their coming, when at last they came, was heralded by an advanceguard of two sporting men, who stationed themselves at either side of the big door.

"Hurry up, now, gents," one of the men said with a shiver, "don't keep this door open no longer'n is needful."

It was not a very large crowd, but it was wonderfully well selected. It ran, in the majority of its component parts, to heavy white coats with pearl buttons. The white coats were shouldered by long blue coats with astrakhan fur trimmings, the wearers of which preserved a cliqueness not remarkable when one considers that they believed every one else present to be either a crook or a prize-fighter.

There were well-fed, well-groomed club-men and brokers in the crowd, a politician or two, a popular comedian with his manager, amateur boxers from the athletic clubs, and quiet, close mouthed sporting men from every city in the country. Their names if printed in the papers would have been as familiar as the types of the papers themselves.

And among these men, whose only thought was of the brutal sport to come, was Hade, with Dwyer standing at ease at his shoulder—Hade, white, and visibly in deep anxiety, hiding his pale face beneath a cloth travelling cap, and with his chin muffled in a wollen scarf. He had dared to come because he feared his danger from the already suspicious Keppler was less than if he stayed away. And so he was there, hovering restlessly on the border of the crowd, feeling his danger and sick with fear.

When Hefflefinger first saw him he started up on his hands and elbows and made a movement forward as if he would leap down then and there and carry off his prisoner single-handed.

"Lie down," growled Gallegher; "an officer of any sort wouldn't live three minutes in that crowd."

The detective drew back slowly and buried himself again in the straw, but never once through the long fight which followed did his eyes leave the person of the murderer. The newspaper men took their places in the foremost row close around the ring, and kept looking at their watches and begging the master of ceremonies to "shake it up, do."

There was a great deal of betting, and all of the men handled the great roll of bills they wagered with a flippant recklessness which could only be accounted for in Gallegher's mind by temporary mental derangement. Some one pulled a box out into the ring and the master of ceremonies mounted it, and pointed out in forcible language that as they were almost all already under bonds to keep the peace, it behooved all to curb their excitement and to maintain a severe silence, unless they wanted to bring the police upon them and have themselves "sent down" for a year or two.

Then two very disreputable-looking persons tossed their respective principals' high hats into the ring, and the crowd, recognizing in this relic of the days when brave knights threw down their gauntlets in the lists as only a sign that the fight was about to begin, cheered tumultuously.

This was followed by a sudden surging forward, and a mutter of admiration much more flattering than the cheers had been, when the principals followed their hats, and slipping out of their great-coats, stood forth in all the physical beauty of the perfect brute.

Their pink skin was as soft and healthy looking as a baby's, and glowed in the lights of the lanterns like tinted ivory, and underneath this silken covering the great biceps and muscles moved in and out and looked like the coils of a snake around the branch of a tree.

Gentlemen and blackguard shouldered each other for a nearer view; the coachmen, whose metal buttons were unpleasantly suggestive of police, put their hands, in the excitement of the moment, on the shoulders of their masters; the perspiration stood out in great drops on the foreheads of the backers, and the newspaper men bit somewhat nervously at the ends of their pencils.

And in the stalls the cows munched contentedly at their cuds and gazed with gentle curiosity at their two fellowbrutes, who stood waiting the signal to fall upon, and kill each other if need be, for the delectation of their brothers.

"Take your places," commanded the master of ceremonies.

In the moment in which the two men faced each other the crowd became so still that, save for the beating of the rain upon the shingled roof and the stamping of a horse in one of the stalls, the place was silent as a church.

"Time," shouted the master of ceremonies.

The two men sprang into a posture of defence, which was lost as quickly as it was taken, one great arm shot out like a piston-rod; there was the sound of bare fists beating on naked flesh; there was an exultant indrawn gasp of savage pleasure and relief from the crowd, and the great fight had begun.

How the fortunes of war rose and fell, and changed and

rechanged that night, is an old story to those who listen to such stories; and those who do not will be glad to be spared the telling of it. It was, they say, one of the bitterest fights between two men that this country has ever known.

But all that is of interest here is that after an hour of this desperate brutal business the champion ceased to be the favorite; the man whom he had taunted and bullied, and for whom the public had but little sympathy, was proving himself a likely winner, and under his cruel blows, as sharp and clean as those from a cutlass, his opponent was rapidly giving way.

The men about the ropes were past all control now; they drowned Keppler's petitions for silence with oaths and in inarticulate shouts of anger, as if the blows had fallen upon them, and in mad rejoicings. They swept from one end of the ring with those of the man they favored, and when a New York correspondent muttered over his shoulder that this would be the biggest sporting surprise since the Heenan-Sayers fight, Mr. Dwyer nodded his head sympathetically in assent.

In the excitement and tumult it is doubtful if any heard the three quickly repeated blows that fell heavily from the outside upon the big doors of the barn. If they did, it was already too late to mend matters, for the door fell, torn from its hinges, and as it fell a captain of police sprang into the light from out of the storm, with his lieutenants and their men crowding close as his shoulder.

In the panic and stampede that followed, several of the men stood as helplessly immovable as though they had seen a ghost; others made a mad rush into the arms of the officers and were beaten back against the ropes of the ring; others dived headlong into the stalls, among the horses and cattle, and still others shoved the rolls of money they held into the hands of the police and begged like children to be allowed to escape.

The instant the door fell and the raid was declared Hefflefinger slipped over the cross rails on which he had been lying, hung for an instant by his hands, and then dropped into the centre of the fighting mob on the floor. He was out of it in an instant with the agility of a pickpocket, was across the room and at Hade's throat like a dog. The murderer, for the moment, was the calmer man of the two.

"Here," he panted, "hands off, now. There's no need for all this violence. There's no great harm in looking at a fight, is there? There's a hundred-dollar bill in my right hand; take it and let me slip out of this. No one is looking. Here."

But the detective only held him the closer.

"I want you for burglary," he whispered under his breath. "You've got to come with me now, and quick. The less fuss you make, the better for both of us. If you don't know who I am, you can feel my badge under my coat there. I've got the authority. It's all regular, and when we're out of this d—d row I'll show you the papers."

He took one hand from Hade's throat and pulled a pair of handcuffs from his pocket.

"It's a mistake. This is an outrage," gasped the murderer, white and trembling, but dreadfully alive and desperate for his liberty. "Let me go, I tell you! Take your hands off of me! Do I look like a burglar, you fool?"

"I know who you look like," whispered the detective, with his face close the face of his prisoner. "Now, will you go easy as a burglar, or shall I tell these men who you are and what I *do* want you for? Shall I call out your real name or not? Shall I tell them? Quick, speak up; shall I?"

There was something so exultant—something so unnecessarily savage in the officer's face that the man he held saw that the detective knew him for what he really was, and the hands that had held his throat slipped down around his shoulders, or he would have fallen. The man's eyes opened and closed again, and he swayed weakly backward and forward, and choked as if his throat were dry and burning. Even to such a hardened connoisseur in crime as Gallegher, who stood closely by drinking it in, there was something so abject in the man's terror that he regarded him with what was almost a touch of pity.

"For God's sake," Hade begged, "let me go. Come with me to my room and I'll give you half the money. I'll divide with you fairly. We can both get away. There's a fortune for both of us there. We both can get away. You'll be rich for life. Do you understand—for life!"

But the detective, to his credit, only shut his lips the tighter. "That's enough," he whispered, in return. "That's more than I expected. You've sentenced yourself already. Come!"

Two officers in uniform barred their exit at the door, but Hefflefinger smiled easily and showed his badge.

"One of Byrnes's men," he said, in explanation; "came over expressly to take this chap. He's a burglar; 'Arlie' Lane, *alias* Carleton. I've shown the papers to the captain. It's all regular. I'm just going to get his traps at the hotel and walk him over to the station. I guess we'll push right on to New York tonight."

The officers nodded and smiled their admiration for the representative of what is, perhaps, the best detective force in the world, and let him pass.

Then Hefflefinger turned and spoke to Gallegher, who still stood as watchful as a dog at his side. "I'm going to his room to get the bonds and stuff," he whispered; "then I'll march him to the station and take that train. I've done my share; don't forget yours!"

"Oh, you'll get your money right enough," said Gallegher. "And, sa-ay," he added, with the appreciative nod of an expert, "do you know, you did it rather well."

Mr. Dwyer had been writing while the raid was settling down, as he had been writing while waiting for the fight to begin. Now he walked over to where the other correspondents stood in angry conclave.

The newspaper men had informed the officers who hemmed them in that they represented the principal papers of the country, and were expostulating vigorously with the captain, who had planned the raid, and who declared they were under arrest.

"Don't be an ass, Scott," said Mr. Dwyer, who was too excited to be polite or politic. "You know our being here isn't a matter of choice. We came here on business, as you did, and you've no right to hold us."

"If we don't get our stuff on the wire at once," protested a New York man, "we'll be too late for tomorrow's paper, and—"

Captain Scott said he did not care a profanely small amount for tomorrow's paper, and that all he knew was that to the station house the newspaper men would go. There they would have a hearing, and if the magistrate chose to let them off, that was the magistrate's business, but that his duty was to take them into custody.

"But then it will be too late, don't you understand?" shouted Mr. Dwyer. "You've got to let us go *now,* at once."

"I can't do it, Mr. Dwyer," said the captain, "and that's all there is to it. Why, haven't I just sent the president of the Junior Republican Club to the patrol wagon, the man that put this coat on me, and do you think I can let you fellows go after that? You were all put under bonds to keep the peace not three days ago, and here you're at it—fighting like badgers. It's worth my place to let one of you off."

What Mr. Dwyer said next was so uncomplimentary to the gallant Captain Scott that that overwrought individual seized the sporting editor by the shoulder, and shoved him into the hands of two of his men.

This was more than the distinguished Mr. Dwyer could brook, and he excitedly raised his hand in resistance. But before he had time to do anything foolish his wrist was gripped by one strong, little hand, and he was conscious that another was picking the pocket of his great-coat.

He slapped his hands to his sides, and looking down, saw Gallagher standing close behind him and holding him by the wrist. Mr. Dwyer had forgotten the boy's existence, and would have spoken sharply if something in Gallegher's innocent eyes had not stopped him.

Gallegher's hand was still in that pocket, in which Mr. Dwyer had shoved his note-book filled with what he had written of Gallegher's work and Hade's final capture, and with a running descriptive account of the fight. With his eyes fixed on Mr. Dwyer, Gallegher drew it out, and with a quick movement shoved it inside his waistcoat. Mr. Dwyer gave a nod of comprehension. Then glancing at his two guardsmen, and finding that they were still interested in the wordy battle of the correspondents with their chief, and had seen nothing, he stooped and whispered to Gallegher: "The forms are locked at twenty minutes to three. If you don't get there by that time it will be of no use, but if you're on time you'll beat the town—and the country too."

Gallegher's eyes flashed significantly, and nodding his head to show he understood, started boldly on a run toward the door. But the officers who guarded it brought him to an abrupt halt, and, much to Mr. Dwyer's astonishment, drew from him what was apparently a torrent of tears.

"Let me go to me father. I want me father," the boy shrieked, hysterically. "They've 'rested father. Oh, daddy, daddy. They're a-goin' to take you to prison."

"Who is your father, sonny?" asked one of the guardians of the gate.

"Keppler's me father," sobbed Gallegher. "They're a-goin' to lock him up, and I'll never see him no more."

"Oh, yes, you will," said the officer, good-naturedly; "he's there in that first patrol-wagon. You can run over and say good night to him, and then you'd better get to bed. This ain't no place for kids of your age."

"Thank you, sir," sniffed Gallegher, tearfully, as the two officers raised their clubs, and let him pass out into the darkness.

The yard outside was in a tumult, horses were stamping, and plunging, and backing the carriages into one another; lights were flashing from every window of what had been apparently an uninhabited house, and the voices of the prisoners were still raised in angry expostulation.

Three police patrol-wagons were moving about the yard, filled with unwilling passengers, who sat or stood, packed together like sheep, and with no protection from the sleet and rain.

Gallegher stole off into a dark corner, and watched the scene until his eyesight became familiar with the position of the land.

Then with his eyes fixed fearfully on the swinging light of a lantern with which an officer was searching among the carriages, he groped his way between horses' hoofs and behind the wheels of carriages to the cab which he had himself placed at the furthermost gate. It was still there, and the horse, as he had left it, with its head turned toward the city. Gallegher opened the big gate noiselessly, and worked nervously at the hitching strap. The knot was covered with a thin coating of ice, and it was several minutes before he could loosen it. But his teeth finally pulled it apart, and with the reins in his hands he sprang upon the wheel. And as he stood so, a shock of fear ran down his back like an electric current, his breath left him, and he stood immovable, gazing with wide eyes into the darkness.

The officer with the lantern had suddenly loomed up from behind a carriage not fifty feet distant, and was standing perfectly still, with his lantern held over his head, peering so directly toward Gallegher that the boy felt that he must see him. Gallegher stood with one foot on the hub of the wheel and with the other on the box waiting to spring. It seemed a minute before either of them moved, and then the officer took a step forward, and demanded sternly, "Who is that? What are you doing there?"

There was no time for parley then. Gallegher felt that he had been taken in the act, and that his only chance lay in open flight. He leaped up on the box, pulling out the whip as he did so, and with a quick sweep lashed the horse across the head and back. The animal sprang forward with a snort, narrowly clearing the gate-post, and plunged off into the darkness.

"Stop!" cried the officer.

So many of Gallegher's acquaintances among the 'longshoremen and mill hands had been challenged in so much the same manner that Gallegher knew what would probably follow if the challenge was disregarded. So he slipped from his seat to the footboard below, and ducked his head.

The three reports of a pistol, which rang out briskly from behind him, proved that his early training had given him a valuable fund of useful miscellaneous knowledge.

"Don't you be scared," he said, reassuringly, to the horse; "he's firing in the air."

The pistol-shots were answered by the impatient clangor of a patrol-wagon's gong, and glancing over his shoulder Gallegher saw its red and green lanterns tossing from side to side and looking in the darkness like the side-lights of a yacht plunging forward in a storm.

"I hadn't bargained to race you against no patrol-wagons," said Gallegher to his animal; "but if they want a race, we'll give them a tough tussle for it, won't we?"

Philadelphia, lying four miles to the south, sent up a faint yellow glow to the sky. It seemed very far away, and Gallegher's braggadocio grew cold within him at the loneliness of his adventure and the thought of the long ride before him.

It was still bitterly cold.

The rain and sleet beat through his clothes, and struck his skin with a sharp chilling touch that set him trembling.

Even the thought of the over-weighted patrol wagon probably sticking in the mud some safe distance in the rear, failed to cheer him, and the excitement that had so far made him callous to the cold died out and left him weaker and nervous.

But his horse was chilled with the long standing, and now leaped eagerly forward, only too willing to warm the half-frozen blood in its veins.

"You're a good beast," said Gallegher, plaintively. "You've got more nerve than me. Don't you go back on me now. Mr. Dwyer says we've got to beat the town." Gallegher had no idea what time it was as he rode through the night, but he knew the would be able to find out from a big clock over a manufactory at a point nearly three-quarters of the distance from Keppler's to the goal.

He was still in the open country and driving recklessly, for he knew the best part of his ride must be made outside the city limits.

He raced between desolate-looking corn-fields with bare stalks and patches of muddy earth rising above the thin covering of snow, truck farms and brick-yards fell behind him on either side. It was very lonely work, and once or twice the dogs ran yelping to the gates and barked after him.

Part of his way lay parallel with the railroad tracks, and he drove for some time beside long lines of freight and coal cars as they stood resting for the night. The fantastic Queen Anne suburban stations were dark and deserted, but in one or two of the block-towers he could see the operators writing at their desks, and the sight in some way comforted him.

Once he thought of stopping to get out the blanket in which he had wrapped himself on the first trip, but he feared to spare the time, and drove on with his teeth chattering and his shoulders shaking with the cold.

He welcomed the first solitary row of darkened houses with a faint cheer of recognition. The scattered lamp-posts lightened his spirits, and even the badly paved streets ran under the beats of his horse's feet like music. Great mills and manufactories, with only a night-watchman's light in the lowest of their many stories, began to take the place of the gloomy farm-houses and gaunt trees that had startled him with their grotesque shapes. He had been driving nearly an hour, he calculated, and in that time the rain had changed to a wet snow, that fell heavily and clung to whatever it touched. He passed block after block of trim workmen's houses, as still and silent as the sleepers within them, and at last he turned the horse's head into Broad Street, the city's great thoroughfare, that stretches from its one end to the other and cuts it evenly in two.

He was driving noiselessly over the snow and slush in the street, with his thoughts bent only on the clock-face he wished so much to see, when a hoarse voice challenged him from the sidewalk. "Hey, you, stop there, hold up!" said the voice.

Gallegher turned his head, and though he saw that the voice came from under a policeman's helmet, his only answer was to hit his horse sharply over the head with his whip and to urge it into a gallop.

This, on his part, was followed by a sharp, shrill whistle from the policeman. Another whistle answered it from a street-corner one block ahead of him. "Whoa," said Gallegher, pulling on the reins. "There's one too many of them," he added, in apologetic explanation. The horse stopped, and stood, breathing heavily, with great clouds of steam rising from its flanks.

"Why in hell didn't you stop when I told you to?" demanded the voice, now close at the cab's side.

"I didn't hear you," returned Gallegher, sweetly. "But I

heard you whistle, and I heard your partner whistle, and I thought maybe it was me you wanted to speak to, so I just stopped."

"You heard me well enough. Why aren't your lights lit?" demanded the voice.

"Should I have 'em lit?" asked Gallegher, bending over and regarding them with sudden interest.

"You know you should, and if you don't, you've no right to be driving that cab. I don't believe you're the regular driver, anyway. Where'd you get it?"

"It ain't my cab, of course," said Gallegher, with an easy laugh. "It's Luke McGovern's. He left it outside Cronin's while he went in to get a drink, and he took too much, and me father told me to drive it round to the stable for him. I'm Cronin's son. McGovern ain't in no condition to drive. You can see yourself how he's been misusing the horse. He puts it up at Bachman's livery stable, and I was just going around there now."

Gallegher's knowledge of the local celebrities of the district confused the zealous officer of the peace. He surveyed the boy with a steady stare that would have distressed a less skilful liar, but Gallegher only shrugged his shoulders slightly, as if from the cold, and waited with apparent indifference to what the officer would say next.

In reality his heart was beating heavily against his side, and he felt that if he was kept on a strain much longer he would give way and break down. A second snow-covered form emerged suddenly from the shadow of the houses.

"What is it, Reeder?" it asked.

"Oh, nothing much," replied the first officer. "This kid hadn't any lamps lit, so I called to him to stop and he didn't do it, so I whistled to you. It's all right, though. He's just taking it round to Bachman's. Go ahead," he added, sulkily.

"Get up!" chirped Gallegher. "Good night," he added, over his shoulder.

Gallegher gave an hysterical little gasp of relief as he trotted away from the two policemen, and poured bitter maledictions on their heads for two meddling fools as he went.

"They might as well kill a man as scare him to death," he

said, with an attempt to get back to his customary flippancy. But the effort was somewhat pitiful, and he felt guiltily conscious that a salt, warm tear was creeping slowly down his face, and that a lump that would not keep down was rising in his throat.

"'Tain't no fair thing for the whole police force to keep worrying at a little boy like me," he said, in shame-faced apology. "I'm not doing nothing wrong, and I'm half froze to death, and yet they keep a-nagging at me."

It was so cold that when the boy stamped his feet against the footboard to keep them warm, sharp pains shot up through his body, and when he beat his arms about his shoulders, as he had seen real cabmen do, the blood in his finger-tips tingled so acutely that he cried aloud with the pain.

He had often been up that late before, but he had never felt so sleepy. It was as if some one was pressing a sponge heavy with chloroform near his face, and he could not fight off the drowsiness that lay hold of him.

He saw, dimly hanging above his head, a round disc of light that seemed like a great moon, and which he finally guessed to be the clock-face for which he had been on the look-out. He had passed it before he realized this; but the fact stirred him into wakefulness again, and when his cab's wheels slipped around the City Hall corner, he remembered to look up at the other big clockface that keeps awake over the railroad station and measures out the night.

He gave a gasp of consternation when he saw that it was half-past two, and that there was but ten minutes left to him. This, and the many electric lights and the sight of the familiar pile of buildings, startled him into a semi-consciousness of where he was and how great was the necessity for haste.

He rose in his seat and called on the horse, and urged it into a reckless gallop over the slippery asphalt. He considered nothing else but speed, and looking neither to the left nor right dashed off down Broad Street into Chestnut, where his course lay straight away to the office, now only seven blocks distant.

Gallegher never knew how it began, but he was suddenly assaulted by shouts on either side, his horse was thrown back on its haunches, and he found two men in cabmen's livery hanging at its head, and patting its sides, and calling it by name. And the other cabmen who have their stand at the corner were swarming about the carriage, all of them talking and swearing at once, and gesticulating wildly with their whips.

They said they knew the cab was McGovern's, and they wanted to know where he was, and why he wasn't on it; they wanted to know where Gallegher had stolen it, and why he had been such a fool as to drive it into the arms of its owner's friends; they said that it was about time that a cab-driver could get off his box to take a drink without having his cab run away with, and some of them called loudly for a policeman to take the young thief in charge.

Gallegher felt as if he had been suddenly dragged into consciousness out of a bad dream, and stood for a second like a half-awakened somnambulist.

They had stopped the cab under an electric light, and its glare shone coldly down upon the trampled snow and the faces of the men around him.

Gallegher bent forward, and lashed savagely at the horse with his whip.

"Let me go," he shouted, as he tugged impotently at the reins. "Let me go, I tell you. I haven't stole no cab, and you've got no right to stop me. I only want to take it to the *Press* office, he begged. "They'll send it back to you all right. They'll pay you for the trip. I'm not running away with it. The driver's got the collar—he's 'rested—and I'm only a-going to the *Press* office. Do you hear me?" he cried, his voice rising and breaking in a shriek of passion and disappointment. "I tell you to let go those reins. Let me go, or I'll kill you. Do you hear me? I'll kill you." And leaning forward, the boy struck savagely with his long whip at the faces of the men about the horse's head.

Some one in the crowd reached up and caught him by the ankles, and with a quick jerk pulled him off the box, and threw him on to the street. But he was up on his knees in a moment, and caught at the man's hand.

"Don't let them stop me, mister," he cried, "please let me go. I didn't steal the cab, sir. S'help me, I didn't. I'm telling you the truth. Take me to the *Press* office, and they'll prove it to you.

They'll pay you anything you ask 'em. It's only such a little ways now, and I've come so far, sir. Please don't let them stop me," he sobbed, clasping the man about the knees. "For Heaven's sake, mister, let me go!"

The managing editor of the *Press* took up the india-rubber speaking-tube at his side, and answered, "Not yet" to an inquiry the night editor had already put to him five times within the last twenty minutes.

Then he snapped the metal top of the tube impatiently, and went upstairs. As he passed the door of the local room, he noticed that the reporters had not gone home, but were sitting about on the tables and chairs, waiting. They looked up inquiringly as he passed, and the city editor asked, "Any news yet?" and the managing editor shook his head.

The compositors were standing idle in the composing-room, and their foreman was talking with the night editor.

"Well," said that gentleman, tentatively.

"Well," returned the managing editor, "I don't think we can wait; do you?"

"It's a half-hour after time now," said the night editor, "and we'll miss the suburban trains if we hold the paper back any longer. We can't afford to wait for a purely hypothetical story. The chances are all against the fight's having taken place or this Hade's having been arrested."

"But if we're beaten on it—" suggested the chief. "But I don't think that is possible. If there were any story to print, Dwyer would have had it here before now."

The managing editor looked steadily down at the floor.

"Very well," he said, slowly, "we won't wait any longer. Go ahead," he added, turning to the foreman with a sigh of reluctance. The foreman whirled himself about, and began to give his orders; but the two editors still looked at each other doubtfully.

As they stood so, there came a sudden shout and the sound of people running to and fro in the reportorial rooms below. There was the tramp of many footsteps on the stairs, and above the confusion they heard the voice of the city editor telling some one to "run to Madden's and get some brandy, quick."

No one in the composing-room said anything; but those compositors who had started to go home began slipping off their overcoats, and every one stood with his eyes fixed on the door.

It was kicked open from the outside, and in the doorway stood a cab-driver and the city editor, supporting between them a pitiful little figure of a boy, wet and miserable, and with the snow melting on his clothes and running in little pools to the floor. "Why, it's Gallegher," said the night editor, in a tone of the keenest disappointment.

Gallegher shook himself free from his supporters, and took an unsteady step forward, his fingers fumbling stiffly with the buttons of his waistcoat.

"Mr. Dwyer, sir," he began faintly, with his eyes fixed fearfully on the managing editor, "he got arrested—and I couldn't get here no sooner, 'cause they kept a-stopping me, and they took me cab from under me—but—" he pulled the notebook from his breast and held it out with its covers from his breast and held it out with its covers damp and limp from the rain, "but we got Hade, and here's Mr. Dwyer's copy."

And then he asked, with a queer note in his voice, partly of dread and partly of hope, "Am I in time, sir?"

The managing editor took the book, and tossed it to the foreman, who ripped out its leaves and dealt them out to his men as rapidly as a gambler deals out cards.

Then the managing editor stooped and picked Gallegher up in his arms, and, sitting down, began to unlace his wet and muddy shoes.

Gallegher made a faint effort to resist this degradation of the managerial dignity; but his protest was a very feeble one, and his head fell back heavily on the managing editor's shoulder.

To Gallegher the incandescent lights began to whirl about in circles, and to burn in different colors; the faces of the reporters kneeling before him and chafing his hands and feet grew dim and unfamiliar, and the roar and rumble of the great presses in the basement sounded far away, like the murmur of the sea.

And then the place and the circumstances of it came back to him again sharply and with sudden vividness.

Gallegher looked up, with a faint smile, into the managing editor's face. "You won't turn me off for running away, will you?" he whispered.

The managing editor did not answer immediately. His head was bent, and he was thinking, for some reason or other, of a little boy of his own, at home in bed. Then he said, quietly, "Not this time, Gallegher."

Gallegher's head sank back comfortably on the older man's shoulder, and he smiled comprehensively at the faces of the young men crowded around him. "You hadn't ought to," he said, with a touch of his old impudence, "'cause—I beat the town."

1891

The Red-Headed League

SIR ARTHUR CONAN DOYLE

I had called upon my friend, Mr. Sherlock Holmes, one day in the autumn of last year and found him in deep conversation with a very stout, florid-faced, elderly gentleman with fiery red hair. With an apology for my intrusion, I was about to withdraw when Holmes pulled me abruptly into the room and closed the door behind me.

"You could not possibly have come at a better time, my dear Watson," he said cordially.

"I was afraid that you were engaged."

"So I am. Very much so."

"Then I can wait in the next room."

"Not at all. This gentleman, Mr. Wilson, has been my partner and helper in many of my most successful cases, and I have no doubt that he will be of the utmost use to me in yours also."

The stout gentleman half rose from his chair and gave a bob of greeting, with a quick little questioning glance from his small, fat-encircled eyes.

"Try the settee," said Holmes, relapsing into his armchair and putting his finger-tips together, as was his custom when in judicial moods. "I know, my dear Watson, that you share my love of all that is bizarre and outside the conventions and humdrum routine of everyday life. You have shown your relish for it by the enthusiasm which has prompted you to chronicle, and, if you will excuse my saying so, somewhat to embellish so many of my own little adventures."

"Your cases have indeed been of the greatest interest to me," I observed.

"You will remember that I remarked the other day, just before we went into the very simple problem presented by Miss Mary Sutherland, that for strange effects and extraordinary combinations we must go to life itself, which is always far more daring than any effort of the imagination."

"A proposition which I took the liberty of doubting."

"You did, Doctor, but none the less you must come round to my view, for otherwise I shall keep on piling fact upon fact on you until your reason breaks down under them and acknowledges me to be right. Now, Mr. Jabez Wilson here has been good enough to call upon me this morning, and to begin a narrative which promises to be one of the most singular which I have listened to for some time. You have heard me remark that the strangest and most unique things are very often connected not with the larger but with the smaller crimes, and occasionally, indeed, where there is room for doubt whether any positive crime has been committed. As far as I have heard it is impossible for me to say whether the present case is an instance of crime or not, but the course of events is certainly among the most singular that I have ever listened to. Perhaps, Mr. Wilson, you would have the great kindness to recommence your narrative. I ask you not merely because my friend Dr. Watson has not heard the opening part but also because the peculiar nature of the story makes me anxious to have every possible detail from your lips. As a rule, when I have heard some slight indication of the course of events, I am able to guide myself by the thousands of other similar cases which occur to my memory. In the present instance I am forced to admit that the facts are, to the best of my belief, unique."

The portly client puffed out his chest with an appearance of some little pride and pulled a dirty and wrinkled newspaper from the inside of his great-coat. As he glanced down the advertisement column, with his head thrust forward and the paper flattened out upon his knee, I took a good look at the man and endeavoured, after the fashion of my companion, to read the indications which might be presented by his dress or appearance.

I did not gain very much, however, by my inspection. Our visitor bore every mark of being an average commonplace British tradesman, obese, pompous, and slow. He wore rather baggy gray shepherd's check trousers, a not over-clean black frock-coat, unbuttoned in the front, and a drab waistcoat with a heavy brassy Albert chain, and a square pierced bit of metal dangling down as an ornament. A frayed top-hat and a faded brown overcoat with a wrinkled velvet collar lay upon a chair beside him. Altogether, look as I would, there was nothing remarkable about the man save his blazing red head, and the expression of extreme chagrin and discontent upon his features.

Sherlock Holmes's quick eye took in my occupation, and he shook his head with a smile as he noticed my questioning glances. "Beyond the obvious facts that he has at some time done manual labour, that he takes snuff, that he is a Freemason, that he has been in China, and that he has done a considerable amount of writing lately, I can deduce nothing else."

Mr. Jabez Wilson started up in his chair, with his forefinger upon the paper, but his eyes upon my companion.

"How, in the name of good-fortune, did you know all that, Mr. Holmes?" he asked. "How did you know, for example, that I did manual labour? It's as true as gospel, for I began as a ship's carpenter."

"Your hands, my dear sir. Your right hand is quite a size larger than your left. You have worked with it, and the muscles are more developed."

"Well, the snuff, then, and the Freemasonry?"

"I won't insult your intelligence by telling you how I read that, especially as, rather against the strict rules of your order, you use an arc-and-compass breastpin."

"Ah, of course, I forgot that. But the writing?"

"What else can be indicated by that right cuff so very shiny for five inches, and the left one with the smooth patch near the elbow where you rest it upon the desk?"

"Well, but China?"

"The fish that you have tattooed immediately above your

right wrist could only have been done in China. I have made a small study of tattoo marks and have even contributed to the literature of the subject. That trick of staining the fishes' scales a delicate pink is quite peculiar to China. When, in addition, I see a Chinese coin hanging from your watch-chain, the matter becomes even more simple."

Mr. Jabez Wilson laughed heavily. "Well, I never!" said he. "I thought at first that you had done something clever, but I see that there was nothing in it, after all."

"I begin to think, Watson," said Holmes, "that I make a mistake in explaining. *'Omne ignotum pro magnifico,'* you know, and my poor little reputation, such as it is, will suffer shipwreck if I am so candid. Can you not find the advertisement, Mr. Wilson?"

"Yes, I have got it now," he answered with his thick red finger planted halfway down the column. "Here it is. This is what began it all. You just read it for yourself, sir."

I took the paper from him and read as follows:

To the Red-headed League:

On account of the bequest of the late Ezekiah Hopkins, of Lebanon, Pennsylvania, U.S.A., there is now another vacancy open which entitles a member of the League to a salary of £4 a week for purely nominal services. All red-headed men who are sound in body and mind, and above the age of twenty-one years, are eligible. Apply in person on Monday, at eleven o'clock, to Duncan Ross, at the offices of the League, 7 Pope's Court, Fleet Street.

"What on earth does this mean?" I ejaculated after I had twice read over the extraordinary announcement.

Holmes chuckled and wriggled in his chair, as was his habit when in high spirits. "It is a little off the beaten track, isn't it?" said he. "And now, Mr. Wilson, off you go at scratch and tell us all about yourself, your household, and the effect which this advertisement had upon your fortunes. You will first make a note, Doctor, of the paper and the date."

"It is *The Morning Chronicle* of April 27, 1890. Just two months ago."

"Very good. Now, Mr. Wilson?"

"Well, it is just as I have been telling you, Mr. Sherlock Holmes," said Jabez Wilson, mopping his forehead; "I have a small pawnbroker's business at Coburg Square, near the City. It's not a very large affair, and of late years it has not done more than just give me a living. I used to be able to keep two assistants, but now I only keep one; and I would have a job to pay him but that he is willing to come for half wages so as to learn the business."

"What is the name of this obliging youth?" asked Sherlock Holmes.

"His name is Vincent Spaulding, and he's not such a youth, either. It's hard to say his age. I should not wish a smarter assistant, Mr. Holmes; and I know very well that he could better himself and earn twice what I am able to give him. But, after all, if he is satisfied, why should I put ideas in his head?"

"Why, indeed? You seem most fortunate in having an employee who comes under the full market price. It is not a common experience among employers in this age. I don't know that your assistant is not as remarkable as your advertisement."

"Oh, he has his faults, too," said Mr. Wilson. "Never was such a fellow for photography. Snapping away with a camera when he ought to be improving his mind, and then diving down into the cellar like a rabbit into its hole to develop his pictures. That is his main fault, but on the whole he's a good worker. There's no vice in him."

"He is still with you, I presume?"

"Yes, sir. He and a girl of fourteen, who does a bit of simple cooking and keeps the place clean—that's all I have in the house, for I am a widower and never had any family. We live very quietly, sir, the three of us; and we keep a roof over our heads and pay our debts, if we do nothing more.

"The first thing that put us out was that advertisement. Spaulding, he came down into the office just this day eight weeks, with this very paper in his hand, and he says:

" 'I wish to the Lord, Mr. Wilson, that I was a red-headed man.' "

" 'Why that?' I asks."

" 'Why,' says he, 'here's another vacancy on the League of the Red-headed Men. It's worth quite a little fortune to any man who gets it, and I understand that there are more vacancies than there are men, so that the trustees are at their wits' end what to do with the money. If my hair would only change colour, here's a nice little crib all ready for me to step into.'"

" 'Why, what is it, then?' I asked. You see, Mr. Holmes, I am a very stay-at-home man, and as my business came to me instead of my having to go to it, I was often weeks on end without putting my foot over the door-mat. In that way I didn't know much of what was going on outside, and I was always glad of a bit of news.

" 'Have you never heard of the League of the Red-headed Men?' he asked with his eyes open.

" 'Never.'

" 'Why, I wonder at that, for you are eligible yourself for one of the vacancies.'

" 'And what are they worth?' I asked.

" 'Oh, merely a couple of hundred a year, but the work is slight, and it need not interfere very much with one's other occupations.'

"Well, you can easily think that that made me prick up my ears, for the business has not been over-good for some years, and an extra couple of hundred would have been very handy.

" 'Tell me all about it,' said I.

" 'Well,' said he, showing me the advertisement, 'you can see for yourself that the League has a vacancy, and there is the address where you should apply for particulars. As far as I can make out, the League was founded by an American millionaire, Ezekiah Hopkins, who was very peculiar in his ways. He was himself red-headed, and he had a great sympathy for all red-headed men; so when he died it was found that he had left his enormous fortune in the hands of trustees, with instructions to apply the interest to the providing of easy berths to men whose hair is of that colour. From all I hear it is splendid pay and very little to do.'

" 'But,' said, I, 'there would be millions of red-headed men who would apply.'

" 'Not so many as you might think,' he answered. 'You see it is really confined to Londoners, and to grown men. This American had started from London when he was young, and he wanted to do the old town a good turn. Then, again, I have heard it is no use your applying if your hair is light red, or dark red, or anything but real bright, blazing, fiery red. Now, if you cared to apply, Mr. Wilson, you would just walk in; but perhaps it would hardly be worth your while to put yourself out of the way for the sake of a few hundred pounds.'

"Now, it is a fact, gentlemen, as you may see for yourselves, that my hair is of a very full and rich tint, so that it seemed to me that if there was to be any competition in the matter I stood as good a chance as any man that I had ever met. Vincent Spaulding seemed to know so much about it that I thought he might prove useful, so I just ordered him to put up the shutters for the day and to come right away with me. He was very willing to have a holiday, so we shut the business up and started off for the address that was given us in the advertisement.

"I never hope to see such a sight as that again, Mr. Holmes. From north, south, east, and west every man who had a shade of red in his hair had tramped into the city to answer the advertisement. Fleet Street was choked with red-headed folk, and Pope's Court looked like a coster's orange barrow. I should not have thought there were so many in the whole country as were brought together by that single advertisement. Every shade of colour they were—straw, lemon, orange, brick, Irish-setter, liver, clay; but, as Spaulding said, there were not many who had the real vivid flame-coloured tint. When I saw how many were waiting, I would have given it up in despair; but Spaulding would not hear of it. How he did it I could not imagine, but he pushed and pulled and butted until he got me through the crowd, and right up to the steps which led to the office. There was a double stream upon the stair, some going up in hope, and some coming back dejected; but we wedged in as well as we could and soon found ourselves in the office."

"Your experience has been a most entertaining one," remarked Holmes as his client paused and refreshed his memory with a huge pinch of snuff. "Pray continue your very interesting statement."

"There was nothing in the office but a couple of wooden chairs and a deal table, behind which sat a small man with a head that was even redder than mine. He said a few words to each candidate as he came up, and then he always managed to find some fault in them which would disqualify them. Getting a vacancy did not seem to be such a very easy matter, after all. However, when our turn came the little man was much more favourable to me than to any of the others, and he closed the door as we entered, so that he might have a private word with us.

" 'This is Mr. Jabez Wilson,' said my assistant, 'and he is willing to fill a vacancy in the League.'

" 'And he is admirably suited for it,' the other answered. 'He has every requirement. I cannot recall when I have seen anything so fine.' He took a step backward, cocked his head on one side, and gazed at my hair until I felt quite bashful. Then suddenly he plunged forward, wrung my hand, and congratulated me warmly on my success.

" 'It would be injustice to hesitate,' said he. 'You will, however, I am sure, excuse me for taking an obvious precaution.' With that he seized my hair in both his hands, and tugged until I yelled with the pain. 'There is water in your eyes,' said he as he released me. 'I perceive that all is as it should be. But we have to be careful, for we have twice been deceived by wigs and once by paint. I could tell you tales of cobbler's wax which would disgust you with human nature.' He stepped over to the window and shouted through it at the top of his voice that the vacancy was filled. A groan of disappointment came up from below, and the folk all trooped away in different directions until there was not a red head to be seen except my own and that of the manager.

" 'My name, said he, 'is Mr. Duncan Ross, and I am myself

one of the pensioners upon the fund left by our noble benefactor. Are you a married man, Mr. Wilson? Have you a family?'

"I answered that I had not.

"His face fell immediately.

"'Dear me!' he said gravely, 'that is very serious indeed! I am sorry to hear you say that. The fund was, of course, for the propagation and spread of the red-heads as well as for their maintenance. It is exceedingly unfortunate that you should be a bachelor.'

"My face lengthened at this, Mr. Holmes, for I thought that I was not to have the vacancy after all; but after thinking it over for a few minutes he said that it would be all right.

"'In the case of another,' said he, 'the objection might be fatal, but we must stretch a point in favour of a man with such a head of hair as yours. When shall you be able to enter upon your new duties?'

"'Well, it is a little awkward, for I have a business already,' said I.

"'Oh, never mind about that, Mr. Wilson!' said Vincent Spaulding. 'I should be able to look after that for you.'

"'What would be the hours?' I asked.

"'Ten to two.'

"Now a pawnbroker's business is mostly done of an evening, Mr. Holmes, especially Thursday and Friday evening, which is just before pay-day; so it would suit me very well to earn a little in the mornings. Besides, I knew that my assistant was a good man, and that he would see to anything that turned up.

"'That would suit me very well,' said I. 'And the pay?'

"'Is £4 a week.'

"'And the work?'

"'Is purely nominal.'

"'What do you call purely nominal?'

"'Well, you have to be in the office, or at least in the building, the whole time. If you leave, you forfeit your whole position forever. The will is very clear upon that point. You don't comply with the conditions if you budge from the office during that time.'

"'It's only four hours a day, and I should not think of leaving,' said I.

"'No excuse will avail,' said Mr. Duncan Ross; 'neither sickness nor business nor anything else. There you must stay, or you lose your billet.'

"'And the work?'

"'Is to copy out the Encyclopædia Britannica. There is the first volume of it in that press. You must find your own ink, pens, and blotting-paper, but we provide this table and chair. Wil you be ready tomorrow?'

"'Certainly,' I answered.

"'Then, good-bye, Mr. Jabez Wilson, and let me congratulate you once more on the important position which you have been fortunate enough to gain.' He bowed me out of the room, and I went home with my assistant, hardly knowing what to say or do, I was so pleased at my own good fortune.

"Well, I thought over the matter all day, and by evening I was in low spirits again; for I had quite persuaded myself that the whole affair must be some great hoax or fraud, though what its object might be I could not imagine. It seemed altogether past belief that anyone could make such a will, or that they would pay such a sum for doing anything so simple as copying out the Encyclopædia Britannica. Vincent Spaulding did what he could to cheer me up, but by bedtime I had reasoned myself out of the whole thing. However, in the morning I determined to have a look at it anyhow, so I bought a penny bottle of ink, and with a quill-pen, and seven sheets of foolscap paper, I started off for Pope's Court.

"Well, to my surprise and delight, everything was as right as possible. The table was set out ready for me, and Mr. Duncan Ross was there to see that I got fairly to work. He started me off upon the letter A, and then he left me; but he would drop in from time to time to see that all was right with me. At two o'clock he bade me good-day, complimented me upon the amount that I had written, and locked the door of the office after me.

"This went on day after day, Mr. Holmes, and on Saturday the manager came in and planked down four golden sovereigns for my week's work. It was the same next week, and the same the week after. Every morning I was there at ten, and every afternoon I left at two. By degrees Mr. Duncan Ross took to coming in only once of a morning, and then, after a time, he did not come in at all. Still, of course, I never dared to leave the room for an instant, for I was not sure when he might come, and the billet was such a good one, and suited me so well, that I would not risk the loss of it.

"Eight weeks passed away like this, and I had written about Abbots and Archery and Armour and Architecture and Attica, and hoped with diligence that I might get on to the B's before very long. It cost me something in foolscap, and I had pretty nearly filled a shelf with my writings. And then suddenly the whole business came to an end."

"To an end?"

"Yes, sir. And no later than this morning. I went to my work as usual at ten o'clock, but the door was shut and locked, with a little square of card-board hammered on to the middle of the panel with a tack. Here it is, and you can read for yourself."

He held up a piece of white card-board about the size of a sheet of note-paper. It read in this fashion:

THE RED-HEADED LEAGUE
IS
DISSOLVED.
OCTOBER 9, 1890.

Sherlock Holmes and I surveyed this curt announcement and the rueful face behind it, until the comical side of the affair so completely overtopped every other consideration that we both burst out into a roar of laughter.

"I cannot see that there is anything very funny," cried our client, flushing up to the roots of his flaming head. "If you can do nothing better than laugh at me, I can go elsewhere."

"No, no," cried Holmes, shoving him back into the chair from which he had half risen. "I really wouldn't miss your case for the world. It is most refreshingly unusual. But there is, if you will excuse my saying so, something just a little funny about it.

Pray what steps did you take when you found the card upon the door?"

"I was staggered, sir. I did not know what to do. Then I called at the offices round, but none of them seemed to know anything about it. Finally, I went to the landlord, who is an accountant living on the ground-floor, and I asked him if he could tell me what had become of the Red-headed League. He said that he had never heard of any such body. Then I asked him who Mr. Duncan Ross was. He answered that the name was new to him.

" 'Well,' said I, 'the gentlemen at No. 4.'

" 'What, the red-headed man?'

" 'Yes.'

" 'Oh,' said he, 'his name was William Morris. He was a solicitor and was using my room as a temporary convenience until his new premises were ready. He moved out yesterday.'

" 'Where could I find him?'

" 'Oh, at his new offices. He did tell me the address. Yes, 17 King Edward Street, near St. Paul's.'

"I started off, Mr. Holmes, but when I got to that address it was a manufactory of artificial knee-caps, and no one in it had ever heard of either Mr. William Morris or Mr. Duncan Ross."

"And what did you do then?" asked Holmes.

"I went home to Saxe-Coburg Square, and I took the advice of my assistant. But he could not help me in any way. He could only say that if I waited I should hear by post. But that was not quite good enough, Mr. Holmes. I did not wish to lose such a place without a struggle, so, as I had heard that you were good enough to give advice to poor folk who were in need of it, I came right away to you."

"And you did very wisely," said Holmes. "Your case is an exceedingly remarkable one, and I shall be happy to look into it. From what you have told me I think that it is possible that graver issues hang from it than might at first appear."

"Grave enough!" said Mr. Jabez Wilson. "Why, I have lost four pound a week."

"As far as you are personally concerned," remarked Holmes, "I do not see that you have any grievance against this extraordinary league. On the contrary, you are, as I understand, richer by some £30, to say nothing of the minute knowledge which you have gained on every subject which comes under the letter A. You have lost nothing by them."

"No, sir. But I want to find out about them, and who they are, and what their object was in playing this prank—if it was a prank—upon me. It was a pretty expensive joke for them, for it cost them two and thirty pounds."

"We shall endeavour to clear up these points for you. And, first, one or two questions, Mr. Wilson. This assistant of yours who first called your attention to the advertisement—how long had he been with you?"

"About a month then."

"How did he come?"

"In answer to an advertisement."

"Was he the only applicant?"

"No, I had a dozen."

"Why did you pick him?"

"Because he was handy and would come cheap."

"At half-wages, in fact."

"Yes."

"What is he like, this Vincent Spaulding?"

"Small, stout-built, very quick in his ways, no hair on his face, though he's not short of thirty. Has a white splash of acid upon his forehead."

Holmes sat up in his chair in considerable excitement. "I thought as much," said he. "Have you ever observed that his ears are pierced for earrings?"

"Yes, sir. He told me that a gypsy had done it for him when he was a lad."

"Hum!" said Holmes, sinking back in deep thought. "He is still with you?"

"Oh, yes, sir; I have only just left him."

"And has your business been attended to in your absence?"

"Nothing to complain of, sir. There's never very much to do of a morning."

"That will do, Mr. Wilson. I shall be happy to give you an opinion upon the subject in the course of a day or two. Today is

Saturday, and I hope that by Monday we may come to a conclusion."

"Well, Watson," said Holmes when our visitor had left us, "what do you make of it all?"

"I make nothing of it," I answered frankly. "It is a most mysterious business."

"As a rule," said Holmes, "the more bizarre a thing is the less mysterious it proves to be. It is your commonplace, featureless crimes which are really puzzling, just as a commonplace face is the most difficult to identify. But I must be prompt over this matter."

"What are you going to do, then?" I asked.

"To smoke," he answered. "It is quite a three-pipe problem, and I beg that you won't speak to me for fifty minutes." He curled himself up in his chair, with his thin knees drawn up to his hawk-like nose, and there he sat with his eyes closed and his black clay pipe thrusting out like the bill of some strange bird. I had come to the conclusion that he had dropped alseep, and indeed was nodding myself, when he suddenly sprang out of his chair with the gesture of a man who has made up his mind and put his pipe down upon the mantelpiece.

"Sarasate plays at the St. James's Hall this afternoon," he remarked. "What do you think, Watson? Could your patients spare you for a few hours?"

"I have nothing to do today. My practice is never very absorbing."

"Then put on your hat and come. I am going through the City first, and we can have some lunch on the way. I observe that there is a good deal of German music on the programme, which is rather more to my taste than Italian or French. It is introspective, and I want to introspect. Come along!"

We travelled by the Underground as far as Aldersgate; and a short walk took us to Saxe-Coburg Square, the scene of a singular story which we had listened to in the morning. It was a poky, little, shabby-genteel place, where four lines of dingy two-storied brick houses looked out into a small railed-in enclosure, where a lawn of weedy grass and a few clumps of faded laurel-bushes made a hard fight against a smoke-laden and uncongenial atmosphere. Three gilt balls and a brown board with "JABEZ WILSON" in white letters, upon a corner house, announced the place where our red-headed client carried on his business. Sherlock Holmes stopped in front of it with his head on one side and looked it all over, with his eyes shining brightly between puckered lids. Then he walked slowly up the street, and then down again to the corner, still looking keenly at the houses. Finally he returned to the pawnbroker's, and, having thumped vigorously upon the pavement with his stick two or three times, he went up to the door and knocked. It was instantly opened by a bright-looking, clean-shaven young fellow, who asked him to step in.

"Thank you," said Holmes, "I only wished to ask you how you would go from here to the Strand."

"Third right, fourth left," answered the assistant promptly, closing the door.

"Smart fellow, that," observed Holmes as we walked away. "He is, in my judgement, the fourth smartest man in London, and for daring I am not sure that he has not a claim to be third. I have known something of him before."

"Evidently," said I, "Mr. Wilson's assistant counts for a good deal in this mystery of the Red-headed League. I am sure that you inquired your way merely in order that you might see him."

"Not him."

"What then?"

"The knees of his trousers."

"And what did you see?"

"What I expected to see."

"Why did you beat the pavement?"

"My dear doctor, this is a time for observation, not for talk. We are spies in an enemy's country. We know something of Saxe-Coburg Square. Let us now explore the parts which lie behind it."

The road in which we found ourselves as we turned round the corner from the retired Saxe-Coburg Square presented as great a contrast to it as the front of a picture does to the back. It was one of the main arteries which conveyed the traffic of the

City to the north and west. The roadway was blocked with the immense stream of commerce flowing in a double tide inward and outward, while the foot-paths were black with the hurrying swarm of pedestrians. It was difficult to realize as we looked at the line of fine shops and stately business premises that they really abutted on the other side upon the faded and stagnant square which we had just quitted.

"Let me see," said Holmes, standing at the corner and glancing along the line, "I should like just to remember the order of the houses here. It is a hobby of mine to have an exact knowledge of London. There is Mortimer's, the tobacconist, the little newspaper shop, the Coburg branch of the City and Suburban Bank, the Vegetarian Restaurant, and McFarlane's carriage-building depot. That carries us right on to the other block. And now, Doctor, we've done our work, so it's time we had some play. A sandwich and a cup of coffee, and then off to violin-land, where all is sweetness and delicacy and harmony, and there are no red-headed clients to vex us with their conundrums."

My friend was an enthusiastic musician, being himself not only a very capable performer but a composer of no ordinary merit. All the afternoon he sat in the stalls wrapped in the most perfect happiness, gently waving his long, thin fingers in time to the music, while his gently smiling face and his languid, dreamy eyes were as unlike those of Holmes, the sleuthhound, Holmes the relentless, keen-witted, ready-handed criminal agent, as it was possible to conceive. In his singular character the dual nature alternately asserted itself, and his extreme exactness and astuteness represented, as I have often thought, the reaction against the poetic and contemplative mood which occasionally predominated in him. The swing of his nature took him from extreme languor to devouring energy; and, as I knew well, he was never so truly formidable as when, for days on end, he had been lounging in his armchair amid his improvisations and his black-letter editions. Then it was that the lust of the chase would suddenly come upon him, and that his brilliant reasoning power would rise to the level of intuition, until those who were unacquainted with his methods would look askance at him as on a man whose knowledge was not that of other mortals. When I saw him that afternoon so enwrapped in the music at St. James's Hall I felt that an evil time might be coming upon those whom he had set himself to hunt down.

"You want to go home, no doubt, Doctor," he remarked as we emerged.

"Yes, it would be as well."

"And I have some business to do which will take some hours. This business at Coburg Square is serious."

"Why serious?"

"A considerable crime is in contemplation. I have every reason to believe that we shall be in time to stop it. But today being Saturday rather complicates matters. I shall want your help tonight."

"At what time?"

"Ten will be early enough."

"I shall be at Baker Street at ten."

"Very well. And, I say, Doctor, there may be some little danger, so kindly put your army revolver in your pocket." He waved his hand, turned on his heel, and disappeared in an instant among the crowd.

I trust that I am not more dense than my neighbours, but I was always oppressed with a sense of my own stupidity in my dealings with Sherlock Holmes. Here I had heard what he had heard, I had seen what he had seen, and yet from his words it was evident that he saw clearly not only what had happened but what was about to happen, while to me the whole business was still confused and grotesque. As I drove home to my house in Kensington I thought over it all, from the extraordinary story of the red-headed copier of the Encyclopædia down to the visit to Saxe-Coburg Square, and the ominous words with which he had parted from me. What was this nocturnal expedition, and why should I go armed? Where were we going, and what were we to do? I had the hint from Holmes that this smooth-faced pawnbroker's assistant was a formidable man—a man who might play a deep game. I tried to puzzle it out, but gave it up in despair and set the matter aside until night should bring an explanation.

It was a quarter-past nine when I started from home and made my way across the Park, and so through Oxford Street to Baker Street. Two hansoms were standing at the door, and as I entered the passage I heard the sound of voices from above. On entering his room I found Holmes in animated conversation with two men, one of whom I recognized as Peter Jones, the official police agent, while the other was a long, thin, sad-faced man, with a very shiny hat and oppressively respectable frock-coat.

"Ha! our party is complete," said Holmes, buttoning up his pea-jacket and taking his heavy hunting crop from the rack. "Watson, I think you know Mr. Jones, of Scotland Yard? Let me introduce you to Mr. Merryweather, who is to be our companion in tonight's adventure."

"We're hunting in couples again, Doctor, you see," said Jones in his consequential way. "Our friend here is a wonderful man for starting a chase. All he wants is an old dog to help him to do the running down."

I hope a wild goose may not prove to be the end of our chase," observed Mr. Merryweather gloomily.

"You may place considerable confidence in Mr. Holmes, sir," said the police agent loftily. "He has his own little methods, which are, if he won't mind my saying so, just a little too theoretical and fantastic, but he has the makings of a detective in him. It is not too much to say that once or twice, as in that business of the Sholto murder and the Agra treasure, he has been more nearly correct than the official force."

"Oh, if you say so, Mr. Jones, it is all right," said the stranger with deference. "Still, I confess that I miss my rubber. It is the first Saturday night for seven-and-twenty years that I have not had my rubber."

"I think you will find," said Sherlock Holmes, "that you will play for a higher stake tonight than you have ever done yet, and that the play will be more exciting. For you, Mr. Merryweather, the stake will be some £30,000; and for you, Jones, it will be the man upon whom you wish to lay your hands."

"John Clay, the murderer, thief, smasher, and forger. He's a young man, Mr. Merryweather, but he is at the head of his profession, and I would rather have my bracelets on him than on any criminal in London. He's a remarkable man, is young John Clay. His grandfather was a royal duke, and he himself has been to Eton and Oxford. His brain is as cunning as his fingers, and though we meet signs of him at every turn, we never know where to find the man himself. He'll crack a crib in Scotland one week, and be raising money to build an orphanage in Cornwall the next. I've been on his track for years and have never set eyes on him yet."

"I hope that I may have the pleasure of introducing you tonight. I've had one or two little turns also with Mr. John Clay, and I agree with you that he is at the head of his profession. It is past ten, however, and quite time that we started. If you two will take the first hansom, Watson and I will follow in the second."

Sherlock Holmes was not very communicative during the long drive and lay back in the cab humming the tunes which he had heard in the afternoon. We rattled through an endless labyringh of gas-lit streets until we emerged into Farringdon Street.

"We are close there now," my friend remarked. "This fellow Merryweather is a bank director, and personally interested in the matter. I thought it as well to have Jones with us also. He is not a bad fellow, though an absolute imbecile in his profession. He has one positive virtue. He is as brave as a bulldog and as tenacious as a lobster if he gets his claws upon anyone. Here we are, and they are waiting for us."

We had reached the same crowded thoroughfare in which we had found ourselves in the morning. Our cabs were dismissed, and, following the guidance of Mr. Merryweather, we passed down a narrow passage and through a side door, which he opened for us. Within there was a small corridor, which ended in a very massive iron gate. This also was opened, and led down a flight of winding stone steps, which terminated at another formidable gate. Mr. Merryweather stopped to light a lantern, and then conducted us down a dark, earth-smelling passage, and so, after opening a third door, into a huge vault or cellar, which was piled all round with crates and massive boxes.

"You are not very vulnerable from above," Holmes remarked as he held up the lantern and gazed about him.

"Nor from below," said Mr. Merryweather, striking his stick upon the flags which lined the floor. "Why, dear me, it sounds quite hollow!" he remarked, looking up in surprise.

"I must really ask you to be a little more quiet!" said Holmes severely. "You have already imperilled the whole success of our expedition. Might I beg that you would have the goodness to sit down upon one of those boxes, and not to interfere?"

The solemn Mr. Merryweather perched himself upon a crate, with a very injured expression upon his face, while Holmes fell upon his knees upon the floor and, with the lantern and a magnifying lens, began to examine minutely the cracks between the stones. A few seconds sufficed to satisfy him, for he sprang to his feet again and put his glass in his pocket.

"We have at least an hour before us," he remarked, "for they can hardly take any steps until the good pawnbroker is safely in bed. Then they will not lose a minute, for the sooner they do their work the longer time they will have for their escape. We are at present, Doctor—as no doubt you have divined—in the cellar of the City branch of one of the principal London banks. Mr. Merryweather is the chairman of directors, and he will explain to you that there are reasons why the more daring criminals of London should take a considerable interest in this cellar at present."

"It is our French gold," whispered the director. "We have had several warnings that an attempt might be made upon it."

"Your French gold?"

"Yes. We had occasion some months ago to strengthen our resources, and borrowed for that purpose 30,000 napoleons from the Bank of France. It has become known that we have never had occasion to unpack the money, and that it is still lying in our cellar. The crate upon which I sit contains 2,000 napoleons packed between layers of lead foil. Our reserve of bullion is much larger at present than is usually kept in a single branch office, and the directors have had misgivings upon the subject."

"Which were very well justified," observed Holmes. "And now it is time that we arranged our little plans. I expect that within an hour matters will come to a head. In the meantime, Mr. Merryweather, we must put the screen over that dark lantern."

"And sit in the dark?"

"I am afraid so. I had brought a pack of cards in my pocket, and I thought that, as we were a *partie carrée*, you might have your rubber after all. But I see that the enemy's preparations have gone so far that we cannot risk the presence of a light. And, first of all, we must choose our positions. These are daring men, and though we shall take them at a disadvantage, they may do us some harm unless we are careful. I shall stand behind this crate, and do you conceal yourselves behind those. Then, when I flash a light upon them, close in swiftly. If they fire, Watson, have no compunction about shooting them down."

I placed my revolver, cocked, upon the top of the wooden case behind which I crouched. Holmes shot the slide across the front of his lantern and left us in pitch darkness—such an absolute darkness as I have never before experienced. The smell of hot metal remained to assure us that the light was still there, ready to flash out at a moment's notice. To me, with my nerves worked up to a pitch of expectancy, there was something depressing and subduing in the sudden gloom, and in the cold dank air of the vault.

"They have but one retreat," whispered Holmes. "That is back through the house into Saxe-Coburg Square. I hope that you have done what I asked, Jones?"

"I have an inspector and two officers waiting at the front door."

"Then we have stopped all the holes. And now we must be silent and wait."

What a time it seemed! From comparing notes afterwards it was but an hour and a quarter, yet it appeared to me that the night must have almost gone, and the dawn be breaking above us. My limbs were weary and stiff, for I feared to change my position; yet my nerves were worked up to the highest pitch of tension, and my hearing was so acute that I could not only hear the gentle breathing of my companions, but I could distinguish the deeper, heavier in-breath of the bulky Jones from the thin, sighing note of the bank director. From my position I could look over the case in the direction of the floor. Suddenly my eyes caught the glint of a light.

At first it was but a lurid spark upon the stone pavement. Then it lengthened out until it became a yellow line, and then, without any warning or sound, a gash seemed to open and a hand appeared; a white, almost womanly hand, which felt about in the centre of the little area of light. For a minute or more the hand, with its writhing fingers, protruded out of the floor. Then it was withdrawn as suddenly as it appeared, and all was dark again save the single lurid spark which marked a chink between the stones.

Its disappearance, however, was but momentary. With a rending, tearing sound, one of the broad, white stones turned over upon its side and left a square, gaping hole, through which streamed the light of a lantern. Over the edge there peeped a clean-cut, boyish face, which looked keenly about it, and then, with a hand on either side of the aperture, drew itself shoulder-high and waist-high, until one knee rested upon the edge. In another instant he stood at the side of the hole and was hauling after him a companion, lithe and small like himself, with a pale face and a shock of very red hair.

"It's all clear," he whispered. "Have you the chisel and the bags? Great Scott! Jump, Archie, jump, and I'll swing for it!"

Sherlock Holmes had sprung out and seized the intruder by the collar. The other dived down the hole, and I heard the sound of rending cloth as Jones clutched at his skirts. The light flashed upon the barrel of a revolver, but Holmes's hunting crop came down on the man's wrist, and the pistol clinked upon the stone floor.

"It's no use, John Clay," said Holmes blandly. "You have no chance at all."

"So I see," the other answered with the utmost coolness. "I fancy that my pal is all right, though I see you have got his coat-tails."

"There are three men waiting for him at the door," said Holmes.

"Oh, indeed! You seem to have done the thing very completely. I must compliment you."

"And I you," Holmes answered. "Your red-headed idea was very new and effective."

"You'll see your pal again presently," said Jones. "He's quicker at climbing down holes than I am. Just hold out while I fix the derbies."

"I beg that you will not touch me with your filthy hands," remarked our prisoner as the handcuffs clattered upon his wrists. "You may not be aware that I have royal blood in my veins. Have the goodness, also, when you address me always to say 'sir' and 'please.'"

"All right," said Jones with a stare and a snigger. "Well, would you please, sir, march upstairs, where we can get a cab to carry your Highness to the police-station?"

"That is better," said John Clay serenely. He made a sweeping bow to the three of us and walked quietly off in the custody of the detective.

"Really, Mr. Holmes," said Mr. Merryweather as we followed them from the cellar, "I do not know how the bank can thank you or repay you. There is no doubt that you have detected and defeated in the most complete manner one of the most determined attempts at bank robbery that have ever come within my experience."

"I have had one or two little scores of my own to settle with Mr. John Clay," said Holmes. "I have been at some small expense over this matter, which I shall expect the bank to refund, but beyond that I am amply repaid by having had an experience which is in many ways unique, and by hearing the very remarkable narrative of the Red-headed League."

"You see, Watson," he explained in the early hours of the morning as we sat over a glass of whisky and soda in Baker Street, "it was perfectly obvious from the first that the only possible object of this rather fantastic business of the advertisement of the League, and the copying of the Enclyclopædia, must be to get this not over-bright pawnbroker out of the way for a number of hours every day. It was a curious way of managing it, but, really, it would be difficult to suggest a better. The method was no doubt suggested to Clay's ingenious mind by the colour of his accomplice's hair. The £4 a week was a lure which must draw him, and what was it to them, who were playing for thousands? They put in the advertisement, one rogue has the temporary office, the other rogue incites the man to apply for it, and together they manage to secure his absence every morning in the week. From the time that I heard of the assistant having come for half wages, it was obvious to me that he had some strong motive for securing the situation."

"But how could you guess what the motive was?"

"Had there been women in the house, I should have suspected a mere vulgar intrigue. That, however, was out of the question. The man's business was a small one, and there was nothing in his house which could account for such elaborate preparations, and such an expenditure as they were at. It must, then, be something out of the house. What could it be? I thought of the assistant's fondness for photography, and his trick of vanishing into the cellar. The cellar! There was the end of this tangled clue. Then I made inquiries as to this mysterious assistant and found that I had to deal with one of the coolest and most daring criminals in London. He was doing something in the cellar—something which took many hours a day for months on end. What could it be, once more? I could think of nothing save that he was running a tunnel to some other building.

"So far I had got when we went to visit the scene of action. I surprised you by beating upon the pavement with my stick. I was ascertaining whether the cellar stretched out in front or behind. It was not in front. Then I rang the bell, and, as I hoped, the assistant answered it. We have had some skirmishes, but we had never set eyes upon each other before. I hardly looked at his face. His knees were what I wished to see. You must yourself have remarked how worn, wrinkled, and stained they were. They spoke of those hours of burrowing. The only remaining point was what they were burrowing for. I walked round the corner, saw that the City and Suburban Bank abutted on our friend's premises, and felt that I had solved my problem. When you drove home after the concert I called upon Scotland Yard and upon the chairman of the bank directors, with the result that you have seen."

"And how could you tell that they would make their attempt tonight?" I asked.

"Well, when they closed their League offices that was a sign that they cared no longer about Mr. Jabez Wilson's presence—in other words, that they had completed their tunnel. But it was essential that they should use it soon, as it might be discovered, or the bullion might be removed. Saturday would suit them better than any other day, as it would give them two days for their escape. For all these reasons I expected them to come tonight."

"You reasoned it out beautifully," I exclaimed in unfeigned admiration. "It is so long a chain, and yet every link rings true."

"It saved me from ennui," he answered, yawning. "Alas! I already feel it closing in upon me. My life is spent in one long effort to escape from the commonplaces of existence. These little problems help me to do so."

"And you are a benefactor of the race," said I.

He shrugged his shoulders. "Well, perhaps, after all, it is of some little use. *'L'homme c'est rien—l'œuvre c'est tout,'* as Gustave Flaubert wrote to George Sand."

1893

Cheating the Gallows

ISRAEL ZANGWILL

They say that a union of opposites makes the happiest marriage, and perhaps it is on the same principle that men who chum together are always so oddly assorted. You shall find a man of letters sharing diggings with an auctioneer, and a medical student pigging with a stockbroker's clerk. Perhaps each thus escapes the temptation to talk "shop" in his hours of leisure, while he supplements his own experiences of life by his companion's.

There could not be an odder couple than Tom Peters and Everard G. Roxdal—the contrast began with their names, and ran through the entire chapter. They had a bedroom and a sitting-room in common, but it would not be easy to find what else. To his landlady, worthy Mrs. Seacon, Tom Peter's profession was a little vague, but everybody knew that Roxdal was the manager of the City and Suburban Bank, and it puzzled her to think why a bank manager should live with such a seedy-looking person, who smoked clay pipes and sipped whiskey and water all the evening when he was at home. For Roxdal was as spruce and erect as his fellow-lodger was round-shouldered and shabby; he never smoked, and he confined himself to a small glass of claret at dinner.

It is possible to live with a man and see very little of him. Where each of the partners lives his own life in his own way, with his own circle of friends and external amusements, days may go by without the men having five minutes together. Perhaps this explains why these partnerships jog along so much more peaceably than marriages, where the chain is drawn so much more tightly and galls the wedded rather than links them. Diverse, however, as were the hours and habits of Peters and Roxdal, they often breakfasted together, and they agreed in one thing—they never stayed out at night. For the rest, Peters sought his diversions in the company of journalists, and frequented debating rooms, where he propounded the most iconoclastic views; while Roxdal had highly respectable houses open to him in the suburbs and was, in fact, engaged to be married to Clara Newell, the charming daughter of a retired corn merchant, a widower with no other child.

Clara naturally took up a good deal of Roxdal's time, and he often dressed to go to the play with her, while Peters stayed at home in a faded dressing-gown and loose slippers. Mrs. Seacon like to see gentlemen about the house in evening dress, and made comparisons not favorable to Peters. And this in spite of the fact that he gave her infinitely less trouble than the younger man. It was Peters who first took the apartments, and it was characteristic of his easy-going temperament that he was so openly and naïvely delighted with the view of the Thames obtainable from the bedroom window, that Mrs. Seacon was emboldened to ask twenty-five per cent more than she had intended. She soon returned to her normal terms, however, when his friend Roxdal called the next day to inspect the rooms, and overwhelmed her with a demonstration of their numerous shortcomings. He pointed out that their being on the ground floor was not an advantage, but a disadvantage, since they were nearer the noises of the street—in fact, the house being a corner one, the noises of two streets. Roxdal continued to exhibit the same finicking temperament in the petty details of the ménage. His shirt fronts were never sufficiently starched, nor his boots sufficiently polished. Tom Peters, having no regard for rigid linen, was always good-tempered and satisfied, and never acquired the respect of his landlady. He wore blue-check shirts and loose ties even on Sundays. It is true he did not go to church, but slept on till Roxdal returned from morning service, and even then it was difficult to get him out of bed, or to make him hurry up his toilette operations. Often the midday meal would be smoking on the table while Peters would still be smoking in the bed, and Roxdal, with his head thrust through the folding doors that separated the bedroom from the sitting-room, would be adjuring the sluggard to arise and shake off his slumbers, and threatening to sit down without him, lest the dinner be spoiled. In revenge, Tom was usually up first on week-days, sometimes at such unearthly hours that Polly had not yet removed the boots from outside the bedroom door, and would bawl down to the kitchen for his shaving water. For Tom, lazy and indolent as he was, shaved with the unfailing regularity of a man to whom shaving has become an instinct. If he had not kept fairly regular hours, Mrs. Seacon would have set him down as an actor, so clean shaven was he. Roxdal did not shave. He wore a full beard, and being a fine figure of a man to boot, no uneasy investor could look upon him without being reassured as to the stability of the bank he managed so successfully. And thus the two men lived in an economical comradeship, all the firmer, perhaps, for their incongruities.

It was on a Sunday afternoon in the middle of October, ten days after Roxdal had settled in his new rooms, that Clara Newell paid her first visit to him there. She enjoyed a good deal of liberty, and did not mind accepting his invitation to tea. The corn merchant, himself indifferently educated, had an exaggerated sense of the value of culture, and so Clara, who had artistic tastes without much actual talent, had gone in for painting, and might be seen, in pretty smocks, copying pictures in the Museum. At one time it looked as if she might be reduced to working seriously at her art, for Satan, who still finds mischief for idle hands to do, had persuaded her father to embark the fruits of years of toil in bubble companies. However, things turned out not so bad as they might have been; a little was saved from the wreck, and the appearance of a suitor, in the person of Everard G. Roxdal, insured her a future of competence, if not of the luxury she had been entitled to expect. She had a good deal of affection for Everard, who was unmistakably a clever man, as well as a good-looking one. The prospect seemed fair and cloudless. Nothing presaged the terrible storm that was about to break over these two lives. Nothing had ever for a moment come to vex their mutual contentment, till this Sunday afternoon. The October sky, blue and sunny, with an Indian summer sultriness, seemed an exact image of her life, with its aftermath of a happiness that had once seemed blighted.

Everard had always been so attentive, so solicitous, that she was as much surprised as chagrined to find that he had apparently forgotten the appointment. Hearing her astonished interrogation of Polly in the passage, Tom shambled from the sitting-room in his loose slippers and his blue-check shirt, with his eternal clay pipe in his mouth, and informed her that Roxdal had gone out suddenly.

"G-g-one out," stammered poor Clara, all confused. "But he asked me to come to tea."

"Oh, you're Miss Newell, I suppose," said Tom.

"Yes, I am Miss Newell."

"He has told me a great deal about you, but I wasn't able honestly to congratulate him on his choice till now."

Clara blushed uneasily under the compliment, and under the ardor of his admiring gaze. Instinctively she distrusted the man. The very first tones of his deep bass voice gave her a peculiar shudder. And then his impoliteness in smoking that vile clay was so gratuitous.

"Oh, then you must be Mr. Peters," she said in return. "He has often spoken to me of you."

"Ah," said Tom, laughingly, "I suppose he's told you all my vices. That accounts for your not being surprised at my Sunday attire."

She smiled a little, showing a row of pearly teeth. "Everard ascribes to you all the virtues," she said.

"Now that's what I call a friend!" he cried, ecstatically. "But won't you come in? He must be back in a moment. He surely would not break an appointment with you." The admiration latent in the accentuation of the last pronoun was almost offensive to her.

She shook her head. She had a just grievance against Everard, and would punish him by going away indignantly.

"Do let me give you a cup of tea," Tom pleaded. "You must be awfully thirsty this sultry weather. There! I will make a bargain with you! If you will come in now, I promise to clear out the moment Everard returns, and not spoil your tête-à-tête." But Clara was obstinate; she did not at all relish this man's society, and besides, she was not going to throw away her grievance against Everard. "I know Everard will slang me dreadfully when he comes in if I let you go," Tom urged. "Tell me at least where he can find you."

"I am going to take the 'bus at Charing Cross, and I'm going straight home," Clara announced determinedly. She put up her parasol, and went up the street into the Strand. A cold shadow seemed to have fallen over all things. But just as she was getting into the 'bus, a hansom dashed down Trafalgar Square, and a well-known voice hailed her. The hansom stopped, and Everard got out and held out his hand.

"I'm so glad you're a bit late," he said. "I was called out unexpectedly, and have been trying to rush back in time. You wouldn't have found me if you had been punctual. But I thought," he added, laughing, "I could rely on you as a woman."

"I was punctual," Clara said angrily. "I was not getting out of this 'bus, as you seem to imagine, but into it, and was going home."

"My darling!" he cried remorsefully. "A thousand apologies." The regret on his handsome face soothed her. He took the rose he was wearing in the buttonhole of his fashionably cut coat and gave it to her.

"Why were you so cruel?" he murmured, as she nestled against him in the hansom. "Think of my despair if I had come home to hear you had come and gone. Why didn't you wait a few moments?"

A shudder traversed her frame. "Not with that man, Peters!" she murmured.

"Not with that man, Peters!" he echoed sharply. "What is the matter with Peters?"

"I don't know," she said. "I don't like him."

"Clara," he said, half sternly, half cajolingly, "I thought you were above these feminine weaknesses. You are punctual, strive also to be reasonable. Tom is my best friend. There is nothing

Tom would not do for me, or I for Tom. You must like him, Clara; you must, if only for my sake."

"I'll try," Clara promised, and then he kissed her in gratitude and broad daylight.

"You'll be very nice to him at tea, won't you?" he said anxiously. "I shouldn't like you two to be bad friends."

"I don't want to be bad friends," Clara protested; "only the moment I saw him a strange repulsion and mistrust came over me."

"You are quiet wrong about him—quite wrong," he assured her earnestly. "When you know him better, you'll find him the best of fellows. Oh, I know," he said suddenly, "I suppose he was very untidy, and you women go so much by appearance!"

"Not at all," Clara retorted. "'Tis you men who go by appearances."

"Yes, you do. That's why you care for me," he said, smiling.

She assured him it wasn't, that she didn't care for him only because he plumed himself, but he smiled on. His smile died away, however, when he entered his rooms and found Tom nowhere.

"I daresay you've made him run about hunting for me," he grumbled unhappily.

"Perhaps he knew I'd come back, and went away to leave us together," she answered. "He said he would when you came."

"And yet you say you don't like him!"

She smiled reassuringly. Inwardly, however, she felt pleased at the man's absence.

If Clara Newell could have seen Tom Peters carrying on with Polly in the passage, she might have felt justified in her prejudice against him. It must be confessed, though, that Everard also carried on with Polly. Alas! it is to be feared that men are much of a muchness where women are concerned; shabby men and smart men, bank managers and journalists, bachelors and semi-detached bachelors. Perhaps it was a mistake after all to say the chums had nothing patently in common. Everard, I am afraid, kissed Polly rather more often than Clara, and although it was because he respected her less, the reason would perhaps not have been sufficiently consoling to his affianced wife. For Polly was pretty, especially on alternate Sunday afternoons, and when at ten P.M. she returned from her outings, she was generally met in the passage by one or the other of the men. Polly liked to receive the homage of real gentlemen, and set her white cap at all indifferently. Thus, just before Clara knocked on that memorable Sunday afternoon, Polly, being confined to the house by the unwritten code regulating the lives of servants, was amusing herself by flirting with Peters.

"You are fond of me a little bit," the graceless Tom whispered, "aren't you?"

"You know I am, sir," Polly replied.

"You don't care for anyone else in the house?"

"Oh, no, sir, and never let anyone kiss me but you. I wonder how it is, sir?" Polly replied ingenuously.

"Give me another," Tom answered.

She gave him another and tripped to the door to answer Clara's knock.

And that very evening, when Clara was gone and Tom still out, Polly turned without the faintest atom of scrupulosity, or even jealousy, to the more fascinating Roxdal, and accepted his amorous advances. If it would seem at first sight that Everard had less excuse for such frivolity than his friend, perhaps the seriousness he showed in this interview may throw a different light upon the complex character of the man.

"You're quite sure you don't care for anyone but me?" he asked earnestly.

"Of course not, sir!" Polly replied indignantly. "How could I?"

"But you care for that soldier I saw you out with last Sunday?"

"Oh, no, sir, he's only my young man," she said apologetically.

"Would you give him up?" he asked suddenly.

Polly's pretty face took a look of terror. "I couldn't, sir! He'd kill me. He's such a jealous brute, you've no idea."

"Yes, but suppose I took you away from here?" he whispered eagerly. "Some place where he couldn't find you— South America, Africa, somewhere thousands of miles away."

"Oh, sir, you frighten me!" whispered Polly, cowering before his ardent eyes, which shone in the dimly lit passage.

"Would you come with me?" he entreated. She did not answer; she shook herself free and ran into the kitchen, trembling with a vague fear.

One morning, earlier than his earliest hour of demanding shaving water, Tom rang the bell violently and asked the alarmed Polly what had become of Mr. Roxdal.

"How should I know, sir?" she gasped. "Ain't he been in, sir?"

"Apparently not," Tom answered anxiously. "He never remains out. We have been here for weeks now, and I can't recall a single night he hasn't been home before twelve. I can't make it out." All inquiries proved futile. Mrs. Seacon reminded him of the thick fog that had come on suddenly the night before.

"What fog?" asked Tom.

"Lord! didn't you notice it, sir?"

"No, I came in early, smoked, read, and went to bed about eleven. I never thought of looking out of the window."

"It began about ten," said Mrs. Seacon, "and got thicker and thicker. I couldn't see the lights of the river from my bedroom. The poor gentleman has been and gone and walked into the water." She began to whimper.

"Nonsense, nonsense," said Tom, though his expression belied his words. "At the worst I should think he couldn't find his way home, and couldn't get a cab, so put up for the night at some hotel. I daresay it will be all right." He began to whistle as if in restored cheerfulness. At eight o'clock there came a letter for Roxdal, marked *Immediate*, but as he did not turn up for breakfast, Tom went round personally to the City and Suburban Bank. He waited half an hour there, but the manager did not make his appearance. Then he left the letter with the cashier and went away with an anxious countenance.

That afternoon it was all over London that the manager of

the City and Surburban had disappeared, and that many thousands of pounds in gold and notes had disappeared with him.

Scotland Yard opened the letter marked *Immediate*, and noted that there had been a delay in its delivery, for the address had been obscure, and an official alteration had been made. It was written in a feminine hand and said: "On second thought I cannot accompany you. Do not try to see me again. Forget me. I shall never forget you."

There was no signature.

Clara Newell, distracted, disclaimed all knowledge of this letter. Polly deposed that the fugitive had proposed flight to her, and the routes to Africa and South America were especially watched.

Yet months passed without result. Tom Peters went about overwhelmed with grief and astonishment. The police took possession of all the missing man's effects.

Gradually the hue and cry dwindled, and died.

"At last we meet!" cried Tom Peters, his face lighting up in joy. "How are you, dear Miss Newell?"

Clara greeted him coldly. Her face had an abiding pallor now. Her lover's flight and shame had prostrated her for weeks. Her soul was the arena of contending instincts. Alone of all the world she still believed in Everard's innocence, felt that there was something more than met the eye, divined some devilish mystery behind it all. And yet that damning letter from the anonymous lady shook her sadly. Then, too, there was the deposition of Polly. When she heard Peter's voice accosting her, all her old repugnance resurged. It flashed upon her that this man—Roxdal's boon companion—must know far more than he had told to the police. She remembered how Everard had spoken of him, with what affection and confidence! Was it likely he was utterly ignorant of Everard's movements?

Mastering her repugnance, she held out her hand. It might be well to keep in touch with him; he was possibly the clue to the mystery. She noticed he was dressed a shade more trimly, and was smoking a meerschaum. He walked along at her side, making no offer to put his pipe out.

"You have not heard from Everard?" he asked. She flushed.

"Do you think I'm an accessory after the fact?" she cried.

"No, no," he said soothingly. "Pardon me, I was thinking he might have written—giving no exact address, of course. Men do sometimes dare to write thus to women. But, of course, he knows you too well—you would have told the police."

"Certainly," she exclaimed, indignantly. "Even if he is innocent he must face the charge."

"Do you still entertain the possibility of his innocence?"

"I do," she said boldly, and looked him full in the face. His eyelids drooped with a quiver. "Don't you?"

"I have hoped against hope," he replied, in a voice faltering with emotion. "Poor old Everard! But I am afraid there is no room for doubt. Oh, this wicked curse of money—tempting the noblest and the best of us."

The weeks rolled on. Gradually she found herself seeing more and more of Tom Peters, and gradually, strange to say, he grew less repulsive. From the talks they had together, she began to see that there was really no reason to put faith in Everard; his criminality, his faithlessness, were too flagrant. Gradually she grew ashamed of her early mistrust of Peters; remorse bred esteem, and esteem ultimately ripened into feelings so warm that when Tom gave freer vent to the love that had been visible to Clara from the first, she did not repulse him.

It is only in books that love lives forever. Clara, so her father thought, showed herself a sensible girl in plucking out an unworthy affection and casting it from her heart. He invited the new suitor to his house, and took to him at once. Roxdal's somewhat supercilious manner had always jarred upon the unsophisticated corn merchant. With Tom the old man got on much better. While evidently quite as well informed and cultured as his whilom friend, Tom knew how to impart his superior knowledge with the accent on the knowledge rather than on the superiority, while he had the air of gaining much information in return. Those who are most conscious of the defects in early education are most resentful of other people sharing their consciousness. Moreover, Tom's *bonhomie* was far more to the old fellow's liking than the studied politeness of his predecessor, so that on the whole Tom made more of a conquest of the father than of the daughter. Nevertheless, Clara was by no means unresponsive to Tom's affection, and when, after one of his visits to the house, the old man kissed her fondly and spoke of the happy turn things had taken, and how, for the second time in their lives, things had mended when they seemed at their blackest, her heart swelled with a gush of gratitude and joy and tenderness, and she fell sobbing into her father's arms.

Tom calculated that he made a clear five hundred a year by occasional journalism, besides possessing some profitable investments which he had inherited from his mother, so that there was no reason for delaying the marriage. It was fixed for Mayday, and the honeymoon was to be spent in Italy.

But Clara was not destined to happiness. From the moment she had promised herself to her first love's friend, old memories began to rise up and reproach her. Strange thoughts stirred in the depths of her soul, and in the silent watches of the night she seemed to hear Everard's voice, charged with grief and upbraiding. Her uneasiness increased as her wedding day drew near. One night, after a pleasant afternoon spent in being rowed by Tom among the upper reaches of the Thames, she retired full of vague forebodings. And she dreamed a terrible dream. The dripping figure of Everard stood by her bedside, staring at her with ghastly eyes. Had he been drowned on the passage to his land of exile? Frozen with horror, she put the question.

"I have never left England!" the vision answered.

Her tongue clove to the roof of her mouth.

"Never left England?" she repeated, in tones which did not seem to be hers.

The wraith's stony eyes stared on.

"Where have you been?" she asked in her dream.

"Very near you," came the answer.

"There has been foul play then!" she shrieked.

The phantom shook its head in doleful assent.

"I knew it!" she shrieked. "Tom Peters—Tom Peters has done away with you. Is it not he? Speak!"

"Yes, it is he—Tom Peters—whom I loved more than all the world."

Even in the terrible oppression of the dream she could not resist saying, woman-like:

"Did I not warn you against him?"

The phantom stared on silently and made no reply.

"But what was the motive?" she asked at length.

"Love of gold—and you. And you are giving yourself to him," it said sternly.

"No, no, Everard! I will not! I swear it! Forgive me!"

The spirit shook its head skeptically.

"You love him. Women are false—as false as men."

She strove to protest again, but her tongue refused to speak.

"If you marry him, I shall always be with you! Beware!"

The dripping figure vanished as suddenly as it came, and Clara awoke in a cold perspiration. Oh, it was horrible! The man she had learned to love was the murderer of the man she had learned to forget! How her original prejudice had been justified! Distracted, shaken to her depths, she would not take counsel even of her father, but informed the police of her suspicions. A raid was made on Tom's rooms, and lo! the stolen notes were discovered in a huge bundle. It was found that he had several banking accounts, with a large, recently paid amount in each bank.

Tom was arrested. Attention was now concentrated on the corpses washed up by the river. It was not long before the body of Roxdal came to shore, the face distorted beyond recognition by long immersion, but the clothes patently his, a pocket book in the breast-pocket removing the last doubt. Mrs. Seacon and Polly and Clara Newell all identified the body. Both juries returned a verdict of murder against Tom Peters, the recital of Clara's dream producing a unique impression in the court and throughout the country. The theory of the prosecution was that Roxdal had brought home the money, whether to fly alone or to divide it, or even for some innocent purpose, as Clara believed; that Peters determined to have it all, that he had gone out for a walk with the deceased, and taking advantage of the fog, had pushed him into the river, and that he was further impelled to the crime by his love for Clara Newell, as was evident from his subsequent relations with her. The judge put on the black cap. Tom Peters was duly hanged by the neck till he was dead.

Brief Résumé of the Culprit's Confession
     When you all read this I shall be dead and laughing at you. I have been hanged for my own murder. I am Everard G. Roxdal. I am also Tom Peters. *We two were one!*
     When I was a young man my mustache and beard wouldn't come. I bought false ones to improve my appearance. One day, after I had become manager of the City and Suburban Bank, I took off my beard and mustache at home, and then the thought crossed my mind that nobody would know me without them. I was another man. Instantly it flashed upon me that if I ran away from the Bank, that other man could be left in London, while the police were scouring the world for a non-existant fugitive.
     But this was only the crude germ of the idea. Slowly I matured my plan. The man who was going to be left in London must be known to a circle of acquaintances beforehand. It would be easy enough to masquerade in the evenings in my beardless condition, with other disguises of dress and voice. But this was not brilliant enough. *I conceived the idea of living with him!* It was Box and Cox reversed.
     We shared rooms at Mrs. Seacon's. It was a great strain, but it was only for a few weeks. I had trick clothes in my bedroom like those of quickchange artists; in a moment I could pass from Roxdal to Peters and from Peters to Roxdal. Polly had to clean two pairs of boots each morning, cook two dinners, and so on. She and Mrs. Seacon saw one or the other of us every moment; it never dawned upon them that *they never saw both of us together!*
     At meals I would not be interrupted, ate off two plates, and conversed with my friend in loud tones. At other times we dined at different hours. On Sundays one was supposed to be asleep when the other was in church. There is no landlady in the

world to whom the idea would have occurred that one man was troubling himself to be two (and to pay for two, including washing).

I worked up the idea of Roxdal's flight, asked Polly to go with me, manufactured that feminine letter that arrived on the morning of my disappearance. As Tom Peters I mixed with a journalistic set. I had another room where I kept the gold and notes till I mistakenly thought the thing had blown over. Unfortunately, returning from the other room on the night of my disappearance, with Roxdal's clothes in a bundle I intended to drop into the river, the bundle was stolen from me in the fog, and the man into whose possession it ultimately came appears to have committed suicide.

What, perhaps, ruined me was my desire to keep Clara's love, and to transfer it to the survivor. Everard told her I was the best of fellows. Once married to her, I would not have had anything to fear. Even if she had discovered the trick, a wife cannot give evidence against her husband, and often does not want to. I made none of the usual slips, but no man can guard against a girl's nightmare after a day up the river and a supper at the Star and Garter. I might have told the judge he was an ass, but then I should have had penal servitude for bank robbery, and that sentence would have been a great deal worse than death.

The only thing that puzzles me, though, is whether the law has committed murder or I have committed suicide.

1893

The Chemistry of Anarchy

ROBERT BARR

It has been said in the London papers that the dissolution of the Soho Anarchist League was caused by want of funds. This is very far from being the case. An Anarchist League has no need for funds, and so long as there is money enough to buy beer the League is sure of continued existence. The truth about the scattering of the Soho organization was told me by a young newspaper man who was chairman at the last meeting.

The young man was not an anarchist, though he had to pretend to be one in the interests of his paper, and so joined the Soho League, where he made some fiery speeches that were much applauded. At last Anarchist news became a drug in the market, and the editor of the paper young Marshall Simkins belonged to, told him that he would now have to turn his attention to Parliamentary work, as he would print no more Anarchist news in the sheet.

One might think that young Simkins would have been glad to get rid of his Anarchist work, as he had no love for the cause. He was glad to get rid of it, but he found some difficulty in sending in his resignation. The moment he spoke of resigning, the members became suspicious of him. He had always been rather better dressed than the others, and, besides, he drank less beer. If a man wishes to be in good standing in the League he must not be fastidious as to dress, and he must be constructed to hold at least a gallon of beer at a sitting. Simkins was merely a "quart" man, and this would have told against him all along if it had not been for the extra gunpowder he put in his speeches. On several occasions seasoned Anarchists had gathered about him and begged him to give up his designs on the Parliament buildings.

The older heads claimed that, desirable as was the obliteration of the Houses of Parliament, the time was not yet ripe for it. England, they pointed out, was the only place where Anarchists could live and talk unmolested, so, while they were quite anxious that Simkins should go and blow up Vienna, Berlin, or Paris, they were not willing for him to begin on London. Simkins was usually calmed down with much difficulty, and finally, after hissing "Cowards!" two or three times under his breath, he concluded with, "Oh, very well, then, you know better than I do—I am only a young recruit; but allow me at least to blow up Waterloo Bridge, or spring a bomb in Fleet Street just to show that we are up and doing."

But this the Anarchists would not sanction. If he wanted to blow up bridges, he could try his hand on those across the Seine. They had given their word that there would be no explosions in London so long as England afforded them an asylum.

"But look at Trafalgar Square," cried Simkins angrily; "we are not allowed to meet there."

"Who wants to meet there?" said the chairman. "It is ever so much more comfortable in these rooms, and there is no beer in Trafalgar Square." "Yes, yes," put in several others; "the time is not yet ripe for it." Thus was Simkins calmed down, and beer allowed to flow again in tranquility, while some foreign Anarchist, who was not allowed to set foot in his native country, would get up and harangue the crowd in broken English and tell them what great things would yet be done by dynamite.

But when Simkins sent in his resignation a change came over their feelings towards him, and he saw at once that he was a marked man. The chairman, in a whisper, advised him to withdraw his resignation. So Simkins, who was a shrewd young fellow, understanding the temper of the assembly, arose and said:

"I have no desire to resign, but you do nothing except talk, and I want to belong to an Anarchist Society that acts." He stayed away from the next meeting, and tried to drop them in that way, but a committee from the League called upon him at his lodgings, and his landlady thought that young Simkins had got into bad ways when he had such evil-looking men visiting him.

Simkins was in a dilemma, and could not make up his mind what to do. The Anarchists apparently were not to be shaken off. He applied to his editor for advice on the situation, but that good man could think of no way out of the trouble.

"You ought to have known better," he said, "than to mix up with such people."

"But how was I to get the news?" asked Simkins, with some indignation. The editor shrugged his shoulders. That was not his part of the business; and if the Anarchists chose to make things uncomfortable for the young man, he could not help it.

Simkins' fellow lodger, a student who was studying chemistry in London, noticed that the reporter was becoming gaunt with anxiety.

"Simkins," said Sedlitz to him one morning, "you are haggard and careworn: what is the matter with you? Are you in love, or is it merely debt that is bothering you?"

"Neither," replied Simkins.

"Then cheer up," said Sedlitz. "If one or the other is not interfering with you, anything else is easily remedied."

"I am not so sure of that," rejoined Simkins; and then he sat down and told his friend just what was troubling him.

"Ah," said Sedlitz, "that accounts for it. There has been an unkempt ruffian marching up and down watching this house. They are on your track, Simkins, my boy, and when they discover that you are a reporter, and therefore necessarily a traitor, you will be nabbed some dark night."

"Well, that's encouraging," said Simkins, with his head in his hands.

"Are these Anarchists brave men, and would they risk their lives in any undertaking?" asked Sedlitz.

"Oh, I don't know. They talk enough, but I don't know

what they would do. They are quite capable, though, of tripping me up in a dark lane."

"Look here," said Sedlitz, "suppose you let me try a plan. Let me give them a lecture on the Chemistry of Anarchy. It's a fascinating subject."

"What good would that do?"

"Oh, wait till you have heard the lecture. If I don't make the hair of some of them stand on end, they are braver men than I take them to be. We have a large room in Clement's Inn, where we students meet to try experiments and smoke tobacco. It is half club, and half a lecture room. Now, I propose to get those Anarchists in there, lock the doors, and tell them something about dynamite and other explosives. You give out that I am an Anarchist from America. Tell them that the doors will be locked to prevent police interference, and that there will be a barrel of beer. You can introduce me as a man from America, where they know as much about Anarchism in ten minutes as they do here in ten years. Tell them that I have spent my life in the study of explosives. I will have to make-up a little, but you know that I am a very good amateur actor, and I don't think there will be any trouble about that. At the last you must tell them that you have an appointment and will leave me to amuse them for a couple of hours."

"But I don't see what good it is all going to do, though I am desperate," said Simkins, "and willing to try anything. I have thought some of firing a bomb off myself at an Anarchist meeting."

When the Friday night of meeting arrived the large hall in Clement's Inn was filled to the doors. Those assembled there saw a platform at one end of the apartment, and a door that led from it to a room at the back of the hall. A table was on the platform, and boxes, chemical apparatus, and other scientific-looking paraphernalia were on it. At the hour of eight young Simkins appeared before the table alone.

"Fellow Anarchists," he said, "you are well aware that I am tired of the great amount of talk we indulge in, and the little action which follows it. I have been fortunate enough to secure the cooperation of an Anarchist from America, who will tell you something of the cause there. We have had the doors locked, and those who keep the keys are not down at the entrance of the Inn, so that if a fire should occur they can quickly come and let us out. There is no great danger of fire, however, but the interruption of the police must be guarded against very carefully. The windows, as you see, are shuttered and barred, and no ray of light can penetrate from this room outside. Until the lecture is over no one can leave the room, and by the same token no one can enter it, which is more the purpose.

"My friend, Professor Josiah P. Slivers, has devoted his life to the Chemistry of Anarchy, which is the title of this lecture. He will tell you of some important discoveries, which are now to be made known for the first time. I regret to say that the Professor is not in a very good state of health, because the line of life which he has adopted has its drawbacks. His left eye has been blown away by a premature explosion during his experiments. His right leg is also permanently disabled. His left arm, as you will notice, is in a sling, having been injured by a little disaster in his workshop since he came to London. He is a man, as you will see, devoted body and soul to the cause, so I hope you will listen to him attentively. I regret that I am unable to remain with you tonight, having other duties to perform which are imperative. I will therefore, if you will permit me, leave by the back entrance after I have introduced the Professor to you."

At this moment the stumping of a wooden leg was heard, and those in the audience saw appear a man on crutches, with one arm in a sling and a bandage over an eye, although he beamed upon them benevolently with the other.

"Fellow Anarchists," said Simkins, "allow me to introduce to you Professor Josiah P. Slivers, of the United States."

The Professor bowed and the audience applauded. As soon as the applause began the Professor held up his unmaimed arm and said, "Gentlemen, I beg that you will not applaud."

It seems the fashion in America to address all sorts and conditions of men as "Gentlemen." The Professor continued, "I have here some explosives so sensitive that the slightest vibration will cause them to go off, and I therefore ask you to listen in silence to what I have to say. I must particularly ask you also not to stamp on the floor."

Before these remarks were concluded Simkins had slipped out by the back entrance, and somehow his desertion seemed to have a depressing effect upon the company, who looked upon the broken-up Professor with eyes of wonder and apprehension.

The Professor drew towards him one of the boxes and opened the lid. He dipped his one useful hand into the box and, holding it aloft, allowed something which looked like wet sawdust to drip through his fingers. "That, gentlemen," he said, with an air of the utmost contempt, "is what is known to the world as dynamite. I have nothing at all to say against dynamite. It has, in its day, been a very powerful medium through which our opinions have been imparted to a listening world, but its day is past. It is what the lumbering stage-coach is to the locomotive, what the letter is to the telegram, what the sailing-vessel is to the steamship. It will be my pleasant duty tonight to exhibit to you an explosive so powerful and deadly that hereafter, having seen what it can accomplish, you will have nothing but derision for such simple and harmless compounds as dynamite and nitroglycerine."

The Professor looked with kindly sympathy over his audience as he allowed the yellow mixture to percolate slowly through his fingers back into the box again. Ever and anon he took up a fresh handful and repeated the action.

The Anarchists in the audience exchanged uneasy glances one with the other.

"Yet," continued the Professor, "it will be useful for us to consider this substance for a few moments, if but for the purpose of comparison. Here," he said, diving his hand into another box and bringing up before their gaze a yellow brick, "is dynamite in a compressed form. There is enough here to wreck all this part of London, were it exploded. This simple brick would lay St. Paul's Cathedral in ruins, so, however antiquated dynamite may become, we must always look upon it with respect, just as we look upon reformers of centuries ago who perished for their opinions, even though their opinions were far behind what ours are now. I shall take the liberty of performing some experiments with this block of dynamite." Saying which the Professor, with his free arm, flung the block of dynamite far down the aisle, where it fell on the floor with a sickening thud. The audience sprang from their seats and tumbled back one over the other. A wild shriek went up into the air, but the Professor gazed placidly on the troubled mob below him with a superior smile on his face. "I beg you to seat yourselves," he said, "and for reasons which I have already explained, I trust that you will not applaud any of my remarks. You have just now portrayed one of the popular superstitions about dynamite, and you show by your actions how necessary a lecture of this sort is in order that you may comprehend thoroughly the substance with which you have to deal. That brick is perfectly harmless, because it is frozen. Dynamite in its frozen state will not explode—a fact well understood by miners and all those who have to work with it, and who, as a rule, generally prefer to blow themselves to pieces trying to thaw the substance before a fire. Will you kindly bring that brick back to me, before it thaws out in the heated atmosphere of this room?"

One of the men stepped gingerly forward and picked up the brick, holding it far from his body, as he tip-toed up to the platform, where he laid it down carefully on the desk before the Professor.

"Thank you," said the Professor, blandly.

The man drew a long breath of relief as he went back to his seat.

"That is frozen dynamite," continued the Professor, "and is, as I have said, practically harmless. Now, it will be my pleasure to perform two startling experiments with the unfrozen substance," and with that he picked up a handful of the wet sawdust and flung it on a small iron anvil that stood on the table. "You will enjoy these experiments," he said, "because it will show you with what ease dynamite may be handled. It is a popular error that concussion will cause dynamite to explode. There is enough dynamite here to blow up this hall and to send into oblivion every person in it, yet you will see whether or not concussion will explode it." The Professor seized a hammer and struck the substance on the anvil two or three sharp blows, while those in front of him scrambled wildly back over their comrades, with hair standing on end. The Professor ceased his pounding and gazed reproachfully at them; then something on the anvil appeared to catch his eye. He bent over it and looked critically on the surface of the iron. Drawing himself up to his full height again, he said:

"I was about to reproach you for what might have appeared to any other man as evidence of fear, but I see my mistake. I came very near making a disastrous error. I have myself suffered from time to time from similar errors. I notice upon the anvil a small spot of grease; if my hammer had happened to strike that spot you would all now be writhing in your death-agonies under the ruins of this building. Nevertheless, the lesson is not without its value. That spot of grease is free nitro-glycerine that has oozed out from the dynamite. Therein rests, perhaps, the only danger in handling dynamite. As I have shown you, you can smash up dynamite on an anvil without danger, but if a hammer happened to strike a spot of free nitroglycerine it would explode in a moment. I beg to apologize to you for my momentary neglect."

A man rose up in the middle of the hall, and it was some little time before he could command voice enough to speak, for he was shaking as if from palsy. At last he said, after he had moistened his lips several times:

"Professor, we are quite willing to take your word about the explosive. I think I speak for all my comrades here. We have no doubt at all about your learning, and would much prefer to hear from your own lips what you have to say on the subject, and not have you waste any more valuable time with experiments. I have not consulted with my comrades before speaking, but I think I voice the sense of the meeting." Cries of "You do, you do," came from all parts of the hall. The Professor once more beamed upon them benevolently.

"Your confidence in me is indeed touching," he said, "but a chemical lecture without experiments is like a body without a soul. Experiment is the soul of research. In chemistry we must take nothing for granted. I have shown you how many popular errors have arisen regarding the substance with which we are dealing. It would have been impossible for these errors to have arisen if every man had experimented for himself; and although I thank you for the mark of confidence you have bestowed upon me, I cannot bring myself to deprive you of the pleasure which my experiments will afford you. There is another very common error to the effect that fire will explode dynamite. Such, gentlemen, is not the case."

The Professor struck a match on his trousers' leg and lighted the substance on the anvil. It burnt with a pale bluish flame, and the Professor gazed around triumphantly at his fellow Anarchists.

While the shuddering audience watched with intense fascination the pale blue flame the Professor suddenly stooped over and blew it out. Straightening himself once more he said, "Again I must apologize to you, for again I have forgotten the small spot of grease. If the flame had reached the spot of nitro-glycerine it would have exploded, as you all know. When a man has his thoughts concentrated on one subject he is apt to forget something else. I shall make no more experiments with dynamite. Here, John," he said to the trembling attendant, "take this box away, and move it carefully, for I see that the nitro-glycerine is oozing out. Put it as tenderly down in the next room as if it were a box of eggs."

"As the box disappeared there was a simultaneous long-drawn sigh of relief from the audience.

"Now, gentlemen," said the Professor, "we come to the subject that ought to occupy the minds of all thoughtful men." He smoothed his hair complacently with the palm of his practicable hand, and smiled genially around him.

"The substance that I am about to tell you of is my own invention, and compares with dynamite as prussic acid does with new milk as a beverage." The Professor dipped his fingers in his vest pocket and drew out what looked like a box of pills. Taking one pill out he placed it upon the anvil and as he tip-toed back he smiled on it with a smile of infinite tenderness. "Before I begin on this subject I want to warn you once more that if any man as much as stamps upon the floor, or moves about except on tip-toe this substance will explode and will lay London from here to Charing Cross, in one mass of indistinguishable ruins. I have spent ten years of my life in completing this invention. And these pills, worth a million a box, will cure all ills to which the flesh is heir."

"John," he said, turning to his attendant, "bring me a basin of water!" The basin of water was placed gingerly upon the table, and the Professor emptied all the pills into it, picking up also the one that was on the anvil and putting it with the others.

"Now," he said, with a deep sigh, "we can breathe easier. A man can put one of these pills in a little vial of water, place the vial in his vest-pocket, go to Trafalgar Square, take the pill from the vial, throw it in the middle of the Square, and it will shatter everything within the four-mile radius, he himself having the glorious privilege of suffering instant martyrdom for the cause. People have told me that this is a drawback to my invention, but I am inclined to differ with them. The one who uses this must make up his mind to share the fate of those around him. I claim that this is the crowning glory of my invention. It puts to instant test our interest in the great cause. John, bring in very carefully that machine with the electric-wire attachment from the next room."

The machine was placed upon the table. "This," said the Professor, holding up some invisible object between his thumb and forefinger, "is the finest cambric needle. I will take upon the point of it an invisible portion of the substance I speak of." Here he carefully picked out a pill from the basin, and as carefully placed it upon the table, where he detached an infinitesimal atom of it and held it up on the point of the needle. "This particle," he said, "is so small that it cannot be seen except with aid of a microscope. I will now place needle and all on the machine and touch it off with electric current"; and as his hand hovered over the push-button there were cries of "Stop! stop!" but the finger descended, and instantly there was a terrific explosion. The very foundation seemed shaken, and a dense cloud of smoke rolled over the heads of the audience. As the Professor became visible through the thinning smoke, he looked around for his audience. Every man was under the benches, and groans came from all parts of the hall. "I hope," said the Professor, in anxious tones, "that no one has been hurt. I am afraid that I took up too much of the substance on the point of the needle, but it will enable you to imagine the effect of a larger quantity. Pray seat yourselves again. This is my last experiment."

As the audience again seated itself, another mutual sigh ascended to the roof. The Professor drew the chairman's chair towards him and sat down, wiping his grimy brow.

A man instantly arose and said, "I move a vote of thanks to Professor Slivers for the interesting—"

The Professor raised his hand. "One moment," he said, "I have not quite finished. I have a proposal to make to you. You see that cloud of smoke hovering over our heads? In twenty minutes that smoke will percolate down through the atmosphere. I have told you but half of the benefits of this terrific explosive. When that smoke mixes with the atmosphere of the room it becomes a deadly poison. We all can live here for the next nineteen minutes in perfect safety, then at the first breath we draw we expire instantly. It is a lovely death. There is no pain, no contortion of the countenance, but we will be found here in the morning stark and stiff in our seats. I propose, gentlemen, that we teach London the great lesson it so much needs. No cause is without its martyrs. Let us be the martyrs of the great religion of Anarchy. I have left in my room papers telling just how and why we died. At midnight these sheets will be distributed to all the newspapers of London, and tomorrow the world will ring with our heroic names. I will now put the motion. All in favor of this signify it by the usual upraising of the right hand."

The Professor's own right hand was the only one that was raised.

"Now all of a contrary opinion," said the Professor, and at once every hand in the audience went up.

"The noes have it," said the Professor, but he did not seem to feel badly about it. "Gentlemen," he continued, "I see that you have guessed my second proposal, as I imagined you would, and though there will be no newspapers in London tomorrow to chronicle the fact, yet the newspapers of the rest of the world will tell of the destruction of this wicked city. I see by your looks that you are with me in this, my second proposal, which is the most striking thing ever planned, and is that we explode the whole of these pills in the basin. To make sure of this, I have sent to an agent in Manchester the full account of how it was done, and the resolutions brought forward at this meeting, and which doubtless you will accept.

"Gentlemen, all in favor of the instant destruction of London signify it in the usual manner."

"Mr. Professor," said the man who had spoken previously, "before you put that resolution I would like to move an amendment. This is a very serious proposal, and should not be lightly undertaken. I move as an amendment, therefore, that we adjourn this meeting to our rooms at Soho, and do the exploding there. I have some little business that must be settled before this grand project is put in motion."

The Professor then said, "Gentlemen, the amendment takes precedence. It is moved that this meeting be adjourned, so that you may consider the project at your club rooms in Soho."

"I second that amendment," said fifteen of the audience rising together to their feet.

"In the absence of the regular chairman," said the Professor, "it is my duty to put the amendment. All in favor of the amendment signify it by raising the right hand."

Every hand was raised. "The amendment, gentlemen, is carried. I shall be only too pleased to meet you tomorrow night at your club, and I will bring with me a larger quantity of my explosive. John, kindly go round and tell the man to unlock the doors."

When Simkins and Slivers called round the next night at the regular meeting place of the Anarchists, they found no signs of a gathering, and never since the lecture has the Soho Anarchist League been known to hold a meeting. The Club has mysteriously dissolved.

The Sheriff
of Gullmore

MELVILLE DAVISSON POST

[The crime of embezzlement here dealt with is statutory. The venue of this story could have been laid in many other States; the statutes are similar to a degree. See the Code of West Virginia; also the late case of The State *vs*. Bolin, 19 Southwestern Reporter, 650; also the long list of ancient cases in Russell on Crimes, 2d volume.]

I.

"It is hard luck, Colonel," said the broker, "but you are not the only one skinned in the deal; the best of them caught it today. By Jupiter! the pit was like Dante's Inferno!"

"Yes, it's gone, I reckon," muttered the Colonel, shutting his teeth down tight on his cigar; "I guess the devil wins every two out of three."

"Well," said the broker, turning to his desk, "it is the fortune of war."

"No, young man," growled the Colonel, "it is the blasted misfortune of peace. I have never had any trouble with the fortune of war. I could stand on an ace high and win with war. It is peace that queers me. Here in the fag-end of the nineteenth century, I, Colonel Moseby Allen, sheriff of Gullmore County, West Virginia, go up against another man's game—yes, and go up in the daytime. Say young man, it feels queer at the mellow age of forty-nine, after you have been in the legislature of a great commonwealth, and at the very expiration of your term as sheriff of the whitest and the freest county in West Virginia—I say it feels queer, after all those high honors, to be suddenly reminded that you need to be accompanied by a business chaperon."

The Colonel stood perfectly erect and delivered his oration with the fluency and the abandon of a southern orator. When he had finished, he bowed low to the broker, pulled his big slouch hat down on his forehead, and stalked out of the office and down the steps to the street.

Colonel Moseby Allen was built on the decided lines of a southern mountaineer. He was big and broad-shouldered, but he was not well proportioned. His body was short and heavy, while his legs were long. His eyes were deep-set and shone like little brown beads. On the whole, his face indicated cunning, bluster, and rashness. The ward politician would have recognized him among a thousand as a kindred spirit, and the professional gambler would not have felt so sure of himself with such a face across the table from him.

When the Colonel stepped out on the pavement, he stopped, thrust his hands into his pockets, and looked up and down Wall Street; then he jerked the cigar out of his mouth, threw it into the gutter, and began to deliver himself of a philippic upon the negative merits of brokers in general, and his broker in particular. The Virginian possessed a vocabulary of smooth billingsgate that in vividness and diversity approached the sublime. When he had consigned some seven generations of his broker's ancestry to divers minutely described localities in perdition, he began to warm to his work, and his artistic profanity rolled forth in startling periods.

The passers-by stopped and looked on in surprise and wonder. For a moment they were half convinced that the man was a religious fanatic, his eloquent, almost poetic, tirade was so thoroughly filled with holy names. The effect of the growing audience inspired the speaker. He raised his voice and began to emphasize with sweeping gestures. He had now finished with the broker's ancestry and was plunging with a rush of gorgeous pyrotechnics into the certain future of the broker himself, when a police officer pushed through the crowd and caught the irate Virginian by the shoulder.

Colonel Allen paused and looked down at the officer.

"You," he said, calmly, "I opine are a minion of the law; a hireling of the municipal authorities."

"See here," said the officer, "you are not allowed to preach on the street. You will have to come with me to the station house."

The Colonel bowed suavely. "Sir," he said, "I, Colonel Moseby Allen, sheriff of Gullmore County in the Mountain State of West Virginia, am a respecter of the law, even in the body of its petty henchmen, and if the ordinances of this God-forsaken Gomorrah are such that a free-born American citizen, twenty-one years old and white, is not permitted the inalienable privilege of expressing his opinion without let or hindrance, then I am quite content to accompany you to the confines of your accursed jail-house."

Allen turned round and started down the street with the officer. He walked a little in advance, and continued to curse glibly in a low monotone. When they were half way to the corner below, a little man slipped out of the crowd and hurried up to the policeman. "Mike," he whispered, putting his hand under the officer's, "here is five for you. Turn him over to me."

The officer closed his hand like a trap, stepped quickly forward, and touched his prisoner on the shoulder.

As the Virginian turned, the officer said in a loud voice: "Mr. Parks, here, says that he knows you, and that you are all right, so I'll let you go this time." Then, before any reply could be made, he vanished around the corner.

Colonel Allen regarded his deliverer with the air of a world-worn cynic. "Well," he said, "one is rarely delivered from the spoiler by the hand of his friend, and I cannot now recall ever having had you for an enemy. May I inquire what motive prompts this gracious courtesy?"

"Don't speak so loud," said Parks, stepping up close to the man. "I happen to know something about your loss. Colonel

Allen, and perhaps also a way to regain it. Will you come with me?"

The Virginian whistled softly. "Yes," he said.

II.

"This is a fine hotel," observed Colonel Allen, beginning to mellow under the mystic spell of a five-course dinner and a quart of Cliquot. "Devilish fine hotel, Mr. Parks. All the divers moneys which I in my official capacity have collected in taxes from the fertile county of Gullmore, would scarcely pay for the rich embellishment of the barber shop of this magnificent edifice."

"Well, Colonel," said the bald Parks, with a sad smile, "that would depend upon the amount of the revenues of your county. I presume that they are large, and consequently the office of sheriff a good one."

"Yes, sir," answered the Virginian, "it is generally considered desirable from the standpoint of prominence. The climate of Gullmore is salubrious. Its pasture lands are fertile, and its citizens cultured and refined to a degree unusual even in the ancient and aristocratic counties of the Old Dominion. And, sir,"—here the Colonel drew himself up proudly, and thrust his hand into the breast of his coat,—"I am proud, sir,—proud to declare that from time to time the good citizens of Gullmore, by means of their suffrage, and with large and comfortable majorities, have proclaimed me their favorite son and competent official. Six years ago I was in the legislature at Charleston as the trusted representative of this grand old county of Gullmore; and four years ago, after the fiercest and most bitterly contested political conflict of all the history of the South, I was elected to that most important and honorable office of sheriff,—to the lasting glory of my public fame, and the great gratification of the commonwealth."

"That gratification is now four years old?" mused Parks.

Colonel Moseby Allen darted a swift, suspicious glance at his companion, but in a moment it was gone, and he had dropped back into his grandiloquent discourse. "Yes, sir, the banner county of West Virginia, deserting her ancient and sacred traditions, and forgetting for the time the imperishable precepts of her patriotic fathers, has gone over to affiliate with the ungodly. We were beaten, sir—beaten in this last engagement,—horse, foot, and dragoons,—beaten by a set of carpetbaggers,—a set of unregenerate political tricksters of such diabolical cunning that nothing but the gates of hell could have prevailed against them. Now, sir, now,—and I say it mournfully, there is nothing left to us in the county of Gullmore, save only honor."

"Honor," sneered Parks, "an imaginary rope to hold fools with! It won't fill a hungry stomach, or satisfy a delinquent account." The little clerk spoke the latter part of his sentence slowly and deliberately.

Again the suspicious expression passed over the face of Colonel Allen, leaving traces of fear and anxiety in its wake. His eyes, naturally a little crossed, drew in toward his nose, and the muscles around his mouth grew hard. For a moment he was silent, looking down into his glass; then, with an effort, he went on: "Yes, the whole shooting-match is in the hands of the Philistines. From the members of the County Court up to the important and responsible position which I have filled for the last four years, and when my accounts are finally wound up, I—"

"Your accounts," murmured Parks, "when they are finally wound up, what then?"

Every trace of color vanished from the Virginian's face, his heavy jaws trembled, and he caught hold of the arms of the chair to steady himself.

Parks did not look up. He seemed deeply absorbed in studying the bottom of his glass. For a moment Colonel Moseby Allen had been caught off his guard, but it was only for a moment. He straightened up and underwent a complete transformation. Then, bending forward, he said, speaking low and distinctly. "Look here, my friend, you are the best guesser this side of hell. Now, if you can pick a winning horse we will divide the pool."

The two men were at a table in a corner of the Hoffman café, and, as it chanced, alone in the room. Parks glanced around quickly, then he leaned over and said: "That depends on just one thing, Colonel."

"Turn up the cards," growled the Virginian, shutting his teeth down tight on his lip."

"Well," said Parks, "you must promise to stick to your rôle to the end, if you commence with the play."

The southerner leaned back in his chair and stroked his chin thoughtfully. Finally he dropped his hand and looked up. "All right," he muttered; "I'll stand by the deal; throw out the cards."

Parks moved his chair nearer to the table and leaned over on his elbow. "Colonel," he said, "there is only one living man who can set up a successful counter-plot against fate, that is dead certain to win, and that man is here in New York to-day. He is a great lawyer, and besides being that, he is the greatest plotter since the days of Napoleon. Not one of his clients ever saw the inside of a prison. He can show men how to commit crimes in such a way that the law cannot touch them. No matter how desperate the position may be, he can always show the man who is in it a way by which he can get out. There is no case so hopeless that he cannot manage it. If money is needed, he can show you how to get it—a plain, practical way, by which you can get what you need and as much as you need. He has a great mind, but he is strangely queer and erratic, and must be approached with extreme care, and only in a certain way. This man," continued the little clerk, lowering his voice, "is named Randolph Mason. You must go to him and explain the whole matter, and you must do it just in the way I tell you."

Again the Virginian whistled softly. "My friend," he said, "there is a little too much mystery about this matter. I am not afraid of you, because you are a rascal; no one ever had a face like you that was not a rascal. You will stick to me because you are out for the stuff, and there is no possible way to make a dollar by throwing the game. I am not afraid of any living man, if I have an opportunity to see his face before the bluff is made. You are all right; your game is to use me in making some haul that is a little too high for yourself. That is what you have been working up to, and you are a smooth operator, my friend. A greenhorn would have concluded long ago that you were a detective, but I knew a blamed sight better than that the moment you made your first lead. In the first place, you are too sharp to waste your time with any such bosh, and in the second place, it takes cash to buy detectives, and there is nobody following me with cash. Gullmore county has no kick coming to it until my final settlements are made, and there is no man treading shoe leather that knows anything about the condition of my official business except myself, and perhaps also that shrewd and mysterious guesser—yourself. So, you see, I am not standing on ceremonies with you. But here, young man, comes in a dark horse, and you want me to bet on him blindfolded. Those are not the methods of Moseby Allen. I must be let in a little deeper on this thing."

"All I want you to do," said Parks, putting his hand confidentially on the Virginian's arm, "is simply to go and see Randolph Mason, and approach him in the way I tell you, and when you have done that, I will wager that you stay and explain everything to him."

Colonel Allen leaned back in his chair and thrust his hands into his pockets. "Why should I do that?" he said curtly.

"Well," murmured the little man mournfully, "one's bondsmen are entitled to some consideration; and then, there is the penitentiary. Courts have a way of sending men there for embezzlement."

"You are correct," said Allen, quietly, "and I have not time to go."

"At any rate," continued Parks, "there can be no possible danger to you. You are taking no chances. Mr. Mason is a member of the New York bar, and anything you may tell him he dare not reveal. The law would not permit him to do so if he desired. The whole matter would be kept as thoroughly inviolate as though it were made in the confessional. Your objectons are all idle. You are a man in a desperate position. You are up to your waist in the quicksand, now, and, at the end of the year, it is bound to close over your head. It is folly to look up at the sky and attempt to ignore this fact. I offer to help you— not from any goodness of heart, understand, but because we can both make a stake in this thing. I need money, and you must have money,—that is the whole thing in a nutshell. Now," said Parks, rising from his chair, "what are you going to do?"

"Well," said the Virginian, drawing up his long legs and spreading out his fat hands on the table, "Colonel Moseby Allen, of the county of Gullmore, will take five cards, if you please."

III.

"This must be the place," muttered the Virginian, stopping under the electric light and looking up at the big house on the avenue. "That fellow said I would know the place by the copper-studded door, and there it is, as certain as there are back taxes in Gullmore." With that, Colonel Moseby Allen walked up the granite steps and began to grope about in the dark door-way for the electric bell. He could find no trace of this indispensable convenience, and was beginning to lapse into a flow of half-suppressed curses, when he noticed for the first time an ancient silver knocker fastened to the middle of the door. He seized it and banged it vigorously.

The Virginian stood in the dark and waited. Finally he concluded that the noise had not been heard, and was about to repeat the signal when the door was flung suddenly open, and a tall man holding a candle in his hand loomed up in the door-way.

"I am looking," stammered the southerner, "for one Randolph Mason, an attorney-at-law."

"I am Randolph Mason,' said the man, thrusting the silver candlestick out before him. "Who are you, sir?"

"My name is Allen," answered the southerner, "Moseby Allen, of Gullmore county, West Virginia."

"A Virginian," said Mason, "what evil circumstance brings you here?"

Then Allen remembered the instructions which Parks had given him so minutely. He took off his hat and passed his hand across his forehead. "Well," he said, "I suppose the same thing that brings the others. We get in and plunge along just as far as

we can. Then Fate shuts down the lid of her trap, and we have
either to drop off the bridge or come here."

"Come in," said Mason. Then he turned abruptly and
walked down the hall-way. The southerner followed, impressed
by this man's individuality. Allen had pushed his way through
life with bluff and bluster, and like that one in the scriptural
writings, "neither feared God nor regarded man." His unlimited
assurance had never failed him before any of high or low
degree, and to be impressed with the power of any man was to
him strange and uncomfortable.

Mason turned into his library and placed the candlestick on
a table in the centre of the floor. Then he drew up two chairs and
sat down in one of them motioning Allen to the other on the
opposite side of the table. The room was long and empty, except
for the rows of heavy book-cases standing back in the darkness.
The floor was bare, and there was no furniture of any kind
whatever, except the great table and the ancient highback chairs.
There was no light but the candle standing high in its silver
candlestick.

"Sir," said Mason, when the Virginian had seated himself,
"which do you seek to evade, punishment or dishonor?"

The Virginian turned round, put his elbows on the table,
and looked squarely across at his questioner. "I am not fool
enough to care for the bark," he answered, "provided the dog's
teeth are muzzled."

"It is well," said Mason, slowly, "there is often difficulty in
dealing with double problems, where both disgrace and punishment are sought to be evaded. Where there is but one difficulty
to face, it can usually be handled with ease. What others are
involved in your matter?"

"No others," answered the Virginian; "I am seeking only to
save myself."

"From the law only," continued Mason, "or does private
vengeance join with it?"

"From the law only," answered Allen.

"Let me hear it all," said Mason.

"Well," said the Virginian, shifting uneasily in his chair,
"my affairs are in a very bad way, and every attempt that I have

made to remedy them has resulted only in disaster. I am walking, with my hands tied, straight into the penitentiary, unless some miracle can be performed in my favor. Everything has gone dead against me from my first fool move. Four years ago I was elected sheriff of Gullmore county in the State of West Virginia. I was of course required by law to give a large bond. This I had much difficulty in doing, for the reason that I have no estate whatever. Finally I induced my brother and my father, who is a very old man, to mortgage their property and thereby secured the requisite bond. I entered upon the duties of my office, and assumed entire control of the revenues of the county. For a time I managed them carefully and kept my private business apart from that of the county. But I had never been accustomed to strict business methods, and I soon found it most difficult to confine myself to them. Little by little I began to lapse into my old habit of carelessness. I neglected to keep up the settlements, and permitted the official business to become intermixed with my private accounts. The result was that I awoke one morning to find that I owed the county of Gullmore ten thousand dollars. I began at once to calculate the possibility of my being able to meet this deficit before the expiration of my term of office, and soon found that by no possible means would I be able to raise this amount out of the remaining fees. My gambling instincts at once asserted themselves. I took five thousand dollars, went to Lexington, and began to play the races in a vain, reckless hope that I might win enough to square my accounts. I lost from the very start. I came back to my county and went on as before, hoping against hope that something would turn up and let me out. Of course this was the dream of an idiot, and when the opposition won at the last election, and a new sheriff was installed, and I was left but a few months within which to close up my accounts, the end which I had refused to think of arose and stared me in the face. I was now at the end of my tether, and there was nothing there but a tomb. And even that way was not open. If I should escape the penitentiary by flight or by suicide, I would still leave my brother and my aged father to bear the entire burden of my defalcations; and when they, as my bondsmen, had paid the sum to the county, they would all be paupers."

The man paused and mopped the perspiration from his face. He was now terribly in earnest, and seemed to be realizing the gravity and the hopelessness of his crime. All his bluster and grandiloquent airs had vanished.

"Wreckless and unscrupulous as I am," he went on, "I cannot bear to think of my brother's family beggars because of my wrong, or my father in his extreme old age turned out from under his own roof and driven into the poor-house, and yet it must come as certainly as the sun will rise tomorrow."

The man's voice trembled now, and the flabby muscles of his face quivered.

"In despair, I gathered up all the funds of the county remaining in my hands and hurried to this city. Here I went to the most reliable broker I could find and through him plunged into speculation. But all the devils in hell seemed to be fighting for my ruin. I was caught in that dread and unexpected crash of yesterday and lost everything. Strange to say, when I realized that my ruin was now complete, I felt a kind of exhilaration,— such, I presume, as is said to come to men when they are about to be executed. Standing in the very gaping jaws of ruin, I have to-day been facetious, even merry. Now, in the full glare of this horrible matter, I scarcely remember what I have been doing, or how I came to be here, except that this morning in Wall Street I heard some one speak of your ability, and I hunted up your address and came without any well defined plan, and, if you will pardon me, I will add that it was also without any hope."

The man stopped and seemed to settle back in his chair in a great heap.

Randolph Mason arose and stood looking down at the Virginian.

"Sir," said Mason, "none are ever utterly lost but the weak. Answer my question."

The Virginian pulled himself together and looked up.

"Is there any large fund," continued Mason, "in the hands of the officers of your county?"

"My successor," said Allen, "has just collected the amount

of a levy ordered by the county court for the purpose of paying
the remainder due on the court-house. He now has that fund in
his hands."

"When was the building erected?" said Mason.

"It was built during the last year of my term of office, and
paid for in part out of levies ordered while I was active sheriff.
When my successor came in there still remained due the
contractors on the work some thirty thousand dollars. A levy
was ordered by the court shortly before my term expired, but
the collection of this levy fell to the coming officer, so this money
is not in my hands, although all the business up to this time has
been managed by me, and the other payments on the building
made from time to time out of moneys in my hands, and I have
been the chief manager of the entire work and know more about
it than any one else. The new sheriff came into my office a few
days ago to inquire how he was to dispose of this money."

Mason sat down abruptly. "Sir," he said almost bitterly,
"there is not enough difficulty in your matter to bother the
cheapest intriguer in Kings county. I had hoped that yours was a
problem of some gravity."

"I see," said the Virginian, sarcastically, "I am to rob the
sheriff of this money in such a manner that it won't be known
who received it, and square my accounts. That would be very
easy indeed. I would have only to kill three men and break a
bank. Yes, that would be very easy. You might as well tell me to
have blue eyes."

"Sir," said Randolph Mason, slowly, "you are the worst
prophet unhung."

"Well," continued the man, "there can be no other way, If it
were turned over to me in my official capacity what good would
it do? My bondsmen would be responsible for it. I would then
have it to account for, and what difference, in God's name, can it
make whether I am sent to the penitentiary for stealing money
which I have already used, or for stealing this money? It all
belongs to the county. It is two times six one way, and six times
two the other way."

"Sir," said Mason, "I retract my former statement in regard

to your strong point. Let me insist that you devote your time to prophecy. Your reasoning is atrocious."

"I am wasting my time here," muttered the Virginian, "there is no way out of it."

Randolph Mason turned upon the man. "Are you afraid of courts?" he growled.

"No," said the southerner, "I am afraid of nothing but the penitentiary."

"Then," said Mason, leaning over on the table, "listen to me, and you will never see the shadow of it."

IV.

"I suppose you are right about that," said Jacob Wade, the newly elected sheriff of Gullmore county, as he and Colonel Moseby Allen sat in the office of that shrewd and courteous official. "I suppose it makes no difference which one of us takes this money and pays the contractors,—we are both under good bonds, you know."

"Certainly, Wade, certainly," put in the Colonel, "your bond is as good as they can be made in Gullmore county, and I mean no disrespect to the Omnipotent Ruler of the Universe when I assert that the whole kingdom of heaven could not give a better bond than I have. You are right, Wade; you are always right; you are away ahead of the ringleaders of your party. I don't mind if I do say so. Of course, I am on the other side, but it was miraculous, I tell you, the way you swung your forces into line in the last election. By all the limping gods of the calendar, we could not touch you!"

Colonel Moseby Allen leaned over and patted his companion on the shoulder. "You are a sly dog, Wade," he continued. "If it had not been for you we would have beaten the bluebells of Scotland out of the soft-headed farmers who were trying to run your party. I told the boys you would pull the whole ticket over with you, but they didn't believe me. Next time they will have more regard for the opinion of Moseby Allen of Gullmore." The Colonel burst out into a great roar of laughter, and brought his fat hand down heavily on his knee.

Jacob Wade, the new sheriff, was a cadaverous-looking

countryman, with a face that indicated honesty and egotism. He had come up from a farm, and had but little knowledge of business methods in general, and no idea of how the duties of his office should be properly performed. He puffed up visibly under the bald flattery of Allen, and took it all in like a sponge.

"Well," said Wade, "I suppose the boys did sort of expect me to help them over, and I guess I did. I have been getting ready to run for a long time, and I ain't been doing no fool things. When the Farmers Alliance people was organizing, I just stayed close home and sawed wood, and when the county was all stirred up about that there dog tax, I kept my mouth shut, and never said nothing."

"That's what you did, Wade," continued the Colonel, rubbing his hands; "you are too smooth to get yourself mixed up with a lot of new-fangled notions that would brand you all over the whole county as a crank. What a man wants in order to run for the office of sheriff is a reputation for being a square, solid, substantial business man, and that is what you had, Wade, and besides that you were a smooth, shrewd, far-sighted, machine politician."

Jacob Wade flushed and grew pompous under this eloquent recital of his alleged virtues. Allen was handling his man with skill. He was a natural judge of men, and possessed in no little degree the rare ability of knowing how to approach the individual in order to gain his confidence and good will.

"No," he went on, "I am not partisan enough to prevent me from appreciating a good clear-headed politician, no matter what his party affiliations may be. I am as firm and true to my principles as any of those high up in the affairs of state. I have been honored by my party time and again in the history of this commonwealth, and have defended and supported her policies on the stump, and in the halls of legislation, and I know a smooth man when I see him, and I honor him, and stick to him out of pure love for his intelligence and genius."

The Colonel arose. He now felt that his man was in the proper humor to give ready assent to the proposition which he had made, and he turned back to it with careless indifference.

"Now, Jacob," he said lowering his voice, "this is not all

talk. You are a new officer, and I am an old one. I am familiar with all the routine business of the sheriffalty, and I am ready and willing and anxious to give all the information that can be of any benefit to you, and to do any and everything in my power to make your term of office as pleasant and profitable as it can be made. I am wholly and utterly at your service, and want you to feel that you are more than welcome to command me in any manner you see fit. By the way, here is this matter that we were just discussing. I am perfectly familiar with all that business. I looked after the building for the county, collected all the previous levies, and know all about the contracts with the builders—just what is due each one and just how the settlements are to be made,—and I am willing to take charge of this fund and settle the thing up. I suppose legally it is my duty to attend to this work, as it is in the nature of unfinished business of my term, but I could have shifted the whole thing over on you and gotten out of the trouble of making the final settlements with the contractors. The levy was ordered during my term, but has been collected by you, and on that ground I could have washed my hands of the troublesome matter if I had been disposed to be ugly. But I am not that kind of a man, Wade; I am willing to shoulder my lawful duties, and wind this thing up and leave your office clear and free from any old matters."

Jacob Wade, sheriff of Gullmore county, was now thoroughly convinced of two things. First, that he himself was a shrewd politician, with an intellect of almost colossal proportions, and second, that Colonel Moseby Allen was a great and good man, who was offering to do him a service out of sheer kindness of heart.

He arose and seized Allen's hand. "I am obliged to you, Colonel, greatly obliged to you," he said; "I don't know much about these matters yet, and it will save me a deal of trouble if you will allow me to turn this thing over to you, and let you settle it up. I reckon from the standpoint of law it is a part of your old business as sheriff."

"Yes," answered Allen, smiling broadly, "I reckon it is, and I reckon I ought n't to shirk it."

"All right," said Wade, turning to leave the office, "I'll just hand the whole thing over to you in the morning." Then he went out.

The ex-sheriff closed the door, sat down in his chair, and put his feet on the table. "Well, Moseby, my boy," he said, "that was dead easy. The Honorable Jacob Wade is certainly the most irresponsible idiot west of the Alleghany mountains. He ought to have a committee,—yes, he ought to have two committees, one to run him, and one to run his business." Then he rubbed his hands gleefully. "It is working like a greased clock," he chuckled, "and by the grace of God and the Continental Congress, when this funeral procession does finally start, it won't be Colonel Moseby Allen of the county of Gullmore who will occupy the hearse."

V.

The inhabitants of the city could never imagine the vast interest aroused in the county of Gullmore by the trial of Colonel Moseby Allen for embezzlement. In all their quiet lives the good citizens had not been treated to such a sweeping tidal wave of excitement. The annual visits of the "greatest show on earth" were scarcely able to fan the interests of the countrymen into such a flame. The news of Allen's arrest had spread through the country like wildfire. Men had talked of nothing else from the moment this startling information had come to their ears. The crowds on Saturday afternoons at the country store had constituted themselves courts of first and last resort, and had passed on the matter of the ex-sheriff's guilt at great length and with great show of learning. The village blacksmith had delivered ponderous opinions while he shod the traveller's horse; and the ubiquitous justice of the peace had demonstrated time and again with huge solemnity that Moseby Allen was a great criminal, and by no possible means could be saved from conviction. It was the general belief that the ex-sheriff would not stand trial; that he would by some means escape from the jail where he was confined. So firm-rooted had this conviction become that the great crowd gathered in the little county seat on the day fixed for the trial were considerably astonished when they saw the ex-sheriff sitting in the dock. In the evening after the first day of the trail, in which certain wholly unexpected things had come to pass, the crowd gathered on the porch of the country hotel were fairly revelling in the huge sensation.

Duncan Hatfield, a long ungainly mountaineer, wearing a red hunting-shirt and a pair of blue jeans trousers, was evidently the Sir-Oracle of the occasion.

"I tell you, boys," he was saying, "old Moseby aint got no more show than a calliker apron in a brush fire. Why he jest laid down and give up; jest naturally lopped his ears and give up like a whipped dog."

"Yes," put in an old farmer who was standing a little back in the crowd, "I reckon nobody calkerlated on jest sich a fizzle."

"When he come into court this mornin'," continued the Oracle, "with that there young lawyer man Edwards, I poked Lum Bozier in the side, and told him to keep his eye skinned, and he would see the fur fly, because I knowed that Sam Lynch, the prosecutin' attorney, allowed to go fer old Moseby, and Sam is a fire-eater, so he is, and he aint afraid of nuthin that walks on legs. But, Jerusalem! it war the tamest show that ever come to this yer town. Edwards jest sot down and lopped over like a weed, and Sam he begun, and he showed up how old Moseby had planned this here thing, and how he had lied to Jake Wade all the way through, and jest how he got that there money, and what an everlasting old rascal he was, and there sot Edwards, and he never asked no questions, and he never paid no attention to nuthin."

"Did n't the lawyer feller do nuthin at all, Dunk?" enquired one of the audience, who had evidently suffered the great mistfortune of being absent from the trial.

"No," answered the Oracle, with a bovine sneer, "he never did nothin till late this evenin. Then he untangled his legs and got up and said somethin to the jedge about havin to let old Moseby Allen go, cause what he had done was n't no crime.

"Then you ought to a heard Sam. He jest naturally took the roof off; he sailed into old Moseby. He called him nine different kinds of horse-thieves, and when he got through, I could see old Ampe Props noddin his head back thar in the jury-box, and then I knowed that it were all up with Colonel Moseby Allen, cause that jury will go the way old Ampe goes, jest like a pack of sheep."

"I reckon Moseby's lawyer were skeered out," suggested Pooley Hornick, the blacksmith.

"I reckon he war," continued the Oracle, "cause when Sam sot down, he got up, and he said to the jedge that he didn't want to do no argufying, but he had a little paper that would show why the jedge would have to let old Moseby go free, and then he asked Sam if he wanted to see it, and Sam he said no, he cared nuthin for his little paper. Then the feller went over and give the little paper to the jedge, and the jedge he took it and he said he would decide in the mornin'."

"You don't reckon," said the farmer, "that the jedge will give the old colonel any show, do you?"

"Billdad Solsberry," said the Oracle, with a grave judicial air, as though to settle the matter beyond question, "you are a plumb fool. If the angel Gabriel war to drop down into Gullmore county, he couldn't keep old Moseby Allen from goin' to the penitentiary."

Thus the good citizens sat in judgment, and foretold the doom of their fellow.

VI.

On Monday night, the eleventh day of May, in the thirty-third year of the State of West Virginia, the judge of the criminal court of Gullmore county, and the judge of the circuit court of Gullmore county were to meet together for the purpose of deciding two matters,— one relating to the trial of Moseby Allen, the retiring sheriff, for embezzling funds of the county, amounting to thirty thousand dollars, and the other, an action pending in the circuit court, wherein the State of West Virginia, at the relation of Jacob Wade, was seeking to recover this sum from the bondsmen of Allen. In neither of the two cases was there any serious doubt as to the facts. It seemed that it was customary for the retiring sheriff to retain an office in the court building after the installation of his successor, and continue to attend to the unfinished business of the county until all his settlements had been made, and until all the matters relating to his term of office had been finally wound up and administered.

In accordance with this custom, Moseby Allen after the expiration of his term, had continued in his office in a quasi-official capacity, in order to collect back taxes and settle up all matters carried over from his regular term.

It appeared that during Allen's term of office the county had built a court-house, and had ordered certain levies for the purpose of raising the necessary funds. The first of the levies had been collected by Allen, and paid over by him to the contractors, as directed by the county court. The remaining levies had not been collected during his term, but had been collected by the new sheriff immediately after his installation. This money, amounting to some thirty thousand dollars, had been turned over to Allen upon his claim that it grew out of the unfinished affairs of his term, and that, therefore, he was entitled to its custody. He had said to the new sheriff that the levy upon which it had been raised was ordered during his term, and the work for which it was to be paid all performed, and the bonds of the county issued, while he was active sheriff, and that he believed it was a part of the matters which were involved in his final settlements. Jacob Wade, then sheriff, believing that Allen was in fact the proper person to rightly administer this fund, and knowing that his bond to the county was good and would cover all his official affairs, had turned the entire fund over to him, and paid no further attention to the matter.

It appeared that, at the end of the year, Moseby Allen had made all of his proper and legitimate settlements fully and satisfactorily, and had accounted to the proper authorities for every dollar that had been collected by him during his term of office, but had refused and neglected to account for the money which he had received from Wade. When approached upon the subject, he had said plainly that he had used this money in unfortunate speculations and could not return it. The man had made no effort to check the storm of indignation that burst upon him; he firmly refused to discuss the matter, or to give any information in regard to it. When arrested, he had expressed no surprise, and had gone to the jail with the officer. At the trial, his attorney had simply waited until the evidence had been introduced, and had then arisen and moved the court to direct a verdict of not guilty, on the ground that Allen, upon the facts shown, had committed no crime punishable under the statutes of West Virginia.

The court had been strongly disposed to overrule this motion without stopping to consider it, but the attorney had insisted that a memorandum which he handed up would sustain his position, and that without mature consideration the judge ought not force him into the superior court, whereupon his Honor, Ephraim Haines, had taken the matter under advisement until morning.

In the circuit court the question had been raised that Allen's bond covered only those matters which arose by virtue of his office, and that this fund was not properly included. Whereupon the careful judge of that court had adjourned to consider.

It was almost nine o'clock when the Honorable Ephraim Haines walked into the library to consult with his colleague of the civil court. He found that methodical jurist seated before a pile of reports, with his spectacles far out on the end of his nose,—an indication, as the said Haines well knew, that the said jurist had arrived at a decision, and was now carefully turning it over in his mind in order to be certain that it was in spirit and truth the very law of the land.

"Well, Judge," said Haines, "have you flipped the penny on it, and if so, who wins?"

The man addressed looked up from his book and removed his spectacles. He was an angular man, with a grave analytical face.

"It is not a question of who wins, Haines," he answered; "it is a question of law. I was fairly satisfied when the objection was first made, but I wanted to be certain before I rendered my decision. I have gone over the authorities, and there is no question about the matter. The bondsmen of Allen are not liable in this action."

"They are not!" said Haines, dropping his long body down

into a chair. "It is public money, and the object of the bond is certainly to cover any defalcations."

"This bond," continued the circuit judge, "provides for the faithful discharge, according to law, of the duties of the office of sheriff during his continuance in said office. Moseby Allen ceased to be sheriff of this county the day his successor was installed, and on that day this bond ceased to cover his acts. This money was handed over by the lawful sheriff to a man who was not then an officer of this county. Moseby Allen had no legal right to the custody of this money. His duties as sheriff had ceased, his official acts had all determined, and there was no possible way whereby he could then perform an official act that would render his bondsmen liable. The action pending must be dismissed. The present sheriff, Wade, is the one responsible to the county for this money. His only recourse is an action of debt, or assumpsit, against Allen individually, and as Allen is notoriously insolvent, Wade and his bondsmen will have to make up this deficit."

"Well," said Haines, "that is hard luck."

"No," answered the judge, "it is not luck at all, it is the law. Wade permitted himself to be the dupe of a shrewd knave, and he must bear the consequences."

"You can depend upon it," said the Honorable Ephraim Haines, criminal judge by a political error, "that old Allen won't get off so easy with me. The jury will convict him, and I will land him for the full term."

"I was under the impression," said the circuit judge, gravely, "that a motion had been made in your court to direct an acquittal on the ground that no crime had been committed."

"It was," said Haines, "but of course it was made as a matter of form, and there is nothing in it."

"Have you considered it?"

"What is the use? It is a fool motion."

"Well," continued the judge, "this matter comes up from your court to mine on appeal, and you should be correct in your ruling. What authorities were cited?"

"Here is the memorandum," said the criminal judge, "you can run down the cases if you want to, but I know it is no use.

The money belonged to the county and old Allen embezzled it,—that is admitted."

To this the circuit judge did not reply. He took the memorandum which Randolph Mason had prepared for Allen, and which the local attorney had submitted, and turned to the cases of reports behind him. He was a hard-working, conscientious man, and not least among his vexatious cares were the reckless decisions of the Honorable Ephraim Haines.

The learned judge of the criminal court put his feet on the table and began to whistle. When at length wearied of this intellectual diversion, he concentrated all the energy of his mammoth faculties on the highly cultured pastime of sharpening his penknife on the back of the Code.

At length the judge of the circuit court came back to the table, sat down, and adjusted his spectacles. "Haines," he said slowly, "you will have to sustain that motion."

"What!" cried the Honorable Ephraim, bringing the legs of his chair down on the floor with a bang.

"That motion," continued the judge, "must be sustained. Moseby Allen has committed no crime under the statutes of West Virginia."

"Committed no crime!" almost shouted the criminal jurist, doubling his long legs up under his chair, "why, old Allen admits that he got this money and spent it. He says that he converted it to his own use; that it was not his money; that it belonged to the county. The evidence of the State shows that he cunningly induced Wade to turn this money over to him, saying that his bond was good, and that he was entitled to the custody of the fund. The old rascal secured the possession of this money by trickery, and kept it, and now you say he has committed no crime. How in Satan's name do you figure it out?"

"Haines," said the judge, gravely, "I don't figure it out. The law cannot be figured out. It is certain and exact. It describes perfectly what wrongs are punishable as crimes, and exactly what elements must enter into each wrong in order to make it a crime. All right of discretion is taken from the trial court; the judge must abide by the law, and the law decides matters of this nature in no uncertain terms."

"Surely," interrupted Haines, beginning to appreciate the gravity of the situation, "old Allen can be sent to the penitentiary for this crime. He is a rank, out and out embezzler. He stole this money and converted it to his own use. Are you going to say that the crime of embezzlement is a dead letter?"

"My friend," said the judge, "you forget that there is no equity in the criminal courts. The crime of embezzlement is a pure creature of the statute. Under the old common law there was no such crime. Consequently society had no protection from wrongs of this nature, until this evil grew to such proportions that the law-making power began by statute to define this crime and provide for its punishment. The ancient English statutes were many and varied, and, following in some degree thereafter, each of the United States has its own particular statute, describing that crime as being composed of certain fixed technical elements. This indictment against Moseby Allen is brought under Section 19 of Chapter 145 of the code of West Virginia, which provides: 'If any officer, agent, clerk or servant of this State, or of any county, district school district or municipal corporation thereof, or of any incorporated bank or other corporation, or any officer of public trust in this State, or any agent, clerk or servant of such officer of public trust, or any agent, clerk or servant of any firm or person, or company or association of persons not incorporated, embezzle or fraudulently convert to his own use, bullion, money, bank notes or other security for money, or any effects or property of another person which shall have come to his possession, or been placed under his care or management, by virtue of his office, place or employment, he shall be guilty of larceny thereof.'

"This is the statute describing the offence sought to be charged. All such statutes must be strictly construed. Applying these requisites of the crime to the case before us, we find that Allen cannot be convicted, for the reason that at the time this money was placed in his hands he was not sheriff of Gullmore county, nor was he in any sense its agent, clerk, or servant. And, second, if he could be said to continue an agent, clerk, or servant of this county, after the expiration of his term, he would continue such agent, clerk, or servant for the purpose only of administering those matters which might be said to lawfully pertain to the unfinished business of his office. This fund was in no wise connected with such unfinished affairs, and by no possible construction could he be said to be an agent, clerk, or servant of this county for the purpose of its distribution or custody. Again, in order to constitute such embezzlement, the money must have come into his possession by virtue of his office. This could not be, for the reason that he held no office. His time had expired; Jacob Wade was sheriff, and the moment Jacob Wade was installed, Allen's official capacity determined, and he became a private citizen, with only the rights and liabilities of such a citizen.

"Nor is he guilty of larceny, for the very evident reason that the proper custodian, Wade, voluntarily placed this money in his hands, and he received it under a *bona fide* color of right."

The Honorable Ephraim Haines arose, and brought his ponderous fist down violently on the table. "By the Eternal!" he said, "this is the cutest trick that has been played in the two Virginias for a century. Moseby Allen has slipped out of the clutches of the law like an eel."

"Ephraim," said the circuit judge, reproachfully, "this is no frivolous matter. Moseby Allen has wrought a great wrong, by which many innocent men will suffer vast injury, perhaps ruin. Such malicious cunning is dangerous to society. Justice cannot reach all wrongs; its hands are tied by the restrictions of the law. Why, under this very statute, one who was *de facto* an officer of the county or State, by inducing some other officer to place in his hands funds to which he was not legally entitled, could appropriate the funds so received with perfect impunity, and without committing any crime of rendering his bondsmen liable. Thus a clerk of the circuit court could use without criminal liability any money, properly belonging to the clerk of the county court, or sheriff, provided he could convince the clerk or sheriff that he was entitled to its custody; and so with any officer of the State or county, and this could be done with perfect ease where the officers were well known to each other and strict business methods were not observed. Hence all the great wrong and injury of embezzlement can be committed, and all the gain and profit of it be secured, without violating the statute or rendering the officer liable to criminal prosecution. It would seem that the rogue must be stupid indeed who could not evade the crime of embezzlement."

The man stopped, removed his spectacles, and closed them up in their case. He was a painstaking, honest servant of the commonwealth, and, like many others of the uncomplaining strong, performed his own duties and those of his careless companion without murmur or comment or hope of reward.

The Honorable Ephraim Haines arose and drew himself up pompously. "I am glad," he said, "that we agree on this matter. I shall sustain this motion."

The circuit judge smiled grimly. "Yes," he said, "it is not reason or justice, but it is the law."

VII.

At twelve the following night Colonel Moseby Allen, ex-sheriff of the county of Gullmore, now acquitted of crime by the commonwealth, hurried across the border for the purpose of avoiding certain lawless demonstrations on the part of his countrymen,—and of all his acts of public service, this was the greatest.

1897

The Episode of the Mexican Seer

GRANT ALLEN

My name is Seymour Wilbraham Wentworth. I am brother-in-law and secretary to Sir Charles Vandrift, the South African millionaire and famous financier. Many years ago, when Charlie Vandrift was a small lawyer in Cape Town, I had the (qualified) good fortune to marry his sister. Much later, when the Vandrift estate and farm near Kimberley developed by degrees into the Cloetedorp Golcondas, Limited, my brother-in-law offered me the not unremunerative post of secretary; in which capacity I have ever since been his constant and attached companion.

He is not a man whom any common sharper can take in, is Charles Vandrift. Middle height, square build, firm mouth, keen eyes—the very picture of a sharp and successful business genius. I have only known one rogue impose upon Sir Charles, and that one rogue, as the Commissary of Police at Nice remarked, would doubtess have imposed upon a syndicate of Vidocq, Robert Houdin, and Cagliostro.

We had run across to the Riviera for a few weeks in the season. Our object being strictly rest and recreation from the arduous duties of financial combination, we did not think it necessary to take our wives out with us. Indeed, Lady Vandrift is absolutely wedded to the joys of London, and does not appreciate the rural delights of the Mediterranean littoral. But Sir Charles and I, though immersed in affairs when at home, both thoroughly enjoy the complete change from the City to the charming vegetation and pellucid air on the terrace at Monte

Carlo. We *are* so fond of scenery. That delicious view over the rocks of Monaco, with the Maritime Alps in the rear, and the blue sea in front, not to mention the imposing Casino in the foreground, appeals to me as one of the most beautiful prospects in all Europe. Sir Charles has a sentimental attachment for the place. He finds it restores and refreshes him, after the turmoil of London, to win a few hundred at roulette in the course of an afternoon among the palms and cactuses and pure breezes of Monte Carlo. The country, say I, for a jaded intellect! However, we never on any account actually stop in the Principality itself. Sir Charles thinks Monte Carlo is not a sound address for a financier's letters. He prefers a comfortable hotel on the Promenade des Anglais at Nice, where he recovers health and renovates his nervous system by taking daily excursions along the coast to the Casino.

This particular season we were snugly ensconced at the Hotel des Anglais. We had capital quarters on the first floor— salon, study, and bedrooms—and found on the spot a most agreeable cosmopolitan society. All Nice, just then, was ringing with talk about a curious imposter, known to his followers as the Great Mexican Seer, and supposed to be gifted with second sight, as well as with endless other supernatural powers. Now, it is a peculiarity of my able brother-in-law's that, when he meets with a quack, he burns to expose him; he is so keen a man of business himself that it gives him, so to speak, a disinterested pleasure to unmask and detect imposture in others. Many ladies at the hotel, some of whom had met and conversed with the Mexican Seer, were constantly telling us strange stories of his doings. He had disclosed to one the present whereabouts of a runaway husband; he had pointed out to another the numbers that would win at roulette next evening; he had shown a third the image on a screen of the man she had for years adored without his knowledge. Of course, Sir Charles didn't believe a word of it; but his curiosity was roused; he wished to see and judge for himself of the wonderful thought-reader.

'What would be his terms, do you think, for a private *séance*?' he asked of Madame Picardet, the lady to whom the Seer had successfully predicted the winning numbers.

'He does not work for money,' Madame Picardet answered, 'but for the good of humanity. I'm sure he would gladly come and exhibit for nothing his miraculous faculties.'

'Nonsense!' Sir Charles answered. 'The man must live. I'd pay him five guineas, though, to see him alone. What hotel is he stopping at?'

'The Cosmopolitan, I think,' the lady answered. 'Oh no; I remember now, the Westminister.'

Sir Charles turned to me quietly. 'Look here, Seymour,' he whispered. 'Go round to this fellow's place immediately after dinner, and offer him five pounds to give a private *séance* at once in my rooms, without mentioning who I am to him; keep the name quite quiet. Bring him back with you, too, and come straight upstairs with him, so that there may be no collusion. We'll see just how much the fellow can tell us.'

I went as directed. I found the Seer a very remarkable and interesting person. He stood about Sir Charles's own height, but was slimmer and straighter, with an aquiline nose, strangely piercing eyes, very large black pupils, and a finely chiselled close-shaven face, like the bust of Antinous in our hall in Mayfair. What gave him his most characteristic touch, however, was his odd head of hair, curly and wavy like Paderewski's, standing out in a halo round his high white forehead and his delicate profile. I could see at a glance why he succeeded so well in impressing women; he had the look of a poet, a singer, a prophet.

'I have come round,' I said, 'to ask whether you will consent to give a *séance* at once in a friend's rooms; and my principal wishes me to add that he is prepared to pay five pounds as the price of the entertainment.'

Señor Antonio Herrera—that was what he called himself—bowed to me with impressive Spanish politeness. His dusky olive cheeks were wrinkled with a smile of gentle contempt as he answered gravely—

'I do not sell my gifts; I bestow them freely. If your friend—your anonymous friend—desires to behold the cosmic wonders that are wrought through my hands, I am glad to show them to him. Fortunately, as often happens when it is necessary to convince and confound a sceptic (for that your friend is a sceptic I feel instinctively), I chance to have no engagements at all this evening.' He ran his hand through his fine, long hair reflectively. 'Yes, I go,' he continued, as if addressing some unknown presence that hovered about the ceiling; 'I go; come with me!' Then he put on his broad sombrero, with its crimson ribbon, wrapped a cloak round his shoulders, lighted a cigarette, and strode forth by my side towards the Hotel des Anglais.

He talked little by the way, and that little in curt sentences. He seemed buried in deep thought; indeed, when we reached the door and I turned in, he walked a step or two farther on, as if not noticing to what place I had brought him. Then he drew himself up short, and gazed around him for a moment. 'Ha, the Anglais,' he said—and I may mention in passing that his English, in spite of a slight southern accent, was idiomatic and excellent. 'It is here, then; it is here!' He was addressing once more the unseen presence.

I smiled to think that these childish devices were intended to deceive Sir Charles Vandrift. Not quite the sort of man (as the City of London knows) to be taken in by hocus-pocus. And all this, I saw, was the cheapest and most commonplace conjurer's patter.

We went upstairs to our rooms. Charles had gathered together a few friends to watch the performance. The Seer entered, wrapt in thought. He was in evening dress, but a red sash round his waist gave a touch of picturesqueness and a dash of colour. He paused for a moment in the middle of the salon, without letting his eyes rest on anybody or anything. Then he walked straight up to Charles, and held out his dark hand.

'Good evening,' he said. 'You are the host. My soul's sight tells me so.'

'Good shot,' Sir Charles answered. 'These fellows have to be quick-witted, you know, Mrs Mackenzie, or they'd never get on at it.'

The Seer gazed about him, and smiled blankly at a person or two whose faces he seemed to recognize from a previous existence. Then Charles began to ask him a few simple questions, not about himself, but about me, just to test him. He answered most of them with surprising correctness. 'His name? His name begins with an S I think—you call him Seymour.' He paused long between each clause, as if the facts were revealed to him slowly. 'Seymour—Wilbraham—Earl of Strafford. No, not Earl of Strafford! Seymour Wilbraham Wentworth. There seems to be some connection in somebody's mind now present between Wentworth and Strafford. I am not English. I do not know what it means. But they are somehow the same name, Wentworth and Strafford.'

He gazed around, apparently for confirmation. A lady came to his resuce.

'Wentworth was the surname of the great Earl of Strafford,' she murmured gently; 'and I was wondering, as you spoke, whether Mr Wentworth might possibly be descended from him.'

'He is,' the Seer replied instantly, with a flash of those dark eyes. And I thought this curious; for though my father always maintained the reality of the relationship, there was one link wanting to complete the pedigree. He could not make sure that the Hon. Thomas Wilbraham Wentworth was the father of Jonathan Wentworth, the Bristol horsedealer, from whom we are descended.

'Where was I born?' Sir Charles interrupted, coming suddenly to his own case.

The Seer clapped his two hands to his forehead and held it between them, as if to prevent it from bursting. 'Africa', he said slowly, as the facts narrowed down, so to speak. 'South Africa; Cape of Good Hope; Jansenville; De Witt Street. 1840.'

'By jove, he's correct,' Sir Charles muttered. 'He seems really to do it. Still, he may have found me out. He may have known where he was coming.'

'I never gave a hint,' I answered; 'till he reached the door, he didn't even know to what hotel I was piloting him.'

The Seer stroked his chin softly. His eye appeared to me to have a furtive gleam in it. 'Would you like me to tell you the number of a bank-note inclosed in an envelope?' he asked casually.

'Go out of the room,' Sir Charles said, 'while I pass it round the company.'

Señor Herrera disappeared. Sir Charles passed it round cautiously, holding it all the time in his own hand, but letting his guests see the number. Then he placed it in an envelope and gummed it down firmly.

The Seer returned. His keen eyes swept the company with a comprehensive glance. He shook his shaggy mane. Then he took the envelope in his hands and gazed at it fixedly. 'AF, 73549,' he answered, in a slow tone. 'A Bank of England note for fifty pounds—exchanged at the Casino for gold won yesterday at Monte Carlo.'

'I see how he did that,' Sir Charles said triumphantly. 'He must have changed it there himself; and then I changed it back again. In point of fact, I remember seeing a fellow with long hair loafing about. Still, it's capital conjuring.'

'He can see through matter,' one of the ladies interposed. It was Madame Picardet. 'He can see through a box.' She drew a little gold vinaigrette, such as our grandmothers used, from her dress-pocket. 'What is in this?' she inquired, holding it up to him.

Señor Herrera gazed through it. 'Three gold coins,' he replied, knitting his brows with the effort of seeing into the box: 'one, an American five dollars; one, a French ten-franc piece; one, twenty marks, German, of the old Emperor William.'

She opened the box and pased it round. Sir Charles smiled a quiet smile.

'Confederacy!' he muttered, half to himself. 'Confederacy!'

The Seer turned to him with a sullen air. 'You want a better sign?' he said, in a very impressive voice. 'A sign that will convince you! Very well: you have a letter in your left waistcoat pocket—a crumpled-up letter. Do you wish me to read it out? I will, if you desire it.'

It may seem to those who know Sir Charles incredible, but, I am bound to admit, my brother-in-law coloured. What that letter contained I cannot say; he only answered, very testily and evasively. 'No, thank you; I won't trouble you. The exhibition you have already given us of your skill in this kind more than amply suffices.' And his fingers strayed nervously to his waistcoat pocket, as if he was half afraid, even then, Señor Herrera would read it.

I fancied too, he glanced somewhat anxiously towards Madame Picardet.

The Seer bowed courteously. 'Your will, señor, is law,' he said. 'I make it a principle, though I can see through all things, invariably to respect the secrecies and sanctities. If it were not so, I might dissolve society. For which of us is it there who could bear the whole truth being told about him?' He gazed around the room. An unpleasant thrill supervened. Most of us felt this uncanny Spanish American knew really too much. And some of us were engaged in financial operations.

'For example,' the Seer continued blandly, 'I happened a few weeks ago to travel down here from Paris by train with a very intelligent man, a company promoter. He had in his bag some documents—some confidential documents:' he glanced at Sir Charles. 'You know the kind of thing, my dear sir: reports from experts—from mining engineers. You may have seen some such; marked *strictly private*.'

'They form an element in high finance,' Sir Charles admitted coldly.

'Pre-cisely,' the Seer murmured, his accent for a moment less Spanish than before. 'And, as they were marked *strictly private*, I respect, of course, the seal of confidence. That's all I wish to say. I hold it a duty, being intrusted with such powers, not to use them in a manner which may annoy or incommode my fellow creatures.'

'Your feeling does you honour,' Sir Charles answered with some acerbity. Then he whispered in my ear: 'Confounded clever scoundrel, Sey; rather wish we hadn't brought him here.'

Señor Herrera seemed intuitively to divine this wish, for he interposed, in a lighter and gayer tone—

'I will now show you a different and more interesting embodiment of occult power, for which we shall need a somewhat subdued arrangement of surrounding lights. Would you mind, señor host—for I have purposely abstained from reading your name on the brain of any one present—would you mind my turning down this lamp just a little? . . . So! That will do. Now, this one; and this one. Exactly! that's right.' He poured a few grains of powder out of a packet into a saucer. 'Next, a match, if you please. Thank you!' It burnt with a strange green light. He drew from his pocket a card, and produced a little ink-bottle. 'Have you a pen?' he asked.

I instantly brought one. He handed it to Sir Charles. 'Oblige me,' he said, 'by writing your name there.' And he indicated a place in the centre of the card, which had an embossed edge, with a small middle square of a different colour.

Sir Charles has a natural disinclination to signing his name without knowing why. 'What do you want with it?' he asked. (A millionaire's signature has so many uses.)

'I want you to put the card in an envelope,' the Seer replied, 'and then to burn it. After that, I shall show you your own name written in letters of blood on my arm, in your own handwriting.'

Sir Charles took the pen. If the signature was to be burned as soon as finished, he didn't mind giving it. He wrote his name in his usual firm clear style—the writing of a man who knows his worth and is not afraid of drawing a cheque for five thousand.

'Look at it long,' the Seer said, from the other side of the room. He had not watched him write it.

Sir Charles stared at it fixedly. The Seer was really beginning to produce an impression.

'Now, put it in that envelope,' the Seer exclaimed.

Sir Charles, like a lamb, placed it as directed.

The Seer strode forward. 'Give me the envelope,' he said. He took it in his hand, walked over towards the fireplace, and solemnly burnt it. 'See—it crumbles into ashes,' he cried. Then he came back to the middle of the room, close to the green light, rolled up his sleeve, and held his arm before Sir Charles. There, in blood-red letters, my brother-in-law read the name, 'Charles Vandrift,' in his own handwriting!

'I see how that's done,' Sir Charles murmured, drawing back. 'It's a clever delusion; but still, I see through it. It's like that ghost-book. Your ink was deep green; your light was green; you made me look at it long; and then I saw the same thing written on the skin of your arm in complementary colours.'

'You think so?' the Seer replied, with a curious curl of the lip.

'I'm sure of it,' Sir Charles answered.

Quick as lightning the Seer rolled up his sleeve. 'That's your name,' he cried, in a very clear voice, 'but not your whole name. What do you say, then, to my right? Is this one also a complementary colour?' He held his other arm out. There, in sea-green letters, I read the name, 'Charles O'Sullivan Vandrift.' It is my brother-in-law's full baptismal designation; but he has dropped the O'Sullivan for many years past, and, to say the truth, doesn't like it. He is a little bit ashamed of his mother's family.

Charles glanced at it hurriedly. 'Quite right,' he said, 'quite right!' But his voice was hollow. I could guess he didn't care to continue the *séance*. He could see through the man, of course; but it was clear the fellow knew too much about us to be entirely pleasant.

'Turn up the lights,' I said, and a servant turned them. 'Shall I say coffee and benedictine?' I whispered to Vandrift.

'By all means," he answered. 'Anything to keep this fellow from further impertinences! And, I say, don't you think you'd better suggest at the same time that the men should smoke? Even these ladies are not above a cigarette—some of them.'

There was sigh of relief. The lights burned brightly. The Seer for the moment retired from business, so to speak. He accepted a partaga with a very good grace, sipped his coffee in a corner, and chatted to the lady who had suggested Strafford with marked politeness. He was a polished gentleman.

Next morning, in the hall of the hotel, I saw Madame Picardet again, in a neat tailor-made travelling dress, evidently bound for the railway station.

'What, off, Madame Picardet?' I cried.

She smiled, and held out her prettily gloved hand. 'Yes, I'm off,' she answered archly. 'Florence, or Rome, or somewhere. I've drained Nice dry—like a sucked orange. Got all the fun I can out of it. Now I'm away again to gain my beloved Italy.'

But it struck me as odd that, if Italy was her game, she went by the omnibus which takes down to the *train de luxe* for Paris.

However, a man of the world accepts what a lady tells him, no matter how improbable; and I confess, for ten days or so, I thought no more about her, or the Seer either. At the end of that time our fortnightly pass-book came in from the bank in London. It is part of my duty, as the millionaire's secretary, to make up this book once a fortnight, and to compare the cancelled cheques with Sir Charles's counterfoils. On this particular occasion I happened to observe what I can only describe as a very grave discrepancy—in fact, a discrepancy of £5,000. On the wrong side, too. Sir Charles was debited with £5,000 more than the total amount that was shown on the counterfoils.

I examined the book with care. The source of the error was obvious. It lay in a cheque to Self or Bearer, for £5,000 signed by Sir Charles, and evidently paid across the counter in London, as it bore on its face no stamp or indication of any other office.

I called in my brother-in-law from the salon to the study. 'Look here, Charles,' I said, 'there's a cheque in the book which you haven't entered.' And I handed it to him without comment, for I thought it might have been drawn to settle some little loss on the turf or at cards, or to make up some other affair he didn't desire to mention to me. These things will happen.

He looked at it and stared hard. Then he pursed up his mouth and gave a long low 'Whew!' At last he turned it over and remarked, 'I say, Sey, my boy, we've just been done jolly well brown, haven't we?'

I glanced at the cheque. 'How do you mean?' I inquired.

'Why, the Seer,' he replied, still staring at it ruefully. 'I don't mind the five thou., but to think the fellow should have gammoned the pair of us like that—ignominious, I call it!'

'How do you know it's the Seer?' I asked.

'Look at the green ink,' he answered. 'Besides, I recollect the very shape of the last flourish. I flourished a bit like that in the excitement of the moment, which I don't always do with my regular signature.'

'He's done us,' I answered, recognising it. 'But how the dickens did he manage to transfer it to the cheque? This looks like your own handwriting, Charles, not a clever forgery.'

'It is,' he said. 'I admit it—I can't deny it. Only fancy him bamboozling me when I was most on my guard! I wasn't to be taken in by any of his silly occult tricks and catchwords; but it never occurred to me he was going to victimize me financially in this way. I expected attempts at a loan or an extortion; but to collar my signature to a blank cheque—atrocious!'

'How did he manage it?' I asked.

'I haven't the faintest conception. I only know those are the words I wrote. I could swear to them anywhere.'

'Then you can't protest the cheque?'

'Unfortunately, no; it's my own true signature.'

We went that afternoon without delay to see the Chief Commissary of Police at the office. He was a gentlemanly Frenchman, much less formal and red-tapey than usual, and he spoke excellent English with an American accent, having acted, in fact, as a detective in New York for about ten years in his early manhood.

'I guess,' he said slowly, after hearing our story, 'you've been victimized right here by Colonel Clay, gentlemen.'

'Who is Colonel Clay?' Sir Charles asked.

'That's just what I want to know,' the Commissary answered, in his curious American-French-English. 'He is a Colonel, because he occasionally gives himself a commission; he is called Colonel Clay, because he appears to possess an india-rubber face, and he can mould it like clay in the hands of the potter. Real name, unknown. Nationality, equally French and English. Address, usually Europe. Profession, former maker of wax figures to the Musée Grevin. Age, what he chooses. Employs his knowledge to mould his own nose and cheeks, with wax additions, to the character he desires to personate. Aquiline this time, you say. *Hein!* Anything like these photographs?'

He rummaged in his desk and handed us two.

'Not in the least,' Sir Charles answered. 'Except, perhaps, as to the neck, everything here is quite unlike him.'

'Then that's the Colonel!' the Commissary answered, with decision, rubbing his hands in glee. 'Look here,' and he took out a pencil and rapidly sketched the outline of one of the two faces—that of a bland-looking young man, with no expression worth mentioning. 'There's the Colonel in his simple disguise. Very good. Now watch me: figure to yourself that he adds here a tiny patch of wax to his nose—an aquiline bridge—just so; well, you have him right there; and the chin, ah, one touch: now, for hair, a wig: for complexion, nothing easier: that's the profile of your rascal, isn't it?'

'Exactly,' we both murmured. By two curves of the pencil, and a shock of false hair, the face was transmuted.

'He had very large eyes, with very big pupils, though,' I objected, looking close; 'and the man in the photograph here has them small and boiled-fishy.'

'That's so,' the Commissary answered. 'A drop of bella-donna expands—and produces the Seer; five grains of opium contract—and give a dead-alive, stupidly innocent appearance. Well, you leave this affair to me, gentlemen. I'll see the fun out. I don't say I'll catch him for you; nobody ever yet has caught Colonel Clay; but I'll explain how he did the trick; and that ought to be consolation enough to a man of your means for a trifle of five thousand!'

'You are not the conventional French office holder, M. le Commissaire,' I ventured to interpose.

'You bet!' the Commissary replied, and drew himself up like a captain of infantry. 'Messieurs,' he continued, in French, with the utmost dignity, 'I shall devote the resources of this office to tracing out the crime, and, if possible, to effectuating the arrest of the culpable.'

We telegraphed to London, of course, and we wrote to the bank, with a full description of the suspected person. But I need hardly add that nothing came of it.

Three days later the Commissary called at our hotel. 'Well, gentlemen,' he said, 'I am glad to say I have discovered everything!'

'What? Arrested the Seer?' Sir Charles cried.

The Commissary drew back, almost horrified at the sugges-tion.

'Arrested Colonel Clay?' he exclaimed. '*Mais*, monsieur, we are only human! Arrested him? No, not quite. But tracked out how he did it. That is already much—to unravel Colonel Clay, gentlemen!'

'Well, what do you make of it?' Sir Charles asked, crest-fallen.

The Commissary sat down and gloated over his discovery. It was clear a well-planned crime amused him vastly. 'In the first place, monsieur,' he said, 'disabuse your mind of the idea that when monsieur your secretary went out to fetch Señor Herrera that night, Señor Herrera didn't know to whose rooms he was coming. Quite otherwise, in point of fact. I do not doubt myself that Señor Herrera, or Colonel Clay (call him which you like), came to Nice this winter for no other purpose than just to rob you.'

'But I sent for him,' my brother-in-law interposed.

'Yes; he *meant* you to send for him. He forced a card, so to speak. If he couldn't do that I guess he would be a pretty poor conjurer. He had a lady of his own—his wife, let us say, or his sister—stopping here at this hotel; a certain Madame Picardet. Through her he induced several ladies of your circle to attend his *séances*. She and they spoke to you about him, and aroused your curiosity. You may bet your bottom dollar that when he came to this room he came ready primed and prepared with endless facts about both of you.'

'What fools we have been, Sey,' my brother-in-law exclaimed. 'I see it all now. That designing woman sent round before dinner to say I wanted to meet him; and by the time you got there he was ready for bamboozling me.'

'That's so,' the Commissary answered. 'He had your name ready painted on both his arms; and he had made other preparations of still greater importance.'

'You mean the cheque. Well, how did he get it?'

The Commissary opened the door. 'Come in,' he said. And a young man entered whom we recognized at once as the chief clerk in the Foreign Department of the Crédit Marseillais, the principal bank all along the Riviera.

'State what you know of this cheque,' the Commissary said, showing it to him, for we had handed it over to the police as a piece of evidence.

'About four weeks since—' the clerk began.

'Say ten days before your *séance*,' the Commissary interposed.

'A gentleman with very long hair and an aquiline nose, dark, strange, and handsome, called in at my department and asked if I could tell him the name of Sir Charles Vandrift's London banker. He said he had a sum to pay in to your credit, and asked if we would forward it for him. I told him it was irregular for us to receive the money, as you had no account with us, but that your London bankers were Darby, Drummond, and Rothenberg, Limited.'

'Quite right,' Sir Charles murmured.

'Two days later a lady, Madame Picardet, who was a customer of ours, brought in a good cheque for three hundred pounds, signed by a first-rate name, and asked us to pay it in on her behalf to Darby, Drummond, and Rothenberg's, and to open a London account with them for her. We did so, and received in reply a cheque-book.'

'From which this cheque was taken, as I learn from the number, by telegram from London,' the Commissary put in. 'Also, that on the same day on which your cheque was cashed, Madame Picardet, in London, withdrew her balance.'

'But how did the fellow get me to sign the cheque?' Sir Charles cried. 'How did he manage the card trick?'

The Commissary produced a similar card from his pocket. 'Was that the sort of thing?' he asked.

'Precisely! A facsimile.'

'I thought so. Well, our Colonel, I find, bought a packet of such cards, intended for admission to a religious function, at a shop in the Quai Masséna. He cut out the centre, and see here—' The Commissary turned it over, and showed a piece of paper pasted neatly over the back; this he tore off, and there, concealed behind it, lay a folded cheque, with only the place where the signature should be written showing through on the face which the Seer had presented to us. 'I call that a neat trick,' the Commissary remarked, with professional enjoyment of a really good deception.

'But he burnt the envelope before my eyes,' Sir Charles exclaimed.

'Pooh!' the Commissary answered. 'What would he be worth as a conjurer, anyway, if he couldn't substitute one envelope for another between the table and the fireplace without your noticing it? And Colonel Clay, you must remember, is a prince among conjurers.'

'Well, it's a comfort to know we've identified our man, and the woman who was with him,' Sir Charles said, with a slight sigh of relief. 'The next thing will be, of course, you'll follow them up on these clues in England and arrest them?'

The Commissary shrugged his shoulders. 'Arrest them!' he exclaimed, much amused. 'Ah, monsieur, but you are sanguine! No officer of justice has ever succeeded in arresting le Colonel Caoutchouc, as we call him in French. He is as slippery as an eel, that man. He wriggles through our fingers. Suppose even we caught him, what could we prove? I ask you. Nobody who has seen him once can ever swear to him again in his next impersonation. He is *impayable*, this good Colonel. On the day when I arrest him, I assure you, monsieur, I shall consider myself the smartest police officer in Europe.'

'Well, I shall catch him yet,' Sir Charles answered, and relapsed into silence.

1897

The Affair of the 'Avalanche Bicycle and Tyre Co., Limited'

ARTHUR MORRISON

I

Cycle companies were in the market everywhere. Immense fortunes were being made in a few days and sometimes little fortunes were being lost to build them up. Mining shares were dull for a season, and any company with the word 'cycle' or 'tyre' in its title was certain to attract capital, no matter what its prospects were like in the eyes of the expert. All the old private cycle companies suddenly were offered to the public, and their proprietors, already rich men, built themselves houses on the Riviera, bought yachts, ran racehorses, and left business for ever. Sometimes the shareholders got their money's worth, sometimes more, sometimes less—sometimes they got nothing but total loss; but still the game went on. One could never open a newspaper without finding, displayed at large, the prospectus of yet another cycle company with capital expressed in six figures at least, often in seven. Solemn old dailies, into whose editorial heads no new thing ever found its way till years after it had been forgotten elsewhere, suddenly exhibited the scandalous phenomenon of 'broken columns' in their advertising sections, and the universal prospectuses stretched outrageously across half or even all the page—a thing to cause apoplexy in the bodily system of any self-respecting manager of the old school.

In the midst of this excitement it chanced that the firm of

Dorrington & Hicks were engaged upon an investigation for the famous and long-established 'Indestructible Bicycle and Tricycle Manufacturing Company,' of London and Coventry. The matter was not one of sufficient intricacy or difficulty to engage Dorrington's personal attention, and it was given to an assistant. There was some doubt as to the validity of a certain patent having reference to a particular method of tightening the spokes and truing the wheels of a bicycle, and Dorrington's assistant had to make inquiries (without attracting attention to the matter) as to whether or not there existed any evidence, either documentary or in the memory of veterans, of the use of this method, or anything like it, before the year 1885. The assistant completed his inquiries and made his report to Dorrington. Now I think I have said that, from every evidence I have seen, the chief matter of Dorrington's solicitude was his own interest, and just at this time he had heard, as had others, much of the money being made in cycle companies. Also, like others, he had conceived a great desire to get the confidential advice of somebody 'in the know'—advice which might lead him into the 'good thing' desired by all the greedy who flutter about at the outside edge of the stock and share market. For this reason Dorrington determined to make this small matter of the wheel patent an affair of personal report. He was a man of infinite resource, plausibility and good-companionship, and there was money going in the cycle trade. Why then should he lose an opportunity of making himself pleasant in the inner groves of that trade, and catch whatever might come his way—information, syndicate shares, directorships, anything? So that Dorrington made himself master of his assistant's information, and proceeded to the head office of the 'Indestructible' company on Holborn Viaduct, resolved to become the entertaining acquaintance of the managing director.

On his way his attention was attracted by a very elaborately fitted cycle shop, which his recollection told him was new. 'The Avalanche Bicycle and Tyre Company' was the legend gilt above the great plate-glass window, and in the window itself stood many brilliantly enamelled and plated bicycles, each labelled on the frame with the flaming red and gold transfer of the firm; and in the midst of all was another bicycle covered with dried mud, of which, however, sufficient had been carefully cleared away to expose a similiar glaring transfer to those that decorated the rest—with a placard announcing that on this particular machine somebody had ridden some incredible distance on bad roads in very little more than no time at all. A crowd stood about the window and gaped respectfully at the placard, the bicycles, the transfers, and the mud, though they paid little attention to certain piles of folded white papers, endorsed in bold letters with the name of the company, with the suffix 'limited' and the word 'prospectus' in bloated black letters below. These, however, Dorrington observed at once, for he had himself that morning, in common with several thousand other people, received one by post. Also half a page of his morning paper had been filled with a copy of that same prospectus, and the afternoon had brought another copy in the evening paper. In the list of directors there was a titled name or two, together with a few unknown names—doubtless the 'practical men.' And below this list there were such positive promises of tremendous dividends, backed up and proved beyond dispute by such ingenious piles of businesslike figures, every line of figures referring to some other line for testimonials to its perfect genuineness and accuracy, that any reasonable man, it would seem, must instantly sell the hat off his head and the boots off his feet to buy one share at least, and so make his fortune for ever. True, the business was but lately established, but that was just it. It had rushed ahead with such amazing rapidity (as was natural with an avalanche) that it had got altogether out of hand, and orders couldn't be executed at all; wherefore the proprietors were reluctantly compelled to let the public have some of the luck. This was Thursday. The share list was to be opened on Monday morning and closed inexorably at four o'clock on Tuesday afternoon, with a merciful extension to Wednesday morning for the candidates for wealth who were so unfortunate as to live in the country. So that it behoved everybody to waste no time lest he be numbered among the unlucky whose subscription-money should be returned in full, failing allotment. The prospectus did not absolutely say it in so many words, but no rational person could fail to feel that the directors were fervently hoping that nobody would get injured in the rush.

Dorrington passed on and reached the well-known establishment of the 'Indestructible Bicycle Company.' This was already a limited company of a private sort, and had been so for ten years or more. And before that the concern had had eight or nine years of prosperous experience. The founder of the firm, Mr Paul Mallows, was now the managing director, and a great pillar of the cycling industry. Dorrington gave a clerk his card, and asked to see Mr Mallows.

Mr Mallows was out, it seemed, but Mr Stedman, the secretary, was in, and him Dorrington saw. Mr Stedman was a pleasant, youngish man, who had been a famous amateur bicyclist in his time, and was still an enthusiast. In ten minutes business was settled and dismissed, and Dorrington's tact had brought the secretary into a pleasant discursive chat, with much exchange of anecdote. Dorrington expressed much interest in the subject of bicycling, and, seeing that Stedman had been a racing man, particularly as to bicyling races.

'There'll be a rare good race on Saturday, I expect,' Stedman said. 'Or rather,' he went on, 'I expect the fifty miles record will go. I fancy our man Gillett is pretty safe to win, but he'll have to move, and I quite expect to see a good set of new records on our advertisements next week. The next best man is Lant—the new fellow, you know—who rides for the "Avalanche" people.'

'Let's see, they're going to the public as a limited company, aren't they?' Dorrington asked casually.

Stedman nodded, with a little grimace.

'You don't think it's a good thing, perhaps,' Dorrington said, noticing the grimace. 'Is that so?'

'Well,' Stedman answered, 'of course I can't say. I don't know much about the firm—nobody does, as far as I can tell—but they seem to have got a business together in almost no time; that is, if the business is as genuine as it looks at first sight. But they want a rare lot of capital, and then the prospectus—well, I've seen more satisfactory ones, you know. I don't say it isn't all right, of course, but still I shan't go out of my way to recommend any friends of mine to plunge on it.'

'You won't?'

'No, I won't. Though no doubt they'll get their capital, or most of it. Almost any cycle or tyre company can get subscribed just now. And this "Avalanche" affair is both, and it is well advertised, you know. Lant has been winning on their mounts just lately, and they've been booming it for all they're worth. By jove, if they could only screw him up to win the fifty miles on Saturday, and beat our man Gillett, that *would* give them a push! Just at the correct moment too. Gillett's never been beaten yet at the distance, you know. But Lant can't do it—though, as I have said, he'll make some fast riding—it'll be a race, I tell you.'

'I should like to see it.'

'Why not come? See about it, will you? And perhaps you'd like to run down to the track after dinner this evening and see our man training—awfully interesting, I can tell you, with all the pacing machinery and that. Will you come?'

Dorrington expressed himself delighted, and suggested that Stedman should dine with him before going to the track. Stedman, for his part, charmed with his new acquaintance—as everybody was at a first meeting with Dorrington—assented gladly.

At that moment the door of Stedman's room was pushed open and a well-dressed, middle-aged man, with a shaven, flabby face, appeared. 'I beg pardon,' he said, 'I thought you were alone. I've just ripped my finger against the handle of my brougham door as I came in—the screw sticks out. Have you a piece of sticking plaster?' He extended a bleeding finger as he spoke. Stedman looked doubtfully at his desk.

'Here is some court plaster,' Dorrington exclaimed, producing his pocket-book. 'I always carry it—it's handier than ordinary sticking plaster. How much do you want?'

'Thanks—an inch or so.'

'This is Mr. Dorrington, of Messrs. Dorrington & Hicks, Mr. Mallows,' Stedman said. 'Our managing director, Mr. Paul Mallows, Mr. Dorrington.'

Dorrington was delighted to make Mr. Mallows' acquaintance, and he busied himself with a careful strapping of the damaged finger. Mr. Mallows had the large frame of a man of strong build who had had much hard bodily work, but there hung about it the heavier, softer flesh that told of a later period of ease and sloth. 'Ah, Mr. Mallows,' Stedman said, 'the bicycle's the safest thing, after all! Dangerous things these broughams!'

'Ah, you younger men,' Mr. Mallows replied, with a slow and rounded enunciation, 'you younger men can afford to be active. We elders—'

'Can afford a brougham,' Dorrington added, before the managing director began the next word. 'Just so—and the bicycle does it all; wonderful thing the bicycle!'

Dorrington had not misjudged his man, and the oblique reference to his wealth flattered Mr. Mallows. Dorrington went once more through his report as to the spoke patent, and then Mr. Mallows bade him good-bye.

'Good day, Mr. Dorrington, good day,' he said. 'I am extremely obliged by your careful personal attention to this matter of the patent. We may leave it with Mr. Stedman now, I think. Good day. I hope soon to have the pleasure of meeting you again.' And with clumsy stateliness Mr. Mallows vanished.

2

'So you don't think the "Avalanche" good business as an investment?' Dorrington said once more as he and Stedman, after an excellent dinner, were cabbing it to the track.

'No, no,' Stedman answered, 'don't touch it! There's better things than that coming along presently. Perhaps I shall be able to put you in for something, you know, a bit later; but don't be in a hurry. As to the "Avalanche," even if everything else were satisfactory, there's too much "booming" being done just now to please me. All sorts of rumours, you know, of their having something "up their sleeve," and so on; mysterious hints in the papers, and all that, as to something revolutionary being in hand with the "Avalanche" people. Perhaps there is. But why they don't fetch it out in view of the public subscription for shares is more than I can understand, unless they don't want too much of a rush. And as to that, well they don't look like modestly shrinking from anything of that sort up to the present.'

They were at the track soon after seven o'clock, but Gillett was not yet riding. Dorrington remarked that Gillett appeared to begin late.

'Well,' Stedman explained, 'he's one of those fellows that afternoon training doesn't seem to suit, unless it is a bit of walking exercise. He just does a few miles in the morning and a spurt or two, and then he comes on just before sunset for a fast ten or fifteen miles—that is, when he is getting fit for such a race as Saturday's. Tonight will be his last spin of that length before Saturday, because tomorrow will be the day before the race. Tomorrow he'll only go a spurt or two, and rest most of the day.'

They strolled about inside the track, the two highly 'banked' ends whereof seemed to a near-sighted person in the centre to be solid erect walls, along the face of which the training riders skimmed, fly-fashion. Only three or four persons beside themselves were in the enclosure when they first came, but in ten minutes' time Mr. Paul Mallows came across the track.

'Why,' said Stedman to Dorrington, 'here's the Governor! It isn't often he comes down here. But I expect he's anxious to see how Gillett's going, in view of Saturday.'

'Good evening, Mr. Mallows,' said Dorrington. 'I hope the finger's all right? Want any more plaster?'

'Good evening, good evening,' responded Mr. Mallows heavily. 'Thank you, the finger's not troubling me a bit.' He held it up, still decorated by the black plaster. 'Your plaster remains, you see—I was a little careful not to fray it too much in washing, that was all.' And Mr. Mallows sat down on a light iron garden chair (of which several stood here and there in the enclosure) and began to watch the riding.

The track was clear, and dusk was approaching when at last the great Gillett made his appearance on the track. He answered a friendly question or two put to him by Mallows and Stedman, and then, giving his coat to his trainer, swung off along the track on his bicycle, led in front by a tandem and closely attended by a triplet. In fifty yards his pace quickened, and he settled down into a swift even pace, regular as clockwork. Sometimes the tandem and sometimes the triplet went to the front, but Gillett neither checked nor heeded as, nursed by his pacers, who were directed by the trainer from the centre, he swept along mile after mile, each mile in but a few seconds over the two minutes.

'Look at the action!" exclaimed Stedman with enthusiasm. 'Just watch him. Not an ounce of power wasted there! Did you ever see more regular ankle work? And did anybody ever sit a machine quite so well as that? Show me a movement anywhere above the hips!"

'Ah,' said Mr. Mallows, 'Gillett has a wonderful style—a wonderful style, really!'

The men in the enslosure wandered about here and there on the grass, watching Gillett's riding as one watched the performance of a great piece of art—which, indeed, was what Gillett's riding was. There were, besides Mallows, Stedman, Dorrington and the trainer, two officials of the Cyclists' Union, an amateur racing man named Sparks, the track superintendent and another man. The sky grew darker, and gloom fell about the track. The machines become invisible, and little could be seen of the riders across the ground but the row of rhythmically working legs and the white cap that Gillett wore. The trainer had just told Stedman that there would be three fast laps and then his man would come off the track.

'Well, Mr. Stedman,' said Mr. Mallows, 'I think we shall be all right for Saturday.'

'Rather!' answered Stedman confidently. 'Gillett's going great guns, and steady as a watch!'

The pace now suddenly increased. The tandem shot once more to the front, the triplet hung on the rider's flank, and the group of swishing wheels flew round the track at a 'one-fifty' gait. The spectators turned about, following the riders round the track with their eyes. And then, swinging into the straight from the top end, the tandem checked suddenly and gave a little jump. Gillett crashed into it from behind, and the triplet, failing to clear, wavered and swung, and crashed over and along the track too. All three machines and six men were involved in one complicated smash.

Everybody rushed across the grass, the trainer first. Then the cause of the disaster was seen. Lying on its side on the track, with men and bicycles piled over and against it, was one of the green painted light iron garden chairs that had been standing in the enclosure. The triplet men were struggling to their feet, and though much cut and shaken, seemed the least hurt of the lot. One of the men of the tandem was insensible, and Gillett, who from his position had got all the worst of it, lay senseless too, badly cut and bruised, and his left arm was broken.

The trainer was cursing and tearing his hair. 'If I knew who'd done this,' Stedman cried, 'I'd *pulp* him with that chair!'

'Oh, that betting, that betting!' wailed Mr. Mallows, hopping about distractedly; 'see what it leads people into doing! It can't have been an accident, can it?'

'Accident? Skittles! A man doesn't put a chair on a track in the dark and leave it there by accident. Is anybody getting away there from the outside of the track?'

'No, there's nobody. He wouldn't wait till this; he'd clear off a minute ago and more. Here, Fielders! Shut the outer gate, and we'll see who's about.'

But there seemed to be no suspicious character. Indeed, except for the ground-man, his boy, Gillett's trainer, and a racing man, who had just finished dressing in the pavilion, there seemed to be nobody about beyond those whom everybody had seen standing in the enclosure. But there had been ample time for anybody, standing unnoticed at the outer rails, to get across the track in the dark, just after the riders had passed, place the obstruction, and escape before the completion of the lap.

The damaged men were helped or carried into the pavilion, and the damaged machines were dragged after them. 'I will give fifty pounds gladly—more, a hundred,' said Mr. Mallows, excitedly, 'to anybody who will find out who put the chair on the track. It might have ended in murder. Some wretched bookmaker, I suppose, who has taken to many bets on Gillett. As I've said a thousand times, betting is the curse of all sport nowadays.'

'The governor excites himself a great deal about betting and bookmakers," Stedman said to Dorrington, as they walked towards the pavilion, 'but, between you and me, I believe some of the "Avalanche" people are in this. The betting bee is always in Mallows' bonnet, but as a matter of fact there's very little betting at all on cycle races, and what there is is little more than a matter of half-crowns or at most half-sovereigns on the day of the race. No bookmaker ever makes a heavy book first. Still there *may* be something in it this time, of course. But look at the "Avalanche" people. With Gillett away their man can certainly win on Saturday, and if only the weather keeps fair he can almost as certainly beat the record; just at present the fifty miles is fairly easy, and it's bound to go soon. Indeed, our intention was that Gillett should pull it down on Saturday. He was a safe winner, bar accidents, and it was good odds on his altering the record, if the weather were any good at all. With Gillett out of it Lant is just about as certain a winner as our man would be if all were well. And there would be a boom for the "Avalanche" company, on the very eve of the share subscription! Lant, you must know, was very second-rate till this season, but he has improved wonderfully in the last month or two, since he has been with the "Avalanche" people. Let him win, and they can point to the machine as responsible for it all. "Here," they will say in effect, "is a man who could rarely get in front, even in second-class company, till he rode an 'Avalanche'. Now he eats the world's record for fifty miles on it, and makes rings round the topmost professionals!" Why, it will be worth thousands of capital to them. Of course the subscription of capital won't hurt us, but the loss of the record may, and to have Gillett knocked out like this in the middle of the season is serious.'

'Yes, I suppose with you it is more than a matter of this one race.'

'Of course. And so it will be with the "Avalanche" company. Don't you see, with Gillett probably useless for the rest of the season, Lant will have it all his own way at anything over ten miles. That'll help to boom up the shares and there'll be big profit made on trading in them. Oh, I tell you this thing seems pretty suspicious to me.'

'Look here,' said Dorrington, 'can you borrow a light for me, and let me run over with it to the spot where the smash took place? The people have cleared into the pavilion and I could go alone.'

'Certainly. Will you have a try for the governor's hundred?'

'Well, perhaps. But anyway there's no harm in doing you a good turn if I can, while I'm here. Some day perhaps you'll do me one.'

'Right you are—I'll ask Fielders, the ground-man.'

A lantern was brought, and Dorrington betook himself to the spot where the iron chair still lay, while Stedman joined the rest of the crowd in the pavilion.

Dorrington minutely examined the grass within two yards of the place where the chair lay, and then, crossing the track and getting over the rails, did the same with the damp gravel that paved the outer ring. The track itself was of cement, and unimpressionable by footmarks, but nevertheless he scrutinized that with equal care, as well as the rails. Then he turned his attention to the chair. It was, as I have said, a light chair made of flat iron strip, bent to shape and riveted. It had seen good service, and its present coat of green paint was evidently far from being its original one. Also it was rusty in places, and parts had been repaired and strengthened with cross-pieces secured by bolts and square nuts, some rusty and loose. It was from the back at the top, that Dorrington secured some object—it might have been a hair—which he carefully transferred to his pocketbook. This done, with one more glance round, he betook himself to the pavilion.

A surgeon had arrived, and he reported well of the chief patient. It was a simple fracture, and a healthy subject. When Dorrington entered, preparations were beginning for setting the limb. There was a sofa in the pavilion, and the surgeon saw no reason for removing the patient till all was made secure.

'Found anything?' asked Stedman in a low tone of Dorrington.

Dorrington shook his head. 'Not much,' he answered at a whisper, 'I'll think it over later.'

Dorrington asked one of the Cyclists' Union officials for the loan of a pencil and, having made a note with it, immediately, in another part of the room, asked Sparks, the amateur, to lend him another.

Stedman had told Mr. Mallows of Dorrington's late employment with the lantern, and the managing director now said quietly, 'You remember what I said about rewarding anybody who discovered the perpetrator of this outrage, Mr. Dorrington? Well, I was excited at the time, but I quite hold to it. It is a shameful thing. You have been looking about the grounds, I hear. I hope you have come across something that will enable you to find something out. Nothing will please me more than to have to pay you, I'm sure.'

'Well,' Dorrington confessed, 'I'm afraid I haven't seen anything very big in the way of a clue, Mr. Mallows; but I'll think a bit. The worst of it is, you never know who these betting men are, do you, once they get away? There are so many, and it may be anybody. Not only that, but they may bribe anybody.'

'Yes, of course—there's no end to their wickedness, I'm afraid. Stedman suggests that trade rivalry may have had something to do with it. But that seems an uncharitable view, don't you think? Of course we stand very high, and there are jealousies and all that, but this is a thing I'm sure no firm would think of stooping to, for a moment. No, it's betting that is at the bottom of this, I fear. And I hope, Mr. Dorrington, that you will make some attempt to find the guilty parties.'

Presently Stedman spoke to Dorrington again. 'Here's something that may help you,' he said. 'To begin with, it must have been done by some one from the outside of the track.'

'Why?'

'Well, at least every probability's that way. Everybody inside was directly interested in Gillett's success, excepting the Union officials and Sparks, who's a gentleman and quite above suspicion, as much so, indeed, as the Union officials. Of course there was the ground-man, but he's all right, I'm sure.'

'And the trainer?'

'Oh, that's altogether improbable—altogether. I was going to say—'

'And there's that other man who was standing about; I haven't heard who he was.'

'Right you are. I don't know him either. Where is he now?' But the man had gone.

'Look here, I'll make some quiet inquiries about that man,' Stedman pursued. 'I forgot all about him in the excitement of the moment. I was going to say that although whoever did it could easily have got away by the gate before the smash came, he might not have liked to go that way in case of observation in passing the pavilion. In that case he could have got away (and indeed he could have got into the grounds to begin with) by way of one of those garden walls that bound the ground just by where the smash occurred. If that were so he must either live in one of the houses, or must know somebody that does. Perhaps you might put a man to smell about along the road—it's only a short one; Chisnall Road's the name.'

'Yes, yes,' Dorrington responded patiently. 'There might be something in that.'

By this time Gillett's arm was in a starched bandage and secured by splints, and a cab was ready to take him home. Mr. Mallows took Stedman away with him, expressing a desire to talk business, and Dorrington went home by himself. He did not turn down Chisnall Road. But he walked jauntily along toward the nearest cab-stand, and once or twice he chuckled, for he saw his way to a delightfully lucrative financial operation in cycle companies, without risk of capital.

The cab gained, he called at the lodgings of two of his men assistants and gave them instant instructions. Then he packed a small bag at his rooms in Conduit Street, and at midnight was in the late fast train for Birmingham.

3

The prospectus of the 'Avalanche Bicycle and Tyre Company' stated that the works were at Exeter and Birmingham. Exeter is a delightful town, but it can scarcely be regarded as the centre of the cycle trade; neither is it in especially easy and short communication with Birmingham. It was the sort of thing that any critic anxious to pick holes in the prospectus might wonder at, and so one of Dorrington's assistants had gone by the night mail to inspect the works. It was from this man that Dorrington, in Birmingham, about noon on the day after Gillett's disaster, received this telegram—

> Works here old disused cloth-mills just out of town. Closed and empty but with big new signboard and notice that works now running are at Birmingham. Agent says only deposit paid—tenancy agreement not signed.—Farrish.

The telegram increased Dorrington's satisfaction, for he had just taken a look at the Birmingham works. They were not empty, though nearly so, nor were they large; and a man there had told him that the chief premises, where most of the work was done, were at Exeter. And the hollower the business the better prize he saw in store for himself. He had already, early in the morning, indulged in a telegram on his own account, though he had not signed it. This was how it ran—

> Mallows, 58, Upper Sandown Place, London, W.
> Fear all not safe here. Run down by 10.10 train without fail.

Thus it happened that at a little later than half past eight Dorrington's other assistant, watching the door of No. 58, Upper Sandown Place, saw a telegram delivered, and immediately afterwards Mr. Paul Mallows in much haste dashed away in a cab which was called from the end of the street. The assistant followed in another. Mr. Mallows dismissed his cab at a theatrical wig-maker's in Bow Street and entered. When he emerged in little more than forty minutes' time, none but a practised watcher, who had guessed the reason for the visit, would have recognized him. He had not assumed the clumsy disguise of a false beard. He was 'made up' deftly. His colour was heightened, and his face seemed thinner. There was no heavy accession of false hair, but a slight crepe-hair whisker at each side made a better and less pronounced disguise. He seemed a younger, healthier man. The watcher saw him safely off to Birmingham by the ten minutes past ten train, and then gave Dorrington note by telegraph of the guise in which Mr. Mallows was travelling.

Now this train was timed to arrive at Birmingham at one, which was the reason Dorrington had named it in the anonymous telegram. The entrance to the 'Avalanche' works was by a large gate, which was closed, but which was provided with a small door to pass a man. Within was a yard, and at a little before one o'clock Dorrington pushed open the small door, peeped, and entered. Nobody was about in the yard, but what little noise could be heard came from a particular part of the building on the right. A pile of solid 'export' crates stood to the left, and these Dorrington had noted at his previous call that morning as making a suitable hiding-place for temporary use. Now he slipped behind them and awaited the stroke of one. Prompt at the hour a door on the opposite side of the yard swung open, and two men and a boy emerged and climbed one after another through the little door in the big gate. Then presently another man, not a workman, but apparently a sort of overseer, came from the opposite door, which he carelessly let fall-to behind him, and he also disappeared through the little door, which he then locked. Dorrington was now alone in the sole active works of the 'Avalanche Bicycle and Tyre Company, Limited.'

He tried the door opposite and found it was free to open. Within he saw in a dark corner a candle which had been left burning, and opposite him a large iron enameling oven, like an immense safe, and round about, on benches, were strewn heaps of the glaring red and gold transfer which Dorrington had observed the day before on the machines exhibited in the Holborn Viaduct window. Some of the frames had the label newly applied, and others were still plain. It would seem that the chief business of the 'Avalanche Bicycle and Tyre Company, Limited' was the attaching of labels to previously nondescript machines. But there was little time to examine further, and indeed Dorrington presently heard the noise of a key in the outer gate. So he stood and waited by the enamelling oven to welcome Mr. Mallows.

As the door was pushed open Dorrington advanced and

bowed politely. Mallows started guiltily, but, remembering his disguise, steadied himself, and asked gruffly, 'Well, sir, and who are you?'

'I,' answered Dorrington with perfect composure, 'I am Mr. Paul Mallows—you may have heard of me in connection with the "Indestructible Bicycle Company."'

Mallows was altogether taken aback. But then it struck him that perhaps the detective, anxious to win the reward he had offered in the matter of the Gillett outrage, was here making inquiries in the assumed character of the man who stood, impenetrably disguised, before him. So after a pause he asked again, a little less gruffly, 'And what may be your business?'

'Well,' said Dorrington, 'I did think of taking shares in this company. I suppose there would be no objection to the managing director of another company taking shares in this?'

'No,' answered Mallows, wondering what all this was to lead to.

'Of course now; I'm sure *you* don't think so, eh?' Dorrington, as he spoke, looked in the other's face with a sly leer, and Mallows began to feel altogether uncomfortable. 'But there's one thing,' Dorrington pursued, taking out his pocket-book, though still maintaining his leer in Mallows' face—'one other thing. And by the way, *will* you have another piece of court plaster now I've got it out? Don't say no. It's a pleasure to oblige you, really.' And Dorrington, his leer growing positively fiendish, tapped the side of his nose with the case of court plaster.

Mallows paled under the paint, gasped, and felt for support. Dorrington laughed pleasantly. 'Come, come,' he said, 'don't be frightened. I admire your cleverness, Mr. Mallows, and I shall arrange everything pleasantly, as you will see. And as to the court plaster, if you'd rather not have it you needn't. You have another piece on now, I see. Why didn't you get them to paint it over at Clarkson's? They really did the face very well, though! And there again you were quite right. Such a man as yourself was likely to be recognized in such a place as Birmingham, and that would have been unfortunate for both of us—*both* of us, I assure you. . . . Man alive, don't look as though I was going to cut your throat! I'm not, I assure you. You're a smart man of business, and I happen to have spotted a little operation of yours, that's all. I shall arrange easy terms for you. . . . Pull yourself together and talk business before the men come back. Here, sit on this bench.'

Mallows, staring amazedly in Dorrington's face, suffered himself to be led to a bench, and sat on it.

'Now,' said Dorrington, 'the first thing is a little matter of a hundred pounds. That was the reward you promised if I should discover who broke Gillett's arm last night. Well, I *have*. Do you happen to have any notes with you? If not, make it a cheque.'

'But—but—how—I mean who!—who—'

'Tut, tut! Don't waste time, Mr. Mallows. *Who?* Why, yourself, of course. I knew all about it before I left you last night, though it wasn't quite convenient to claim the reward then, for reasons you'll understand presently. Come, that little hundred.'

'But what—what proof have you? I'm not to be bounced like this, you know.' Mr. Mallows was gathering his faculties again.

'Proof? Why, man alive, be reasonable! Suppose I have none—none at all? What difference does that make? Am I to walk out and tell your fellow directors where I have met you—here—or am I to have that hundred? More, am I to publish abroad that Mr. Paul Mallows is the moving spirit in the rotten "Avalanche Bicycle Company"?'

'Well,' Mallows answered reluctantly, 'if you put it like that—'

'But I only put it like that to make you see things reasonably. As a matter of fact your connection with this new company is enough to bring your little performance with the iron chair near proof. But I got at it from the other side. See here—you're much too clumsy with your fingers, Mr. Mallows. First you go and tear the tip of your middle finger opening your brougham door, and have to get court plaster from me. Then you let that court plaster get frayed at the edge, and you still keep it on. After that you execute your very successful chair operation. When the eyes of the others are following the bicycles you take the chair in the hand with the plaster on it, catching hold of it at the place where a rough, loose, square nut protrudes, and you pitch it on to the track so clumsily and nervously that the nut carries away the frayed thread of the court plaster with it. Here it is, you see, still in my pocket-book, where I put it last night by the light of the lantern; just a sticky black silk thread, that's all. I've only brought it to show you I'm playing a fair game with you. Of course I might easily have got a witness before I took the thread off the nut, if I had thought you were likely to fight the matter. But I knew you were not. You can't fight, you know, with this bogus company business known to me. So that I am only showing you this thread as an act of grace, to prove that I have stumped you with perfect fairness. And now the hundred. Here's a fountain pen, if you want one.'

'Well,' said Mallows glumly, 'I suppose I must, then.' He took the pen and wrote the cheque. Dorrington blotted it on the pad of his pocket-book and folded it away.

'So much for that!' he said. 'That's just a little preliminary, you understand. We've done these little things just as a guarantee of good faith—not necessarily for publication, though you must remember that as yet there's nothing to prevent it. I've done you a turn by finding out who upset those bicycles, as you so ardently wished me to do last night, and you've loyally fulfilled your part of the contract by paying the promised reward—though I must say that you haven't paid with all the delight and pleasure you spoke of at the time. But I'll forgive you that, and now that the little *hors-d'oeuvre* is disposed of, we'll proceed to serious business.'

Mallows looked uncomfortably glum.

'But you mustn't look so ashamed of yourself, you know,' Dorrington said, purposely misinterpreting his glumness. 'It's all business. You were disposed for a little side flutter, so to speak—a little speculation outside your regular business. Well, you mustn't be ashamed of that.'

'No,' Mallows observed, assuming something of his ordinarily ponderous manner; 'no, of course not. It's a little speculative deal. Everybody does it, and there's a deal of money going.'

'Precisely. And since everybody does it, and there is so much money going, you are only making your share.'

'Of course.' Mr. Mallows was almost pompous by now.

'Of course.' Dorrington coughed slightly. 'Well now, do you know, I am exactly the same sort of man as yourself—if you don't mind the comparison. *I* am disposed for a little side flutter, so to speak—a little speculation outside my regular business. I also am not ashamed of it. And since everybody does it, and there is so much money going—why, *I* am thinking of making *my* share. So we are evidently a pair, and naturally intended for each other!'

Mr. Paul Mallows here looked a little doubtful.

'See here, now,' Dorrington proceeded. 'I have lately taken it into my head to operate a little on the cycle share market. That was why I came round myself about that little spoke affair, instead of sending an assistant. I wanted to know somebody who understood the cycle trade, from whom I might get tips. You see I'm perfectly frank with you. Well, I have succeeded uncommonly well. And I want you to understand that I have gone every step of the way by fair work. I took nothing for granted, and I played the game fairly. When you asked me (as you had anxious reason to ask) if I had found anything, I told you there was nothing very big—and see what a little thing the thread was! Before I came away from the pavilion I made sure that you were really the only man there with black court plaster on his fingers. I had noticed the hands of every man but two, and I made an excuse of borrowing something to see those. I saw your thin pretence of suspecting the betting men, and I played up to it. I have had a telegraphic report on your Exeter works this morning—a deserted cloth mills with nothing on it of yours but a sign-board, and only a deposit of rent paid. *There* they referred to the works here. *Here* they referred to the works there. It was very clear, really! Also I have had a telegraphic report of your make-up adventure this morning. Clarkson does it marvellously, doesn't he? And, by the way, that telegram bringing you down to Birmingham was not from your confederate here, as perhaps you fancied. It was from me. Thanks for coming so promptly. I managed to get a quiet look round here just before you arrived, and on the whole conclusion I come to as to the "Avalanche Bicycle and Tyre Company, Limited," is this: A clever man, whom it gives me great pleasure to know,' with a bow to Mallows, 'conceives the notion of offering the public the very rottenest cycle company ever planned, and all without appearing in it himself. He finds what little capital is required; his two or three confederates help to make up a board of directors, with one or two titled guinea pigs, who know nothing of the company and care nothing, and the rest's easy. A professional racing man is employed to win races and make records, on machines which have been specially made by another firm (perhaps it was the "Indestructible," who knows?) to a private order, and afterwards decorated with the name and style of the bogus company on a transfer. For ordinary sale, bicycles of the "trade" description are bought—so much a hundred from the factors, and put your own name on 'em. They come cheap, and they sell at a good price—the profit pays all expenses and perhaps a bit over; and by the time they all break down the company will be successfully floated, the money—the capital—will be divided, the moving spirit and his confederates will have disappeared, and the guinea-pigs will be left to stand the racket—if there is a racket. And the moving spirit will remain unsuspected, a man of account in the trade all the time! Admirable! All the work to be done at the "works" is the sticking on of labels and a bit of enamelling. Excellent, all round! Isn't that about the size of your operations?'

'Well, yes,' Mallows answered, a little reluctantly, but with something of modest pride in his manner, 'that was the notion, since you speak so plainly.'

'And it shall be the notion. All—everything—shall be as you have planned it, with one exception, which is this. The moving spirit shall divide his plunder with me.'

'You? But—but—why, I gave you a hundred just now!'

'Dear, dear! Why will you harp so much on that vulgar little hundred? That's settled and done with. That's our little personal bargain in the matter of the lamentable accident with the chair. We are now talking of bigger business—not hundreds, but thousands, and not one of them, but a lot. Come now, a mind like yours should be wide enough to admit of a broad and large view of things. If I refrain from exposing this charming scheme of yours I shall be promoting a piece of scandalous robbery. Very well then, I want my promotion money, in the regular way. Can I shut my eyes and allow a piece of iniquity like this to go on unchecked, without getting anything by way of damages for myself? Perish the thought! When all expenses are paid, and the confederates are sent off with as little as they will take, you and I will divide fairly, Mr. Mallows, respectable brothers in rascality. Mind, I might say we'd divide to begin with, and leave you to pay expenses, but I am always fair to a partner in anything of this sort. I shall just want a little guarantee, you know—it's safest in such matters as these; say a bill at six months for ten thousand pounds—which is very low. When a satisfactory division is made you shall have the bill back. Come—I have a bill-stamp ready, being so much convinced of your reasonableness as to buy it this morning, though it cost five pounds.'

'But that's nonsense—you're trying to impose. I'll give you anything reasonable—half is out of the question. What, after all the trouble and worry and risk that I've had?'

'Which would suffice for no more than to put you in gaol if I held up my finger!'

'But hang it, be reasonable! You're a mighty clever man, and you've got me on the hip, as I admit. Say ten per cent.'

'You're wasting time, and presently the men will be back. Your choice is between making half, or making none, and going to gaol into the the bargain. Choose!'

'But just consider—'

'Choose!'

Mallows looked despairingly about him. 'But really,' he said, 'I want the money more than you think. I—'

'For the last time—choose!"

Mallow's desparing gaze stopped at the enamelling oven. 'Well, well,' he said, 'if I must, I must, I suppose. But I warn you, you may regret it.'

'Oh dear no, I'm not so pessimistic. Come, you wrote a cheque—now I'll write the bill. "Six months after date, pay to me or my order the sum of ten thousand pounds for value received"—excellent value too, *I* think. There you are!'

When the bill was written and signed, Mallows scribbled

his acceptance with more readiness than might have been expected. Then he rose, and said with something of brisk cheerfulness in his tone, 'Well, that's done, and the least said the soonest mended. You've won it, and I won't grumble any more. I think I've done this thing pretty neatly, eh? Come and see the "works"'.

Every other part of the place was empty of machinery. There were a good many finished frames and wheels, bought separately, and now in course of being fitted together for sale; and there were many more complete bicycles of cheap but showy make to which nothing needed to be done but to fix the red and gold 'transfer' of the 'Avalanche' company. Then Mallows opened the tall iron door of the enamelling oven.

'See this,' he said; 'this is the enamelling oven. Get in and look round. The frames and other different parts hang on the racks after the enamel is laid on, and all those gas jets are lighted to harden it by heat. Do you see that deeper part there by the back?—go closer.'

Dorrington felt a push at his back and the door was swung to with a bang, and the latch dropped. He was in the dark, trapped in a great iron chamber. 'I warned you,' shouted Mallows from without; 'I warned you you might regret it!' And instantly Dorrington's nostrils were filled with the smell of escaping gas. He realized his peril on the instant. Mallows had given him the bill with the idea of silencing him by murder and recovering it. He had pushed him into the oven and had turned on the gas. It was dark, but to light a match would mean death instantly, and without the match it must be death by suffocation and poison of gas in a very few minutes. To appeal to Mallows was useless—Dorrington knew too much. It would seem that at last a horribly fitting retribution had overtaken Dorrington in death by a mode parallel to that which he and his creatures had prepared for others. Dorrington's victims had drowned in water—and now Dorrington himself was to drown in gas. The oven was of sheet iron, fastened by a latch in the centre. Dorrington flung himself desperately against the door, and it gave outwardly at the extreme bottom. He snatched a loose angle-iron with which his hand came in contact, dashed against the door once more, and thrust the iron through where it strained open. Then, with another tremendous plunge, he drove the door a little more outward and raised the angle-iron in the crack; then once more, and raised it again. He was near to losing his senses, when, with one more plunge, the catch of the latch, not designed for such treatment, suddenly gave way, the door flew open, and Dorrington, blue in the face, staring, stumbling and gasping, came staggering out into the fresher air, followed by a gush of gas.

Mallows had retreated to the rooms behind, and thither Dorrington followed him, gaining vigour and fury at every step. At sight of him the wretched Mallows sank in a corner, sighing and shivering with terror. Dorrington reached him and clutched him by the collar. There should be no more honour between these two thieves now. He would drag Mallows forth and proclaim him aloud; and he would keep that £10,000 bill. He hauled the struggling wretch across the room, tearing off the crêpe whiskers as he came, while Mallows supplicated and whined, fearing that it might be the other's design to imprison *him* in the enamelling oven. But at the door of the room against that containing the oven their progress came to an end, for the escaped gas had reached the lighted candle, and with one loud report the partition wall fell in, half burying Mallows where he lay, and knocking Dorrington over.

Windows fell out of the building, and men broke through the front gate, climbed into the ruined rooms and stopped the still escaping gas. When the two men and the boy returned, with the conspirator who had been in charge of the works, they found a crowd from the hardware and cycle factories thereabout, surveying with great interest the spectacle of the extrication of Mr. Paul Mallows, managing director of the 'Indestructible Bicycle Company,' from the broken bricks, motar, bicycles and transfers of the 'Avalanche Bicycle and Tyre Company, Limited,' and the preparations for carrying him to a surgeon's where his broken leg might be set. As for Dorrington, a crushed hat and a torn coat were all his hurts, beyond a few scratches. And in a couple of hours it was all over Birmingham, and spreading to other places, that the business of the 'Avalanche

Bicycle and Tyre Company' consisted of sticking brilliant labels on factors' bicycles, bought in batches; for the whole thing was thrown open to the general gaze by the explosion. So that when, next day, Lant won the fifty miles race in London, he was greeted with ironical shouts of 'Gum on yer transfer!' 'Hi! mind your label!' 'Where did you steal that bicycle?' 'Sold yer shares?' and so forth.

Somehow the 'Avalanche Bicycle and Tyre company, Limited,' never went to allotment. It was said that a few people in remote and benighted spots, where news never came till it was in the history books, had applied for shares, but the bankers returned their money, doubtless to their extreme disappointment. It was found politic, also, that Mr. Paul Mallows should retire from the directorate of the 'Indestructible Bicycle Company'—a concern which is still, I believe, flourishing exceedingly.

As for Dorrington, he had his hundred pounds reward. But the bill of £10,000 he never presented. Why, I do not altogether know, unless he found that Mr. Mallows' financial position, as he had hinted, was not altogether so good as was supposed. At any rate, it was found among the notes and telegrams in this case in the Dorrington deed-box.

1899

The Nameless Man

RODRIGUEZ OTTOLENGUI

Mr Barnes was sitting in his private room, with nothing of special importance to occupy his thoughts, when his office boy announced a visitor.

'What name?' asked Mr Barnes.

'None!' was the reply.

'You mean,' said the detective, 'that the man did not give you his name. He must have one, of course. Show him in.'

A minute later the stranger entered, and, bowing courteously, began the conversation at once.

'Mr Barnes, the famous detective, I believe?' said he.

'My name is Barnes,' replied the detective. 'May I have the pleasure of knowing yours?'

'I sincerely hope so,' continued the stranger. 'The fact is, I suppose I have forgotten it.'

'Forgotten your name?' Mr Barnes scented an interesting case, and became doubly attentive.

'Yes!' said the visitor. 'That is precisely my singular predicament. I seem to have lost my identity. That is the object of my call. I wish to discover who I am. As I am evidently a full-grown man, I can certainly claim that I have a past history, but to me that past is entirely a blank. I awoke this morning in this condition, yet apparently in possession of all my faculties, so much so that I at once saw the advisability of consulting a first-class detective, and, upon inquiry, I was directed to you.'

'Your case is most interesting, from my point of view, I mean. To you, of course, it must seem unfortunate. Yet it is not unparalleled. There have been many such cases recorded, and,

241

for your temporary relief, I may say that sooner or later, complete restoration of memory usually occurs. But now, let us try to unravel your mystery as soon as possible, that you may suffer as little inconvenience as there need be. I would like to ask you a few questions?'

'As many as you like, and I will do my best to answer.'

'Do you think that you are a New Yorker?'

'I have not the least idea, whether I am or not.'

'You say you were advised to consult me. By whom?'

'The clerk at the Waldorf Hotel, where I slept last night.'

'Then, of course, he gave you my address. Did you find it necessary to ask him how to find my offices?'

'Well, no, I did not. That seems strange, does it not? I certainly had no difficulty in coming here. I suppose that must be a significant fact, Mr Barnes?'

'It tends to show that you have been familiar with New York, but we must still find out whether you live here or not. How did you register at the hotel?'

'M.J.G. Remington, City.'

'You are sure that Remington is not your name?'

'Quite sure. After breakfast this morning I was passing through the lobby when the clerk called me twice by that name. Finally, one of the hall-boys touched me on the shoulder and explained that I was wanted at the desk. I was very much confused to find myself called "Mr Remington", a name which certainly is not my own. Before I fully realised my position, I said to the clerk, "Why do you call me Remington?" and he replied, "Because you registered under that name." I tried to pass it off, but I am sure that the clerk looks upon me as a suspicious character.'

'What baggage have you with you at the hotel?'

'None. Not even a satchel.'

'May there not be something in your pockets that would help us; letters, for example?'

'I am sorry to say that I have made a search in that direction but found nothing. Luckily I did have a pocket-book though.'

'Much money in it?'

'In the neighborhood of five hundred dollars.'

Mr Barnes turned to his table and made a few notes on a pad of paper. While he was so engaged his visitor took out a fine gold watch, and, after a glance at the face, was about to return it to his pocket when Mr Barnes wheeled around in his chair, and said:

'That is a handsome watch you have there. Of a curious pattern too. I am rather interested in old watches.'

The stranger seemed confused for an instant, and quickly put up his watch, saying:

'There is nothing remarkable about it. Merely an old family relic. I value it more for that than anything else. But about my case, Mr Barnes, how long do you think it will take to restore my identity to me? It is rather awkward to go about under a false name.'

'I should think so,' said the detective. 'I will do my best for you, but you have given me absolutely no clue to work upon, so that it is impossible to say what my success will be. Still I think forty-eight hours should suffice. At least in that time I ought to make some discoveries for you. Suppose you call again on the day after to-morrow at noon precisely. Will that suit you?'

'Very well, indeed. If you can tell me who I am at that time I shall be more than convinced that you are a great detective, as I have been told.'

He arose and prepared to go, and upon the instant Mr Barnes touched a button under his table with his foot, which caused a bell to ring in a distant part of the building, no sound of which penetrated the private office. Thus anyone could visit Mr Barnes in his den, and might leave unsuspicious of the fact that a spy would be awaiting him out in the street who would shadow him persistently day and night until recalled by his chief. After giving the signal, Mr Barnes held his strange visitor in conversation a few moments longer to allow his spy opportunity to get to his post.

'How will you pass the time away, Mr Remington?' said he. 'We may as well call you by that name, until I find your true one.'

'Yes, I suppose so. As to what I shall do during the next forty-eight hours, why, I think I may as well devote myself to seeing the sights. It is a remarkably pleasant day for a stroll, and I think I will visit your beautiful Central Park.'

'A capital idea. By all means, I would advise occupation of that kind. It would be best not to do any business until your memory is restored to you.'

'Business. Why, of course, I can do no business.'

'No! If you were to order any goods, for example, under the name of Remington, later on when you resume your proper identity, you might be arrested as an impostor.'

'By George, I had not thought of that. My position is more serious than I had realised. I thank you for the warning. Sightseeing will assuredly be my safest plan for the next two days.'

'I think so. Call at the time agreed upon, and hope for the best. If I should need you before then, I will send to your hotel.'

Then, saying 'Good morning', Mr Barnes turned to his desk again, and, as the stranger looked at him before stepping out of the room, the detective seemed engrossed with some papers before him. Yet scarcely had the door closed upon the retreating form of his recent visitor, when Mr Barnes looked up, with an air of expectancy. A moment later a very tiny bell in a drawer of his desk rang, indicating that the man had left the building, the signal having been sent to him by one of his employés, whose business it was to watch all departures, and notify his chief. A few moments later Mr Barnes himself emerged, clad in an entirely different suit of clothing, and with such an alteration in the colour of his hair, that more than a casual glance would have been required to recognise him.

When he reached the street the stranger was nowhere in sight, but Mr Barnes went to a doorway opposite, and there he found, written in blue pencil, the word 'up', whereupon he walked rapidly up town as far as the next corner, where once more he examined a door-post, upon which he found the word 'right', which indicated the way the men ahead of him had turned. Beyond this he could expect no signals, for the spy shadowing the stranger did not know positively that his chief would take part in the game. The two signals which he had written on the doors were merely a part of a routine, and intended to aid Mr Barnes should he follow; but if he did so, he would be expected to be in sight of the spy by the time the second signal were reached. And so it proved in this instance, for as Mr Barnes turned the corner to the right, he easily discerned his man about two blocks ahead, and pressently was near enough to see 'Remington' also.

The pursuit continued until Mr Barnes was surprised to see him enter the Park, thus carrying out his intention as stated in his interview with the detective. Entering at the Fifth Avenue gate he made his way towards the menagerie, and here a curious incident occurred. The stranger had mingled with the crowd in the monkey-house, and was enjoying the antics of the mischievous little animals, when Mr Barnes, getting close behind him, deftly removed a pocket-handkerchief from the tail of his coat and swiftly transferred it to his own.

On the day following, shortly before noon, Mr Barnes walked quickly into the reading-room of the Fifth Avenue Hotel. In one corner there is a handsome mahogany cabinet, containing three compartments, each of which is entered through double doors, having glass panels in the upper half. About these panels are draped yellow silk curtains, and in the centre of each appears a white porcelain numeral. These compartments are used as public telephone stations, the applicant being shut in, so as to be free from the noise of the outer room.

Mr Barnes spoke to the girl in charge, and then passed into the compartment numbered '2'. Less than five minutes later Mr Leroy Mitchel came into the reading-room. His keen eyes peered about him, scanning the countenances of those busy with the papers or writing, and then he gave the telephone girl a number, and went into the compartment numbered '1'. About ten minutes elapsed before Mr Mitchel came out again, and, having paid the toll, he left the hotel. When Mr Barnes emerged, there was an expression of extreme satisfaction upon his face. Without lingering, he also went out. But instead of following Mr Mitchel through the main lobby to Broadway, he crossed the reading-room and reached 23rd Street through the side door. Thence he proceeded to the station of the Elevated Railroad, and went up town. Twenty minutes later he was ringing the bell of

Mr Mitchel's residence. The buttons, who answered his summons, informed him that his master was not at home.

'He usually comes in to luncheon, however, does he not?' asked the detective.

'Yes, sir,' responded the boy.

'Is Mrs Mitchel at home?'

'No, sir.'

'Miss Rose?'

'Yes, sir.'

'Ah! Then I'll wait. Take my card to her.'

Mr Barnes passed into the luxurious drawing-room, and was soon joined by Rose, Mr Mitchel's adopted daughter.

'I am sorry papa is not at home, Mr Barnes,' said the little lady, 'but he will surely be in to luncheon, if you will wait.'

'Yes, thank you, I think I will. It is quite a trip up, and, being here, I may as well stop awhile and see your father, though the matter is not of any great importance.'

'Some interesting case, Mr Barnes? If so, do tell me about it. You know I am almost as much interested in your cases as papa is.'

'Yes, I know you are, and my vanity is flattered. But I am sorry to say I have nothing on hand at present worth relating. My errand is a very simple one. Your father was saying, a few days ago, that he was thinking of buying a bicycle, and yesterday, by accident, I came across a machine of an entirely new make, which seems to me superior to anything yet produced. I thought he might be interested to see it, before deciding what kind to buy.'

'I am afraid you are too late, Mr Barnes. Papa has bought a bicycle already.'

'Indeed! what style did he choose?'

'I really do not know, but it is down in the lower hall, if you care to look at it.'

'It is hardly worth while, Miss Rose. After all, I have no interest in the new model, and if your father has found something that he likes, I won't even mention the other to him. It might only make him regret his bargain. Still, on second thoughts, I will go down with you, if you will take me, into the dining-room and show me the head of that moose which your father had been bragging about killing. I believe it has come back from the taxidermist's?'

'Oh, yes! He is just a monster. Come on!'

They went down to the dining-room, and Mr Barnes expressed great admiration about the moose's head, and praised Mr Mitchel's skill as a marksman. But he had taken a moment to scrutinize the bicycle which stood in the hall-way, while Rose was opening the blinds in the dining-room. Then they returned to the drawing-room, and after a little more conversation Mr Barnes departed, saying that he could not wait any longer, but he charged Rose to tell her father that he particularly desired him to call at noon on the following day.

Promptly at the time appointed, Remington walked into the office of Mr Barnes, and was announced. The detective was in his private room. Mr Leroy Mitchel had been admitted but a few moments before.

'Ask Mr Remington in,' said Mr Barnes to his boy, and when that gentleman entered, before he could show surprise to find a third party present, he detective said:

'Mr Mitchel, this is the gentleman whom I wish you to meet. Permit me to introduce to you, Mr Mortimer J. Goldie, better known to the sporting fraternity as G.J. Mortimer, the champion short-distance bicycle rider, who recently rode a mile in the phenomenal time of 1•56, on a quarter-mile track.'

As Mr Barnes spoke, he gazed from one to the other of his companions, with a half-quizzical, and wholly pleased expression on his face. Mr Mitchel appeared much interested, but the newcomer was evidently greatly astonished. He looked blankly at Mr Barnes a moment, then dropped into a chair with the query:

'How in the name of conscience did you find that out?'

'That much was not very difficult,' replied the detective. 'I can tell you more; indeed I can supply your whole past history, provided your memory has been sufficiently restored for you to recognise my facts as true.'

Mr Barnes looked at Mr Mitchel and winked one eye in a

most suggestive manner, at which that gentleman burst out into hearty laughter, finally saying:

'We may as well admit that we are beaten, Goldie. Mr Barnes has been too much for us.'

'But I want to know how he has done it,' persisted Mr Goldie.

'I have no doubt that Mr Barnes will gratify you. Indeed, I am as curious as you are to know by what means he has arrived at his quick solution of the problem which we set him.'

'I will enlighten you as to detective methods with pleasure,' said Mr Barnes. 'Let me begin with the visit made to me by this gentleman two days ago. At the very outset his statement aroused my suspicion, though I did my best not to let him think so. He announced to me that he had lost his identity, and I promptly told him that his case was not uncommon. I said that, in order that he might feel sure that I did not doubt his tale. But truly his case, if he were telling the truth, was absolutely unique. Men have lost recollection of their past, and even have forgotten their names. But I have never before heard of a man who had forgotten his name, *and at the same time knew that he had done so.*'

'A capital point, Mr Barnes,' said Mr Mitchel. 'You were certainly shrewd to suspect fraud so early.'

'Well, I cannot say that I suspected fraud so soon, but the story was so unlikely, that I could not believe it immediately. I therefore was what I might call analytically attentive during the rest of the interview. The next point worth noting which came out was that although he had forgotten himself, he had not forgotten New York, for he admitted having come to me without special guidance.'

'I remember that,' interrupted Mr Goldie, 'and I think I even said to you at the time that it was significant.'

'And I told you that it at least showed that you had been familiar with New York. This was better proven when you said that you would spend the day at Central Park, and when, after leaving here, you had no difficulty to find your way thither.'

'Do you mean to say that you had me followed? I made sure that no one was after me.'

'Well, yes, you were followed,' said Mr Barnes, with a smile. 'I had a spy after you, and I followed you as far as the Park myself. But let me come to the other points in your interview and my deductions. You told me that you had registered as "M.J.G. Remington". This helped me considerably, as we shall see presently. A few minutes later you took out your watch, and in that little mirror over my desk, which I use occasionally when I turn my back upon a visitor, I noted that there was an inscription on the outside of the case. I turned and asked you something about the watch, when you hastily returned it to your pocket, with the remark that it was "an old family relic". Now can you explain how you could have known that, supposing that you had forgotten who you were?'

'Neatly caught, Goldie,' laughed Mr Mitchel. 'You certainly made a mess of it there.'

'It was an asinine slip,' said Mr Goldie, laughing also.

'Now then,' continued Mr Barnes, 'you readily see that I had good reason for believing that you had not forgotten your name. On the contrary, I was positive that your name was a part of the inscription on the watch. What, then, could be your purpose in pretending otherwise? I did not discover that for some time. However, I decided to go ahead, and find you out if I could. Next I noted two things. Your coat opened once, so that I saw, pinned to your vest, a bicycle badge, which I recognised as the emblem of the League of American Wheelmen.'

'Oh! Oh!' cried Mr Mitchel. 'Shame on you, Goldie, for a blunderer.'

'I had entirely forgotten the badge,' said Mr Goldie.

'I also observed,' the detective went on, 'little indentations on the sole of your shoe, as you had your legs crossed, which satisfied me that you were a rider even before I observed the badge. Now, then, we come to the name, and the significance thereof. Had you really lost your memory, the choosing of a name when you registered at the hotel, would have been a haphazard matter of no importance to me. But as soon as I decided that you were imposing upon me, I knew that your choice of a name had been a deliberate act of the mind; one from which deductions could be drawn.'

'Ah! Now we come to the interesting part,' said Mr Mitchel. 'I love to follow a detective when he uses his brains.'

'The name as registered, and I examined the registry myself to make sure, was odd. Three initials are unusual. A man without memory, and therefore not quite sound mentally, would hardly have chosen so many. Then why had it been done in this instance? What more natural than that these initials represented the true name? In assuming an alias, it is the most common method to transpose the real name in some way. At least it was a working hypothesis. Then the last name might be very significant. "Remington". The Remingtons make guns, sewing-machines, typewriters, and bicycles. Now, this man was a bicycle rider, I was sure. If he chose his own initials as a part of the alias, it was possible that he selected "Remington" because it was familiar to him. I even imagined that he might be an agent for Remington bicycles, and I had arrived at that point during our interview, when I advised him not to buy anything until his identity was restored. But I was sure of my quarry, when I stole a handkerchief from him at the park, and found the initials "M.J.G." upon the same.'

'Marked linen on your person!' exclaimed Mr Mitchel. 'Worse and worse! We'll never make a successful criminal of you, Goldie.'

'Perhaps not! I shan't cry over it.'

'I felt sure of my success by this time,' continued Mr Barnes, 'yet at the very next step I was baulked. I looked over a list of L.A.W. members and could not find a name to fit my initials, which shows, as you will see presently, that, as I may say, "too many clues spoil the broth." Without the handkerchief I would have done better. Next I secured a catalogue of the Remingtons, which gave a list of their authorized agents, and again I failed. Returning to my office I received information from my spy, sent in by messenger, which promised to open a way for me. He had followed you about, Mr Goldie, and I must say you played your part very well, so far as avoiding acquaintances is concerned. But at last you went to a public telephone, and called up someone. My man saw the importance of discovering to whom you had spoken, and bribed the telephone attendant to give him the information. All that he learned, however, was that you had spoken to the public station at the Fifth Avenue Hotel. My spy thought that this was inconsequent, but it proved to me at once that there was collusion, and that your man must have been at the other station by previous appointment. As that was at noon, a few minues before the same hour on the following day, that is to say, yesterday, I went to the Fifth Avenue Hotel telephone and secreted myself in the middle compartment, hoping to hear what your partner might say to you. I failed in this, as the boxes are too well made to permit sound to pass from one to the other; but imagine my gratification to see Mr Mitchel himself go into the box.'

'And why?' asked Mr Mitchel.

'Why, as soon as I saw you, I comprehended the whole scheme. It was you who had concocted the little diversion to test my ability. Thus, at last, I understood the reason for the pretended loss of identity. With the knowledge that you were in it, I was more than ever determined to get at the facts. Knowing that you were out, I hastened to your house, hoping for a chat with little Miss Rose, as the most likely member of your family to get information from.'

'Oh, fie! Mr Barnes,' said Mr Mitchel, 'to play upon the innocence of childhood! I am ashamed of you!'

'All's fair, etc. Well, I succeeded. I found Mr Goldie's bicycle in your hall-way, and, as I suspected, 'twas a Remington. I took the number and hurried down to the agency, where I readily discovered that wheel number 5,086 is ridden by G.J. Mortimer, one of their regular racing team. I also learned that Mortimer's private name is Mortimer J. Goldie. I was much pleased at this, because it showed how good my reasoning had been about the alias, for you observe that the racing name is merely a transposition of the family name. The watch, of course, is a prize, and the inscription would have proved that you were imposing upon me, Mr Goldie, had you permitted me to see it.'

'Of course. That was why I put it back in my pocket.'

'I said just now,' said Mr Barnes, 'that without the stolen handkerchief I would have done better. Having it, when I looked over the L.A.W. list I went through the "G's" only.

Without it I should have looked through the "G's", "J's", and "M's", not knowing how the letters may have been transposed. In that case I should have found "G.J. Mortimer", and the initials would have proved that I was on the right track.'

'You have done well, Mr Barnes,' said Mr Mitchel. 'I asked Goldie to play the part of a nameless man for a few days, to have some fun with you. But you have had fun with us, it seems. Though, I am conceited enough to say, that had it been possible for me to play the principal part, you would not have pierced my identity so soon.'

'Oh! I don't know,' said Mr Barnes. 'We are both of us a little egotistical, I fear.'

'Undoubtedly. Still, if I ever set another trap for you, I will assign myself the chief rôle.'

'Nothing would please me better,' said Mr Barnes. 'But, gentlemen, as you have lost in this little game, it seems to me that some one owes me a dinner, at least!'

'I'll stand the expense with pleasure,' said Mr Mitchel.

'Not at all,' interrupted Mr Goldie. 'It was through my blundering that we lost, and I'll pay the piper.'

'Settle it between you,' cried Mr Barnes. 'But let us walk on. I am getting hungry.'

Whereupon they adjourned to Delmonico's.

1899

His Defense

HARRY STILLWELL EDWARDS

"What?"

Colonel Rutherford shot a swift glance from the brief he was examining at the odd figure before him, and resumed his occupation quickly, to hide the smile that was already lifting the heavy frown from his face. "Indicted for what?"

"For the cussin' of my mother-in-law; an' I want you ter be on hand at court ter make er speech for me when hit comes up."

"Did you cuss her?"

The lawyer fell easily into the vernacular of his visitor, but he was afraid to lift his eyes again higher than the tips of his own polished boots, resting upon the table in front of him, in the good old Georgia fashion.

"Did I?" The stranger shifted his hat to the other hand and wiped his brow with a cotton handkerchief. His voice was low and plaintive. "I sho'ly did cuss. I cussed 'er comin' an' goin', for'ards and back'ards, all erroun' an' straight through. Ain't no use ter deny hit. I done hit."

He was tall, and in old age would be gaunt. He was also sunburned, and stooped a little, as from hard labor and long walking in plowed ground or long riding behind slow mules. One need not have been a physiognomist to discover that, although yet young, the storms of life had raged about him. But the lawyer noticed that he was neat, and that his jeans suit was homemade, and his pathetic homespun shirt and sewed-on collar—the shirt and collar that never will sit right for any country housewife, however devoted—were ornamented with a black cravat made of a ribbon and tied like a schoolgirl's sash.

The defendant leaned over the table as he finished speaking, resting his hands thereon, and thrusting forward his aquiline features, shame and excitement struggling for expression in his blue eyes.

"Did she cuss you first?"

The stranger looked surprised.

"No."

"Did she abuse you, strike you—did she ever chuck anything at you?"

"Why, no!—you see, hit wasn't edzactly the words—"

"Then it seems to me, my friend, that you have no use for a lawyer. I never take any kind of a criminal case for less than one hundred dollars, and the court will hardly fine you that much if you plead quilty. By your own statement, you see, you are guilty, and I can't help you. Better go and plead guilty and file an exculpatory affidavit—"

"No, sir. That'l do for some folks, but not for me. I never dodged in my life, and I ain't goin' ter dodge now. All you got ter do is ter make er speech. I want you ter tell them for me—"

"But what is the use, my friend? Can't you see—"

"Don't make no difference. You go. I'll be thar with your money."

"All right," was the laughing rejoinder; "but you are simply wasting time and money."

"That's my business. No man ever wasted his time or money when he was settin' himself right before his folks."

Lifting his head with an air the memory of which dwelt with the attorney for many a day, the novel client departed, leaving him still laughing. He opened his docket and wrote, in the absence of further information: "The man who cussed his mother-in-law, Crawford Court, $100."

Court opened in Crawford County as usual. The city lawyers followed the judge over from Macon in nondescript vehicles, their journey enlivened by many a gay jest and well-told tale, to say nothing of refreshments by the way. The autumn woods were glorious in the year's grand sunset. Like masqueraders in some wild carnival, the gums and sumacs and hickories and persimmons and maples mingled their flaunting banners and lifted them against the blue and cloudless skies. Belated cotton-pickers stole the last of the fields' white lint, and sang in harmonies that echoed from the woodlands, seeming to voice the gladness of unseen revelers.

And Knoxville, waking from its dull dreams, took on life and color for the week. Horses tugged at the down-sweeping limbs or dozed contentedly beside the racks; and groups of country folks, white and black, discussed solemnly or with loud jest the ever-changing situation. The session of court, brief though it be, is fraught with meaning for many families, the chief points of friction being the issues between landlord and tenant, factor and farmer, loan associations and deliquent debtors. And there is always the criminal side of court, with its sable fringe of evildoers.

The sheriff, in obedience to time-honored custom, had shouted from the front steps the names of all parties concerned in the case of the State *versus* Hiram Ard, and the State, through its urban solicitor, the Hon. Jefferson Brown, had announced "Ready," when Colonel Rutherford felt a hand upon his shoulder, and, looking up, saw a half-familiar face earnestly bent toward his own.

"Hit's come," said the stranger, his blue eyes full of excitement; "an' thar's your hundred."

"Beg your pardon," said the lawyer; "some mistake! I—don't think—I can exactly locate you."

"What? I'm the man they say that cussed his mother-in-law!"

"Why, of course, of course! One moment, your Honor, until I can consult my client."

The consultation was brief. The lawyer urged a plea of guilty. The client was determined to go to trial.

"Ready for the defense!" said Colonel Rutherford, in despair, waving his client to his seat with a gesture that seemed to disclaim responsibility for anything that might happen.

The usual preliminaries and formalities were soon disposed of, and the jury stricken, twelve good men and true, as their names will show; for to adjudge this case were assembled there Dike Sisson, Bobby Lewis, Zeke Cothern, Tony Hutt, Hob

Garrett, Jack Dermedy, Tommie Liptrot, Jack Doozenbery, Abe Ledzetter, Cran Herringdine, Bunk Durden, and Tim Newberry.

The State, upon this occasion, had but one witness. Mrs. Jessy Gonder was called to the stand. The lady was mild-looking and thin, and something in her bearing unconsciously referred one to a happier past. But the good impression—perhaps it is better to say the soft impression—vanished when she loosened her bonnet-strings and tongue, and with relentless, drooping corners—those dead smiles of bygone days—began to relate her grievance.

Well, Mrs. Gonder was one of those unfortunate women whom adversity sours and time cannot sweeten; and that is all there is of it. In sharp, crisp tones and bitter words she told of her experience with the defendant. The narrative covered years of bitterness, disappointment, wounded vanity, and hatred, and was remarkable for its excess of feeling. It was, from a professional standpoint, overdone. It was an outburst. Members of the admirable jury who had looked with surprise and animosity upon Hiram Ard began to regard him with something like sympathy; for, disguise it as she might, it was plain to all men that the overwhelming cause of her grievance was Hiram's conquest of her only daughter. Bobby Lewis leaned over and whispered to Bunk Durden, and both young men laughed until their neighboring jurors were visibly affected, and the court knocked gently with its gavel. When she came to the cause of war wherein this low-bred son-in-law had cursed around her,— her, Jessy Gonder,—had entered the house she occupied and had forcibly taken away a sewing-machine loaned by her own daughter, her voice trembled and she shook her clenched fist above the rail, her eyes, the while, fairly blazing in the shadow of her black bonnet. She sank back at last, exhausted.

While the witness was testifying the defendant looked straight ahead of him, settling slowly in his seat, until his matched hands, supported by his elbows that rested upon the chair, almost covered his face. From time to time a wave of color flushed his cheeks and brow. Then he seemed to wander off to scenes the woman's words recalled, and he became oblivious to his surroundings. When at last his attorney touched him and called him to the witness-stand, he started violently, and with difficulty regained his composure.

"Tell the jury what you know of this case," said Rutherford; and then to the court: "This seems to be purely a family quarrel, your Honor, and I trust the defendant will be allowed to proceed without interruption of any kind. Go on, sir," he concluded, to the latter.

The defendant seated himself in the witness-stand, his arm on the rail, and said:

"Hit's er long story, my friends, an' if thar warn't nothin' in the case but er fine I wouldn't take your time. But thar's er heap more, an' ef you'll all hear me out, I don't think any of you'll believe I'm much ter be blamed. So far as the cussin' is concerned, thar ain't no dispute erbout that. I done hit, an' I oughtn't er done hit. No gentleman can cuss erroun' er woman, an' for the first time in my life I warn't er gentleman. I could er come here an' pleaded guilty an' quit, but that don't square er gentleman's record. I hired er lawyer ter take my case, an' did hit ter have him put me up here where I could get er chance ter face my people, an' say I was wrong, an' sorry for hit, an' willin' ter take the consequences. That's the kind of man Hiram Ard is."

All the shamefacedness was gone from the man. He had straightened up in his chair, and his blue eyes were beaming with earnestness. His declaration, simple and direct, had penetrated every corner of the room. In a moment he had caught the attention of the crowd, for all the world loves a manly man, and from that moment their attention never wavered.

"But," he continued, when the silence had become intense, "I ain't willin' for you ter think Hiram Ard could cuss erroun' any woman offhand an' for er little matter.

"Some of you knowed me when I was er barefooted boy, with no frien' in the worl' 'ceptin' ma an' pa, an' not them long. This trouble started away back thar—when I was that kind er boy an' goin' ter school. I was 'mos' too big ter go ter school, an' she—I mean Cooney, Cooney Gonder—was 'mos' too young. Somehow I got ter sorter lookin' out for her on the road, gentlemen, an' totin' her books, an' holdin' her steady crossin' the logs over Tobysofkee Creek an' the branches. An' at school, when the boys teased her an' pulled her hair an' hid her dinner-bucket, I sorter tuk up for her; an' the worst fight I ever had was erbout Cooney Gonder.

"Well, so it went on year in an' out. Then pa died, an' the ole home was sold for his debts. An' then ma died. All I had left, gentlemen, was erbout sixty acres on Tobysofkee an' thirty up in Coldneck deestric'; an' not er acre cleared. But I went ter work. I cut down trees an' made er clearin', an' I hired er mule an' planted er little crop. Cotton fetched er big price that year, an' I bought the mule outright. An' then er feller come erlong with er travelin' sawmill, an' I let him saw on halves ter get lumber ter build my house. Hit was just er two-room house, but hit war mine, an' I was the proudes'! I bought ernother mule on credit, an' the new lan' paid for hit too an' lef' me money besides. An' then I put on ernother room.

"Well, all this time I was tryin' ter keep comp'ny with Cooney, gentlemen—I say tryin', 'cause her folks didn't think much of me. My family warn't much, an' Cooney's was good blood an' er little stuckup. An' Cooney—well, Cooney had done growed ter be the prettiest an' sweetest in all the Warrior deestric', as you know, an' they had done made her er teacher, for she was smart as she was pretty. An' she was good—too good for me. Ter this day I don't understan' hit. Cooney say hit was because I was honest an' er man all over; that was the excuse she gave for lovin' me. But I do know that when she said yes, two things happened: I kissed her, an' there was er riot in Cooney's family. Cooney's ma was the last ter come roun', an' I don't think she ever did quite come roun', for she warn't at the wedding; but, so help me God, I never bore her no ill will. Hit must have been hard ter give Cooney up.

"I will never forget the day, gentlemen, she come into that little home. Hit was like bein' born ag'in; I was that happy. I made the po'est crop I ever made in my life; but, bless you, the whole place changed. Little vines come up an' made er shade on the po'ch, an' flowers growed about the yard in places that look like they had been waitin' for flowers always. An' the little fixin's on the bureau and windows, an' white stuff hangin' ter the mantelpieces—well, I never knowed what hit was ter live before.

"Then at last I went ter work. It was four mules then, an' me in debt for two, an' some rented land; but no man who had Cooney could honestly call himself in debt. I worked day in an' out, rain or shine, hot or cold, an' I struck hit right. Cooney was sewin' for two an' sewin' on little white things for another, and we were the happiest. One day I come home 'for' dark ter find Cooney was gone ter her neighbor's. I slipped in on her, an' thar she was er-sewin' on er sewin'-machine, an' proud of the work as I was of the first land I ever laid off. Hit was hard ter pull her away. Well, I didn't say nothin'; I thought, an' I kept hit all ter myself. I went ter town that fall with my cotton, an' when I had done paid my draft at the warehouse I had seventy dollars left. What did I do with hit? What do you reckon I did with hit?"

The aquiline face took on a positively beautiful smile. The speaker leaned over the rail and talked confidentially to the jury.

"Well, here's what I did, gentlemen. I went ter whar that one-arm old soldier stays what keeps sewin'-machines an' the tax-books, an' I planked down sixty of my pile for one of them. An' then I went home an' set the thing in the settin'-room while Cooney was gettin' supper; an' I let her eat, but I couldn't hardly swaller, I was so full of that machine."

He laughed aloud at this point, and several of the jury joined him. The court smiled and lifted a law-book in front of his face.

"When I took her in thar an' turned up the light, Cooney like ter fainted. 'My wife don't have ter sew on no borrowed machine no more,' says I, just so; an' she fell ter cryin' an' huggin' me; an' by an' by we got down ter work. I'll be doggoned if we didn't set up tell one er'clock playin' on that thing! She'd sew, an' then I'd sew, an' then I'd run the wheel underneath an' she'd run the upper works. We hemmed and hawed all the napkins over, an' the table-cloths; an' tucked all the pillow frills; an' Cooney made me er handkerchief out of something. Gentlemen, next ter gettin' Cooney, hit was the happiest night of my life!"

* * *

Hiram paused to take breath, and the tension on the audience being relieved, they moved, looked into one another's faces, and, smiling, exchanged comments. A breath of spring seemed to have invaded the autumn.

"Wouldn't believe he was guilty ef he swore hit," said a voice somewhere, and there was applause, which was promptly suppressed. Hiram did not hear the comment. He was lost in his dream.

"Then the baby come. But before he come I saw Cooney begin ter change. She'd sit an' droop, an' brighten up an' droop erg'in, lookin' away off; an' her step got slow. Then, one day, hit come ter me: she was homesick for her ma. Well, gentlemen, I reck'n 'twas natchul at that time. She never had said nothin', but the way her ma had done an' the way she had talked about me was the grief of her life. She couldn't see how she was goin' ter meet the new trouble erlone. I fixed hit for her. I took her out on the po'ch where she could break down without my seemin' ter know hit, an' I tole her as how hit did look like hit was a shame for her ma ter have ter live off at her sister's, an' her own chile keepin' house, with a comp'ny room; an' I believed I'd drive over an' tell her ter let bygones be bygones, an' come an' live with us; that I didn't set no store by the hard things she's said, an' we would do our best for her. Well, that got Cooney. She dropped her head down in my lap, an' I knowed I'd done hit the nail on the head. Natchully I was happy erlong with her.

"Well, I went an' made my best talk, an' when I got done, gentlemen, what you reck'n Cooney's ma said—what do you reck'n? She said: 'How's Cooney?' 'Po'ly,' says I. 'I thought so,' says she, 'er you wouldn't ter come. I'll get my things an' go.' But Cooney was so happy when she did come, I caught the fever too, an' thought me an' the old lady would get on all right at last. But we didn't. Seemed like pretty soon ma begin ter look for things ter meddle in, an' she got er new name for me ev'y time I come erroun'. I didn't answer back, because she was Cooney's ma. I grit my teeth an' went on. But she'd come out an' lean on the fence, even, when I was plowin', an' talk. 'Look like any fool,' she said one day, 'look like any fool would know better'n ter lay off land with er twister. Whyn't yer git er roun' p'inted shovel?' My lan' was new, gentlemen, an' full of roots; that's why.

"An' she'd look at my hogs an' say: 'I allus did despise Berkshires. Never saw er sow that wouldn't eat pigs after er while. Whyn't you cross 'em on the big Guinea?' An' then, the chickens. 'Thar's them Wyandottes! Never knew one ter raise er brood yet; an' one rooster takes more pasture than er mule.' An' I paid ten dollars for three, gentlemen. An' then, Cooney's mornin'-glories made her sick. An' she didn't like sewin'-machines; they made folks want more clothes than they ought ter have, an' made the wash too big. An' what she called 'jimcracks' was Cooney's pretties in the sittin'-room.

"But I stood it; she was Cooney's ma. Only, when the mockin'-bird's cage door was found open an' he gone, I like to have turned my mind loose, for I had my suspicions, an' have yet. He was a little bird when I found him. I was clearin' my lan', an' one of these new niggers come erlong with er single-barrel gin, an' shot both the old birds right before my eyes with one load. I was that mad I took up er loose root an' frailed him tell he couldn't walk straight, an' I bent the gun roun'er tree an' flung hit after him. Then I went ter the nest in the haw-bush, an' started out ter raise the four young ones. I couldn't find er bug ter save me, though it looked easy for the old birds, so I took them home an' tried eggs an' potato. Well, one by one they died, until but one was left. When Cooney come he was grown, an' with the dash of white on his wings all singers have. But he never would sing—I think he was lonesome. The first night she come, I woke ter hear the little feller singin' away like his heart was too full ter hold hit all. I turned over ter wake Cooney, that she might hear him too, an' what do you reck'n? The moonlight had found er way in through the half-open blinds an' had fell across her face. Hit shone out there in the darkness like an angel's, an' that little lonesome bird had seen hit for the first time. Hit started the song in him just like hit had in me, an' God knows—" His voice quivered a moment and he looked away, a slight gesture supplying a conclusion.

"Then the baby come, an' when Cooney said, 'We'll name hit Jessy, after ma,' I said, 'Good enough. Hit's natchul.'

"Looks like that ought ter have made it easier all erroun', but hit didn't. Hit all got worse. An' ter keep the peace, I got not ter comin' inter the house tell the dinner-bell would ring. I'd jus' set on the fence, pretendin' I was er-watchin' the stock feed. An' after dinner I'd go out erg'in an' set on the fence ter keep the peace. Not that I blamed Cooney's ma so much, for I didn't. Nobody ever said hit for her but me, an' I don't mind sayin' hit now: but she had had trouble ernough for four women; an' her boy died. He was er good boy, if thar ever was one. I remember the time we went ter school togethr; an' when he died of the fever, why, hit was then I sorter took his place an' looked out for Cooney all the time. Her boy died, an' I think er heap er 'lowance ought ter be made for er widow when her boy is buried, for I don't believe there is much else left for her in this world."

The stillness in the room was absolute when the witness paused a moment and for some reason studied his fingers, his face bent down. All eyes were unconsciously turned then toward the prosecutrix. She had moved uncomfortably many times during this narrative, and now lowered her veil, as if she felt the focus of their attention. Afterward she did not look up again. Hiram, whose face had grown singularly tender, raised his eyes, somewhat wearily, at last.

"I know what hit is to lose a child," he said gently, "for I lost Jessy. The fever came; she faded out, an'—well—we jus' put her ter sleep out under the two cedars I had left in the corner of the yard. Then hit was worse than ever, for I had Cooney ter comfort, my own load ter tote, an'—Cooney's ma was harder ter stan' than before. I studied an' studied, an' then I took Cooney out with me ter the field an' tole her what was on my mind. 'Let's go up ter Coldneck,' says I, 'an' build us a little house jus' like the one we started with, an' plant mornin'-glories on the po'ch, an' begin over. Let's give ma this place for life, an' two mules, an' split up. An' let's do hit quick, 'cause I can't hold out much longer.' You see, I was 'fraid er myself. Well, Cooney hugged me, an' I saw her heart was happy over the change.

"So we went. Her ma said we were fools, an' settled down ter run her end of the bargain. An' I'm boun' ter say she made good crops, an' with her nephew ter help her, got erlong well tell he married an' went ter his wife's folks.

"Hit looked like hit was goin' ter be easy, gentlemen, leavin' the little home; an' hit was tell Cooney got in the wagon an' looked back—not at the house, an' the flowers she had planted, an' the white curtains in her winders, but at the two little cedars where Jess was sleepin', an' the mockin-bird balancin' an' singin' on the highest limb. Hit was easy tell then. Her heart jus' broke, an' she cried out ter herself: 'Ma! Ma! I wouldn't er treated you that-er-way—I wouldn't er done hit!'" He pointed his finger at the prosecutrix. "She didn't know Cooney felt that-er-way, gentlemen; this is the first time. An' she didn't know that when I came back from Macon, next fall, an' brought er little marble slab with Jess's name on hit, an' put hit up under the cedars, I got one with her Tom's name on hit, too, an' went ter her ole home, an' cleared away the weeds, an' put hit over Tom's grave. He was er good boy—an' he was Cooney's brother.

"Well," continued the defendant, after a pause, "we did well. I cleared the land an' made er good crop. An' then our own little Tom come. That's what we named him. An' one day Cooney asked me ter go back an' get her sewin'-machine from her ma's. Hit was the first plantin' day we had had in April, an' I hated mightily ter lose er day; but Cooney never had asked me for many things, so I went. When I rode up, ma come out, an' restin' her hands on her sides, she said: 'I did give you credit for some sense! What you donin' here, an' hit the first cotton-plantin' day of the year? I'll be boun' you picked out this day ter come for that ar sewin'-machine.' I tole her I had; an' then she answered back: 'Nobody but er natchul-born fool would come for er sewin'-machine in that sort er wagon. You can't get hit. Thar wouldn't be er whole j'int in hit when you got back!' Well, seein' as how I had brought the thing from Macon once in the same wagon, hit did look unreasonable I couldn't take hit further. But the road ter Coldneck was rougher, an' I couldn't give her no hold on me, so back I went, twelve miles, an' er whole day sp'iled. But Cooney was sorry, I could see; an' she never did ask me for many things, so I borrowed Buck Drawhorn's spring-wagon, an' next day, bright an' early, I put out erg'in. When I got back ter the ole home, she was stan'in' jus' like I left her, with her hands on her sides. I didn't get time ter put in 'fo' she called out: 'Nobody but er natchul-born fool would come here for er machine, an' clouds er-risin' in the rain quarter. Don't you know ef that machine gets wet hit won't be worth hits weight in ole iron? You can't get hit!' Well, gentlemen, seems ter me that with all our kiver mos' still in the house, she might er loant me some ter put on that machine; but she didn't; an' bein' 'fraid er myself, I wheeled roun' an' went back them twelve miles erg'in. Ernother day sp'iled, an' no machine. An' I won't do nobody er injustice, gentlemen. Hit did rain like all-fire, though whar hit come from I don't know tell now, an' I got wet ter the bones.

"But I was determ' then ter git that machine, if I didn't never plant er cotton-seed. Next day I rode up bright an' early, an' thar she was. I hadn't got out the wagon 'fo' she opened: 'You can't git that machine! You go back an' tell Cooney I'm ersewin' for Hester Bloodsworth, an' when I git done I'll let her know. An' don't you come back here no more tell I let her know.' Well, gentlemen, then I knowed I hadn't been 'fraid of myself for nothin'. I started ter cussin'! I cussed all the way up the walk, an' up the steps, an' inter the room, an' while I was shoulderin' that ar machine, an' while I was er-totin' hit out an' while I was er-loadin' hit in the wagon, an' while I was er-drivin' off. An' when I thought of them seventy-odd miles, an' the three days plantin' I'd done lost, I stopped at the rise in the road an' cussed back erg'in. I did hit, an', as I said, hit was ongentlemanly, an' I'm sorry. The only excuse I've got, gentlemen, is I did hit in self-defense, for if I hadn't cussed, so help me God, I'd er busted wide open then an' thar!"

The sensation that followed this remarkable climax was not soon stilled; but when quiet was at length restored, everybody's attention was attracted to the prosecutrix. She had never lifted her face from the time the defendant had mentioned the dead boy. She was still sitting with her face concealed, lost in thought, and it is likely that she never knew the conclusion of the defendant's statement. She looked up at last, impressed by the silence, and seeing the court gazing toward her as he fingered his books, she arose, wearily and unsteadily.

"Can I say a few words, judge?" Her voice was just audible at first. He nodded gravely. "Then I want to say that—I have— probably been wrong—all the way through. I have had—many troubles—many disappointments. Cooney's husband has been a good husband to her, and has always treated me kindly. I don't believe he intended to curse me, and I think if you will let me take it all back—" She hesitated and faltered.

"Be seated, madam," said the court, with something like tenderness in his voice. "Gentlemen of the jury, this case is dismissed."

The defendant came down from the stand, and paused before the woman in black a moment. Then he bent over her, but the only words any one caught were "Cooney" and "little Tom." He patted her shoulder with his rough, sunburnt hand. She hesitated a moment, and then, drawing down her veil, she took his arm and in silence left the courtroom. There was a sudden burst of applause, followed by the sound of the judge's gavel. At the door, Colonel Rutherford, leaning over the rail which separated the bar from the audience, thrust something into Hiram Ard's hand. "The fee goes with the speech," he said, smiling. "Keep it for little Tom."

1899

The Man That Corrupted Hadleyburg

MARK TWAIN

It was many years ago. Hadleyburg was the most honest and upright town in all the region round about. It had kept that reputation unsmirched during three generations, and was prouder of it than of any other of its possessions. It was so proud of it, and so anxious to insure its perpetuation, that it began to teach the principles of honest dealing to its babies in the cradle, and made the like teachings the staple of their culture thenceforward through all the years devoted to their education. Also, throughout the formative years temptations were kept out of the way of the young people, so that their honesty could have every chance to harden and solidify, and become a part of their very bone. The neighboring towns were jealous of this honorable supremacy, and affected to sneer at Hadleyburg's pride in it and call it vanity; but all the same they were obliged to acknowledge that Hadleyburg was in reality an incorruptible town; and if pressed they would also acknowledge that the mere fact that a young man hailed from Hadleyburg was all the recommendation he needed when he went forth from his natal town to seek for responsible employment.

But at last, in the drift of time, Hadleyburg had the ill luck to offend a passing stranger—possibly without knowing it, certainly without caring, for Hadleyburg was sufficient unto itself, and cared not a rap for strangers or their opinions. Still, it would have been well to make an exception in this one's case, for he was a bitter man and revengeful. All through his wanderings during a whole year he kept his injury in mind, and gave all his leisure moments to trying to invent a compensating satisfaction for it. He contrived many plans, and all of them were good, but none of them was quite sweeping enough; the poorest of them would hurt a great many individuals, but what he wanted was a plan which would comprehend the entire town, and not let so much as one person escape unhurt. At last he had a fortunate idea, and when it fell into his brain it lit up his whole head with an evil joy. He began to form a plan at once, saying to himself, "That is the thing to do—I will corrupt the town."

Six months later he went to Hadleyburg, and arrived in a buggy at the house of the old cashier of the bank about ten at night. He got a sack out of the buggy, shouldered it, and staggered with it through the cottage yard, and knocked at the door. A woman's voice said "Come in," and he entered, and set his sack behind the stove in the parlor, saying politely to the old lady who sat reading the *Missionary Herald* by the lamp:

"Pray keep your seat, madam, I will not disturb you. There—now it is pretty well concealed; one would hardly know it was there. Can I see your husband a moment, madam?"

No, he was gone to Brixton, and might not return before morning.

"Very well, madam, it is no matter. I merely wanted to leave that sack in his care, to be delivered to the rightful owner when he shall be found. I am a stranger; he does not know me; I am merely passing through the town to-night to discharge a matter which has been long in my mind. My errand is now completed, and I go pleased and a little proud, and you will never see me again. There is a paper attached to the sack which will explain everything. Good-night, madam."

The old lady was afraid of the mysterious big stranger, and was glad to see him go. But her curiosity was roused, and she went straight to the sack and brought away the paper. It began as follows:

"TO BE PUBLISHED: or, the right man sought out by private inquiry—either will answer. This sack contains gold coin weighing a hundred and sixty pounds four ounces—"

"Mercy on us, and the door not locked!"

Mrs. Richards flew to it all in a tremble and locked it, then pulled down the window-shades and stood frightened, worried, and wondering if there was anything else she could do toward making herself and the money more safe. She listened awhile for burglars, then surrendered to curiosity and went back to the lamp and finished reading the paper:

"I am a foreigner, and am presently going back to my own country, to remain there permanently. I am grateful to America for what I have received at her hands during my long stay under her flag; and to one of her citizens—a citizen of Hadleyburg—I am especially grateful for a great kindness done me a year or two ago. Two great kindnesses, in fact. I will explain. I was a gambler. I say I WAS. I was a ruined gambler. I arrived in this village at night, hungry and without a penny. I asked for help—in the dark; I was ashamed to beg in the light. I begged of the right man. He gave me twenty dollars—that it to say, he gave me life, as I considered it. He also gave me a fortune; for out of that money I have made myself rich at the gaming-table. And finally, a remark which he made to me has remained with me to this day, and has at last conquered me; and in conquering has saved the remnant of my morals: I shall gamble no more. Now I have no idea who that man was, but I want him found, and I want him to have this money, to give away, throw away, or keep, as he pleases. It is merely my way of testifying my gratitude to him. If I could stay, I would find him myself; but no matter, he will be found. This is an honest town, an incorruptible town, and I know I can trust it without fear. This man can be identified by the remark which he made to me; I feel persuaded that he will remember it.

"And now my plan is this: If you prefer to conduct the inquiry privately, do so. Tell the contents of this present writing to any one who is likely to be the right man. If he shall answer, 'I am the man; the remark I made was so-and-so,' apply the test—to wit: open the sack, and in it you will find a sealed envelope containing that remark. If the remark mentioned by the candidate tallies with it, give him the money, and ask no further questions, for he is certainly the right man.

"But if you shall prefer a public inquiry, then publish this present writing in the local paper—with these instructions added, to wit: Thirty days from now, let the candidate appear at the town-hall at eight in the evening (Friday), and hand his remark, in a sealed envelope, to the Rev. Mr. Burgess (if he will be kind enough to act); and let Mr. Burgess there and then destroy the seals of the sack, open it, and see if the remark is correct; if correct, let the money be delivered, with my sincere gratitude, to my benefactor thus identified."

Mrs. Richards sat down, gently quivering with excitement, and was soon lost in thinkings—after this pattern: "What a strange thing it is! . . . And what a fortune for that kind man who set his bread afloat upon the waters! . . . If it had only been my husband that did it! . . . for we are so poor, so old and poor! . . ." Then, with a sigh—"But it was not my Edward; no, it was not he that gave a stranger twenty dollars. It is a pity, too; I see it now . . ." Then, with a shudder—"But it is *gambler's* money! the wages of sin: we couldn't take it; we couldn't touch it. I don't like to be near it; it seems a defilement." She moved to a farther chair . . . "I wish Edward would come, and take it to the bank; a burglar might come at any moment; it is dreadful to be here all alone with it."

At eleven Mr. Richards arrived, and while his wife was saying, "I am *so* glad you've come!" he was saying, "I'm so tired—tired clear out; it is dreadful to be poor, and have to make these dismal journeys at my time of life. Always at the grind, grind, grind, on a salary—another man's slave, and he sitting at home in his slippers, rich and comfortable."

"I am so sorry for you, Edward, you know that; but be comforted: we have our livelihood; we have our good name—"

"Yes, Mary, and that is everything. Don't mind my talk—it's just a moment's irritation and doesn't mean anything. Kiss me—

there, it's all gone now, and I am not complaining any more. What have you been getting? What's in the sack?"

Then his wife told him the great secret. It dazed him for a moment; then he said:

"It weighs a hundred and sixty pounds? Why, Mary, it's for-ty thou-sand dollars—think of it—a whole fortune! Not ten men in this village are worth that much. Give me the paper."

He skimmed through it and said:

"Isn't it an adventure! Why, it's a romance; it's like the impossible things one reads about in books, and never sees in life." He was well stirred up now, cheerful, even gleeful. He tapped his old wife on the cheek, and said, humorously, "Why, we're rich, Mary, rich; all we've got to do is to bury the money and burn the papers. If the gambler ever comes to inquire, we'll merely look coldly upon him and say: 'What is this nonsense you are talking? We have never heard of you and your sack of gold before'; and then he would look foolish, and—"

"And in the meantime, while you are running on with your jokes, the money is still here, and it is fast getting along toward burglar-time."

"True. Very well, what shall we do—make the inquiry private? No, not that: it would spoil the romance. The public method is better. Think what a noise it will make! And it will make all the other towns jealous; for no stranger would trust such a thing to any town but Hadleyburg, and they know it. It's a great card for us. I must get to the printing-office, now, or I shall be too late."

"But stop—stop—don't leave me here alone with it, Edward!"

But he was gone. For only a little while, however. Not far from his own house he met the editor-proprietor of the paper, and gave him the document, and said, "Here is a good thing for you, Cox—put it in!"

"It may be too late, Mr. Richards, but I'll see."

At home again he and his wife sat down to talk the charming mystery over; they were in no condition for sleep. The first question was, "Who could the citizen have been who gave

the stranger the twenty dollars?" It seemed a simple one; both
answered it in the same breath—

"Barclay Goodson."

"Yes," said Richards, "he would have done it, and it would
have been like him, but there's not another in the town."

"Everybody will grant that, Edward—grant it privately,
anyway. For six months, now, the village has been its own
proper self once more—honest, narrow, self-righteous, and
stingy."

"It's what he always called it, to the day of his death—said it
right out publicly, too."

"Yes, and he was hated for it."

"Oh, of course; but he didn't care. I reckon he was the best-
hated man among us, except the Reverend Burgess."

"Well, Burgess deserves it—he will never get another
congregation here. Mean as the town is, it knows how to
estimate *him*. Edward, doesn't it seem odd that the stranger
should appoint Burgess to deliver the money?"

"Well, yes—it does. That is—that is—"

"Why so much that-*is*-ing? Would *you* select him?"

"Mary, maybe the stranger knows him better than this
village does."

"Much *that* would help Burgess!"

The husband seemed perplexed for an answer; the wife
kept a steady eye upon him, and waited. Finally Richards said,
with the hesitancy of one who is making a statement which is
likely to encounter doubt,

"Mary, Burgess is not a bad man."

His wife was certainly surprised.

"Nonsense!" she exclaimed.

"He is not a bad man. I know. The whole of his unpopulari-
ty had its foundation in that one thing—the thing that made so
much noise."

"That 'one thing,' indeed! As if that 'one thing' wasn't
enough, all by itself."

"Plenty. Plenty. Only he wasn't guilty of it."

"How you talk! Not guilty of it! Everybody knows he *was*
guilty."

"Mary, I give you my word—he was innocent."

"I can't believe it, and I don't. How do you know?"

"It is a confession. I am ashamed, but I will make it. I was the only man who knew he was innocent. I could have saved him, and—and—well, you know how the town was wrought up—I hadn't the pluck to do it. It would have turned everybody against me. I felt mean, ever so mean; but I didn't dare; I hadn't the manliness to face that."

Mary looked troubled, and for a while was silent. Then she said, stammeringly:

"I—I don't think it would have done for you to—to—One mustn't—er—public opinion—one has to be so careful—so—" It was a difficult road, and she got mired; but after a little she got started again. "It was a great pity, but—Why, we couldn't afford it, Edward—we couldn't indeed. Oh, I wouldn't have had you do it for anything!"

"It would have lost us the good-will of so many people, Mary; and then—and then—"

"What troubles me now is, what *he* thinks of us, Edward."

"He? *He* doesn't suspect that I could have saved him."

"Oh," exclaimed the wife, in a tone of relief, "I am glad of that. As long as he doesn't know that you could have saved him, he—he—well, that makes it a great deal better. Why, I might have known he didn't know, because he is always trying to be friendly with us, as little encouragement as we give him. More than once people have twitted me with it. There's the Wilsons, and the Wilcoxes, and the Harknesses, they have a mean pleasure in saying, 'Your friend Burgess," because they know it pesters me. I wish he wouldn't persist in liking us so; I can't think why he keeps it up."

"I can explain it. It's another confession. When the thing was new and hot, and the town made a plan to ride him on a rail, my conscience hurt me so that I couldn't stand it, and I went privately and gave him notice, and he got out of the town and staid out till it was safe to come back."

"Edward! If the town had found it out—"

"*Don't!* It scares me yet, to think of it. I repented of it the minute it was done; and I was even afraid to tell you, lest your face might betray it to somebody. I didn't sleep any that night, for worrying. But after a few days I saw that no one was going to suspect me, and after that I got to feeling glad I did it. And I feel glad yet, Mary—glad through and through."

"So do I, now, for it would have been a dreadful way to treat him. Yes, I'm glad; for really you did owe him that, you know. But, Edward, suppose it should come out yet, some day!"

"It won't."

"Why?"

"Because everybody thinks it was Goodson."

"Of course they would!"

"Certainly. And of course *he* didn't care. They persuaded poor old Sawlsberry to go and charge it on him, and he went blustering over there and did it. Goodson looked him over, like as if he was hunting for a place on him that he could despise the most, then he says, 'So you are the Committee of Inquiry, are you?' Sawlsberry said that was about what he was. 'Hm. Do they require particulars, or do you reckon a kind of a *general* answer will do?' 'If they require particulars, I will come back, Mr. Goodson; I will take the general answer first,' 'Very well, then, tell them to go to hell—I reckon that's general enough. And I'll give you some advice, Sawlsberry; when you come back for the particulars, fetch a basket to carry the relics of yourself home in.'"

"Just like Goodson; it's got all the marks. He had only one vanity: he thought he could give advice better than any other person."

"It settled the business, and saved us, Mary. The subject was dropped."

"Bless you, I'm not doubting *that*."

Then they took up the gold-sack mystery again, with strong interest. Soon the conversation began to suffer breaks—interruptions caused by absorbed thinkings. The breaks grew more and more frequent. At last Richards lost himself wholly in thought. He sat long, gazing vacantly at the floor, and by and by he began to punctuate his thoughts with little nervous movements of his hands that seemed to indicate vexation. Meantime his wife too had relapsed into a thoughtful silence, and her movements were beginning to show a troubled discomfort. Finally Richards got up and strode aimlessly about the room, plowing his hands through his hair, much as a somnambulist might do who was having a bad dream. Then he seemed to arrive at a definite purpose; and without a word he put on his hat and passed quickly out of the house. His wife sat brooding, with a drawn face, and did not seem to be aware that she was alone. Now and then she murmured, "Lead us not into t— . . . but—but—we are so poor, so poor! . . . Lead us not into . . . Ah, who would be hurt by it?—and no one would ever know . . . Lead us . . ." The voice died out in mumblings. After a little she glanced up and muttered in a half-frightened, half-glad way—

"He is gone! But, oh dear, he may be too late—too late . . . Maybe not—maybe there is still time." She rose and stood thinking, nervously clasping and unclasping her hands. A slight shudder shook her frame, and she said, out of a dry throat, "God forgive me—it's awful to think such things— but . . . Lord, how we are made—how strangely we are made!"

She turned the light low, and slipped stealthily over and kneeled down by the sack and felt of it ridgy sides with her hands, and fondled them lovingly; and there was a gloating light in her poor old eyes. She fell into fits of absence; and came half out of them at times to mutter, "If we had only waited!—oh, if we had only waited a little, and not been in such a hurry!"

Meantime Cox had gone home from his office and told his wife all about the strange things that had happened, and they had talked it over eagerly, and guessed that the late Goodson was the only man in the town who could have helped a suffering stranger with so noble a sum as twenty dollars. Then there was a pause, and the two became thoughtful and silent. And by and by nervous and fidgety. At last the wife said, as if to herself,

"Nobody knows this secret but the Richardses . . . and us . . . nobody."

The husband came out of his thinkings with a slight start, and gazed wistfully at his wife, whose face was become very pale; then he hesitatingly rose, and glanced furtively at his hat, then at his wife—a sort of mute inquiry. Mrs. Cox swallowed once or twice, with her hand at her throat, then in place of speech she nodded her head. In a moment she was alone, and mumbling to herself.

And now Richards and Cox were hurrying through the deserted streets, from opposite directions. They met, panting, at the foot of the printing-office stairs; by the night-light there they read each other's face. Cox whispered,

"Nobody knows about this but us?"

The whispered answer was,

"Not a soul—on honor, not a soul!"

"If it isn't too late to—"

The men were starting up-stairs; at this moment they were overtaken by a boy, and Cox asked,

"Is that you, Johnny?"

"Yes, sir."

"You needn't ship the early mail—nor *any* mail; wait till I tell you."

"It's already gone, sir."

"*Gone?*" It had the sound of an unspeakable disappointment in it.

"Yes, sir. Time-table for Brixton and all the towns beyond changed to-day, sir—had to get the papers in twenty minutes earlier than common. I had to rush; if I had been two minutes later—'

The men turned and walked slowly away, not waiting to hear the rest. Neither of them spoke during ten minutes; then Cox said, in a vexed tone,

"What possessed you to be in such a hurry, I can't make out."

The answer was humble enough:

"I see it now, but somehow I never thought, you know, until it was too late. But the next time—"

"Next time be hanged! It won't come in a thousand years."

Then the friends separated without a good-night, and dragged themselves home with the gait of mortally stricken men. At their homes their wives sprang up with an eager

"Well?"—then saw the answer with their eyes and sank down sorrowing, without waiting for it to come in words. In both houses a discussion followed of a heated sort—a new thing; there had been discussions before, but not heated ones, not ungentle ones. The discussions tonight were a sort of seeming plagiarisms of each other. Mrs. Richard said,

"If you had only waited, Edward—if you had only stopped to think; but no, you must run straight to the printing-office and spread it all over the world."

"It *said* publish it."

"That is nothing; it also said do it privately, if you liked. There, now—is that true, or not?"

"Why, yes—yes, it is true; but when I thought what a stir it would make, and what a compliment it was to Hadleyburg that a stranger should trust it so—"

"Oh, certainly, I know all that; but if you had only stopped to think, you would have seen that you *couldn't* find the right man, because he is in his grave, and hasn't left chick nor child nor relation behind him; and as long as the money went to somebody that awfully needed it, and nobody would be hurt by it, and—and—"

She broke down crying. Her husband tried to think of some comforting thing to say, and prpesently came out with this:

"But after all, Mary, it must be for the best—it *must* be; we know that. And we must remember that it was so ordered—"

"Ordered! Oh, everything's *ordered*, when a person has to find some way out when he has been stupid. Just the same, it was *ordered* that the money should come to us in this special way, and it was you that must take it on yourself to go meddling with the designs of Providence—and who gave you the right? It was wicked, that is what is was—just blasphemous presumption, and no more becoming to a meek and humble professor of—"

"But, Mary, you know how we have been trained all our lives long, like the whole village, till it is absolutely second nature to us to stop not a single moment to think when there's an honest thing to be done—"

"Oh, I know it, I know it—it's been one everlasting training and training and training in honesty—honesty shielded, from the very cradle, against every possible temptation, and so it's *artificial* honesty, and weak as water when temptation comes, as we have seen this night. God knows I never had shade nor shadow of a doubt of my petrified and indestructible honesty until now—and now, under the very first big and real temptation, I—Edward, it is my belief that this town's honesty is as rotten as mine is; as rotten as yours is. It is a mean town, a hard, stingy town, and hasn't a virtue in the world but this honesty it is so celebrated for and so conceited about; and so help me, I do believe that if ever the day comes that its honesty falls under great temptation, its grand reputation will go to ruin like a house of cards. There, now, I've made confession, and I feel better; I am a humbug, and I've been one all my life, without knowing it. Let no man call me honest again—I will not have it."

"I—well, Mary, I feel a good deal as you do; I certainly do. It seems strange, too, so strange. I never could have believed it—never."

A long silence followed; both were sunk in thought. At last the wife looked up and said,

"I know what you are thinking, Edward."

Richards had the embarrassed look of a person who is caught.

"I am ashamed to confess it, Mary, but—"

"It's no matter, Edward, I was thinking the same question myself."

"I hope so. State it."

"You were thinking, if a body could only guess out *what the remark was* that Goodson made to the stranger.

"It's perfectly true. I feel guilty and ashamed. And you?"

"I'm past it. Let us make a pallet here, we've got to stand watch till the bank vault opens in the morning and admits the sack . . . Oh dear, oh dear—if we hadn't made the mistake!"

The pallet was made, and Mary said:

"The open sesame—what could it have been? I do wonder what that remark could have been? But come; we will get to bed now."

"And sleep?"

"No: think."

"Yes, think."

By this time the Coxes too had completed their spat and their reconciliation, and were turning in—to think, to think, and toss, and fret, and worry over what the remark could possibly have been which Goodson made to the stranded derelict; that golden remark; that remark worth forty thousand dollars, cash.

The reason that the village telegraph office was open later than usual that night was this: The foreman of Cox's paper was the local representative of the Associated Press. One might say its honorary representative, for it wasn't four times a year that he could furnish thirty words that would be accepted. But this time it was different. His dispatch stating what he had caught got an instant answer:

Send the whole thing—all the details—twelve hundred words.

A colossal order! the foreman filled the bill; and he was the proudest man in the State. By breakfast-time the next morning the name of Hadleyburg the Incorruptible was on every lip in America, from Montreal to the Gulf, from the glaciers of Alaska to the orange-groves of Florida; and millions and millions of people were discussing the stranger and his money-sack, and wondering if the right man would be found, and hoping some more news about the matter would come soon—right away.

II

Hadleyburg village woke up world-celebrated—astonished—happy—vain. Vain beyond imagination. Its nineteen principal citizens and their wives went about shaking hands with each other, and beaming, and smiling, and congratulating, and saying *this* thing adds a new word to the dictionary— *Hadleyburg*, synonym for *incorruptible*—destined to live in dictionaries forever! And the minor and unimportant citizens and their wives went around acting in much the same way. Everybody ran to the bank to see the gold-sack; and before noon grieved and envious crowds began to flock in from Brixton and all neighboring towns; and that afternoon and next day reporters began to arrive from everywhere to verify the sack and its history and write the whole thing up anew, and make dashing free-hand pictures of the sack, and of Richards's house, and the bank, and the Presbyterian church, and the Baptist church, and the public square, and the town-hall where the test would be applied and the money delivered; and damnable portraits of the Richardses, and Pinkerton the banker, and Cox, and the foreman, and Reverend Burgess, and the postmaster—and even of Jack Halliday, who was the loafing, good-natured, no-account, irreverent fisherman, hunter, boys' friend, stray-dogs' friend, typical "Sam Lawson" of the town. The little mean, smirking, oily Pinkerton showed the sack to all comers, and rubbed his sleek palms together pleasantly, and enlarged upon the town's fine old reputation for honesty and upon this wonderful endorsement of it, and hoped and believed that the example would now spread far and wide over the American world, and be epoch-making in the matter of moral regeneration. And so on, and so on.

By the end of the week things had quieted down again; the wild intoxication of pride and joy had sobered to a soft, sweet, silent delight—a sort of deep, nameless, unutterable content. All faces bore a look of peaceful, holy happiness.

Then a change came. It was a gradual change; so gradual that its beginnings were hardly noticed; maybe were not noticed at all, except by Jack Halliday, who always noticed everything; and always made fun of it, too, no matter what it was. He began to throw out chaffing remarks about people not looking quite so happy as they did a day or two ago; and next he claimed that the new aspect was deepening to positive sadness; next, that it was taking on a sick look; and finally he said that everybody was become so moody, thoughtful, and absent-minded that he could rob the meanest man in town of a cent out of the bottom of his breeches pocket and not disturb his revery.

At this stage—or at about this stage—a saying like this was dropped at bedtime—with a sigh, usually—by the head of each of the nineteen principal households: "Ah, what *could* have been the remark that Goodson made?"

And straightway—with a shudder—came this, from the man's wife:

"Oh, *don't*! What horrible thing are you mulling in your mind? Put it away from you, for God's sake!"

But that question was wrung from those men again the next night—and got the same retort. But weaker.

And the third night the men uttered the question yet again—with anguish, and absently. This time—and the following night—the wives fidgeted feebly, and tried to say something. But didn't.

And the night after that they found their tongues and responded—longingly,

"Oh, if we *could* only guess!"

Halliday's comments grew daily more and more sparklingly disagreeable and disparaging. He went diligently about, laughing at the town, individually and in mass. But his laugh was the only one left in the village: it fell upon a hollow and mournful vacancy and emptiness. Not even a smile was findable anywhere. Halliday carried a cigar-box around on a tripod, playing that it was a camera, and halted all passers and aimed the thing and said, "Ready!—now look pleasant, please," but not even this capital joke could surprise the dreary faces into any softening.

So three weeks passed—one week was left. It was Saturday evening—after supper. Instead of the aforetime Saturday-evening flutter and bustle and shopping and larking, the streets were empty and desolate. Richards and his old wife sat apart in their little parlor—miserable and thinking. This was become their evening habit now: the lifelong habit which had preceded it, of reading, knitting, and contented chat, or receiving or paying neighborly calls, was dead and gone and forgotten, ages ago—two or three weeks ago; nobody talked now, nobody read, nobody visited—the whole village sat at home, sighing, worrying, silent. Trying to guess out that remark.

The postman left a letter. Richards glanced listlessly at the superscription and the postmark—unfamiliar, both—and tossed the letter on the table and resumed his might-have-beens and his hopeless dull miseries where he had left them off. Two or three hours later his wife got wearily up and was going away to bed wihtout a good-night—custom now—but she stopped near the letter and eyed it awhile with a dead interest, then broke it open, and began to skim it over. Richards, sitting there with his chair tilted back against the wall and his chin between his knees, heard something fall. It was his wife. He sprang to her side, but she cried out:

"Leave me alone, I am too happy. Read the letter—read it!"

He did. He devoured it, his brain reeling. The letter was from a distant State, and it said:

"I am a stranger to you, but no matter: I have something to tell. I have just arrived home from Mexico, and learned about that episode. Of course you do not know who made that remark, but I know, and I am the only person living who does know. It was GOODSON. I knew him well, many years ago. I passed through your village that very night, and was his guest till the midnight train came along. I overheard him make that remark to the stranger in the dark—it was in Hale Alley. He and I talked of it the rest of the way home, and while smoking in his house. He mentioned many of your villagers in the course of his talk—most of them in a very uncomplimentary way, but two or three favorably; among these latter yourself. I say 'favorably'—nothing stronger. I remember his saying he did not actually LIKE any person in the town—not one; but that you—I THINK he said you—am almost sure—had done him a very great service once, possibly without knowing the full value of it, and he wished he had a fortune, he would leave it to you when he died, and a curse apiece for the rest of the citizens. Now, then, if it was you that did him that service, you are his legitimate heir, and entitled to the sack of gold. I know that I can trust to your honor and honesty, for in a citizen of Hadleyburg these virtues are an unfailing inheritance, and so I am going to reveal to you the remark, well satisfied that if you are not the right man you will seek and find the right one and see that poor Goodson's debt of gratitude for the service referred to is paid. This is the remark: 'YOU ARE FAR FROM BEING A BAD MAN: GO AND REFORM.'

"Howard L. Stephenson."

"Oh, Edward, the money is ours, and I am so grateful, *oh*, so grarteful—kiss me, dear, it's forever since we kissed—and we needed it so—the money—and now you are free of Pinkerton and his bank, and nobody's slave any more; it seems to me I could fly for joy."

It was a happy half-hour that the couple spent there on the settee caressing each other; it was the old days come again— days that had begun with their courtship and lasted without a break till the stranger brought the deadly money. By and by the wife said:

"Oh, Edward, how lucky it was you did him that grand service, poor Goodson! I never liked him, but I love him now. And it was fine and beautiful of you never to mention it or brag about it." Then, with a touch of reproach, "But you ought to have told *me*, Edward, you ought to have told your wife, you know."

"Well, I—er—well, Mary, you see—"

"Now stop hemming and hawing, and tell me about it, Edward. I always loved you, and now I'm proud of you. Everybody believes there was only one good generous soul in this village, and now it turns out that you—Edward, why don't you tell me?"

"Well—er—er—Why, Mary, I can't!"

"You *can't*? *Why* can't you?"

"You see, he—well, he—he made me promise I wouldn't."

The wife looked him over, and said, very slowly,

"Made—you—promise? Edward, what do you tell me that for?"

"Mary, do you think I would lie?"

She was troubled and silent for a moment, then she laid her hand within his and said:

"No . . . no. We have wandered far enough from our bearings—God spare us that! In all you life you have never uttered a lie. But now—now that the foundations of things seem to be crumbling from under us, we—we—" She lost her voice for a moment, then said, brokenly, "lead us not into temptation . . . I think you made the promise, Edward. Let it rest so. Let us keep away from that ground. Now—that is all gone by; let us be happy again; it is no time for clouds."

Edward found it something of an effort to comply, for his mind kept wandering—trying to remember what the service was that he had done Goodson.

The couple lay awake the most of the night, Mary happy and busy, Edward busy but not so happy. Mary was planning what she would do with the money. Edward was trying to recall that service. At first his conscience was sore on account of the lie he had told Mary—if it was a lie. After much reflection— suppose it *was* a lie? What then? Was it such a great matter? Aren't we always *acting* lies? Then why not *tell* them? Look at Mary—look what she had done. While he was hurrying off on his honest errand, what was she doing? Lamenting because the papers hadn't been destroyed and the money kept! Is theft better than lying?

That point lost its sting—the lie dropped into the background and left comfort behind it. The next point came to the front: *Had* he rendered that service? Well, here was Goodson's own evidence as reported in Stephenson's letter, there could be no better evidence than that—it was even *proof* that he had rendered it. Of course. So that point was settled . . . No, not quite. He recalled with a wince that his unknown Mr. Stephenson was just a trifle unsure as to whether the performer of it was Richards or some other—and, oh dear, he had put Richards on his honor! He must himself decide whither that money must go—and Mr. Stephenson was not doubting that if he was the wrong man he would go honorably and find the right one. Oh, it was odious to put a man in such a situation—ah, why couldn't Stephenson have left out that doubt! What did he want to intrude that for?

Further reflection. How did it happen that *Richards's* name remained in Stephenson's mind as indicating the right man, and not some other man's name? That looked good. Yes, that looked very good. In fact, it went on looking better and better, straight along—until by and by it grew into positive *proof*. And then Richards put the matter at once out of his mind, for he had a private instinct that a proof once established is better left so.

He was feeling reasonably comfortable now, but there was still one other detail that kept pushing itself on his notice: of course he had done that service—that was settled; but what *was* that service? He must recall it—he would not go to sleep till he had recalled it; it would make his peace of mind perfect. And so he thought and thought. He thought of a dozen things— possible services, even probable services—but none of them seemed adequate, none of them seemed large enough, none of them seemed worth the money—worth the fortune Goodson had wished he could leave in his will. And besides, he couldn't remember having done them, anyway. Now, then—now, then— what *kind* of a service would it be that would make a man so inordinately grateful? Ah—the saving of his soul! That must be it. Yes, he could remember, now, how he once set himself the task of converting Goodson, and labored at it as much as—he was going to say three months; but upon closer examination it shrunk to a month, then to a week, then to a day, then to nothing. Yes, he remembered now, and with unwelcome vividness, that Goodson had told him to go to thunder and mind his own business—*he* wasn't hankering to follow Hadley-burg to heaven!

So that solution was a failure—he hadn't saved Goodson's soul. Richards was discouraged. Then after a little came another idea: had he saved Goodson's property? No, that wouldn't do— he hadn't any. His life? That is it! Of course. Why, he might have thought of it before. This time he was on the right track, sure. His imagination-mill was hard at work in a minute, now.

Thereafter during a stretch of two exhausting hours he was busy saving Goodson's life. He saved it in all kinds of difficult and perilous ways. In every case he got it saved satisfactorily up to a certain point; then, just as he was beginning to get well persuaded that it had really happened, a troublesome detail would turn up which made the whole thing impossible. As in the matter of drowning, for instance. In that case he had swum

out and tugged Goodson ashore in an unconscious state with a
great crowd looking on and applauding, but when he had got it
all thought out and was just beginning to remember all about it,
a whole swarm of disqualifying details arrived on the ground;
the town would have known of the circumstance, Mary would
have known of it, it would glare like a limelight in his own
memory instead of being an inconspicuous service which he had
possibly rendered "without knowing its full value." And at this
point he remembered that he couldn't swim, anyway.

Ah—*there* was a point which he had been overlooking from
the start: it had to be a service which he had rendered "possibly
without knowing the full value of it." Why, really, that ought to
be an easy hunt—much easier than those others. And sure
enough, by and by he found it. Goodson, years and years ago,
came near marrying a very sweet and pretty girl, named Nancy
Hewitt, but in some way or other the match had been broken
off; the girl died; Goodson remained a bachelor, and by and by
became a soured one and a frank despiser of the human species.
Soon after the girl's death the village found out, or thought it
had found out, that she carried a spoonful of negro blood in her
veins. Richards worked at these details a good while, and in the
end he thought he remembered things concerning them which
must have gotten mislaid in his memory through long neglect.
He seemed to dimly remember that it was *he* that found out
about the negro blood; that it was he that told the village; that
the village told Goodson where they got it; that he thus saved
Goodson from marrying the tainted girl; that he had done him
this great service "without knowing the full value of it," in fact
without knowing that he *was* doing it; but that Goodson knew
the value of it, and what a narrow escape he had had, and so
went to his grave grateful to his benefactor and wishing he had a
fortune to leave him. It was all clear and simple now, and the
more he went over it the more luminous and certain it grew; and
at last, when he nestled to sleep satisfied and happy, he
remembered the whole thing just as if it had been yesterday. In
fact, he dimly remembered Goodson's *telling* him his gratitude
once. Meantime Mary had spent six thousand dollars on a new

house for herself and a pair of slippers for her pastor, and then had fallen peacefully to rest.

That same Saturday evening the postman had delivered a letter to each of the other principal citizens—nineteen letters in all. No two of the envelopes were alike, and no two of the superscriptions were in the same hand, but the letters inside were just like each other in every detail but one. They were exact copies of the letter received by Richards—handwriting and all— and were all signed by Stephenson, but in place of Richards's name each receiver's own name appeared.

All night long eighteen principal citizens did what their caste-brother Richards was doing at the same time—they put in their energies trying to remember what notable service it was that they had unconsciously done Barclay Goodson. In no case was it a holiday job; still they succeeded.

And while they were at this work, which was difficult, their wives put in the night spending the money, which was easy. During that one night the nineteen wives spent an average of seven thousand dollars each out of the forty thousand in the sack—a hundred and thirty-three thousand altogether.

Next day there was a surprise for Jack Halliday. He noticed that the faces of the nineteen chief citizens and their wives bore that expression of peaceful and holy happiness again. He could not understand it, neither was he able to invent any remarks about it that could damage it or disturb it. And so it was his turn to be dissatisfied with life. His private guesses at the reasons for the happiness failed in all instances, upon examination. When he met Mrs. Wilcox and noticed the placid ecstasy in her face, he said to himself, "Her cat has had kittens"—and went and asked the cook: but it was not so; the cook had detected the happiness, but did not know the cause. When Halliday found the duplicate ecstasy in the face of "Shadbelly" Billson (village nickname), he was sure some neighbor of Billson's had broken his leg, but inquiry showed that this had not happened. The subdued ecstasy in Gregory Yates's face could mean but one thing—he was a mother-in-law short: it was another mistake. "And Pinkerton—Pinkerton—he has collected ten cents that he thought he was going to lose." And so on, and so on. In some cases the guesses had to remain in doubt, in the others they proved distinct errors. In the end Halliday said to himself, "Anyway it foots up that there's nineteen Hadleyburg families temporarily in heaven: I don't know how it happened; I only know Providence is off duty today."

An architect and builder from the next State had lately ventured to set up a small business in this unpromising village, and his sign had now been hanging out a week. Not a customer yet; he was a discouraged man, and sorry he had come. But his weather changed suddenly now. First one and then another chief citizen's wife said to him privately:

"Come to my house Monday week—but say nothing about it for the present. We think of building."

He got eleven invitations that day. That night he wrote his daughter and broke off her match with her student. He said she could marry a mile higher than that.

Pinkerton the banker and two or three other well-to-do men planned country-seats—but waited. That kind don't count their chickens until they are hatched.

The Wilsons devised a grand new thing—a fancy-dress ball. They made no actual promises, but told all their acquaintanceship in confidence that they were thinking the matter over and thought they should give it—"and if we do, you will be invited, of course." People were surprised, and said, one to another, "Why they are crazy, those poor Wilsons, they can't afford it." Several among the nineteen said privately to their husbands, "It is a good idea: we will keep still till their cheap thing is over, then *we* will give one that will make it sick."

The days drifted along, and the bill of future squanderings rose higher and higher, wilder and wilder, more and more foolish and reckless. It began to look as if every member of the nineteen would not only spend his whole forty thousand dollars before receiving-day, but be actually in debt by the time he got the money. In some cases light-headed people did not stop with planning to spend, they really spent—on credit. They bought land, mortgages, farms, speculative stocks, fine clothes, horses, and various other things, paid down the bonus, and made themselves liable for the rest—at ten days. Presently the sober second thought came, and Halliday noticed that a ghastly anxiety was beginning to show up in a good many faces. Again he was puzzled, and didn't know what to make of it. "The Wilcox kittens aren't dead, for they weren't born; nobody's broken a leg; there's no shrinkage in mother-in-laws; *nothing* has happened—it is an unsolvable mystery."

There was another puzzled man, too—the Rev. Mr. Burgess. For days, wherever he went, people seemed to follow him or to be watching out for him; and if he ever found himself in a retired spot, a member of the nineteen would be sure to appear, thrust an envelope privately into his hand, whisper "To be opened at the town-hall Friday evening," then vanish away like a guilty thing. He was expecting that there might be one claimant for the sack,—doubtful, however, Goodson being dead,—but it never occurred to him that all this crowd might be claimants. When the great Friday came at last, he found that he had nineteen envelopes.

III

The town-hall had never looked finer. The platform at the end of it was backed by a showy draping of flags; at intervals along the walls were festoons of flags; the gallery fronts were clothed in flags; the supporting columns were swathed in flags; all this was to impress the stranger, for he would be there in considerable force, and in a large degree he would be connected with the press. The house was full. The 412 fixed seats were occupied; also the 68 extra chairs which had been packed into the aisles; the steps of the platform were occupied; some distinguished strangers were given seats on the platform; at the horseshoe of tables which fenced the front and sides of the platform sat a strong force of special correspondents who had come from everywhere. It was the best-dressed house the town had ever produced. There were some tolerably expensive toilets there, and in several cases the ladies who wore them had the look of being unfamiliar with that kind of clothes. At least the town thought they had that look, but the notion could have arisen from the town's knowledge of the fact that these ladies had never inhabited such clothes before.

The gold-sack stood on a little table at the front of the platform where all the house could see it. The bulk of the house gazed at it with a burning interest, a mouth-watering interest, a wistful and pathetic interest; a minority of nineteen couples gazed at it tenderly, lovingly, proprietarily, and the male half of this minority kept saying over to themselves the moving little impromptu speeches of thankfulness for the audience's applause and congratulations which they were presently going to get up and deliver. Every now and then one of these got a piece of paper out of his vest pocket and privately glanced at it to refresh his memory.

Of course there was a buzz of conversation going on—there always is; but at last when the Rev. Mr. Burgess rose and laid his hand on the sack he could hear his microbes gnaw, the place was so still. He related the curious history of the sack, then went on to speak in warm terms of Hadleyburg's old and well-earned reputation for spotless honesty, and of the town's pride in this reputation. He said that this reputation was a treasure of priceless value; that under Providence its value had now become inestimably enhanced, for the recent episode had spread this fame far and wide, and thus had focused the eyes of the American world upon this village, and made its name for all time, as he hoped and believed, a synonym for commerical incorruptibility. [*Applause.*] "And who is to be the guardian of this noble treasure—the community as a whole? No! The responsibility is individual, not communal. From this day forth each and every one of you is in his own person its special guardian, and individually responsible that no harm shall come of it. Do you—does each of you—accept this great trust? [*Tumultuous assent.*] Then all is well. Transmit it to your children and to your children's children. Today your purity is beyond reproach—see to it that it shall remain so. Today there is not a person in your community who could be beguiled to touch a penny not his own—see to it that you abide in this grace. ["*We will! We will!*"] This is not the place to make comparisons between ourselves and other communities—some of them ungracious toward us; they have their ways, we have ours; let us be content. [*Applause.*] I am done. Under my hand, my friends, rests a stranger's eloquent recognition of what we are; through him the world will always henceforth know what we are. We do not know who he is, but in your name I utter your gratitude, and ask you to raise your voices in endorsement."

The house rose in a body and made the walls quake with the thunders of its thankfulness for the space of a long minute. Then it sat down, and Mr. Burgess took an envelope out of his pocket. The house held its breath while he slit the envelope open and took from it a slip of paper. He reads its contents— slowly and impressively—the audience listening with tranced attention to this magic document, each of whose words stood for an ingot of gold:

"'The remark which I made to the distressed stranger was this: "You are very far from being a bad man; go, and reform."'" Then he continued:

"We shall know in a moment now whether the remark here quoted corresponds with the one concealed in the sack; and if that shall prove to be so—and it undoubtedly will—this sack of gold belongs to a fellow-citizen who will henceforth stand before the nation as a symbol of the special virtue which has made our town famous throughout the land—Mr. Billson!"

The house had gotten itself all ready to burst into the proper tornado of applause; but instead of doing it, it seemed stricken with a paralysis; there was a deep hush for a moment or two, then a wave of whispered murmurs swept the place—of about this tenor: "*Billson!* oh, come, this is *too* thin! Twenty dollars to a stranger—or anybody—*Billson!* tell it to the marines!" And now at this point the house caught its breath all of a sudden in a new access of astonishment, for it discovered that whereas in one part of the hall Deacon Billson was standing up with his head meekly bowed, in another part of it Lawyer Wilson was doing the same. There was a wondering silence now for a while.

Everybody was puzzled, and nineteen couples were surprised and indignant.

Billson and Wilson turned and stared at each other. Billson asked, bitingly,

"Why do *you* rise, Mr. Wilson?"

"Because I have a right to. Perhaps you will be good enough to explain to the house why *you* rise?"

"With great pleasure. Because I wrote that paper."

"It is an impudent falsity! I wrote it myself."

It was Burgess's turn to be paralyzed. He stood looking vacantly at first one of the men and then the other, and did not seem to know what to do. The house was stupefied. Lawyer Wilson spoke up, now, and said,

"I ask the Chair to read the name signed to that paper."

That brought the Chair to itself, and it read out the name,

" 'John Wharton *Billson*.' "

"There!" shouted Billson, "what have you got to say for yourself, now? And what kind of apology are you going to make to me and to this insulted house for the imposture which you have attempted to play here?"

"No apologies are due, sir; and as for the rest of it, I publicly charge you with pilfering my note from Mr. Burgess and substituting a copy of it signed with your own name. There is no other way by which you could have gotten hold of the test-remark; I alone, of living men, possessed the secret of its wording."

There was likely to be a scandalous state of things if this went on; everybody noticed with distress that the short-hand scribes were scribbling like mad; many people were crying "Chair, Chair! Order! order!" Burges rapped with his gavel, and said:

"Let us not forget the proprieties due. There has evidently been a mistake somewhere, but surely that is all. If Mr. Wilson gave me an envelope—and I remember now that he did—I still have it."

He took one out of his pocket, opened it, glanced at it, looked surprised and worried, and stood silent a few moments. Then he waved his hand in a wandering and mechanical way, and made an effort or two to say something, then gave it up, despondently. Several voices cried out:

"Read it! read it! What is it?"

So he began in a dazed and sleep-walker fashion:

" '*The remark which I made to the unhappy stranger was this:*

"You are far from being a bad man. [The house gazed at him, marveling.] *Go, and reform."'* [*Murmurs:* "Amazing! what can this mean?"] This one," said the Chair, "is signed Thurlow G. Wilson."

"There!" cried Wilson, "I reckon that settles it! I knew perfectly well my note was purloined."

"Purloined!" retorted Billson. "I'll let you know that neither you nor any man of your kidney must venture to—"

The Chair. "Order, gentlemen, order! Take your seats, both of you, please."

They obeyed, shaking their heads and grumbling angrily. The house was profoundly puzzled; it did not know what to do with this curious emergency. Presently Thompson got up. Thompson was the hatter. He would have liked to be a Nineteener; but such was not for him: his stock of hats was not considerable enough for the position. He said:

"Mr. Chairman, if I may be permitted to make a suggestion, can both of these gentlemen be right? I put it to you, sir, can both have happened to say the very same words to the stranger? It seems to me—"

The tanner got up and interrupted him. The tanner was a disgruntled man; he believed himself entitled to be a Nineteener, but he couldn't get recognition. It made him a little unpleasant in his ways and speech. Said he:

"Sho, *that's* not the point! *That* could happen—twice in a hundred years—but not the other thing. *Neither* of them gave the twenty dollars!"

[*A ripple of applause.*]

Billson. "I did!"

Wilson. "I did!"

Then each accused the other of pilfering.

The Chair. "Order! Sit down, if you please—both of you. Neither of the notes has been out of my possession at any moment."

A Voice. "Good—that settles *that!*"

The Tanner. "Mr. Chairman, one thing is now plain: one of these men has been eavesdropping under the other one's bed, and filching family secrets. If it is not unparliamentary to suggest it, I will remark that both are equal to it. [*The Chair.* "Order! order!"] I withdraw the remark, sir, and will confine myself to suggesting that *if* one of them has overheard the other reveal the test-remark to his wife, we shall catch him now."

A Voice. "How?"

The Tanner. "Easily. The two have not quoted the remark in exactly the same words. You would have noticed that, if there hadn't been a considerable stretch of time and an exciting quarrel inserted between the two readings."

A Voice. "Name the difference."

The Tanner. "The word *very* is in Billson's note, and not in the other."

Many Voices. "That's so—he's right!"

The Tanner. "And so, if the Chair will examine the test-remark in the sack, we shall know which of these two frauds—[*The Chair.* "Order!"]—which of these two adventurers—[*The Chair.* "Order! order!"]—which of these two gentlemen—[*laughter and applause*]—is entitled to wear the belt as being the first dishonest blatherskite ever bred in this town—which he has dishonored, and which will be a sultry place for him from now out!" [*Vigorous applause.*]

Many Voices. "Open it!—open the sack!"

Mr. Burgess made a slit in the sack, slid his hand in and brought out an envelope. In it were a couple of folded notes. He said:

"One of these is marked, 'Not to be examined until all written communications which have been addressed to the Chair—if any—shall have been read.' The other is marked 'The Test.' Allow me. It is worded—to wit:

" 'I do not require that the first half of the remark which was made to me by my benefactor shall be quoted with exactness, for it was not striking, and could be forgotten; but its closing fifteen words are quite striking, and I think easily rememberable; unless *these* shall be accurately reproduced, let the applicant be regarded as an impostor. My benefactor began by saying he seldom gave advice to any one, but that it always bore the hallmark of high value when he did give it. Then he said this—and it has never faded from my memory: *"You are far from being a bad man—" ' "*

Fifty Voices. "That settles it—the money's Wilson's! Wilson! Wilson! Speech! Speech!"

People jumped up and crowded around Wilson, wringing his hand and congratulating fervently—meantime the Chair was hammering with the gavel and shouting:

"Order, gentlemen! Order! Order! Let me finish reading, please." When quiet was restored, the reading was resumed— as follows:

> *" ' "Go, and reform—or, mark my words—some day, for your sins, you will die and go to hell or Hadleyburg—*TRY AND MAKE IT THE FORMER*" ' "*

A ghastly silence followed. First an angry cloud began to settle darkly upon the faces of the citizenship; after a pause the cloud began to rise, and a tickled expression tried to take its place; tried so hard that it was only kept under with great and painful difficulty; the reporters, the Brixtonites, and other strangers bent their heads down and shielded their faces with their hands, and managed to hold in by main strength and heroic courtesy. At this most inopportune time burst upon the stillness the roar of a solitary voice—Jack Halliday's:

"*That's* got the hall-mark on it!"

Then the house let go, strangers and all. Even Mr. Burgess's gravity broke down presently, then the audience considered itself officially absolved from all restraint, and it made the most of its privilege. It was a good long laugh, and a tempestuously whole-hearted one, but it ceased at last—long enough for Mr. Burgess to try to resume, and for the people to get their eyes partially wiped; then it broke out again; and afterward yet again; then at last Mr. Burgess was able to get out these serious words:

"It is useless to try to disguise the fact—we find ourselves in the presence of a matter of grave import. It involves the honor of your town, it strikes at the town's good name. The difference of a single word between the test-remarks offered by Mr. Wilson and Mr. Billson was itself a serious thing, since it indicated that one or the other of these gentlemen had committed a theft—"

The two men were sitting limp, nerveless, crushed; but at these words both were electrified into movement, and started to get up—

"Sit down!" said the Chair, sharply, and they obeyed. "That, as I have said, was a serious thing. And it was—but for only one of them. But the matter has become graver; for the honor of *both* is now in formidable peril. Shall I go even further, and say in inextricable peril? *Both* left out the crucial fifteen words." He paused. During several moments he allowed the pervading stillness to gather and deepen its impressive effects, then added: "There would seem to be but one way whereby this could happen. I ask these gentlemen—Was there *collusion?— agreement!*"

A low murmur sifted through the house; its import was, "He's got them both."

Billson was not used to emergencies; he sat in a helpless collapse. But Wilson was a lawyer. He struggled to his feet, pale and worried, and said:

"I ask the indulgence of the house while I explain this most painful matter. I am sorry to say what I am about to say, since it must inflict irreparable injury upon Mr. Billson, whom I have always esteemed and respected until now, and in whose invulnerability to temptation I entirely believed—as did you all. But for the preservation of my *own* honor I must speak—and with frankness. I confess with shame—and I now beseech your pardon for it—that I said to the ruined stranger all of the words contained in the test-remark, including the disparaging fifteen. [*Sensation.*] When the late publication was made I recalled them, and resolved to claim the sack of coin, for by every right I was entitled to it. Now I will ask you to consider this point, and weigh it well: that stranger's gratitude to me that night knew no bounds; he said himself that he could find no words for it that were adequate, and that if he should ever be able he would repay me a thousand fold. Now, then, I ask you this: Could I expect—could I believe—could I even remotely imagine—that, feeling as I did, he would do so ungrateful a thing as to add those quite unnecessary fifteen words to his test?—set a trap for me?—expose me as a slanderer of my own town before my own people assembled in a public hall? It was preposterous; it was impossible. His test would contain only the kindly opening clause of my remark. Of that I had no shadow of doubt. You would have thought as I did. You would not have expected a base betrayal from one whom you had befriended and against whom you had committed no offense. And so, with perfect confidence, perfect trust, I wrote on a piece of paper the opening words—ending with 'Go, and reform,'—and signed it. When I was about to put it in an envelope I was called into my back office, and without thinking I left the paper lying open on my desk." He stopped, turned his head slowly toward Billson, waited a moment, then added: "I ask you to note this: when I returned, a little later, Mr. Billson was retiring by my street door." [*Sensation.*]

In a moment Billson was on his feet and shouting:

"It's a lie! It's an infamous lie!"

The Chair. "Be seated, sir! Mr. Wilson has the floor."

Billson's friends pulled him into his seat and quieted him, and Wilson went on:

"Those are the simple facts. My note was now lying in a different place on the table from where I had left it. I noticed that, but attached no importance to it, thinking a draught had blown it there. That Mr. Billson would read a private paper was a thing which could not occur to me; he was an honorable man, and he would be above that. If you will allow me to say it, I think his extra word '*very*' stands explained; it is atttributable to a defect of memory. I was the only man in the world who could furnish here any detail of the test-remark—by *honorable* means. I have finished."

There is nothing in the world like a persuasive speech to fuddle the mental apparatus and upset the convictions and debauch the emotions of an audience not practiced in the tricks and elusions of oratory. Wilson sat down victorious. The house submerged him in tides of approving applause; friends swarmed to him and shook him by the hand and congratulated him, and Billson was shouted down and not allowed to say a word. The Chair hammered and hammered with its gavel, and kept shouting.

"But let us proceed, gentlemen, let us proceed!"

At last there was a measurable degree of quiet, and the hatter said:

"But what is there to proceed with, sir, but to deliver the money?"

Voices. "That's it! That's it! Come forward, Wilson!"

The Hatter. "I move three cheers for Mr. Wilson, Symbol of the special virtue which—"

The cheers burst forth before he could finish; and in the midst of them—and in the midst of the clamor of the gavel also—some enthusiasts mounted Wilson on a big friend's shoulder and were going to fetch him in triumph to the platform. The Chair's voice now rose above the noise—

"Order! To your places! You forget that there is still a document to read." When quiet had been restored he took up the document, and was going to read it, but laid it down again, saying, "I forgot; this is not to be read until all written communications received by me have first been read." He took an envelope out of his pocket, removed its enclosure, glanced at it—seemed astonished—held it out and gazed at it—stared at it.

Twenty or thirty voices cried out:

"What is it? Read it! read it!

And he did—slowly, and wondering:

" 'The remark which I made to the stranger—[*Voices.* "Hello! how's this?"]—was this: "You are far from being a bad man. [*Voices.* "Great Scott!"] Go, and reform." ' [*Voice.* "Oh, saw my leg off!"] Signed by Mr. Pinkerton the banker."

The pandemonium of delight which turned itself loose now was of a sort to make the judicious weep. Those whose withers were unwrung laughed till the tears ran down; the reporters, in throes of laughter, set down disordered pot-hooks which would never in the world be decipherable; and a sleeping dog jumped up, scared out of its wits, and barked itself crazy at the turmoil. All manner of cries were scattered through the din: "We're getting rich—*two* Symbols of Incorruptibility!—without counting Billson!" "*Three!*—count Shadbelly in—we can't have too many!" "All right—Billson's elected!" "Alas, poor Wilson—victim of *two* thieves!"

A Powerful Voice. "Silence! The chair's fished up something more out of its pocket."

Voices. "Hurrah! Is it something fresh? Read it! read it! read!"

The Chair [reading.] " 'The remark which I made,' etc.: ' "You are far from being a bad man. Go," ' etc. Signed, Gregory Yates.' "

Tornado of Voices. "Four symbols!" " 'Rah for Yates!" "Fish again!"

The house was in a roaring humor now, and ready to get all the fun out of the occasion that might be in it. Several Nineteeners, looking pale and distressed, got up and began to work their way toward the aisles, but a score of shouts went up:

"The doors, the doors—close the doors; no Incorruptible shall leave this place! Sit down, everybody!"

The mandate was obeyed.

"Fish again! Read! read!"

The Chair fished again, and once more the familiar words began to fall from its lips—" 'You are far from being a bad man—"

"Name! name! What's his name?"

" 'L. Ingoldsby Sargent.' "

"Five elected! Pile up the Symbols! Go on, go on!"

" 'You are far from being a bad—' "

"Name! name!"

" 'Nicholas Whitworth.' "

"Hooray! hooray! it's a symbolical day!"

Somebody wailed in, and began to sing this rhyme (leaving out "it's") to the lovely "Mikado" tune of "When a man's afraid, a beautiful maid—"; the audience joined in, with joy; then, just in time, somebody contributed another line—

And don't you this forget—

The house roared it out. A third line was at once furnished—

Corruptibles far from Hadleyburg are—

The house roared that one too. As the last note died, Jack Halliday's voice rose high and clear, freighted with a final line—

But the Symbols are here, you bet!

That was sung with booming enthusiasm. Then the happy house started in at the beginning and sang the four lines through twice, with immense swing and dash, and finished up with a crashing three-times-three and a tiger for "Hadleyburg the Incorruptible and all Symbols of it which we shall find worthy to receive the hall-mark tonight."

Then the shouting at the Chair began again, all over the place:

"Go on! go on! Read! read some more! Read all you've got!"

"That's it—go on! We are winning eternal celebrity!"

A dozen men got up now and began to protest. They said that this farce was the work of some abandoned joker, and was an insult to the whole community. Without a doubt these signatures were all forgeries—

"Sit down! sit down! Shut up! You are confessing. We'll find *your* names in the lot."

"Mr. Chairman, how many of those envelopes have you got?"

The Chair counted.

"Together with those that have been already examined, there are nineteen."

A storm of derisive applause broke out.

"Perhaps they all contain the secret. I move that you open them all and read every signature that is attached to a note of that sort—and read also the first eight words of the note."

"Second the motion!"

It was put and carried—uproariously. Then poor old Richards got up, and his wife rose and stood at his side. Her head bent down, so that none might see that she was crying. Her husband gave her his arm, and so supporting her, he began to speak in a quavering voice:

"My friends, you have known us two—Mary and me—all our lives, and I think you have liked us and respected us—"

The Chair interrupted him:

"Allow me. It is quite true—that which you are saying, Mr. Richards: this town *does* know you two; it *does* like you; it *does* respect you; more—it honors you and *loves* you—"

Halliday's voice rang out:

"That's the hall-marked truth, too! If the Chair is right, let the house speak up and say it. Rise! Now, then—hip! hip! hip!—all together!"

The house rose in mass, faced toward the old couple eagerly, filled the air with a snowstorm of waving handkerchiefs, and delivered the cheers with all its affectionate heart.

The Chair then continued:

"What I was going to say is this: We know your good heart, Mr. Richards, but this is not a time for the exercise of charity toward offenders. [*Shouts of "Right! right!"*] I see your generous purpose in your face, but I cannot allow you to plead for these men—'

"But I was going to—"

"Please take your seat, Mr. Richards. We must examine the rest of these notes—simple fairness to the men who have already been exposed requires this. As soon as that has been done—I give you my word for this—you shall be heard."

Many Voices. "Right!—the Chair is right—no interruption can be permitted at this stage! Go on!—the names! the names!—according to the terms of the motion!"

The old couple sat reluctantly down, and the husband whispered to the wife, "It is pitifully hard to have to wait; the shame will be greater than ever when they find we were only going to plead for *ourselves*."

Straightway the jollity broke loose again with the reading of the names.

" 'You are far from being a bad man—' Signature, Robert J. Titmarsh.'

" 'You are far from being a bad man—' Signature, 'Eliphalet Weeks.'

" 'You are far from being a bad man—' Signature, 'Oscar B. Wilder.' "

At this point the house lit upon the idea of taking the eight words out of the Chairman's hands. He was not unthankful for that. Thenceforward he held up each note in its turn, and waited. The house droned out the eight words in a massed and measured and musical deep volume of sound (with a daringly close resemblance to a well-known church chant)—"'You are f-a-r from being a b-a-a-a-d man.'" Then the Chair said, "Signature, 'Archibald Wilcox.'" And so on, and so on, name after name, and everybody had an increasingly and gloriously good time except the wretched Nineteen. Now and then, when a particularly shining name was called, the house made the Chair wait while it changed the whole of the test-remark from the beginning to the closing words, "And go to hell or Hadleyburg—try and make it the for-or-m-e-r!" and in these special cases they added a grand and agonized and imposing "A-a-a-a-*men!*"

The list dwindled, dwindled, dwindled, poor old Richards keeping tally of the count, wincing when a name resembling his own was pronounced, and waiting in miserable suspense for the time to come when it would be his humiliating privilege to rise with Mary and finish his plea, which he was intending to word thus: ". . . for until now we have never done any wrong thing, but have gone our humble way unreproached. We are very poor, we are old, and have no chick nor child to help us; we were sorely tempted, and we fell. It was my purpose when I got up before to make confession and beg that my name might not be read out in this public place, for it seemed to us that we could not bear it; but I was prevented. It was just; it was our place to suffer with the rest. It has been hard for us. It is the first time we have ever heard our name fall from any one's lips—sullied. Be merciful—for the sake of the better days; make our shame as light to bear as in your charity you can." At this point in his revery Mary nudged him, perceiving that his mind was absent. The house was chanting, "You are f-a-r," etc.

"Be ready," Mary whispered. "Your name comes now; he has read eighteen."

The chant ended.

"Next! next! next!" came volleying from all over the house.

Burgess put his hand into his pocket. The old couple, trembling, began to rise. Burgess fumbled a moment, then said, "I find I have read them all."

Faint with joy and surprise, the couple sank into their seats, and Mary whispered,

"Oh, bless God, we are saved!—he has lost ours—I wouldn't give this for a hundred of those sacks!"

The house burst out with its "Mikado" travesty, and sang it three times with ever-increasing enthusiasm, rising to its feet when it reached for the third time the closing line—

But the Symbols are here, you bet!

and finishing up with cheers and a tiger for "Hadleyburg purity and our eighteen immortal representatives of it."

Then Wingate, the saddler, got up and proposed cheers "for the cleanest man in town, the one solitary important citizen in it who didn't try to steal that money—Edward Richards."

They were given with great and moving heartiness; then somebody proposed that Richards be elected sole guardian and Symbol of the now Sacred Hadleyburg Tradition, with power and right to stand up and look the whole sarcastic world in the face.

Passed, by acclamation; then they sang the "Mikado" again, and ended it with,

And there's one Symbol left, you bet!

There was a pause; then—

A Voice. "Now, then. who's to get the sack?"

The Tanner (with bitter sarcasm). "That's easy. The money has to be divided among the eighteen Incorruptibles. They gave the suffering stranger twenty dollars apiece—and that remark—each in his turn—it took twenty-two minutes for the procession to move past. Staked the stranger—total contribution, $360. All they want is just the loan back—and interest—forty thousand dollars altogether."

Many Voices [derisively.] "That's it! Divvy! divvy! Be kind to the poor—don't keep them waiting!"

The Chair. "Order! I now offer the stranger's remaining document. It says: 'If no claimant shall appear [*grand chorus of groans.*], I desire that you open the sack and count out the money to the principal citizens of your town, they to take it in trust [*cries of "Oh! Oh! Oh!"*], and use it in such ways as to them shall seem best for the propagation and preservation of your community's noble reputation for incorruptible honesty [*more cries*]—a reputation to which their names and their efforts will add a new and far-reaching lustre.' [*Enthusiastic outburst of sarcastic applause.*] That seems to be all. No—here is a postscript:

" 'P.S.—CITIZENS OF HADLEYBURG: There *is* no test-remark—nobody made one. [*Great sensation.*] There wasn't any pauper stranger, nor any twenty-dollar contribution, nor any accompanying benediction and compliment—these are all inventions. [*General buzz and hum of astonishment and delight.*] Allow me to tell my story—it will take but a word or two. I passed through your town at a certain time, and received a deep offense which I had not earned. Any other man would have been content to kill one or two of you and call it square, but to me that would have been a trivial revenge, and inadequate; for the dead do not *suffer*. Besides, I could not kill you all—and, anyway, made as I am, even that would not have satisfied me. I wanted to damage every man in the place, and every woman—and not in their bodies or in their estate, but in their vanity—the place where feeble and foolish people are most vulnerable. So I disguised myself and came back and studied you. You were easy game. You had an old and lofty reputation for honesty, and naturally you were proud of it—it was your treasure of treasures, the very apple of your eye. As soon as I found out that you carefully and vigilantly kept yourselves and your children *out of temptation*, I knew how to proceed. Why, you simple creatures, the weakest of all weak things is a virtue which has not been tested in the fire. I laid a plan, and gathered a list of names. My project was to corrupt Hadleyburg the Incorruptible. My idea was to make liars and thieves of nearly half a hundred smirchless men and women who had never in their lives uttered a lie or stolen a penny. I was afraid of Goodson. He was neither born nor reared in Hadleyburg. I was afraid that if I started to operate my scheme by getting my letter laid before you, you would say to yourselves, "Goodson is the only man among us who would give away twenty dollars to a poor devil"—and then you might not bite at my bait. But Heaven took Goodson; then I knew I was safe, and I set my trap and baited it. It may be that I shall not catch all the men to whom I mailed the pretended test secret, but I shall catch the most of them, if I know Hadleyburg nature. [*Voices.* "Right—he got every last one of them."] I believe they will even steal ostensible *gamble*-money, rather than miss, poor, tempted, and mistrained fellows. I am hoping to eternally and everlastingly squelch your vanity and give Hadleyburg a new reknown—one that will *stick*—and spread far. If I have succeeded, open the sack and summon the Committee on Propagation and Preservation of the Hadleyburg Reputation.'"

A Cyclone of Voices. "Open it! Open it! The Eighteen to the front! Committee on Propagation of the Trandition! Forward—the Incorruptibles!"

The Chair ripped the sack wide, and gathered up a handful of bright, broad, yellow coins, shook them together, then examined them—

"Friends, they are only gilded disks of lead!"

There was a crashing outbreak of delight over this news, and when the noise had subsided, the tanner called out:

"By right of apparent seniority in this business, Mr. Wilson is Chairman of the Committee on Propagation of the Tradition. I suggest that he step forward on behalf of his pals, and receive in trust the money."

A Hundred Voices. "Wilson! Wilson! Wilson! Speech! Speech!"

Wilson [in a voice trembling with anger.] "You will allow me to say, and without apologies for my language, *damn* the money!"

A Voice. "Oh, and him a Baptist!"

A Voice. "Seventeen Symbols left! Step up, gentlemen, and assume your trust!"

There was a pause—no response.

The Saddler. "Mr. Chairman, we've got *one* clean man left, anyway, out of the late aristocracy; and he needs money, and deserves it. I move that you appoint Jack Halliday to get up there and auction off that sack of gilt twenty-dollar pieces, and give the result to the right man—the man whom Hadleyburg delights to honor—Edward Richards."

This was received with great enthusiasm, the dog taking a hand again; the saddler started the bids at a dollar, the Brixton folk and Barnum's representative fought hard for it, the people cheered every jump that the bids made, the excitement climbed moment by moment higher and higher, the bidders got on their mettle and grew steadily more and more daring, more and more determined, the jumps went from a dollar up to five, then to ten, then to twenty, then fifty, then to a hundred, then—

At the beginning of the auction Richards whispered in distress to his wife: "O Mary, can we allow it? It—it—you see, it is an honor-reward, a testimonial to purity of character, and—and—can we allow it? Hadn't I better get up and—O Mary, what ought we to do?—what do you think we—[*Halliday's voice.* "Fifteen I'm bid!—fifteen for the sack!—twenty!—ah, thanks!— thirty—thanks again! Thirty, thirty, thirty!—do I hear forty?—forty it is! Keep the ball rolling, gentlemen, keep it rolling!—fifty!—thanks, noble Roman! going at fifty, fifty, fifty!—seventy!—ninety!—splendid!—a hundred!—pile it up, pile it up!—hundred and twenty!— forty!—just in time!—hundred and fifty!—two hundred!—superb! Do I hear two h—thanks!—two hundred and fifty!—*"]

"It is another temptation, Edward—I'm all in a tremble— but, oh, we've escaped *one* temptation, and that ought to warn us to— [*"Six did I hear?—thanks!—six fifty, six f—SEVEN hundred!"*] And yet, Edward, when you think—nobody susp— [*"Eight hundred dollars!—hurrah!—make it nine!—Mr. Parsons, did I hear you say—thanks—nine!—this noble sack of virgin lead going at only nine hundred dollars, gilding and all—come! do I hear—a thousand!— gratfully yours!—did some one say eleven?—a sack which is going to be the most celebrated in the whole Uni—"*] O Edward" (beginning to sob), "we are *so* poor!—but—but—do as you think best—do as you think best."

Edward fell—that is, he sat still; sat with a conscience which

was not satisfied, but which was overpowered by circumstances.

Meantime a stranger, who looked like an amateur detective
gotten up as an impossible English earl, had been watching the
evenings's proceedings with manifest interest, and with a
contented expression in his face; and he had been privately
commenting to himself. He was now soliloquizing somewhat
like this: "None of the Eighteen are bidding; that is not
satisfactory; I must change that—the dramatic unities require it;
they must buy the sack they tried to steal; they must pay a heavy
price, too—some of them are rich. And another thing, when I
make a mistake in Hadleyburg nature the man that puts that
error upon me is entitled to a high honorarium, and some one
must pay it. This poor old Richards has brought my judgment to
shame; he is an honest man:—I don't understand it, but I
acknowledge it. Yes, he saw my deuces *and* with a straight flush,
and by rights the pot is his. And it shall be a jack-pot, too, if I
can manage it. He disappointed me, but let that pass."

He was watching the bidding. At a thousand, the market
broke; the prices tumbled swiftly. He waited—and still watched.
One competitor dropped out, then another, and another. He put
in a bid or two, now. When the bids had sunk to ten dollars, he
added a five; some one raised him a three; he waited a moment,
then flung in a fifty-dollar jump, and the sack was his—at
$1,282. The house broke out in cheers—then stopped; for he
was on his feet, and had lifted his hand. He began to speak.

"I desire to say a word, and ask a favor. I am a speculator in
rarities, and I have dealings with persons interested in numis-
matics all over the world. I can make a profit on this purchase,
just as it stands; but there is a way, if I can get your approval,
whereby I can make every one of these leaden twenty-dollar
pieces worth its face in gold, and perhaps more. Grant me that
approval, and I will give part of my gains to your Mr. Richards,
whose invulnerable probity you have so justly and so cordially
recognized to-night; his share shall be ten thousand dollars, and
I will hand him the money to-morrow. [*Great applause from the
house.* But the "invulnerable probity" made the Richardses blush
prettily; however, it went for modesty, and did no harm.] If you

will pass my proposition by a good majority—I would like a two-thirds vote—I will regard that as the town's consent, and that is all I ask. Rarities are always helped by any device which will rouse curiosity and compel remark. Now if I may have your permission to stamp upon the faces of each of these ostensible coins the names of the eighteen gentlemen who—"

Nine-tenths of the audience were on their feet in a moment—dog and all—and the proposition was carried with a whirlwind of approving applause and laughter.

They sat down, and all the Symbols except "Dr." Clay Harkness got up, violently protesting against the proposed outrage, and threatening to—

"I beg you not to threaten me," said the stranger, calmly. "I know my legal rights, and am not accustomed to being frightened at bluster." [*Applause.*] He sat down. "Dr." Harkness saw an opportunity here. He was one of the two very rich men of the place, and Pinkerton was the other. Harkness was proprietor of a mint; that is to say, a popular patent medicine. He was running for the Legislature on one ticket, and Pinkerton on the other. It was a close race and a hot one, and getting hotter every day. Both had strong appetites for money; each had bought a great tract of land, with a purpose; there was going to be a new railway, and each wanted to be in the Legislature and help locate the route to his own advantage; a single vote might make the decision, and with it two or three fortunes. The stake was large, and Harkness was a daring speculator. He was sitting close to the stranger. He leaned over while one or another of the other Symbols was entertaining the house with protests and appeals, and asked, in a whisper,

"What is your price for the sack?"

"Forty thousand dollars."

"I'll give you twenty."

"No."

"Twenty-five."

"No."

"Say thirty."

"The price is forty thousand dollars; not a penny less."

"All right, I'll give it. I will come to the hotel at ten in the morning. I don't want it known; will see you privately."

"Very good." Then the stranger got up and said to the house:

"I find it late. The speeches of these gentlemen are not without merit, not without interest, not without grace; yet if I may be excused I will take my leave. I thank you for the great favor which you have shown me in granting my petition. I ask the Chair to keep the sack for me until to-morrow, and to hand these three five-hundred-dollar notes to Mr. Richards." They were passed up to the Chair. "At nine I will call for the sack, and at eleven will deliver the rest of the ten thousand to Mr. Richards in person, at his home. Good night."

Then he slipped out, and left the audience making a vast noise, which was composed of a mixture of cheers, the "Mikado" song, dog-disapproval, and the chant, "You are f-a-r from being a b-a-a-d man—a-a-a-a-men!"

IV

At home the Richardses had to endure congratulations and compliments until midnight. Then they were left to themselves. They looked a little sad, and they sat silent and thinking. Finally Mary sighed and said,

"Do you think we are to blame, Edward—*much* to blame?" and her eyes wandered to the accusing triplet of big bank notes lying on the table, where the congratulators had been gloating over them and reverently fingering them. Edward did not answer at once; then he brought out a sigh and said, hesitatingly:

"We—we couldn't help it, Mary. It—well, it was ordered. *All* things are."

Mary glanced up and looked at him steadily, but he didn't return the look. Presently she said:

"I thought congratulations and praises always tasted good. But—it seems to me, now—Edward?"

"Well?"

"Are you going to stay in the bank?"

"N-no."

"Resign?"

"In the morning—by note."

"It does seem best."

Richards bowed his head in his hands and muttered: "Before, I was not afraid to let oceans of people's money pour through my hands, but—Mary, I am so tired, so tired—"

"We will go to bed."

At nine in the morning the stranger called for the sack and took it to the hotel in a cab. At ten Harkness had a talk with him privately. The stranger asked for and got five checks on a metropolitan bank—drawn to "Bearer,"—four for $1,500 each, and one for $34,000. He put one of the former in his pocketbook, and the remainder, representing $38,500, he put in an envelope, and with these he added a note, which he wrote after Harkness was gone. At eleven he called at the Richards house and knocked. Mrs. Richards peeped through the shutters, then went and received the envelope, and the stranger disappeared without a word. She came back flushed and a little unsteady on her legs, and gasped out:

"I am sure I recognized him! Last night it seemed to me that maybe I had seen him somewhere before."

"He is the man that brought the sack here?"

"I am almost sure of it."

"Then he is the ostensible Stephenson, too, and sold every important citizen in this town with his bogus secret. Now if he has sent checks instead of money, we are sold, too, after we thought we had escaped. I was beginning to feel fairly comfortable once more, after my night's rest, but the look of that envelope makes me sick. It isn't fat enough; $8,500 in even the largest bank notes makes more bulk than that."

"Edward, why do you object to checks?"

"Checks signed by Stephenson! I am resigned to take the $8,500 if it could come in bank notes—for it does seem that it was so ordered, Mary—but I have never had much courage, and I have not the pluck to try to market a check signed with that disastrous name. It would be a trap. That man tried to catch me, we escaped somehow or other; and now he is trying a new way. If it is checks—"

"Oh, Edward, it is *too* bad!" and she held up the checks and began to cry.

"Put them in the fire! quick! we mustn't be tempted. It is a trick to make the world laugh at *us*, along with the rest, and— Give them to *me*, since you can't do it!" He snatched them and tried to hold his grip till he could get to the stove; but he was human, he was a cashier, and he stopped a moment to make sure of the signature. Then he came near to fainting.

"Fan me, Mary, fan me! They are the same as gold!"

"Oh, how lovely, Edward! Why?"

"Signed by Harkness. What can the mystery of that be, Mary?"

"Edward, do you think—"

"Look here—look at this! Fifteen—fifteen—fifteen—thirty-four. Thirty-eight thousand five hundred! Mary, the sack isn't worth twelve dollars, and Harkness—apparently—has paid about par for it."

"And does it all come to us, do you think—instead of the ten thousand?"

"Why, it looks like it. And the checks are made to 'Bearer,' too."

"Is that good, Edward? What is it for?"

"A hint to collect them at some distant bank, I reckon. Perhaps Harkness doesn't want the matter known. What is that—a note?"

"Yes. It was with the checks."

It was in the "Stephenson" handwriting, but there was no signature. It said:

> "*I am a disappointed man. Your honesty is beyond the reach of temptation. I had a different idea about it, but I wronged you in that and I beg pardon, and do it sincerely. I honor you—and that is sincere too. This town is not worthy to kiss the hem of your garment. Dear sir, I made a square bet with myself that there were nineteen debauchable men in your self-righteous community. I have lost. Take the whole pot, you are entitled to it.*"

Richards drew a deep sigh, and said:

"It seems written with fire—it burns so. Mary—I am miserable again."

"I, too. Ah, dear, I wish—"

"To think, Mary—he *believes* in me."

"If those beautiful words were deserved, Mary—and God knows I believed I deserved them once—I think I could give the forty thousand dollars for them. And I would put that paper away, as representing more than gold and jewels, and keep it always. But now—We could not live in the shadow of its accusing presence, Mary."

He put it in the fire.

A messenger arrived and delivered an envelope.

Richards took from it a note and read it; it was from Burgess.

You saved me in a difficult time. I saved you last night. It was at cost of a lie, but I made the sacrifice freely, and out of a grateful heart. None in this village knows so well as I know how brave and good and noble you are. At bottom you cannot respect me, knowing as you do of that matter of which I am accused, and by the general voice condemned; but I beg that you will at least believe that I am a grateful man; it will help me to bear my burden.

[*Signed*] **Burgess**

"Saved, once more. And on such terms!" He put the note in the fire. "I—I wish I were dead, Mary, I wish I were out of it all."

"Oh, these are bitter, bitter days, Edward. The stabs, through their very generosity, are so deep—and they come so fast!"

Three days before the election each of two thousand voters suddenly found himself in possession of a prized memento— one of the renowned bogus double-eagles. Around one of its faces was stamped these words: "THE REMARK I MADE TO THE POOR STRANGER WAS—" Around the other face was stamped these: "GO AND REFORM. [SIGNED] PINKERTON." Thus the entire remaining refuse of the renowned joke was emptied upon a single head, and with calamitous effect. It revived the recent vast laugh and concentrated it upon Pinkerton; and Harkness's election was a walkover.

Within twenty-four hours after they Richardses had received their checks their consciences were quieting down, discouraged; the old couple were learning to reconcile themselves to the sin which they had committed. But they were to learn, now, that a sin takes on new and real terrors when there seems a chance that it is going to be found out. This gives it a fresh and most substantial and important aspect. At church the morning sermon was of the usual pattern; it was the same old things said in the same old way; they had heard them a thousand times and found them innocuous, next to meaningless, and easy to sleep under; but now it was different: the sermon seemed to bristle with accusations; it seemed aimed straight and specially at people who were concealing deadly sins. After church they got away from the mob of congratulators as soon as they could, and hurried homeward, chilled to the bone at they did not know what—vague, shadowy, indefinite fears. And by chance they caught a glimpse of Mr. Burgess as he turned a corner. He paid no attention to their nod of recognition! He hadn't seen it; but they did not know that. What could his conduct mean? It might mean—it might mean—oh, a dozen dreadful things. Was it possible that he knew that Richards could have cleared him of guilt in that by gone time, and had been silently waiting for a chance to even up accounts? At home, in their distress they got to imagining that their servant might have been in the next room listening when Richards revealed the secret to his wife that he knew of Burgess's innocence; next, Richards began to imagine that he had heard the swish of a gown in there at that time; next, he was sure he *had* heard it. They would call Sarah in, on a pretext, and watch her face: if she had been betraying them to Mr. Burgess, it would show in her manner. They asked her some questions—questions which were so random and incoherent and seemingly purposeless that the girl felt sure that the old people's minds had been affected by their sudden good fortune; the sharp and watchful gaze which they bent upon her frightened her, and that completed the business. She blushed, she became nervous and confused, and to the old people these

were plain signs of guilt—guilt of some fearful sort or other—
without doubt she was a spy and a traitor. When they were
alone again they began to piece many unrelated things together
and get horrible results out of the combination. When things
had got about to the worst, Richard was delivered of a sudden
gasp, and his wife asked,

"Oh, what is it?— what is it?"

"The note—Burgess's note! Its language was sarcastic, I see
it now." He quoted: "'At bottom you cannot respect me,
knowing, as you do, of *that matter* of which I am accused'—oh, it
is perfectly plain, now, God help me! He knows that I know! You
see the ingenuity of the phrasing. It was a trap—and like a fool, I
walked into it. And Mary—?"

"Oh, it is dreadful—I know what you are going to say—he
didn't return your transcript of the pretended test-remark."

"No—kept it to destroy us with. Mary, he has exposed us to
some already. I know it—I know it well. I saw it in a dozen faces
after church. Ah, he wouldn't answer our nod of recognition—
he knew what he had been doing!"

In the night the doctor was called. The news went around
in the morning that the old couple were rather seriously ill—
prostrated by the exhausting excitement growing out of their
great windfall, the congratulations, and the late hours, the
doctor said. The town was sincerely distressed; for these old
people were about all it had left ot be proud of, now.

Two days later the news was worse. The old couple were
delirious, and were doing strange things. By witness of the
nurses, Richards had exhibited checks—for $8,500? No—for an
amazing sum—$38,500! What could be the explanation of this
gigantic piece of luck?

The following day the nurses had more news—and wonderful. They had concluded to hide the checks, lest harm come
to them; but when they searched they were gone from under the
patient's pillow—vanished away. The patient said:

"Let the pillow alone; what do you want?"

"We thought it best that the checks—"

"You will never see them again—they are destroyed. They
came from Satan. I saw the hell-brand on them, and I knew they

were sent to betray me to sin." Then he fell to gabbling strange and dreadful things which were not clearly understandable, and which the doctor admonished them to keep to themselves.

Richards was right; the checks were never seen again.

A nurse must have talked in her sleep, for within two days the forbidden gabblings were the property of the town; and they were of a surprising sort. They seemed to indicate that Richards had been a claimant for the sack himself, and that Burgess had concealed that fact and then maliciously betrayed it.

Burgess was taxed with this and stoutly denied it. And he said it was not fair to attach weight to the chatter of a sick old man who was out of his mind. Still, suspicion was in the air, and there was much talk.

After a day or two it was reported that Mrs. Richards's delirious deliveries were getting to be duplicates of her husband's. Suspicion flamed up into conviction, now, and the town's pride in the purity of its one undiscredited important citizen began to dim down and flicker toward extinction.

Six days passed, then came more news. The old couple were dying. Richards's mind cleared in his latest hour, and he sent for Burgess. Burgess said:

"Let the room be cleared. I think he wishes to say something in privacy."

"No!" said Richards: "I want witnesses. I want you all to hear my confession, so that I may die a man, and not a dog. I was clean—artificially—like the rest; and like the rest I fell when temptation came. I signed a lie, and claimed the miserable sack. Mr. Burgess remembered that I had done him a service, and in gratitude (and ignorance) he suppressed my claim and saved me. You know the thing that was charged against Burgess years ago. My testimony, and mine alone, could have cleared him, and I was a coward, and left him to suffer disgrace—"

"No—no—Mr. Richards, you—"

"My servant betrayed my secret to him—"

"No one has betrayed anything to me—"

—"and then he did a natural and justifiable thing, he repented of the saving kindness he had done me, and he *exposed* me—as I deserved—"

"Never!—I make oath—"

"Out of my heart I forgive him."

Burgess's impassioned protestations fell upon deaf ears; the dying man passed away without knowing that once more he had done poor Burgess a wrong. The old wife died that night.

The last of the sacred Nineteen had fallen a prey to the fiendish sack; the town was stripped of the last rag of its ancient glory. Its mourning was not showy, but it was deep.

By act of the Legislature—upon prayer and petition—Hadleyburg was allowed to change its name to (never mind what—I will not give it away), and leave one word out of the motto that for many generations had graced the town's official seal.

It is an honest town once more, and the man will have to rise early that catches it napping again.

ABOUT THE AUTHORS

Grant Allen

Charles Grant Blairfindie Allen (1848-1899) is best remembered in the mystery genre for his humorous stories about Colonel Clay, the first heroic rogue of short crime fiction (*An African Millionaire*, 1897). However, Allen also wrote a number of popularly received fantastic novels and short stories. Among his contemporaries, Allen was most noted for *The Woman Who Did* and *The British Barbarians*, two controversial novels of 1895. The first novel outraged moralists by suggesting justification for a girl's desire to avoid marriage while conducting an affair resulting in a love child. The second outraged nearly everybody by suggesting a twenty-fifth century anthropologist would find Victorian customs irrational, parochial, and incomprehensible. Allen's shorter works of science fiction and fantasy are very well written. Many can be found in *Strange Stories* (1884) and *Twelve Tales* (1899), but they have never been assembled into one volume. His final work, a novel called *Hilda Wade*, was a collaboration with his good friend Sir Arthur Conan Doyle, who followed Allen's deathbed instructions for its completion.

Robert Barr

The family of Robert Barr (1850-1912) emigrated from Glasgow, Scotland, to Canada when he was four. Educated in Toronto, Barr became headmaster of a junior school while still in his teens. After marrying in 1876, he became a reporter for the *Free Press* in Detroit. There he is said to have "rifled mail bags, crossed a river on ice floes, and run a revolver gauntlet—all in pursuit of news." In 1881 his paper sent him to England as a correspondent. He started a British edition, made friends with Kipling and Doyle and, in 1892, along with Jerome K. Jerome, founded his own magazine, *The Idler*. A parody of Sherlock Holmes, "Detective Stories Gone Wrong: The Adventures of Sherlaw Kombs," appeared in *The Idler* (May 1892) under Barr's pseudonym, Luke Sharp. (The story was subsequently retitled "The Great Pegram Mystery.") The magazine was a literary and financial success, but a lawsuit ended its life five years later.

Barr remained in England, earning his living as a writer, and is chiefly remembered for fast-moving tales that were extremely popular with mass audiences. Many featured his egomaniacal French detective, Eugene Valmont, collected in the 1906 volme, *The Triumphs of Eugene Valmont*. Barr's mystery novels and short story collections include *Strange Happenings* (1883), *From Whose Bourne* (1893), *The Face and the Mask* (1894), *Revenge!* (1896), *Jennie Baxter, Journalist* (1899), *Tales of Two Continents* (1902), *The Triumphs of Eugene Valmont* (1906), and *The Girl in the Case* (1910).

Wilkie Collins

William Wilkie Collins (1824-1889), often called "the father of the English detective story," wrote his first novel, *Antonina* at the age of seventeen while apprenticed to a tea merchant. Following its publication in 1850, Collins completed his law degree and subsequently met Charles Dickens during an amateur theatrical. The two writers forged an enormously fruitful lifelong friendship. Each man influenced the other's work; Collins' mastery of plot paralleled Dickens' expert characterizations. Often they collaborated on articles and ideas.

Always in poor health, Collins' dedication to writing bordered on valor for he often was in extreme pain and dictated text to secretaries, none of whom could endure his cries and groans for long.

His two most famous works, *The Woman in White* (1860) and *The Moonstone* (1868) were based, in part, on actual events. These long novels with complex plots, suspense, and red-herrings, neared the popularity of Dickens' work. *The Woman in White* appeared in serial form in England in *All the Year Round* and America in *Harper's Weekly* (November 1859). T.S. Eliot called *The Moonstone* "the first, the longest, and the best of modern English detective novels." It featured Sergeant Cuff, who was based on a contemporary detective. A number of Collins' short stories concern mystery and detection. His collections *After Dark* (1856), *The Queen of Hearts* (1859), *Little Novels* (1887) and *Alicia Warlock, A Mystery, and Other Stories* (1875) all contain such works. Some are milestones, as "The Biter Bit," the first humorous detective story.

Richard Harding Davis

It was probably inevitable that Richard Harding Davis (1864-1916) became a fiction writer and perhaps the best known reporter of his day. His father, L. Clarke Davis, editor of the *Philadelphia Public Ledger*, and his mother, pioneer naturalistic novelist Rebecca Harding Davis, not only passed on their literary enthusiasm, but also gave their son entree to their peers: writers, actors, and playwrights.

During college at Swarthmore, Lehigh, and Johns Hopkins, Davis began writing fiction. He landed his first newspaper job in 1886 at the Philadelphia *Record*. Always, his work as reporter was fodder for fiction, and his first important story, "Gallegher," was the product of this job. It appeared in *Scribner's* in August 1890, became an immediate hit, was translated into French and German, and incorporated into his first collection, *Gallegher and Other Stories*, in 1891.

He wove his travels, many of them as a war correspondent, into novels, twenty-five plays, non-fiction travelogues and eleven short story collections. A love of cities, perhaps for the abundance of situations they afford, an ability to create memorable characters, and an instinct for contrasts, especially moral contrasts, fill Davis' work. Stories based on his newspaper experiences perhaps ring truest, amalgamating fiction and reporting.

Sir Arthur Conan Doyle

Sir Arthur Conan Doyle (1859-1930) was a strange blend of rationalist, idealist, romantic, and mystic who produced outstanding works of adventure, fantasy, science fiction, and horror. Doyle began writing while studying medicine at the University of Edinburgh in 1879. It was there he met his models for George Challenger and Sherlock Holmes: Professors Rutherford and Bell. After graduating in 1881, Doyle had difficulty building a successful practice, so he signed on as ship's doctor for an Arctic whaler and an African steamer, while continuing to supplement his income through writing.

In 1891, the editors of *The Strand Magazine*, impressed by Doyle's first Sherlock Holmes novel, *A Study in Scarlet* (1882), commissioned him to write a series featuring the same character. The public went wild over these short stories, and, by escalating prices for subsequent series, Doyle gained financial security. Thereafter he began devoting his energies to what interested him more: participating in current affairs and writing nonfiction. His two books explaining and justifying the Boer War (*The Great Boer War*, 1900, and *The War in South Africa: Its Cause and Conduct*, 1902) resulted in his knighthood.

When his son Kingsley died of pneumonia after being severely wounded in World War I, Doyle became an avid spiritualist and expended much of his remaining life penning books about psychic phenomena and the existence of an afterlife. Ironically, it is his character, Sherlock Holmes, whom he tried to kill off, who has brought him "literary immortality."

Harry Stillwell Edwards

Harry Stillwell Edwards (1855-1938) spent all but three years of his life in Macon, Georgia. He began writing in private school and, after receiving a Bachelor of Law from Mercer University at age twenty one, continued, contributing to the Macon *Telegraph* and the Macon *Evening News*. He married children's writer Mary Roxie Lane in 1881, and she encouraged him to submit his first story, "Elder Brown's Backslide" to *Harper's Magazine*. This, and his second, "Two Runaways," published in the *Century*, showed great sensitivity to black dialect and culture.

A love of the South, its traditions, speech, and culture pervades Edwards' work. In his approximately one hundred stories, he wrote of real people, often empathetically about blacks, as in his best known tale, *Eneas Africanus*. Most famous for his newspaper work, Edwards won a $10,000 prize for his first novel, *Sons and Fathers*, which has been called the best mystery novel ever written by an American.

Thomas Hardy

Thomas Hardy (1840-1928) was thought dead when born, and his extreme delicacy was the reason he was taught at home until the age of eight. He lived to be eighty-seven, his mind clear to the last, dying of a cold.

At sixteen, apprenticed to a local ecclesiastical architect, Hardy studied more philosophy and poetry than architecture, but still worked for six years, after 1867, as a practising architect. In 1874 he married Emma Lavinia Gifford, the sister-in-law of the vicar of one of his projects, and devoted himself in off-hours to poetry, although none was published until 1898. His first well-received novel, *Far From the Madding Crowd* (1874), gave Hardy enough success to support his wife, and settle near London. Although he produced his novels annually or biennially, he never took them seriously. Everyone else did, however. Critical acclaim and notoriety greeted each one. *Tess of the D'Urbervilles* (1891) and *Jude the Obscure* (1896), both had to be "expurgated" when published in magazines, especially in America. Called "obscene" and "filthy" when they came out, they offended Victorian sensibilities. As years went by, they were reevaluated as masterpieces, and Hardy received numerous honors for his work. By that time he had abandoned fiction for his first, his true, literary love, poetry. After his first wife died, he married his secretary in 1914, when he was seventy-four. She devoted herself to him and wrote his biography. Hardy's heart is buried in his first wife's grave; his ashes rest in the Poet's Corner of Westminster Abbey.

Nathaniel Hawthorne

Born in Salem, Massachussetts, Nathaniel Hawthorne (1804-1864) came from a long line of Puritans, some of whom had been cursed by a victim of the Salem witch trials. Most of his work is strongly allegorical and a warning against pride, particularly intellectual pride. After majoring in literature at Bowdoin College, where he made some extremely valuable contacts, he was determined to become a writer. The lack of international copyright laws made it very difficult for a young American writer to succeed, however. American publishers found it more profitable to reprint British authors, to whom no royalties were paid, than to cultivate costly native talent.

In 1828 Hawthorne completed *Fanshawe*, a vanity novel, which caught the attention of Boston publisher Samuel Goodrich. During the next eleven years Goodrich published more than twenty-five of Hawthorne's anonymous works in his annual short story collections, *The Token*. Attempts to support his family by writing faltered until Boston publisher James T. Fields stumbled across the first draft of *The Scarlet Letter*. This novel made its triumphant appearance in 1850 and was followed a year later by the Poelike masterpiece, *The House of the Seven Gables*. When old college chum Franklin Pierce became president in 1853, Hawthorne was rewarded with a consulship in Liverpool, England. Increasing royalties, plus five years of lucrative service, finally provided financial security. So he retired, and after a two-year sojourn in Italy returned home to continue writing, rather unsuccessfully, until his death four years later.

Arthur Morrison

Born in a slum near London, self-educated Arthur Morrison (1863-1945) was secretive about his private life. In his public life, he was many things; art expert, dramatist, journalist, but he is probably best remembered for his twenty-five Martin Hewett stories—making him about the only contemporary rival of Sherlock Holmes to stand the test of time. The stories are well-structured, often imaginative, and nicely written. They were collected as *Martin Hewitt, Investigator* (1894), *Chronicles of Martin Hewett* (1895), and *Adventures of Martin Hewett* (1896). Ironically, Morrison had little enthusiasm for them.

Other mystery-related books he wrote are *The Dorrington Deed-Box* (1897), *Cunning Murrell* (1900), *The Hole in the Wall* (1902), and *The Green Eye of Goona* (1903). Morrison is considered one of the leaders in the development of naturalistic fiction in England in the 1890s. His *Tales of Mean Streets* (1894) and *A Child of the Jago* (1896) are classic studies of the hopelessness of slum life, and were instrumental in initiating social reforms.

After the turn of the century, he devoted much of his time to the study of Oriental art, became the owner of one of the great collections of English and Oriental masters and a noted authority on the subject. During this time his writing centered around the monumental *The Painters of Japan* (1911).

Rodriguez Ottolengui

A well known dentist, Rodriguez Ottolengui (1861?-1937) published one volume of short detective stories, called *The Final Proof; or, The Value of Evidence* (Putnam 1898). Never published in England, four stories from it appeared in the *Idler* magazine (See Robert Barr), which seldom published detective stories.

Ottolengui's stories have been faulted for stilted dialogue and melodramatic disclosures, but they're told without pretensiousness, in a straight forward way, and all the pieces of the puzzle work out. These stories about professional detective Mr. Barnes and the rich amateur, Mr. Mitchel, contain enjoyable interactions between the two, but were discounted by his peers, who delighted in his expertise in root canal therapy. When he died, his book, *Methods of Filling Teeth*, was considered his masterpiece.

Edgar Allan Poe

Edgar Allan Poe (1809-1849), often called "the founder in the modern detective story," was the seminal genre writer of the nineteenth century. He popularized stories of science fiction and psychological terror in England, America, and France. He invented stories of detection and he influenced Arthur Conan Doyle, Jules Verne, and Guy de Maupassant. Despite his place in history, his life was filled with poverty, failure, and tragedy.

Shortly after Poe's birth in Boston, his father ran away; his mother succumbed to consumption three years later. Cared for by the John Allans, to whom he initially brought great joy, Poe lost their favor by behaving disgracefully at the University of

Virginia. After two abortive tries at an army career, Poe began to write full-time. Winning the 1833 Baltimore *Sunday Visitor* short story contest ("Ms Found in a Bottle") brought his first of several editorial jobs. But he was invariably fired by his employers because of his arrogance, strong views, and antisocial behavior.

He moved to New York, living and writing in abject poverty, as his cousin-bride wasted away. Masterpieces such as "The Raven" and "The Purloined Letter," brought scant funds, or were simply given away. Yet he was prolific, producing a short science fiction novel and several volumes worth of poems and short stories in a brief period of time.

In 1849, just as he seemed on the verge of straightening out his life, he disappeared and was discovered dying in a Baltimore gutter.

Melville Davisson Post

Melville Davisson Post (1871-1930) was born in rural Romines Milles, West Virginia, an area that was to become the setting of much of his fiction. Graduating from West Virginia University, he practiced criminal law and was in Democratic politics for several years before deciding to write full-time. He became one of the best paid magazine writers in America, and was admired for technical plotting skill.

His mission always to entertain the reader, he created two antithetical series characters, both of whom stemmed from his upbringing and interests. The first was the strange, embittered lawyer, Randolph Mason. On the verge of insanity, Mason used his impeccable knowledge of the law to circumvent it, enabling criminals to escape punishment. In 1911, Mason repented, and subsequently Post replaced him with one of the most original detectives in America literature. Uncle Abner, who had no known surname, a god-fearing, Bible-toting Methodist frontier man, sought justice in the untamed West Virginia of the early nineteenth century. His mission was to mete out God's justice, which didn't always equate with the letter of the law, to his countrymen, in the most practical way possible. The well made stories, which often began after the crime was committed and much of the evidence was in hand, were immediately popular. Abner sought truth through reasoning and painstaking examination of the evidence, tension growing as the mystery simultaneously unfolded with its solution.

William Russell

Almost nothing is known of William Russell's life. Even his name is incorrectly printed as *Thomas* Russell on some early American editions of his book. He is best known by his pseudonym, "Waters," but he also wrote novels about the sea as "Lieutenant Warneford."

His tales, told in the first person, of a London police detective, first appeared in *Chamber's Edinburgh Journal* on July 28, 1849. The first short detective stories by an English author, they were collected in *The Recollections of a Policeman*, published in New York in 1852, in England in 1856, and reprinted numerous times under numerous titles.

"Waters," the writer-narrator, a member of the Metropolitan Police, solves cases with the help of two assistants. Approximately thirteen collections of these stories, issued from 1857 to 1870, appeared, and numerous ersatz Waters soon surfaced in his wake.

Mark Twain (Samuel Langhorne Clemens)

Samuel Clemens (1835-1910) grew up in Hannibal, Missouri, and was educated largely in the printing offices of the *Missouri Courier* and the *Hannibal Journal*. He worked as a journalist, and did a stint as a Mississippi steamboat pilot. When on the river, he met an older pilot, Isaiah Sellers, who wrote stories for the New Orleans *Picayune*, under the pseudonym of "Mark Twain," a river term. Clemens so well imitated and exceeded Sellers' style in a river story published by the New Orleans *True Delta*, Sellers stopped writing. Clemens thereafter used his pen name, in apology, perhaps.

His humorous, anecdotal, seemingly spontaneous stories mixed memory with improbability and were often told with an imperturbable innocence. He wrote tirelessly, in almost every genre imaginable, his short stories succeeding more often than longer works. The best of these tales appear effortless. Many, written for ready cash, have not aged well. His forté was a romantic realism, seen through the eyes of a young boy. Indeed, his wife's name for him, "Youth," reveals his secret: the voice he used for Tom Sawyer and Huck Finn rang true; his stories had such vitality, because he never grew old.

Israel Zangwill

The son of a Russian Jewish refugee, Israel Zangwill (1864-1926) grew up in a London ghetto, and had a life-long devotion to Jewish causes. His outspoken views on zionism, woman's suffrage and the League of Nations (he supported the first two, denounced the latter as the "League of Damnations") were not always well received.

Because of his novel, *The Big Bow Mystery* (1892), he has gone down in mystery history as the "father of the locked-room mystery." Although Poe's "The Murders in the Rue Morgue" preceded him (1841), *The Big Bow Mystery*, a parody on detective stories, is the first longer work (a novelette) to use this plot device. It was written in two weeks, first published in the *London Star*. Several films have been based on Zangwill's work, including *The Perfect Crime*, 1928, and *The Verdict*, 1946.